RED HIBISCUS

Red Hibiscus

Jane August

The Holix Club

Contents

for my parents & our divine ancestors

Trigger Warning

TO THE READERS:

The contents discussed in this book are for entertainment purposes only.
**Before you get too comfortable & indulge in one of my fantasies; this
content comes with a Trigger warning:**

**Content not suitable for children or those under the age of 18. Must
be 18+ to ride the seas. Furthermore, content can potentially harm the
reader, triggering mental stress or behaviors. Content MAY or MAY
NOT include highlighted mentions or discussions on uncomfortable,
adult, & controversial topics such as, but not limited to; SEX, INAPPRO-
PRIATE LANGUAGE, DEATH, FAMILY OR CHILDHOOD TRAUMA,
BULLYING, VIOLENCE, BDSM & FETISH, SEXUAL ABUSE & RAPE,
GENERAL ABUSES, MENTAL HEALTH CONDITIONS, DRUG & ALCO-
HOL; SUBSTANCE ABUSE, SUICIDE & DEPRESSION & other triggers
that may have not been mentioned, but forewarned.**

- *CONTENT INCLUDING SETTINGS, CHARACTERS, NAMES, &
  SITUATIONS ARE ALL **FICTIONAL** (make-believe)
- **STORIES ARE FOR ENTERTAINMENT PURPOSES **ONLY.**
- ***ALL CONTENT AUTHENTICALLY **WRITTEN BY** JEM AUGUST
- ****THE CONTENT YOU'RE ABOUT TO READ is POSITIVE
  ROMANTIC AND EROTIC ESCAPADES. THIS IS A SAFE PLACE
  DEDICATED TO MAKING YOU FEEL SAFE, EMPOWERED & SEX-

POSITIVE. Please take trigger warnings into consideration and mostly, Enjoy!!

1

**Beautiful Truths &
Reckless Lies**

Prolog

I was never a romantic, so 'hopeless' was throwing it WAY out of the ballpark. Landon could testify to that. The whole thing about someone being your 'Rib,' the Adam to your Eve, soul mates, and star-crossed lovers; well, I never had too much time to sit and consider that it was possible in MY life. I was a realist, and true love was for the surrealistic. My thought of it? You have a partner in crime that you marry by law and stick by til death. Someone to help you tackle adulthood. Marriage for the government. Home. Career. Family. Bills. Taxes. Retirement. Death. But that was before I met the real me. That was before I learned that this thing *'LOVE'* was way more complicated than I cared to realize. Sometimes fate decides to use a fucked up way of internally waking you up. Making it clear you have a destiny even if you don't want it. They give you the key to your future despite total disregard of knowing it'll still ruin all the reckless lies you built around yourself.

1

Live a Loveless life?

Or death by a touch of true love?

After Haven, I would have picked death every time without question. It's corny but truthful when I say I didn't want to live in a world Haven didn't exist in. I reflect on my earth life because I want to remember why; before that night of the storytelling, before the nightmares, before I knew of the curse before I saw the truth. The girl I used to be was too numb to feel emotions. She was too numb to feel love, so she's faded into a blue-gray background. The new me, dangerous and lustful, glittered and flourished in the light of eternal Sun, with no remorse for killing the old me.

I wanted to really feel,

Even though I cared for the old me, she was naive, too careful at times, quiet, shy, submissive, and reserved. She was so innocent and easily manipulated. 'New' Daya loves being reckless and has a craving for freedom like never before. The 'old' me, I didn't know of all the damage that was. The 'old' me only had the memories of the nightmares, while the new me couldn't stop the monsters from coming until he saved me from it all. A melodically daunting contrast, keeping me enslaved to the dark past without causing much pain. But, someone incredibly wise once taught me; *you can't break what's blessed.* I was only one Princess out of millions, whose birth had been gifted a thousand times by my ancestor mother. My blood would lead me to my destiny. My name was Dayanara Managualt; a Taino Princess.

Daca Taino

The night before

"So like, freaking centuries ago RIGHT, there lived a tribe by the sea... A Taino tribe but not just any Taino tribe. A tribe of sexy beautiful Classy Tainos of the enchanting island of *Boriken*. So among them was this beautiful Taino Princess named *Guanina*. *Guanina* was the fairest of them all. She had a crazy sexy body, a pretty face, and long hair. Nice rack, little booty, tiny waist; everybody wanted to know her, if you know what I mean. Anyway, Guanina's older brother was the Tribesmen Chief, *Cacique Guaybana*. Some say he was a gracious and good Cacique to his people. Other's say he was a ruthless savage king that led his tribe with pride, honor, and strength. No one crossed them, up until these John Smith-looking Iberian and Latin assholes washed up ashore with Christopher Columbus. Soon after, the entire island of Boriken was overtaken by these conquistadors running around,d killing us off, stealing goods, taking territories and slaves. TAKING and mistreating OUR Taino women... And among these men was *Don Cristobal de Sotomayor*. And not for nothing; he wasn't a bad-looking fellow. It was inevitable that *Guanina* and *Don Cristobal* would end up meeting and falling *"in love."* And so they did. Of course, Cacique Guaybana was disgusted by this madness. But the princess swore he was her one true love. Guanina- tired of the same handsome and strong Taino warriors, must have thought, damn okay; sophisticated and God-like and is looking hella sexy-"

"-Dad, cut it out!" Leyla, heavily annoyed, demanded. Honestly, I also have had enough of my uncle's hip opera. We both playfully hit my uncle. Leyla caught his head, and I got him on the shoulder. He and Landon chuckled, "Alright, Alright, I'll be myself about it," My uncle was too old and too educated to talk like a young millennial, which is why it was so cringe-stinging. The four of us gazed off into a dark, shallow lake underneath a pale yellow waxing moon. Sitting at the edge of our boat dock, listening to my uncle retell Taino *Legends* and watching fireflies. It was calm. We listened to the waves crash up against the dock posts. *Atabey*, I honored silently. The late summer night air smelled of cedar pine and firewood from the dying firepit in the yard. That smell always reminded me how quickly this sleepy honey dusk would turn into colorful brisk fall nights. It was September, and the last couple of hours were depleting because it was nearly midnight and tonight was my birthday.

The *Legend of Guanina and the 'Red Hibiscus,'* so he calls it. It was the same every year, but nonetheless, the versions varied.

"-In my defense, I'm just trying to appeal to a younger but more mature audience," my uncle would end up explaining as he reached in the cooler and handed me a cold wine cooler to replace the 2nd empty bottle I had next to me. So innocent for 18 years old, he thought. But as I was sitting there feeling blissful and loopy at the same time, he couldn't help catch my imbalance. Guilt washed over his face already as he tried remembering where he had left off.

"... So one day, Cacique Guaybana was told that their unwanted guests planned to go to Caparra and overrun it. The Cacique had enough. All was fair in love and war, but his people weren't weak nor feeble. They were kind to the wrong people and realized too late. They were not going to let them take over. He planned a counter sneak attack, and *Guanina* overheard this plot. So out of what must have been blinding lust, she and one of Don Cristobal's servant men went to warn him. But he never took the warning seriously. Landon, did you know this is historical-"

"- Relevant to the Rebellion of 1511, Jinx!!" We raced to mimic him, leaving an interrupted look on his face.

"Can I finish? Please and thank you. So like I was saying, this is historically relevant to the 1511 Taino Rebellion. So then, Don Cristobal Soto de Mayor went on to *Caparra,* and the Taino warriors all awaited him. Do you know what happened? Guaybana showed no mercy as he and the tribesmen won this battle. And he made sure that he, himself, was the one who killed his sister's lover, Don Cristobal Soto de Mayor. Many claim they were star-crossed soul mates, stuck in a crossfire, but The Taino Tribesmen refused to believe love can blind someone from their people and family. They claimed it was an act of betrayal. So they dragged Guanina, *the traitor,* to Soto de Mayor's grave and killed her too. Soon after, a magical Ceiba tree grows over their graves, ravished by white lilies and tons of red hibiscus flowers. They say that when they had killed Guanina, Guaybana offered her soul as a sacrificial gift to the Taino Ancestor of Darkness, Death, and Destruction; Moboyas. They wanted to celebrate the successful battle. That night a curse was put upon all the women of the Classic Taino tribesmen. So shall they never taint the bloodline and let immediate death shadow her all of her life. Moboyas makes sure of it. That's it that's the tale."

Uncle Misa clapped his hands together and let out a little laugh as he reached for his Rum on rocks, shaking his head lightly. He might have been a little drunk. Leyla and I had looked at him strangely, side blinded by the ominous turn the story took. Yes, he has always told us this story. But, no. He was never passionately dark about their deaths. Usually, he had more of a pitied and sad; Romeo & Juliet; *'that sucks';* kinda vibe about it. But, this birthday was more like, **'that's what they deserve.'** I can almost read it in his face.

"-I have Joe taking care of stuff at the warehouse this weekend, so I'll be at your game on Saturday, Landon."

My uncle's love for American sports, all that is manly, and the deep desire to father a son made Landon more than just the ideal suitor for me. He treated him like a son.

"Yeah, it's going to be a big one."

Landon's sport was Lacrosse, but he excelled in almost everything, and it was just the beginning of the school year. So yes, I dated the Quarterback, even though I wasn't the cheeky popular cheerleader; that was Leyla. I was the loner, but Landon never minded that. He claims he's loved me the minute he saw me. I never really felt that from him, but he never gave me a reason to doubt him. Since I introduced them two years ago, my uncle pulled Landon under his wing. My uncle Misa only had Leyla and me. He has always wanted a boy around the house. Landon grew up without a father and was raised solo by his wealthy and seemingly always busy mother; undoubtedly, the pair were inseparable once brought together. He supported Landon's prospecting college picks and his 5-year plan, among other telling signs. At the beginning of last spring, I realized how strong their bond was. My uncle hired him down at the Lumberyard, gave him the spare key to the place, and even bought him a brand new truck to drive Ley and me around in. He trusted him, I knew.

As children, things were never 'normal' for Leyla and me. We lived a unique lifestyle. Like most Puerto Ricans, our bloodline dated back to the divine Classic Taino Tribesmen of Boriken. My uncle ensured that while he loved the American soil, we lived with **Taino** customs and culture. Puertorican. Yes, it was where we were from, formally known as Boriken. But the average Puerto Rican was so much more than 'Puerto Rican.' So many bloodlines of ancient indigenous peoples were destroyed and altered. Boriken went from being the only home of the Taino to a place where people from all tribes and corners of the world could come and settle. So many cultures blended and bent. Today, we are the same, but we aren't the last bit of the Taino peoples; Puertoricans are richly indigenous.

You can imagine that we had our fair share of rituals and traditions. Our blood was of Taino color magic, Caciques and Bohiques powerful. A bloodline well protected throughout centuries, protected by our natural gardens and remedies were the most beautiful and potent. That was the blood that coursed through me. This storytelling Misa was doing was one of the sacred rituals and many other rituals. Misa had a very severe passion for the arts of Taino color magic. Still, he lived two very different lives, and the magical part of things was of a secret life he didn't care to share with anyone. Although pretty private about his magical connections, my uncle cherished his Taino magic and rituals. This would be Landon's first time at one of Misael's rituals. That says all I need to know about my uncle's stance with Landon.

When I met Landon, I felt like he cared. I felt like he supported me. I saw qualities in him that made him an *ideal* partner. I did care for Landon. Almost even loved him. But as I said, I wasn't much of a romantic. Not like he was. And certainly not like Leyla. Landon says he loved me the day he met me. He never pressured me to say the same until I was ready, and he never pressured me to have sex. He was a gentleman. The kind of guy you wanted your daughter or niece to date. But Over the years, I've grown pretty skeptical; I would find reasons to write them off as silly stories. I'd never find the love of my life because that wasn't something tangible. Perfection is not natural. Trust and effort are real. And even that very night, I still wasn't that romantic child, even though Landon was resilient to the cold, apathetic muscle I called a heart. He held onto me as if it were immoral to let go.

Although, that night did have a different feel to it. The story-telling was not as personal and intimate. No real coziness. It was solid and cold, and the air felt strangely thick.

When we were younger, Leyla and I would come out here in our pj's, running into the dewy grass-ridden backyard where the fire pit burned sticks of marshmallows for s'mores. The wind would blow warm kisses. Crickets would sing like tonight, and the moon always witnessed from above Misa's storytelling. Afterward, we would dance to my uncle's guitar or congas. I remember seeing this colorful rainbow dust forming at our feet as we danced. It looked like glitter against the Bonfire flames. I once asked what it was, but my uncle never answered. I can't remember much of my childhood after that memory. Still, it's a faint memory I can attest has happened and strangely floated in my mind that night.

Over the years, my uncle's expression to the legends he told grew wearier, almost unsure. I never put much thought into it until this day. As I watched the shadows dance on the side of his tired, wrinkled face, staring off into the dark waters beyond the dock on our land. He seemed to slip into an odd trance. He was lost in his thoughts, trying to concentrate on the silence of the night.

"Is something bothering you, uncle?" I asked him out of curiosity, with no other reasons to ask. Then, startled out of his train of thought, he peered at me and smiled weakly.

"No… No, it's just been a long day. But, hey, you three don't get too drunk out here." He slowly stood up.

"Are you going in now, Papa?" Leyla asked.

"Yeah… I'm getting old."

"I'm coming up with you,"

"Hey Land, make sure my girl is in the house by midnight… I'll see you in the morning… be careful on the road tonight. Text me when you get in. Daya, be careful out there. There are creatures in the dark, dark night that just might-"

"Bite in the dark, dark night." I finished his sentence. He smiled and reached to caress my hair before planting a kiss on my forehead. He patted Landon's shoulder before throwing a tired arm over Leyla and walking off into the grassy backyard.

We were left alone, staring at the moon. Our legs were dangling off the dock. The wind fluttered around our innocent innuendo's as he slowly reached over for my hand. "I love being here with you," he said earnestly.

"Yeah, my uncle loves seeing you here."

"How about you? You love seeing me here?"

He was doing that romanticizing thing again.

Shit- look away, "...Of course." He smiled, stood up, and helped me to my feet. It was nearing midnight, and Landon never disobeyed my uncle. "Let's get you to the house."

We trailed through the grassy backyard and around the lodge house to the front door. I leaned my back against the door, my hand already on the knob.

"Happy Birthday, Beautiful..." He leaned in and kissed me. I held back. By now, Landon was used to this from me.

"Thanks," He pulled off of me.

"See you tomorrow?" His brow raised, and he smiled that perfect smile. I twisted the knob and fell back into the open door. Not a moment later, I peered through the foyer window and saw his truck gone before I had a chance to lock up.

2

Nightmares

I looked at his face, perfectly shaped lips, deeply royal blue eyes, and a smile that could knock any girl out. So beautiful. Everything about Landon is gorgeous, and it made me insecure sometimes. I knew he deserved more than I was willing to give; I had no love to give. Landon was kind, sweet, romantic, and he was mine.

I don't deserve him.

Landon and I met during a track meet in the spring of our sophomore year. I had only heard of *Landon Upton* from Leyla and her gal pals. *'The Stallion,'* they called him; for more reasons than one. Cross country was MY sport. I took the lead in my team, and when Landon came threatening my winning streak, he took away my attention. *'Show off,'* I'd mimic behind his back. He just strolled into the track field, sporting charming glowing glitz of lime in his blue eyes. After that day, he always seemed to want to spark up a conversation with me. He would ignore everyone, and everyone hated it. Down to the coach, as he vied for my attention. Being a loner, I couldn't deny the royalty feeling I got from his undying attention. He made it easy to like him. I felt bad as I lay there in my bed thinking of Landon. The year and a half of being with him had been *too* perfect, to the point of vanilla. There wasn't much room to criticize. But, honestly, I was kind of coerced into dating him. It was Leyla's doing. I wasn't even in their *'clique'* in school. I had no friends or desire for teenage puppy love, and I was comfortable with that until he made me uncomfortable.

From what I could remember from childhood, Ley and I were home-schooled. When my uncle finally decided to enroll in high school, I was sure everyone thought I was strange. I thought they were odd, for sure. I quickly became this outsider, struggling to relate to my classmates, while Leyla became this social butterfly. Right away, they crowned her the teenage dream Queen. Beautiful, sweet, funny, confident; they all loved her. Not even Landon couldn't deny it. He was, after all, Leyla's friend. Once Landon realized he couldn't have Leyla, I figured he just sought after me. I was the next best thing. He never strikes me as true love, let alone a *soul mate*. Maybe that's why I've always been so cold towards him.

I could see the bright night sky and the stars twinkling from my bed. Staring out into the free world, I realized that only out in the natural world is where I'd felt true love. The trees. The grass. The mud. Nothing filled that hollowness in my heart more than running through the forest, preferably at night. My fingertips were scratching against bark and feet, hitting the rich terrain. The delicious smell of cedar and pine. The crisp taste of the berries and apples. The refreshing river water where I swam. Maybe there wasn't someone out there for me, but rather a place. I wasn't a fortune teller, but for sure, Landon wasn't it. Sadly, I was content with that.

Remember I said I had childhood nightmares? I can't tell you how old I was when I first had them, only that I had stopped having them when I was 5- or 6. Sometimes the dreams would get so real I could feel the sweat trickle down my shoulder and my long wavy hair, sticking to my skin.

The same routine. There are the same tropical clouds above; familiar sounds and smells in the same moist salty air. And the same feeling of fear. Clear midnight runs through the *El Yunque Rain forest*, the holy ground that cradled the heart of *Boriken*. I'd run to *El Morro* and back down into the golden pathways of the city's alleyways. The Moon shone over, reflecting into my light honey cognac eyes, and kissed the sweat from my warm skin. I could hear the coquis singing their midnight song against the wind, and even from the alleyways, I could taste the salt in the air from the sea up ahead. After a while, those golden streets turned dark, and I was running down a trail into the rainforest. I never knew what I was looking for, but the more I ran, the darker things became. I'd get this feeling of fear. It was all happening AGAIN. I was no longer looking for something, but rather, something was looking for me. Again, I was being chased, and the dream dramatically changed; I was no longer on the Island of Enchantment. I was now on the mainland. North country, running down a familiar forest trail from an unspeakable creation of evil. For years I couldn't see its face. It was only that night I had come face to face with it—this dark and bony silhouette of a figure that I stared at from a distance. For a split second, I kept a strong pace through the woods. But I couldn't outrun the faceless monster, with rotten, moldy branch horns and sharp splinter teeth; I could only see through the glimmer of a Northern moonlight. Owls

hooted, and wolves cried. It was cold, freezing. For a moment, I believed I could make it out of the woods. That's when I hit a Ceiba tree, randomly sitting there in a Northern forest. I instantly tripped on the entanglements of its elegant roots. My hands pierced the mud. I immediately looked up, noticing the extensive trail of fire that the monster was leaving behind.

Those flames lit my eyes up without scandal.

Red. Orange. Yellow.

Flares and flickers on the monster before me, breaking and cracking its long meatless limbs, pulling at the dead earth to reach me. The fire came all around me, and the heat blared on my back as I watched its dry earthly sheering claws running for me. Ready to gut my heart right out, I screamed so hard and for so long until my lungs gave out. I could hear a roar of a bear and then-

-I'm sitting up in my bed, breathless and heart speeding at the rate of sound. My eyes searched the bright bedroom like a scanner; I was safely in my bed. My 6 o'clock alarm was going off, and the dainty blue morning light was peering through the window.

Oh- And my uncle was standing there in the doorway, face as pale as the light blue curtains, looking like he just took a hit to his stomach with a cannon. He was worried but primarily scared. He stood back with hesitation, almost afraid to ask as he watched me continue to shake in cold body sweat, palms still gripping my bed-sheets. "Are you okay?" He asked me halfway through the door.

I badly scoffed switched my eyes to the window.

"... Yeah, it was just a-"

"-A night terror?"

At first, I didn't answer.

I looked up at him. He stood there trying to hide behind a concerned look. He was more scared than he appeared. I don't remember seeing that look on his face since I was a 5-year-old child. "I'm okay… it's just a dream", I told him as I loosened the grip to my bed. He walked further in; the last thing you want your parents to do when you finally hit 18. He reached over and rubbed my head, leaving my long black waves destroyed and a considerable look of irritation on my face. "Happy Birthday Kiddo…"

It was a warm and bright Friday morning. Perfect weather, and yet, there was no mistake; that dream was an omen. Because after that nightmare, the Fever began to seep in.

I finally came downstairs for breakfast. Eyes sunken in and pale like sheer ivory, I nodded. Aunt Charlotte leaned over the island table, greeting me with a smile. She kissed my cheek. "Cute outfit but the ugly face? Did you get any sleep last night, honey?" My aunt asked as I sat down and poured myself a glass of orange juice.

"Yeah, you look like you fell on your face Daya. You Okay?"

Leyla walked in mid-conversation. My uncle held onto a suspect look on his face; he slid my breakfast across the table. Runny, barely cooked eggs, burnt toast, and burnt bacon. Not his best. He was just as distracted as I was, and this inedible breakfast was proof. I exhaled hard. My insides still shook from the nightmare. I looked at Leyla from across the table, and she choked over her toast. Looking away, she coughed while trying to force words out, "Jesus Daya-" she sipped her juice, "...Can you at least warn someone before you go burning your eyes in their soul? You're doing it again."

She must have meant my eyes doing that weird rapid color-changing thing it does to accommodate whatever emotions I was locking in internally. It was like a light switch to match behaviors, moods, or feelings. Indeed, one of the many strange traits within my inner workings. Leyla and I were 'special.' It took them years to confess that our bodies harvested Great Taino power and magic... whatever that meant. To me, it was just something we were "born" with. Natural like hair and skin. We never questioned it—none of the odd 'magical' traits Leyla and I had. It did freak Leyla out, even her own eyes when she did it. It was always random and usually out of the blue. Sometimes our eyes would intensely glow. Misael and Charlotte found it unique, but they encouraged us to hide it from the world. I think that's why Leyla was freaked by it, as extroverted as she was. I found the mood identifier pretty cool, but Leyla's disgust over it made me want to hide it too. Over the years, she and I learned to control it to a degree, but times like this were just inevitable. "Did you go to bed late?" I disagreed.

"No... I had a nightmare last night."

The room was quiet and still. Leyla looked at her parents; her mouth was partially open in utter disbelief. My uncle looked away, though my aunt wanted an explanation. He cleared his throat.

"Yeah ... uh... I woke up to Daya, well, you know, screaming."

"Misael, she hasn't dreamt since she was 6? I thought you said-"

She stopped, looked at Leyla, and then she looked at me. A solid moment passed before my aunt's reaction carried on. She walked over to me and weaved her manicured fingers into my wavy midnight hair. My uncle stared at her with an annoyed look on his face. *Dramatic,* he thought. My aunt and uncle had a 'tic for tac' relationship. "-Charlotte, please let's not talk about this right now... it's Daya's birthday." He was seriously annoyed, looking up from his coffee. Finally, my uncle made it clear that we shouldn't talk about it with a solid glance. Misael was only reserved because the nightmares were such a traumatic part of our lives, despite somehow forgetting a while. Now sitting here, I remember why. My uncle blamed himself for all the Taino teachings he embedded in our heads when the nightmares stopped. He was depressed for months.

Maybe we were too young to learn of the Taino and Carib tribes-men and their Zeni Gods, Taino princesses, and magical gardens and rainforests. But if that were the case, why didn't Leyla have nightmares? Maybe she was much more resilient? Perhaps it was because she was a Puertorican Half breed. For a very long time, I knew my mother was dead. My father; I have no clue who he was. Misa was close to my mother, so her death took a toll on him. They were twins, so it was always hard for him to talk about her, especially to me. I still don't know much about her. All I knew was that her name was Anais, she was 18 when she had me, and she died of a *rare* sickness hours after I was born. As the years passed, begging my uncle for more details was useless, and my interest in her faded. Now it didn't matter. I deeply loved the family I have, without biological parents.

Our family was more than reasonably close; it had always been my uncle Misa, Leyla, and aunt Charlotte.

I grew up in the small quiet town of Grey Wolf Hollow. A lovely picturesque town up in the Northern mountainous hills of upstate New York, just at the rim of the Canadian border. The town was split in two by a beautiful calming river that flowed from the top of one mountain to another mountain. Grey Wolf Hollow was most heavenly in the fall, with the colors, footbridges, hiking trails, and rustic scenery. Everyone lived peacefully here.

The locals shared this piece of Heaven with those who lived on the Grey Wolf River Reservation. The Reserve wasn't like tradi-tional reserves. This indigenous Reserve was multicultural. It had become a haven for those who ran blood with any American soil Indigenous tribe. They welcomed different people of different in-digenous tribes from all over for whatever good reason they came.

Despite the mix of cultures, traditions, and beliefs, the Grey Wolf River tribe was of strength, teamwork, and trust and had welcomed all Indigenous peoples. It was where my aunt and uncle met. Charlotte greeted Misael and Anais when they arrived here from Puerto Rico over 20 years ago. They were only 15 at the time, running from something; I could only presume. They couldn't just settle anywhere because they were the last of the Royal tribesmen. They were too special.

Our family lineage was among the last royal bloodlines preserved throughout the centuries. So they 'joked' that we were little princesses all the time. The blood that courses through me was the last Pureblood of the Managualt Royal dynasty. It wasn't to be tainted by foreign heritage. Although our lives revolved around Puerto Rico, my uncle chopped it all down to ancient history, and we adopted the American lifestyle into our own culture. After my mother passed, my uncle and aunt took full responsibility for me, raising me like their own with lots of love, trust, and guidance. They were young parents. Misa knew he loved Charlotte and married her the moment he could. After that, he pushed on with his education, and later on, college, working and creating a network of great friends to help him climb the career ladder. By the age of 22, he owned his own Lumber business; by 26, his land and home. Now, he was heading towards early retirement. His lumber company was very well off. My aunt and uncle eventually separated. Aunt Charlotte moved out with Leyla when I was 6, a little after the nightmares. They were always at each other's throats.

Nevertheless, they co-parented decently, and to this very day, you could still see the love they had for each other. They remained close no matter how stubborn the other was acting. I loved them dearly but sometimes feel like it was my fault they split. Raising me wasn't easy with all of my 'special' attributes. With Charlotte out of the house, it gave my uncle tons of free time to breathe down our backs. I didn't mind too much. Introverted, homebound, realistic, bookworm; ambitious with a lustful desire for nature while staying quiet at heart. My hobbies included:

Minding my own business.

Gardening. Painting. Reading.

Running. Exploring.

And I loved reading, mostly Shakespeare.

I spent a lot of time outside by the lake or down by the river on the weekends. I also spent tons of time running track in the woods, exploring and finding new trails. But, as I grew into a teen, I found no interest in friends, parties, or teenage wildlife antics. I owed a cellphone that had no purpose but to read from. I had one person I considered a 'friend' because she was Charlotte's neighbor. Her name was Sunny, and Sunny was trouble. But Sunny worked at the only bookstore in town, which was the only attachment I had to her.

Leyla was my only *real* friend. Although we were very different, we were very close and protective of each other. Misa says we remind him of how he and Anais were. But, he says, I'm more like him, and Leyla was a lot like Anais. It's strange; I felt like it was probably the reason why I loved being around Leyla so much. Leyla Managualt was impressionable and attractive, but she was also charismatic. By the end of that first week of high school, everyone knew the Managualt girls because of Leyla.

The *'home-schooled kids'* that lived up on that mountain. We were all they could talk about. Down to the upper-classmen knew who we were. 'The quiet and snotty Daya' is how they perceived me; 'She's the one with the long raven locks of waves and perfect long-running legs.' I had dimples they would only see rare on occasion if you happen to catch me smiling, and I was the taller one, at 5'7. The one with sharp cognac eyes that were *'too beautiful'* to look into has all the curiosity hidden behind ball caps and sunglasses. The even prettier and more outgoing Managualt girl is Leyla. The boy magnet. Cream olive skin and a perfect coke bottle body. Boys hung to her perfect smile and loved how short she was at 5'2. She always flipped her black shoulder-length waves that lifted one side by the crease. She also had sharp, beautiful eyes, but they were magnetic bottle green and effortlessly pulled everyone in with a contagious laugh. All the girls wanted to be her frenemy. All the boys wanted to sleep with her.

But that was just it. It wasn't just our looks that set us apart from the other girls, although some may argue. We were also virgins and proud of it. Something considered rare in this fast era. My uncle made a point to mesh in our minds at a young age.

'No one is worthy or would EVER be.'

I could tell you I wasn't interested in love, let alone sex. It was for marriage. Leyla's thoughts, on the other hand, I couldn't tell you. She says she is a virgin, and mostly I believe her. But truthfully, I've had my doubts. She was romantic and always dating. Leyla, unlike me, was always open to falling in and out of love. She wasn't afraid to be passionate or weak from love. She seemed to have the courage for it that I never did. I envied her. Unfortunately for her suitors, her lust never lasted long. Leyla was quite choosy, and she recycled them as quickly as she pulled them in.

When Landon walked into the kitchen, he had interrupted my rushing thoughts. He greeted everyone as I jumped to my feet and began to clear the table before me. I handed my uncle the dirty kitchenware as Landon lightly tugged my free hand. And then I did something strange. I turned to kiss my boyfriend. Usually, I hated that so early in the morning. "Happy birthday," He says again romantically, trying to find my eyes.

"Well, family, I hate to cut this morning's meeting short, but we have school…. it's been interesting. Come on, Daya." Leyla picked up her book bag and tapped Landon's shoulder, cocking her head towards the door. Her beautiful eyes shot at it and then back at us. I managed to grab my bookbag in time to say goodbye to my aunt and uncle. Leyla hauled me out of the house and to Landon's truck. Misa peered his head from the doorway. A suspicion still leaking from his eyes as he managed to sneak in, "Have a good day..."

Leyla was seemingly excited this strange morning. Whenever she acted this way, it was because she had something up her sleeve she knew I would disapprove of. That mind of hers was always brewing up some master plan. The radio was blaring as the truck crept down the mountain recklessly. Landon turned the music down and slowed, "What does Misa have planned for tonight? Birthday dinner?" His soft eyes found mine first, and then he glanced at Leyla.

"Yeah, classic birthday dinner... I'm bringing your buddy, Logan. He's been after me for weeks now."

"Logan? Really?" Scoffing with disbelief.

Leyla chewed on her recent manicure.

"Sure, why not? Why? Are you jealous?" She poked her head from the back and smacked his shoulder. He giggled nervously.

"-He's an airhead. You're too smart for him. All I'm saying is don't use big words when talking to him." He continued to chop as I caught her eyes roll,

"-Should I dress formally?"

"Cash... dress cash. Daya, I have your gift at mom's house. I'll bring it later, and you can wear it for dinner."

Landon reached for my hand.

"-Daya... I also have a surprise for you. But later." His voice was sweet and calm. I nearly drifted into his eyes before I realized I couldn't possibly have my emotions under control, so my eyes darted outside of the window. He has seen my eyes rapidly change before, but never-ending questions always followed.

What was on his mind? I thought, holding onto him,

Sex?

-Sex, out of all things, wasn't in my plan, nor did I think he had it in his plans when the thought slipped in my brain. But once the idea popped up, I suddenly couldn't leave it alone. I'd be lying if I said I wasn't a little intrigued, which took me off guard almost immediately.

I, Daya Managualt, have never been intrigued or curious about,

Sex.

Ever. Until right now, this moment. And it was already beginning to suffocate me.

By the time we reached the senior parking lot, I was sweating and avoiding all eye contact. Landon helped me out of the truck and walked hand-in-hand with me into the school like any other day. All I could think of was, how am I going to let this go?

Throughout Social Studies, I twitched in my seat.

Despite my rough start, I woke up this morning feeling noticeably different. Mature and sexual. Confident even and oddly enough, powerful. After that nightmare episode, I couldn't help but masturbate for the first time; after looking at myself while clearing up a foggy mirror after my steamy shower, I felt more into myself. I checked myself out in the mirror for the first time when I dropped my towel. I looked terrific naked and overcome with suppressed sexual tension I didn't know existed in me. I never knew I looked so tempting, completely natural. I could finally see the hype in Landon's eyes. It was a dusty thought that blew over almost instantly and thrown behind many other thoughts as I sat in class, wondering if turning 18 affected my sexual desire,

It seems to be growing.

Now I thought of Landon, his smile, and those love-addicted eyes that go loco over me. Heat flushed from an intimate place. I was beginning to turn myself on. I slipped my hands between my warm thighs, my fingers digging into my blue jeans under the desk.

His lips.

His God-forsaken lips were my next thought.

How he talked to me, in that low sexy voice.

How his bottom lip seemed to quiver when he said 'surprise,' and how he licked his lips right after. I couldn't stop the thoughts from coming in. I tried to tell myself I wasn't ready for those invading thoughts, but apparently, my body was otherwise. I couldn't knock it off. I was beginning to wonder how I would act when I saw Landon in a short couple of hours for lunch. I had to avoid him until these feelings went away.

I never felt as near translucent as I did with Landon in the cafe for lunch. Landon stood leaned up against the table, awaiting me. The closer I got, the more nervous I got. I was beginning to wish I had skipped lunch. But when I was face to face with him, I was also faced with the urge to get inside his head. For the first time since we started dating, I looked at him. His eyes weren't just blue or green. They were sapphire with a wisp of stardust. They glittered a little when they focused on me, like when we first met. I didn't know it at that moment, but the corner of my lip creased up. I was smiling at him, and he took notice.

"-Hey," he had optimism in his voice while trying to pull me into his arms. For the first time since he asked me to be his girlfriend, he made me perfectly anxious, and it was slowly beginning to scare me.

"You seem different." He admitted as he tried to chase the color in my eyes. I avoided him again. I knew I'd be reckless and unsettled. His cold hands ran up my arm, sending goosebumps to the front line. I felt that too. "I feel different-" I mirrored him, sitting down, our legs straddling the bench as we faced each other.

"Yeah… there's something different in your eyes today…" and he seemed to like it. Very offish-ly, it made me excited in more than just one way. My body heated up.

"That surprise I had for you… it can't wait."

Of course, the thought of it was eating me alive.

I was nearly begging to hear about it. Unshelved even. I took a deep breath and tried to relax before looking into his eyes. I knew my emotions now; they were controlled.

"I've been thinking Landon and … I think-"

"-Dayanara…" He stopped me just as I was about to tell him how I've been feeling about blossoming up for him. Instead, he took both my hands into his and looked at me. Nervously he cracked a smile and glanced away before looking back at me.

"Dayanara Managualt, will you please do me the honor and accept my ring?" His right hand slid behind him, and he forced out a box too big for his slim-fit pocket. So nervous, he no longer searched to find my eyes but tried to keep from dropping the box.

"I'm not going to sugarcoat it, Daya… It's an engagement ring, and I was going to propose. I spent all summer saving and planning. But I know how fickle you could be about love, and I don't want to scare you off, so it's just a promise ring for now."

"Fickle?" I repeated, unaware of how bad I played in love.

"I know you love me, Daya, but let's be honest, you're not exactly the romantic type. But, I do know that I love you, and I care about your family like my own. I know you make me want to do and be better, and I want a future with you. You're my motivation in life, and I need you. Will you accept it?"

My heart sank deep.

I felt like he knocked the wind right out of my chest. The truth was, it's not what I wanted to hear. I barely knew how to act coming in here, which was about sex. Marriage, right now? And wait a minute; what about sex? I can't tell him what I was thinking now. He could either run from my advances or take full advantage of it, although that idea kind of lifted me. I looked down at his hands. He popped the box open, and over a tiny silver band, there was a beautiful diamond rock. It made the entire thing so fundamental.

"Landon… I don't know what to say."

"It doesn't have to mean anything now." I reluctantly agreed, taking the box and holding it in my hands. I couldn't help but stare at the ring, glimmering underneath the dim cafeteria lights.

He wants to marry me? Keep me forever?

Why did that make me so sad? I couldn't say anything.

"Hey, Day-" He lifted my chin, "One more thing, I haven't had a chance to talk to Misael about this… so please, don't say anything."

Landon's eyes shot towards a happy-go-lucky Leyla, strutting into the cafe. She was clicking her booties on the vinyl flooring, like a supermodel. I looked at him as he leaned in quickly and kissed me fast. My lips felt a strange sensation I had never felt before. Passion perhaps caused my eyes to shimmer into a tomato red and back to the rusty color it was before.

Shit- Landon noticed.

"Your eyes … it's doing it again."

Leyla slapped her hands down right between us. It shook our heavy thoughts away, and I snapped the box shut, shoving it into my sweater just in time for Leyla not to notice.

"What are you guys up to?" She casually asked as she sat down.

A wave of relief washed over. I realized that this was my moment to escape, "-I'm going to go use the bathroom. I'll be back." I peeled off the bench and out of the cafeteria. Landon watched me run away; his face played how deep his heart sank. I spent the rest of my lunch underneath the west wing staircase. I couldn't bring myself to face Landon after his surprise, so I hid for cover. I sat there in solitude, reflecting on my relationship with Landon.

I never saw it heading in this direction, though the signs all pointed to one door. Of course, I was just as giddy as any girl initially. But not before testing him. It took me a while to trust his intentions. It was a day just like this. He was nervous to talk to me but confident nonetheless. By then, my reputation as a shrew was perpetuated through the grapevine like a ghostwriter. No one was shocked when he asked me, except for me.

I gave him a hard time that first week of him pursuing me. I refused to believe that Mr. Popular, Mr. Grey Wolf Hollow High, Mr. Home-coming king, wanted *me* out of all the girls in school.

He was tall, athletic, and charming. Despite being raised by a single mother, he wasn't a delinquent, running around causing chaos and smoking cigarettes and weed. He came from Old money, dressed well and proper. Respectful and well-spoken. My uncle loved that about him. All the while, there was nothing special about me. But he insisted.

I refused to let him take me out, and then I refused to hear him out. By the end of that first week of serenading, he was beginning to get frustrated. He recruited Leyla, who tried her best every day to convince me he was a good guy. Finally, I insisted that someone paid him to ask me out or that he only wanted my virginity under his belt. He didn't want me; he wanted Leyla. But she was anything but loyal to one suitor at the time.

She defended him.

"He's just not that type of guy Daya. He's not that stupid."

I'd thought so otherwise.

Leyla insisted that I stop thinking too hard about this.

"Dayanara, he's the hottest and sweetest guy in school. Give me one good reason why not?"

"It's because he is the hottest and sweetest guy in school that I don't want to," I admitted that early Spring day by the gym lockers. She stared at me with desperate eyes, her stare echoing, '*please,*'

"Fine, I'll go out with him. But one little thing goes wrong, and I'm leaving," I warned.

Our first date was casual. So casual, it was a double date at *Billy's,* the local gaming and Pub hangout, with Leyla and her boy toy at the time. Even in a place so crowded, the unthinkable happened. I was caving in. Leyla didn't warn how easy it would be for him to break down the volcanic breccia hedges I built around my heart. He didn't even mind ripping down the old thorny vines that grew like wild grass inside my heart. Landon was that invested. So determined to make me his that the more he pushed, the more I broke. He was kind and very well-mannered. He opened doors and pulled chairs out for me. The *nicer* he got, the *ruder* I got.

I challenged him with everything. But, in brief honesty, our conversation kept going to shit because of my unwillingness to give up my vulnerability. Challenging him turned into being rude until I was no longer my quiet and sweet self anymore.

By the time we were sitting in the bed of his truck at Lancer's Drive-In, Landon was infuriated but mostly frustrated with me; he pretended to be okay. He had offered me popcorn, soda pop, and nachos, but I refused. He even offered his Letterman to me when my teeth began to chatter, and I turned him down. All the while, Leyla was texting me death threats from a few car rows down. She was horrified, watching from a distance. I was destroying all faith in Landon, and that had distracted her from her date.

Now she was summoning my immediate death.

I finally broke Landon when I snapped at him.

"-*You don't have to get me anything!!*"

Looking down, he took a moment before he scoffed. I knew he had enough, and it wasn't just the look of disgust on his face,

"... You're right, I don't have to get you anything. I wanted to..."

"Well, don't. I don't know what you're expecting out of me, Landon, but you're not getting laid...." And then he snapped back.

"-You're kidding me, right? Is that what this is all about? You think I'm trying to get in your pants? I wasn't hoping to get laid, I was hoping to get to know the girl I have a crush on, but you're acting like a bitch. Is this how you always are? Because I'm beginning to think you're exactly the girl that everyone makes you up to be. *My* mistake." Ultimately his sad eyes turned me soft. He kicked off the tailgate and trailed into a dark background. My heart sank in shame. What a fucking bitch I had become to protect myself from something I knew nothing about, love. The sad part was that we all knew I was purposely sabotaging the night. I never gave him a chance, and he had been so kind and sincere. So what the hell did I do?

When he recoiled back to his truck, I had a swift change of heart. He avoided me as he walked to the driver's seat to grab his jacket. When he came back, his tone had switched. So serious, "You think Leyla can give you a lift home? I'm checking out for the night..." I sighed miserably and blurted out, "I'm sorry!" And I was.

"I've been at your tail for weeks now, and I don't want to waste your time. It's clear you don't want to be here, at least not with me." I did want to be there. With Landon, no one else. "I do want to be here... Look, I'm sorry for acting like a sketchy bitch. I never had this before, it's my first date, and I'm just nervous and paranoid."

"Paranoid? Why?"

"Come on, Landon... You're perfect. You could have anyone you want. So what would you want from a girl like me? I only have one thing to offer." He rolled his eyes and chuckled.

"Yes. You are very paranoid, Daya. Why wouldn't I want some-one to like you? There's so much depth I can only glance in from the outside, and I want to know more. You're unique and smart as hell. Beautiful and different, you're not a follower or after every guy you see. I pay attention to all of that Daya, not just what you look like in a skirt. Although that also seems to turn my head too. Now I'm just humiliated, and I feel kind of ridiculous that a girl like you would ever even consider me...." Shadows and honesty crept on his face. He still looked perfect even in solemn anguish.

"I'm a fucking spaz... this is my fault. I never meant to make you feel that way. I'm sorry, and you don't deserve any of it. You've been so kind and sweet and respectful. Can we start over?" I asked him timidly. He shook his head in disbelief and looked at the woods behind us. He played with the jacket zipper in his hands as he thought about it, "No... no, we can't."

Ugh- I wanted to take a thorny stake to my heart.

"-Kidding.... I'm just kidding. You deserve that..." He laughed and joked as he came close. Relieved, I cracked a smile.

"I'll take that jacket now."

I reached over and softly ripped it from his grips. He smiled before handing me a chocolate bar. I smirked back at him, glad to be in his good graces once again. I made him nervous.

"How about some popcorn?" Sitting back on the bed of the truck.

"That's just going too far now." I joked.

By the end of the movie, he had his arms wrapped around me. After that night, the drive-in and the late-night talks on the dock turned into a routine every Friday night.

Any other Friday night, I'd worry about what movie we'd watch at the drive-in. But instead, I was more worried about the conver-sation Landon would have with my uncle at dinner. Even so, all that intensity wasn't strong enough to throw away the thoughts of being underneath Landon, nonetheless on top of him. Sex was still zooming in my mind, and it was clear that the thought wasn't going to wash away. Not even the school bell could shake the idea out.

When the last bell rang, my heart was racing like a thousand wild horses across the midwest. I tried to feel normal about seeing Landon. But, unfortunately, I wasn't normal. I stalled. I stopped at my locker and then stopped by the art department to grab my pastel case from Mr. Brook's class. I purposely took my time, and by the time I reached the parking lot, I had convinced myself that I would be just fine. My eyes found Leyla first, sitting on Logan's car. Her arms around him and his knees between her knees, picking at each other's faces in puppy love. I immediately found Landon at his truck a moment later, and I started towards him.

He was looking down at his phone when I came over. His one arm winged open and caught me, pulling me in softly. "Where did you go?" He finally looked away from his phone. Disappointment in his tone, I had to come up with something. "I had to go see Mrs. Laurie … about my College applications. Sorry, I should have texted you." I pecked a kiss on his cheek.

"Scared me half to death, babe. Everything okay?"

"Yeah… I just wanted to get some advice on writing my essays."

"I doubt you need to worry about that; you are beauty and brains... So Daya. About the ring. You don't have to accept it if you don't want to..." Typical me; overthinking things and making him feel insecure. Now he sounded unsure. The same skeptical tone he had that night at Lancer's drive-in. "I accept… it,"

I still don't understand what drove me to say that.

"You know I love you, right?" He suddenly kissed me. Each grasp was made to make my body tingle and sore. Why was I feeling so intense? I had never felt this way before. My eyes effortlessly closed in the bliss of his lips. His fingers traced away at the sides of me. I giggled before opening my eyes. He was smiling back, eyes glowing, completely mesmerized.

"Right..." The way he looked at me nearly took my breath away. I blushed as he exhaled slowly. We both felt something different in the air. For once, I wasn't holding back. I was completely open. He broke an easy-going smile, "Come on. I'll take you to Billy's for a not-so-virgin, Shirley Temple."

Though his words made my heart skip a beat, I loved the sound of that. Accepting his offer, I hopped into my boyfriend's truck.

3

Birthday

My uncle was in rare form when I got home that afternoon. He was sitting in the living room in a gloomy dark corner, tweaking the strings to his *quarto*. A little ominous if you asked me, sitting there alone in the dark, all paranoid. My uncle's melancholia mood carried on into today. It was enough to make him pull out his old Congo's and even the guitar. "You haven't played that thing in years...." I said as I walked in, and it was quiet for a moment until,

"Hey, you don't have to stay home for your birthday,"

The thought seemed idealistic. I could stop Landon from talking about the proposal, and I could be alone with him and bail on everyone. I peered into the kitchen from where I stood, the dinner table elegantly set and dinner already cooking. Misa seemed more depressed than ever today, and that worried me. I had the same feeling as I did last night. Something wasn't right with him.

"I love our little rituals, and I have all I want here."

My uncle took a minute to take in my words, "18... really blows my mind... It seems like yesterday you and Leyla were dancing around the Batey in your pj's. Now here you are... 18 and off to college. My girls. I feel like I'm losing them." Fuck. An engagement would wreck his world. Exhausted, I started up the steps.

"-I almost forgot... a package came in for you today,"

It sat on the edge of my bed, a brown package ribbon with dry twine. "*For Dayanara... Utado, Puerto Rico*" No Name. I slowly began to tear away at the brown wrapping paper, eventually breaking, surfacing the face of an old, dusty Journal. Seriously OLD Journal. It was thick but worn down and brown. The binds were beginning to give out, and the metallic gold lining of the book was fading. I flipped it open to the middle of the book. Stained; blue ink cursive. Some, in plain Taino petroglyphs, while the margins had translation and notes written in Spanish. Interesting; the journal took my curiosity to another level. I noticed that the margin had names written by others who had once possessed the book before landing here in my bedroom. My eyes danced around the words until I stopped at two that I recognized. *Salome Managualt*, my cousin. *Anais Managualt*, my mother. My fingers traced over her handwriting. I never felt more elastic and sentimental than I did when my prints brushed over the old ink. I almost felt like I could feel her for the first time.

Mom. My heart yearned in a foreign way. All this time, I was suppressing all these emotions I thought I had never felt. Feelings over Landon and now emotions I had thrown aside over my mom. For so long, I pretended not to care. I was curious about love. And sex. I was curious about Anais. All of her and especially how she died. But my uncle Misa wouldn't have it. I already knew that. I was never allowed to bring her name up, and he was always so quiet about her. He only brought her up when he wanted to, which wasn't often. I picked up the book and held on to it, closing my eyes thinking of the last picture I'd seen of my mom. I couldn't remember.

A Polaroid floated onto my lap from magic, and it was her.

My heart had felt warm because I looked so much like her. Long sparrow hair. Long legs. Hypnotizing eyes. She seemed happy, clutching on the pretty pearl necklace around her neck. Beautiful in her royal tribal attire. Her crown is made of Parrot feathers and a big beautiful smile. I didn't feel so empty for once. And Landon? I could feel something beautiful beginning to erupt inside me. Something was up. I barely explored the book. I was too cautious about it. Not to mention my mother's writing still hypnotized me. It was going to take some time to translate.

I meditated for an hour before I fell into a slumber. I was hoping that a small nap wouldn't rejuvenate such violent dreams. I was wrong. I had the same nightmare. All over again. My mind was tormented by that awful noise IT made; bone cracking. IT drove me up the wall insane. I had to watch the monster draw closer as I lay hopelessly. The monster continued to leave behind that trail of flames and black acid spit, dragging its abnormally skeletal, elongated structure and its terrifying stag crown made of sharp branches and needles. It was so close. I watched the blood run like river streams, down the creases of its burning skin. Cheekbones rise as it laughs, pulling himself a foot closer. He can eat my face off if he wants to. But, looking away, I could only see something rustling in the forest background. Something I've only heard but never seen before in the nightmare.

A Big. Fucking. Bear.

What then started as a tingle sensation turned into pain. My wrist burned and bled. I screamed, awaking from the nightmare. It was painful, and I cried as I ran into my bathroom. I turned on the cold water and let the faucet run over the bleeding burn.

That shit almost touched me through the dream.

That much was confirmed; as I looked down to the burn. It was already beginning to scar before my eyes. So what was I to tell everyone? Did I get burnt by something sharp, or something sharp burnt me? What in the hell? None of it made sense. Something more profound *is* going on, and my uncle's been pretty shady since yesterday. *Someone* was hiding something from me.

It was too much of an eventful 18th Birthday, and all of these emotions weren't 'normal' for me. So it's not a coincidence that these nightmares are coming back. Neither was it a coincidence that I acquired the journal. Not to mention Landon's half-ass proposal and this sudden sexual hunger. Everyone was acting weird today, and I was hoping someone would tell me why? I took a cold shower. I needed it with the concupiscent aching I had. I was hoping Landon had nothing to do with this so I could move on with my plans with him. Yes. Now I had plans with him. Maybe it was the stress with everything going on, but he lingered in my head, screaming **'cure'**; I honestly wanted him on top of me. Tonight. And as I brushed my hair, I thought of a plan of attack.

Music in the background, I tried to pretend everything was *fantastic.* I patched my wrist up smoothed my lips over with balm; I looked classic. I was on my knees before the closet when Leyla walked in. She closed the door behind her and stopped before me, "Girl, what are you doing?" Handing me the gift bag.

"Thank you…"

One glance into the bag, and I was super pleased. I pulled out a long sleeve Navy bodycon dress. It was scandalously short and was going to show too much skin, but I didn't care, "I love it. It's perfect," Leyla was catching onto my new attitude. In the mirror, I grazed myself with my lilac eyes. It was as short and skanky as I imagined. My eyes fluttered a deeper lilac color as my hips moved in the thin cotton dress. My panty line was showing. I reached under the skin-tight dress and pulled my underwear down, kicking it to the side. I took a glimpse of Leyla in the mirror. I was too excited. I turned to her, "... How do I look?"

"Stunning, and I hate you... everyone is here, so we should head down." It came out like sarcasm but could have passed as truth. I shrugged my shoulders at her before ditching the shoes and went down barefooted behind her. The room shined amber. Everyone around the elegant dining table. My aunt and uncle, Sunny, Leyla's date Logan, and Landon. I rudely ignored everyone and walked straight over to Landon without realizing it. I quickly found myself in his hands. "Hey-" His eyes went big in a way I had never noticed before. I liked it.

"-You look amazing... did Leyla get that for you?" I nodded as I let him take my waist and pull me closer. Landon was more than pleased with my warming heart. My uncle, although, was less than satisfied. He was noticing and looked positively scared.

"What are you wearing? Did Leyla get you that?"

"Yes, yes she did."

My uncle looked at her and shook his head disapprovingly.

"What? Mom said it was okay, so don't bag me on it." She sat down next to Logan and crossed her arms and legs. I was too distracted with Landon to start questioning my uncle about strange things. Besides, there are too many guests to start exposing secrets and whatnot. So I shook the idea away and decided to wait for later when our guests were gone. Dinner dragged some. My aunt and uncle bombarded me with questions about my prom, graduation, summer, and college plans. Sunny tried her best to catch up with me between them. Logan was too busy with Leyla and Leyla with Logan. Landon sat next to me quietly and unmoved. It was like he was waiting for his chance to grasp my full attention.

Still, the dinner went on.

After dinner, my uncle played a very embarrassing flip video of me in which I had to hide my sapphire eyes. Then, we told some stories in the living room and played dance music. That gave me a chance to get a little closer to Landon. Although he was terrible, dancing brought us unspeakably close without raising any questions. He noticed the sudden surge in me and deemed it suspicious. Suddenly, I seemed more attentive, more passionate, more comfortable. I was looking at him in his eyes and showing PDA. He wasn't sure how to handle it, but he never rejected it.

Gifts. Toasts. Birthday wishes. My aunt and uncle both whined and cried; the two went on about watching me *grow up fast* and *how proud* they were. But, when Landon took the floor, he brought a different energy. Subtle but sweet until he said he had a gift.

"-First off, I want to say; Misa- Charlotte, you raised a beautiful, smart, amazing girl; you should be very proud of her. I love you, Daya. I always have, always will. I know that I want to be with you forever. So- just so I'm clear- Mr. and Mrs. Managualt, I want to ask Dayanara to marry me."

The music didn't stop, but the room got silent.

Although I saw this coming, my jaw dropped, as did everyone else. I turned to Landon and lightly hit him in the gut, mouthing the words, *'what the hell are you doing?'*

Everyone was stunned. Except for my uncle,

Whose response was to laugh then say,

"Landon, of course, you have my blessing."

"-Misael, what!?" Charlotte was just as confused as the rest of us. Leyla threw her hands up,

"-This has nothing to do with me," Leyla argued, hauling ass. So Landon and I were left alone with my uncle and aunt very quickly.

"Misa? What do you mean they have your blessing? No offense, kids, but you're only kids. This is not what we discussed, Misael..."

I agreed while Landon shook his head in disagreement.

"Charlotte, I trust Landon… especially with Daya… they're just kids. Just like we were, and sometimes kids fall in love. Let them make their own decision."

"*Their OWN decision?* You know why I don't like this."

My aunt was so unconvinced. She seemed to take the news harder than Misael. My uncle surprised me. He was so understanding, maybe too understanding. What a change of heart, I thought.

"Daya… how do you feel about all of this? Are you okay with this?" She turned to me. I looked at Landon, his hands on his hips, shaking his head and his eyes to his still feet. I looked at my uncle, who wanted to know as much as my aunt. Careful, I told myself.

"Well… he did say it was just a promise ring for now… until I'm ready." My aunt finally let the tension go. Exhaling, she looked at me with a concerned look,

"Are you sure you're okay with this?"

I timidly nodded. Looking at Landon, I tried visualizing him without the preppy polo shirt. His sweet eyes pulled a smile out of me. I blushed and rolled my eyes, "-I'm with him."

"Okay. That settles it then. Just don't do anything behind our backs." Misael settled.

Easy. We cut the cake, but everyone was gone. Charlotte said her goodbyes after they sang *happy birthday*. When Misa began with his nightly business phone calls, I was finally free to spend alone with Landon. We walked out onto the porch—one small piece of flaky coconut Birthday cake with strawberry filling to share. I followed Landon's lead to the porch steps and sat with him. We were quiet when Landon began to eat off the plate. I watched him a moment and couldn't help but kiss him, leaving him breathless, and caught off guard. I seized him with my lilac-rose eyes once we pulled off each other, "You sure you want to do this?" He broke the silence.

There was fear in his eyes, and I could feel it. "Are *you* sure about this?" He seemed unsure.

"Yes… I am." He leaned in and kissed me. I closed my eyes, letting his emotions infiltrate into me. Empathy was quickly becoming an addiction. I set the plate aside and wrapped my arms around him, pulling him in hard. I wanted to let him know how much I wanted him on my body. How bad I wanted him IN my body. I couldn't stop kissing him as his hands searched me; I trembled under his fingerprints. It was what I imagined feeling all day. It felt just as good as I knew it would. I pushed him away, finally ripping our lips apart, "-You want to go sit in your truck?"

THE TRUCK? No, I didn't mean the truck. The sound of it was just as unromantic as the thought. But there was no way I could get him upstairs to my bedroom. Fine. The truck will do until I come up with a plan to get him in my room. He was confused for a moment. Understandable; he wasn't used to this odd behavior from me.

"…Uh yeah… Come on." He carried me to the truck. Giggling, I admired him as he admired my eyes. He was about to kiss me when we were distracted by a rustling in the woodlands. We couldn't see anything, but we could hear something, even feel something watching us. I heard another snap from the darkness, but my eyes only found my uncle peering at us from the window. His eyes were on the abyss of the nightly outside, but he was too busy into his conversation. Curfew wasn't for another hour anyway.

Landon tossed me into the passenger seat and ran over to the driver's side. He slammed the door shut and looked at me scandalously. His arms reached for me, but I was much more manic, seductively crawling to straddle his lap.

Yes, in that tiny dress.

I finally got to where I wanted, on top of him. Our eyes locked magnetically. I held him, pinning down his shoulders, throwing my hair to one side. He cracked a shy smile. "-**Woah**."

He was amazed. His eyes were glowing, flexing even as mine were sparkling that fresh and mysterious Lilac color I've never had before. *"I want you so bad,"* The words ached out my mouth shamelessly. I slowly began to rub myself on him. He looked so nervous underneath, slowly submitting to my body's will, at a loss for words. I kissed him. He was shaking and seemed apprehensive.

"Don't be scared... I want you to." I slid his hand up my bare thigh, and I kissed him again, slowly guiding his hand closer. The feeling of his skin stringing along mine was teasing. I threw my head back and moaned. I could feel him rising underneath me like a tent, which reminded me that I wore nothing underneath my dress. Now Landon seems to notice. He suddenly flinched back, retreating his touches and sexual glances.

"I can't... I can't do this...." Landon pulled away. His gut feeling was contagious. I retreated to my seat, crossing my legs instantly.

"-I-I promised your uncle we wouldn't do anything crazy. Besides, wouldn't you rather wait for our wedding night?"

With one sentence, he had ruined the whole moment.

I looked at him and appealed.

"Why does it matter what you promised my uncle?"

"Because I respect him as a man, and I respect you as my girl. I know you; this is not what you want. I don't know what has gotten into you lately, and trust. It'sit's not that I don't like it because clearly, I do. But Daya, you don't want this, not in my truck," looking down at his towering hard-on, he grabbed his football jersey from the back seat to cover it.

"-I want to make a good impression... let's just take it slow?" He meant it. I could tell. Like a preschooler caught running with scissors, I looked down and agreed. He lifted my chin and kissed me,

"I have to head home now... you'll be okay, right?" I nodded.

What a Don.

"Lemme bring you back." He scooped me into his arms and carried me back to my porch. The eerie feeling of watching, still lingering from the dense midnight forest.

I kissed him once more before I let him go. Disappointment dripped down my face as I watched him pull off down the mountain. I let the night air blow it all away and exhaled long. That was intense. Not as intense as the feeling I got standing outside in the creepy night.

Something was watching me.

Leaning against the front door, I discovered that terrible feeling of being left turned on. My heart couldn't stop its repetitive thundering inside, and my eyes were going ballistic from the emotions. An urgent tingling spread all over, and I was red from the excessive thoughts of sex. Throbbing, dripping like a leaky faucet.

Relief; Masturbate

The thought left me cheeky to the point of ache. Adrenaline flowed through me; it was an adventure, literally at hand. But I came down to reality when my uncle's voice pulled me out of my perverted thoughts. He was still on his phone, sitting in the kitchen.

I checked my watch, 11:52 pm. I stayed in the shadows.

I still had a chance to walk up the stairs and mind my own business; the old me warned the new me. But a suspicion arose in my uncle's fainting tone, so I stayed a moment. I couldn't help but eavesdrop. I listened in on his colorful conversation with "*unknown.*" He laughed before continuing,

"Awe, man, I'm excited. -Of course, brother, I haven't seen you in what? 15 years- right. Right, when do you think you'll be arriving in town? October? Wow, that's soon. Yeah, of course. Hey, don't say that; we had our times in the past, but we're still family by spirit, right? We're still best friends, right? Great, so there's no problem. Last you said you were going off-grid to connect with your roots from your father's side of things."

I had to listen more. I wanted to know who *unknown* was.

"... It's strange you bring that up. I don't know. I thought the tribal dances and tea were the cure. -No, Dean- The nightmares have come back. I'm glad you *happen* to call. There's a lot that we need to catch up on. You're the only one I know who could help us, brother. I'm stressed out, and I spoke to the elders down at the res this morning. Oh- they did. I see. So this call wasn't just a coincidence. But, hey, I need you, so please feel free if you're coming to town. I know it might cause some complications. The boys can be tamed, my girls, not so much."

That was enough. I lingered in the shadows long enough.

I walked in, clearing my throat. My uncle already sported a look of guilt. I stared directly at him, and he tried to pretend I wasn't there. All calm, as if everything was just fine. But his contradicting shaky tone made it hard to go along. Finally, the look in my eye forced him to continue, "-Just come back home. We can deal with it; I'm not upset, but we don't have a choice. Yeah sure. Call me when you get into town."

"-Who was that?" I could barely wait till he hung up,

"A good friend. He's the *first person* your mother and I met here. He brought us to the res and introduced me to Charlotte after. He helped me settle here."

"Why did he leave?" My uncle looked at me evasively.

"Dean? He was looking to raise his boys off-grid to give them a more Indigenous life. He didn't want to raise them entitled. The boy's maternal relatives were trying to force their superficial ego influence. Dean didn't have it."

"-Why is he coming back?"

My uncle, exhausted, slid his hand down his face and exhaled.

"Why are you asking so many questions? Why do you care?"

"You told him about my nightmares... Why would you tell a stranger about my nightmares? Did I know him?"

"...You did... when you were little. God, I remember those days. He was my best friend. The only one I could trust. Dean could help with the nightmares. But, trust me when I tell you, everything is going to be fine. You don't need to worry." He sounded like he was trying to convince himself. It wasn't compelling. Be smart.

"... It'll be great for you to have a friend again to do man stuff. Also, it'll give me more time with Landon."

"Yeah, exactly. I love Landon's company, but it would be great to have someone my age who can do real man things like legally drink and go to strip clubs. He has two of his own, so I'm sure Landon won't feel so alone. Soon enough, we men will end up outnumbering you gals here." He meant it as a joke, but it left a bitter taste in his mouth. Great, I thought. More testosterone in the house during this sensitive phase I'm in. I faked a smile, "Goodnight."

"-Daya, there are creatures in the dark, dark night that might-"

"-Bite in the dark, dark night, I love you."

By the time I got in my room, all the sexual frustration in me had drained. I pulled off my dress and pulled on some shorts before crawling into my colorful quilts. Laying there, I remembered the burn and how no one bothered to notice. I had to prepare myself for another sleepless night. Another nightmare was sure to follow. And another nightmare did follow, but not as severe, not as vivid. Tolerable. Even more strange enough, the suffering slipped into a sweet wet slumber that was anything but a nightmare. I began to dream of Landon, and when I woke up, I felt heavenly. As if I had been sleeping on a bed of clouds and baby breath all night.

Almost reborn.

4

Magic Garden

Weeks later, my senses were never sharper.

The burning smell of the turkey bacon turned me on. Everything seemed to turn me on. Apple juice in my hand, and toast with fresh wild berry jam in another; I had more hunger for the life around me. I threw my long legs up on the table in a white cropped sweatshirt and matching shorts. I was amazed by **FOOD**.

"Good morning," My uncle says as he grabs a full plate and takes a seat across from me, "-What are your plans for the day? Hanging out with Landon?" I shook my head as I started to clean up the table. My uncle was already prying into my schedule.

"Maybe later... he has practice."

"Right- So what are *we* doing today?" I looked at him with a skeptical look. '*We?* I beg your pardon? It wasn't like Misa to stay home and hang out with me. Misa ran and took care of his entire business; he was a workaholic. Only on occasion, he would have someone cover for a few hours on the evenings we had a game or something school-related going on. He should be at work, but he was here, trying to plan the day I already had planned.

"Shouldn't you be down at the lumber yard?" I questioned, "-It's Saturday; I go running and meditate; do my errands, and check out the new arrivals at the book store."

"Well, I took a personal day." I looked at him, skeptical.

"-Why would you do that?"

"Because I'm my boss, and I can do that. I wanted to spend time with you and Leyla. Maybe have a movie night or something? We can watch those oldies you two love so much."

"That's what we do with Charlotte already," I shot him down.

"Eh- fine. I'll just find something to do. I've meant to clear out that spot for your garden anyway."

Curiosity spiking, I looked at him.

"You've been promising me that garden since I could remember. Don't you think it's a little late now?" He scoffed.

"-Better late than never. Besides, I have no choice. It's your magic, and the garden gates appeared in the azalea's this morning; your magic will find you regardless. Besides, the excessive potted plants on the deck are a fire hazard."

"-What?" His use of language made me shiver.

"... Well, the gates around your magic garden appeared. Before Ana died, she had mentioned something like this to me; *'The garden gates will rise from the ground.'* I thought you had seen them, honestly." He was casual but gave me the stern, 'don't **ask**' face.

It's fall, early October, which means harvest time in upstate NY. Late that morning, I started on weekend errands. The town was busy. I headed to the post office to pick up and drop off mail. And even though I knew it would be chaotic, I went by the farmer's market. It was nearly impossible to get out of in 15 minutes, but the checkout lines were predictably long. I stopped for hot coffee and munched on an apple on my way to the bookstore. I glanced to the forest woods across the quiet street and noticed something rustling in the bushes. I squinted. It was a vast brown animal, but it was too far into the woodland to be sure.

A bear perhaps; not odd around these parts.

"Got that copy of *Troilus and Cressida*," Sunny handed me a small shopping bag from behind the counter when I caught up with her minutes later. I peered in the bag, my heart warmed.

"Thanks… I appreciate this. When are you getting out?"

"Right about now… give me a few minutes."

I pulled out the book, and I skimmed through the pages for a moment as Sunny disappeared into the background. I was in love with it. I had been a fan of Shakespeare since I first read *Romeo and Juliet* when I was ten, and over the years, I've added to my collection.

Love. Hate. Toxicity. Sex. Tragedy.

That's what life was like; duality, with no punches held.

It was also everything I lacked out of my own life.

"-Excuse me," a jolting voice echoed over me. My eyes never left the book pages, despite the stranger. He lightly bumped me, and I saw the sparks fly unexpectedly over it. Ugh, I wouldn't say I liked these random magical happenings. They were hard to be discreet about, harder to discredit. So I pretended not to notice and ignored the stranger, keeping my eyes hidden within the book and even turning from him to let him pass by.

"Sorry," I finally looked up, but the tall stranger swiftly disappeared behind the bookcases as Sunny returned to me.

The Grey Wolf River was my favorite place on earth; aside from the El Yunque rainforest, we'd visit once a year. Not only was Grey Wolf River jolting with natural beauty, but it was also a place where I could get away from everything, on occasion. The mixed indigenous cultures made it an ideal place for learning, which I loved. It was always peaceful and straightforward here.

Hot summer days called for swimming, fishing, and sports, and there was always something going on at the ceremonial courts. My favorite pastime was to run the nature trails. I'd find different paths that led right up the mountain, back home. I don't know what it was about this place that made me feel so free, but I loved it here.

It was my second home.

Our bloodline was exceptionally different; Rare Royal Native blood. When mama and Misa arrived here, they were greeted and taken in by loving and caring arms; and the people of Grey Wolf River welcomed our family name with blessings. We were blessed with a second home and family, collecting 'outsider' friends over the years. The kind and humbling people were always easygoing and respectful, peacefully following their cultural lifestyles without judgment or interference. We took care of each other. They protected each other. Helped each other, no matter what part of the world your indigenous roots were snatched from, as long as you treated everyone with respect and kindness. A sacred and private place;

When I got to Wolf Creek River that afternoon, Misa stood outside Charlotte's cabin, seemingly waiting for me. It's been a while since my uncle has loitered these parts.

"What are you doing here?"

"You've been asking many questions lately," My uncle stopped me, "-I need to speak to you."

Misa's suspicious nature made me cynical,

"I've been finding a lot of reasons to ask questions."

"The elders asked me to bring you to the village... they want to talk to us." The look on his face said it was going to be a while. The defeat on his face should have warned me. I gave Sunny the okay to go on without me. She nodded and trailed on home. I raised my hands over my head and held them there for a long while. Then, after deep thought, I swung my arms down, slapping on my thighs, and faced him, "... What's the meaning of this?"

More sketchy shit, I thought.

Misael kept quiet and led me across the reservation. We stopped outside the elder's village hall, and not a moment passed when Charlotte poked her head from inside the hall, "-They're ready."

5 Elders in royal thrones, each to their respective royal tribe on the reserve. *The Cree, the Navajo, the Cherokee, the Aztecs, and the Blackfoot.* They were the watchers of Grey Wolf River Reserve. It was intimidating to stand before the wise men. From what I understood, the elders summoned only a select few to the sacred conference hall, which was either good or bad.

"Miss Dayanara, you've grown so much," The spokesmen for the group spoke. He sat in the middle, and I recognized him the most because he was Charlotte's Grandfather. The watcher of the Cree born, "I'm sure your uncle told you why you're here."

"-I had no time," My uncle Misael stared to the ground.

"-A imminent curse takes a higher degree of ritual. It was ignorant of you to believe such a thing would pass." Troubled, My uncle turned to me, "Daya, as you know, the Managualt lineage is one of the last Taino Royal blood families; But it is also one of the many **Moboyas** cursed in the name of Princess Guanina and her un-matched lust. The same pure blood courses through your veins, which means you inherited the curse like all Managualt women. I hadn't said anything before because Dean and I had thought we had cured you of the curse, as we did Leyla. But your nightmares have returned, which means the fever is setting in."

"Fever? What fever?"

"The fever inflicted to kill you," I suddenly became distrusting with my uncle, now that I was thinking about it. It all made sense. Tears dropped from my ebony clouded eyes as I tried to keep my attention upfront with the elders.

"I thought we had cured you. We all thought we had everything figured out to save you. But the magic failed." My uncle made eye contact with the elders, and they nudged him to continue, "-the curse is a dark blockage ignited by your natural lust, only to suppress your heart chakra. All romantic emotions within you exist, but the attempt to cure you failed. The curse begins with nightmares; then, they become severe fevers. You'll keep having these fevers until the last fever consumes you into the darkness. Unless we find a cure, the curse will prevent you from falling in love with anyone who is not pure Taino-born. But you're much more than a Taino princess Daya; **Moboyas,** a dark spirit of our tribe, fell in love with your mother's shining beauty. He was obsessed with her light and followed her around. She went missing for weeks before she washed up on the river banks. When we got her home, we found out she was pregnant. Moboyas, the Taino spirit of Darkness and Death, is your true father, and he took your mother from us the day you were born. Moboyas is at fault for conjuring the creature you see in your nightmares.

"He's angry. We've seen your future Dayanara. You're star-crossed with one of *our* boys-" The watcher of the Cree stood. "-the *wendigo* is the creature after you, child. The jealousy and distrust this divine love will brew can kill the both of you if you are not smart about it." He warned.

"-Grandfather, we don't need to scare her; we can cure a curse."

"-We are here to help Charlotte, but we know nothing... that's why we called Dean Tyson. He'll be moving back to town, and he's unsteady. You can only imagine why. We only know of the great danger because of the boy; the Spirits have warned us."

"What about Landon?" I cried to Charlotte.

"Honey, even if Landon were your soulmate, there would be no future between you. It's the one permanent part of the curse healers can not reverse. Daya, you're a goddess half-ling. In Moboyas mind, you are his creation. Therefore, he will indefinitely make sure that you return to your home in *Turey*. Even if we break the curse, Moboyas will relinquish your freedom to love on earth. Whatever you're starting to feel now will be taken from you, and you'll be numb like you were before." That last part hurt most. This new thing called *'feelings'* was a beautiful gift, and my respected father threatened to take it from me. All this euphoria I felt, gone with the wind, "-As Watcher of Cree, I refuse to lose our most powerful spirit warrior over this love affair. For now, we are waiting for the Tyson family. We wanted to make sure Misael did the right thing, and that was to tell you-" Misael and Charlotte chased me as I stormed out of the conference hall, breathing in the cold fall air. Dusk was settling; dark navy sky with a stride of neon orange. The pathway lights were turning on as we walked. The two continued to argue behind me,

"-Just stop! You're both making this worse, so please,"

"She's right," My uncle suddenly went from eighty to zero and looked at Charlotte peacefully. The two kept quiet as they walked on before me. I stayed behind and cried there in the middle of the reservation. It was seemingly empty, with no one to notice me standing there, gracelessly crying, until one of the res boys appeared from the blue. It was dark out, so I didn't see him right away. I only noticed Skylar there when he spoke. "Daya," he reached over and gently took my arm. Aztec blood, I thought as I looked in his brown russet eyes. God, I'm paranoid. Although I already knew Skylar, he felt kind and inviting. I found myself violating him with my eyes, unintentionally. His arms were like boulders; I cried right into his big arms, and he didn't resist. He pulled me close and let me cry. I looked up at his chest and admired the beauty of the male form through him. My eyes met his very hopeful eyes. Slowly. I hoped he would kiss me, and for a moment, I thought he would but,

"-Daya, what are you doing?"

Leyla snapped out of it, and I fell right out of Skylar's arms. Quickly. Leyla pulled me away from him; I was oblivious to my magic, hungry to inflict lust on whomever. A downpour of sad tears ensued. As I lay in bed that night, everything sunk into me.

I locked myself in my room for three days as I hid from the world and avoided everyone. It was so hard to accept what was happening. My fate was inescapable, according to the elders. I was a slave to these nightmares and this sexual hunger, destined to be enslaved. I had thought I was born to resist love. I've only been hypnotized and lied to for 12 years. I was blinded to withstand love, passion, emotions, and sex. Now out of the blue, it was the only thing I obsessed over. I was never going to have it now. What was my uncle's plan? Use Landon to keep me from the truth? Was that the only reason why he was okay with our engagement? I didn't know what to think, so I ignored Landon and eventually lashed out when he asked me why I blew off his phone calls and texts. I had only one honest answer; I had become curious about *'the Cree boy.'*

Who was he? Where was he? Was he looking for me?

And not knowing precisely who Landon's father was, there was still that slim possibility it could be him. These questions only made me want to find *'him.'* It was killing me slower than poison, and I just wanted to die already. Dying would be a process for me. However, the nightmares seemed to wind down in intensity. Since my birthday, they appeared to be fading each day. By the 3rd day of isolation, I was binge-watching my favorite old romance movies; *West Side story, Casa Blanca, Philadelphia Story, A Bronx Tale,* to name a few. This new emotion felt like I was watching them all for the first time. Feeling every stretch of the human emotion, **love,** run within me, while I still had the feeling. By noon, I decided to forgive my uncle. I couldn't hold onto the anger anymore. Not while Misa acted so normal about everything; he was still so kind and caring, as he always had been. Besides, I still had questions, and I wanted more answers. He was the only one who could give me that.

Around eight that evening, he finally walked into the living room. With a smile on his face, he seemed like he was in a good mood. That was until he reviewed the selection of movies I was watching. "How was your day," he was almost afraid to ask.

"Good, and yours?" In my sweetest voice ever; His fear subsided.

"Good. Hey, you're not still mad at me, are you?"

"No, not at all... but I have questions," I smiled at him. I was serious but not trying to fight. My uncle sighed, defeated. Then, as if he was waiting for it, he sat down on the couch, nervously rubbing the crown of his head. I wasn't sure of what I wanted to know, except for the identity of the Cree boy "-Who is he?" I dove right in.

"I have no idea... But, honestly- **(LIES)** -even if I did know, I wouldn't hide it from you. As Charlotte said, there are plenty of cures for this curse. But no matter which you choose, you can't be with him or anyone else. So I need to keep you away from him, for your own sake. You used to be pretty great at staying away from boys-" I cracked a smile, and then a chuckle came out. My uncle was relieved to hear it, "-You've had any nightmares lately?"

"No, and please don't bring it up." He nodded in agreement.

"I finished the garden. Want to go take a look?"

I followed him to the dark backyard. We were empty of all we had left from the summer, but the water well next to the fire pit. Misa had the patio glowing with furniture and the fire pit flaring in the summertime. The freshly cut lawn with sun chairs and summertime decorations would be on display; The trampoline and pitched tents. The place would radiate with patches of flowers, fruits, and veggies scattered throughout the yard because I had no space for a greenhouse garden. But tonight, it was completely vacant. My uncle led me near the forest, where the trail led deeper into the Northern abyss. In the distance, I saw the flower ravished gates.

Ultimately in the dark, my uncle guides me forward. I could hear the crunchy fall leaves underneath each step I took until we stopped. Then, I listened to the sound of a squeaky and possibly very rusty old metal garden gate scrape against the earth. There was something here. I took another step and no longer felt or heard the crunch of the dried leaves. I took several more steps and noticed the terrain had become squishy, like walking on sand. Finally, we stopped, and I heard the gates close behind us. It was suddenly hot and humid.

What an Enchantment.

How did we get here? But this wasn't the backyard, and it sure the fuck wasn't upstate New York in the fall. But this magical garden we found ourselves in was not so foreign. It was the strangest thing; I've been here before, in my dreams—that cross-world between El Yunque and the Adirondacks. "Where the hell are we?" -We were in a perfect 90 degrees, jungle-like realm, glamourized by the sea-rolling beachfront like a hidden cove. Goosebumps seem to peak over my skin. The palm trees swayed against the oak and pine. I could see sunlight rays peering, from which was impossible; I had seen the sun go down hours ago.

"This place is **your Magic Garden**,"

The garden was a pleasant surprise. Like never before, I could feel the magic and power pulse within my veins in the garden. I was excited, and he urged me to explore, "Go ahead," he said when I looked back at him. I took off running.

Breathtaking. So surreal. I found myself surrounded by bright Flamboyans and palms. Patches of colorful wildflowers grew wildly.

There were hundreds of beautiful flowers, some known to produce in the Caribbean and others from Northern America. This infinite natural realm hoarded red hibiscus, sunflowers, yellow Brugmansia, and musk rainbow plumerias; exotic flowers and rose vines everywhere; Egrets and Lilies, phalaenopsis orchids, daisies; anything and everything I could imagine. Trees of coconut, banana, grapefruits, mangoes, papayas, and sour-sop. Star apples, oranges, strawberries, avocados, and pineapples. Trees, vines of bell peppers, plantains, Quenepas, Yautia, Cassavas, and much more to eat, hear, smell, touch, and see. Rich ivory sand glittered in and around a small *Batey.* It was of color rainbow fluorite. Next to it stood a yellow Flamboyan tree. Waterfalls ravished into a surrounding lagoon—colors of turquoise, Cerulean, and seafoam, and hedges of stone, grass, and flowers. The fire sun beating behind the trees; the entire place had a visible golden tint. I could see all the living species in the glowing light inhabited the garden. Most of the air and water; colorful butterflies and peacocks. Raintree frogs. Fishes glittering in the water and beautiful birds singing from above. Parrots, and even a couple of horses snacking in the bushes.

Only one beautiful Ceiba grew its roots wildly in the middle of the garden. Bright red *dinnerplate* hibiscus and classic white lilies rose savagely all over the tree. The colors and visuals were enchanting, putting a spell on my eyes until I realized it was all real, as it was growing and breathing before my eyes.

"Uncle, how is this possible?" Unsure if it were an illusion.

"Ancient magic; it courses through the Managualt blood. Everyone has their magic garden once their magic awakens. The magic inside will always protect you from the wendigo. It will make you stronger. Heal you from anything."

I was intrigued; A healing paradise of my own.

"I could live here?"

"You can. If you wanted to, you could live here forever."

Looking at the dusky coloring sky, my hands brisked through the lagoon. It all seemed surreal. Everything seemed perfect here.

"Once you learn your powers, you'll be able to manipulate every aspect of the garden and grow as much as you want. If you choose to bind your life here, you will be young and live forever. But you could **never** leave, nor ever bring in a living soul, because everyone has their garden, so their souls will be ravished, trapped, attached, and entwined into your garden, and your realm will make them a part of its beauty. If you choose to stay here, we'll have Dean do that binding thing, and you'll be safe here."

I was charmed by its beauty; smiling as I paced around,

"I love it… thank you; it's beautiful."

"You have mother Gaia to thank,"

Leaving the garden was as dramatic as going in. We returned to the cold, dark backyard. The garden gates behind us looked how I imagined; white, old, and rusty. I watched my uncle lock the bolt and slip the key into his pocket. Then, in the dark, cold evening, we walked back to the house for tea and apple slices.

I returned to school the next day hoping to apologize to Landon; after a few harsh text messages back and forth, unfortunately, I had thrown him to the back of my mind, and he hadn't surfaced until now, while he was standing behind me at my locker.

"Still mad at me?" I asked as I slammed the locker door shut and turned to him. My back rested on the cold metal.

"I knew you were a brat when I started dating you. I miss you," He kissed me sincerely, and I watched his eyes glow tints of green, as it does on occasion. He glanced at my hand and took notice of his ring. He smiled. "What are you doing in an hour? Want to ditch and hang out in my truck?" I looked at him. He had this planned, and I was glad he did. Although Landon wasn't my soul mate, and I couldn't be left alone with him, I still very much wanted him. My hands balled into knuckles as I gripped his tee-shirt. I kissed him hard and excitedly. He stared at me with those glowing eyes, so severe but handsome.

"-Yes, I'll skip class with you." With a hazed voice, as if he had said something utterly romantic. My thoughts danced with expectations. We would be alone, parked off somewhere out of sight. He'd tell me some crazy story about how he's always been the one, and I'll be ready to take it all away without a single thought.

My heart pumped excitedly. My stomach fluttered.

Then Landon crushed all my hopes,

"Cool, so meet me here after the next class. Logan and Leyla are on their way up to your house now. She had mentioned that Misa had a couple of lunch meetings..." As the bell rang, I exhaled all the broken hopes, and Landon hurried to his next class. Great.

The lyrics to *sex & candy* set a legit mood in Landon's car. Parked to the farthest side of the dirt driveway, Landon and I hid under the pine needles and the forest shadows. Just perfect for privacy. His new truck smelled of the cheap air fresheners from the rearview mirror. The backseat was a mess; jackets and clothing we stripped off, tossed into the pile of random stuff. He must have been in a hurry to clean the truck because the leather shined and smelled clean, but his dirty jerseys and football gear were now in the back seat with all the mail and papers he once hoarded between the seat console. After that, it was easier to slide onto his lap.

Admiring his ripped and hairless statue, I had him bare-chested and unbuckled. As if it matters; I had been straddling him for the last 45 minutes but not getting anywhere. My anticipation was leaking down my thighs. When we got up to the house, Ley seemed annoyed with me, and strangely Landon was getting to the same point. Logan drooled over my overheated body and the littlest sexual innuendo I threw into the universe. Once I got Landon alone, I figured he'd relax, but his body was still so tense underneath me. Eventually, he brushed away any lingering doubts and allowed things to heat up between us.

I couldn't get enough of Landon's lips. His fingernails dug deep into my hips, grinding me slowly against him. The bulge in his jeans has been teasing me through the thin fabric of the biker shorts I wore. I could see the resistance in his mind, but his body said so otherwise, so I held him pinned down. My free hand explored his abs and chest. Both of us are sweating; nerves perhaps. He looked away, his arms off to the side. Barely holding my eyes, his brows underlining the curved wrinkles on his head. He was distracted.

Logan and Leyla.

The two had been bickering innocently before making out on top of Logan's car, all out in the open. I took Landon's chin and redirected his emerald eyes onto me. He seemed upset, but that couldn't steer me away from what I desired. I continued to kiss and hump him, despite him. The friction I was laying on him could have quickly started a fire—the truck rocking suspiciously.

"I want you so bad," I whispered before licking the rim of his earlobe. It must have been too much for him. His hands took control of my arms, and he harshly pushed me away.

"We should stop." He was serious as his arms pushed me back into the passenger's seat. The truck rocked more. The confusion reflected in my eyes of pasty hoary clouding over my once lilac pupils. He refused them as he looked back over to his buddy Logan cradling Leyla. I exhaled viciously with irritation. He glared at me and said,

"-Dayanara, your eyes again. Can you control them?"

I rolled them for him.

"You're killing my mood," I confessed as he rolled down the windows. I looked towards a suspicious rustling in the woods. He took a deep breath from the crisp mid-October air. The smell of fire logs and crops blew in with the brisk wind.

"-What are you two doing?" Leyla interrogated Landon through the widow. He huffed a slightly nervous laugh, "-Nothing," he promised her. I crossed my legs tightly and reached for my jacket. *Son of a bitch.* I watched in envy as Logan pulled Leyla into him, aggressively grabbing a handful of her ass and kissing her like he was leaving for good. My eyes clouded over a bright emerald, abet Logan's seducing glance at me, "-What are you doing?" Landon was itching paranoia. My eyes stayed on Logan putting his Letterman over Leyla's shoulders. Logan lifted her onto his front bumper. Her legs split in two, despite the skirt she was wearing. His hands grappled the skin on her thighs. I knew Landon could see the longing for it in my eyes as I also watched the pair, near to arousal;

"-Can I say something to you without you jumping down my throat?" Landon interrupted. I knew I wasn't going to like what he had to say. His fingers ran through his soft brown hair before pulling on his tee-shirt. I sucked my teeth and nodded to my disappointment, giving him the go. "You're amazing. You're smart and serious and kind. Your beauty is blinding. Daya, you have no idea how much you turn me on. I love you, and I want to make you my wife; you know that, right?" The way he stared at me made me feel bad. I kept my eyes on the rustling trees.

"I want to… but I can't. We've talked about this. I'm only doing it for you," Landon's eyes of humility meeting inferno had pierced me some. He looked away and began to eyestalk Leyla. I watched him curiously before saying, "I hope I'm what you want, Landon…" the words came crackling out, low and alienated. He pretended to ignore me as he watched the brewing drama between Leyla and

Logan. I barely notice them squabbling before us with the rustling in the woods.

"Just stop," Landon was more aggravated now.

"You know what, I'm tired. So I'm going to call it a night."

"It's the damn afternoon; what do you mean?"

"You don't have to deal with me..." I grabbed my book bag.

"You're acting like a whore." Did he call me *a whore?* Landon has never disrespected my name before. I never gave him a reason. I looked at him with excruciating eyes, and he instantly regretted the words. I don't know what color my eyes were getting, but I know it made him feel shameful. I was suddenly dropping tears as he was speechless. Our toxic moment was stolen by Leyla screaming. Landon and I jumped out of the truck and ran over to them. The two were fussing about a big bear near the rustling trees until Leyla asked me, "Were you two having sex? "

"-No." Leyla was utterly dejected. I gave her a loathing look,

"-That's not any of your business." That hit a nerve in her.

"You're so reckless, Daya! You can't do it with Landon."

Was she joking? She had to be. I turned to Landon.

"You're holding back, and if I didn't know any better, I'd say **she's** the reason why." Her eyes flickered in undecided color as he choked on excuses. I ignored him and turned to stand before Logan and smile. Logan licked his lips at me and smiled back, shooting his shot amid everything. That's when Landon punched him in the face. We watched as the two grappled in front of us and yelled to stop, but they continued until they broke blood.

It wasn't until my uncle came crashing down between them, out of the woodworks. None of us noticed him pulling into the driveway. He separated them both and scolded us. "-The school called, said they saw you all hauling ass out the parking lot. You two are best friends. What the hell?"

"-I can't do this. I can't." Landon seemed to confess.

"What do you mean? Pull it together."

The confused look on my face was telling; my stare burned into my uncle before he shut it down, "-Daya, I want you in the truck." He tossed orders around. I looked at him skeptically while Logan was already slamming the door to his Honda coup, taking off.

"Now, Dayanara!" I watched my uncle talk to Leyla and Landon from behind the window. Their body movements confused me. I wasn't sure what was going on out there; my uncle nodded at them, kissed his daughter's forehead, then sent them on their way.

Misa didn't say much in the car, and neither did I. I couldn't help but feel so transparent, as if he knew everything I was thinking, from skipping school to forcing myself on Landon. When we arrived at the reserve, I rushed to the village hall, and my uncle followed behind, trying to keep up. When he finally caught up with me, he pulled me to a halt, "-Jesus, what's wrong with you girls lately? Daya, I don't want to see Landon around the house unless I bring him to the house. Do I make myself clear?"

"Did you ever consider that encouraging this engagement would lead to conflicting feelings?" He exhaled in defeat. Knowing my fate, no matter what will lead to the grave, "I'm trying to help you."

We walked into the Conference Hall. It felt like a good 15 minutes that the elders did nothing but whisper back and forth. Sometimes they would address Misa. I watched the wood fire burning colors dance in tune with the shadows on their long stiff faces. The elders continued to talk amongst each other until they drew silent again. They acknowledged one another with nods and silent glares; as if they were agreeing. Then the watcher of the Cree spoke,

"-Child of the sand, sea, and sun… your uncle tells us that you have become very fond of this boy, Landon? Bring him to the Harvest Festival. We want to meet Landon."

Hopeless. I didn't ask why. I had only agreed and settled on the feeling that I could trust what the elders were doing.

5

Fever

Fuck me, I thought.

I couldn't possibly be back where I was;

I sprinted through the rainforest barefoot, panting, scared, waiting for something terrible to happen. But when the black soil's cold and gelatinous pulp squished through my toes, I realized this was different. The air went from warm to cold. Every element changed instantly before me. I could see my uneasy breath fog into the air. The path I was running down was a familiar one. One, I usually jogged down any given day. I knew my way around. The moon overhead glittered in gold, and I realized I was right; This dream was different. Like the other nightmares, the creature had clawed its razor nails into the dirt and dragged its molted body behind me, holding up its stag skull. That part hasn't changed, nor did the fact that the monster was leaving behind that trail of fire. It was a fire that immediately destroyed all in its path with its grotesque, burning body. Arms and hands wrapped around my shoulders, pulling me in. My heart stopped, and when I looked up, it was

Landon. Only Landon. I felt relief, but my heart revs up. My fingers gripped him, and I threw my head on his rugged chest. Cold and stiff, his facial expression was completely monotone. He never moved, even with the fire behind us. I glanced back. The creature crawled through the footsteps I left behind and gained on us. "GO!" I screamed at Landon, trying to push him, but he stood there stiff like stone. Unable to move. "Damn it, Landon, Go!" I cried again as I attempted to snap him out of the trance. The heat climbed up my back; it was getting too close. I screamed again.

A roar. A ridiculously heralding roar bellowed throughout the forest, possibly waking the dead. Birds flew from the trees—all but one owl hooting from above me, like a warning siren. I hesitated to look at the monster, who I was sure was right behind me. 4 feet away, Landon was still frozen. I couldn't save myself; how could I save him too? I squeezed my eyes shut and hunkered down my rapid heart, embracing that this creature would devour us now—another staggering roar. My eyes fluttered open. Behold, before my eyes, standing on two feet, an abnormally large brown bear. It was bigger than a polar bear or anything I had ever seen before. Larger than I could imagine a bear already getting. When I went to scream, nothing but stinging silence came out. Again, I squeezed my eyes shut. I turned over and flipped my body to jump into Landon's arms, but he puffed into thin air. A dust cloud of glitters and colors puffed in my face. I looked up slowly, and my head had escalated back, scaling face to face with the bear towering over me. Thirteen feet, I thought. The bear, who had paid not a single mind to me, roared again. Everything around me seemed to tremble, but the wendigo monster, who sized up to the challenge—growing taller and longer.

I only had two options. Both ended in death.

Die by the grips of this disgusting monstrous creature, or die by the claws of this beautiful animal? I turned back to the bear and finally caught its dark precious eyes of intrusive but delectable Sable. Its mouth expanding to consume me,

Nothing came out—only stinging silence.

Harrowing was the freezing late October wind. The cold rain was pouring down on me, and I was stuck screaming even after realizing I was staring up at a soft cornflower morning sky. I was lying completely nude, in a puddle of mud right at the break of the trail, near my garden gates. My skin was warm like freshly baked bread. My cheeks rose red like my trembling lips. I could hear Charlotte calling my name, running towards me. Then, a warm embrace with a thick quilt. Sheer sickness bled from my uncle's face as my uncle scooped me up and carried me back to the house.

After a hot shower and some dry clothes, I lay wrapped up in a bundle of warm blankets on the sofa. I was crying. I felt hopeless. *'What the hell is happening?'* No one could understand how I ended up outside, naked, amid a nightmare. By now, I was running a high fever. My aunt handed me a tea of sweetgrass and sage.

"... It's the fever. It has set in. -I'm calling the behike-" Charlotte began looking for her cellphone. My uncle, who mainly said nothing, sat there still pretty out of it. Pondering for a solution, he cleared his throat and finally spoke,

"Charlotte... we have to keep her in the Garden-"

For some reason, those words sent my aunt into a panic.

"You said we weren't going to do that this time. You promised."

"-If the fever doesn't kill her, the lust will..."

I looked down at the burn on my wrist.

"Dean must bind the garden first or-"

Leyla left the room in distress when the two began to argue. Everything was fading for her. Every day. Day and night. The constant back and forth weakened our family, and I hated myself. The tension was so thick, and I just wanted it to stop. But, I was too weak to scream. However, lately, I've been practicing and playing with the magic everyone keeps saying I have. Using meditation, I learned my magic. So, I closed my eyes, and like some *'emotion controller,'* I tricked their energy to mimick calm and loving energy. The two settled in voices and movement. I put them under a calming spell, and the two retracted their aggression. They looked at me at the same time. Shit- This is working, I thought.

"Daya, what do you suppose we do?"

My uncle looked at me, nearly dazed. My aunt glitched to keeping me in the garden; I'd keep away from Misael's 'suggestions.' Charlotte was sure Dean was the answer. I trusted Charlotte more than Misa these days. Best we wait for him. Besides, no one was helping the current situation. A new perspective would do justice. I cleared my throat, "... As soon as Dean gets here, he can bind the garden, but I won't bind myself until I'm ready. I'll decide when. Is that okay?" And, like under hypnosis, they both seriously agreed. I eased my influence off slowly until Misa and Charlotte were back to themselves. I looked at the two, smitten. The air felt different than it had in a long while. Lighter, for the most part. But in the near, it felt more sexual. Primal even. Something vital was coming. Now that I could feel the fever settling into the cracks of my bones, I was no longer looking for a reason or asking questions.

It's time I made the decisions.

Today was Samhain. And the day of the annual fall festival at Grey Wolf River. A rainy Halloween morning, and it was already starting scary. Landon had avoided me and all my calls; it's been days, and he still hasn't apologized. Tonight the elders want to meet him. No questions asked, and I haven't even spoken to him. The truth was that I didn't want to. But since I **had** to, I would instead do it in person. I asked Leyla to reach out to him, but she refused; she said it was none of her business, contrary to the excessive time. Everyone avoided me, but nothing bothered me more than Landon and Leyla. Nearly every day, I watched them from afar, laughing and joking. I was raging with jealousy, and I let it show shamelessly. I knew they were close, but they never made me feel uncomfortable.

I thought about it more that evening, as I got dressed for the Festival. The fever finally subsided, and I regained control of my body after Charlotte's special tea. I felt physically better, but weak, fucking depressed, and slightly pale. I pulled myself together. I wanted to reclaim Landon. I cared enough for him to concede if that's what it takes. Only time would tell whether or not this jealousy would kill me sooner rather than later. For now, he was still important to me. I studied my vintage look. A long-sleeved ribbed red bodysuit and a light tan corduroy short skirt with matching boots. I tend to give off too much sex appeal for any outfit these days. I released my waves from a messy ponytail. Fingernails and lips stained red.

When I came down into the kitchen, it was clear that I wouldn't have to look for Landon. He was sitting in the living room with my uncle. He looked handsome in his gray hooded jean jacket. His hands in his pockets and his brown hair hiding under his hood. His green puppy dog eyes. *Damn it.* I hated fighting with him.

"What are you doing here?" In a stiff tone.

"Came to say sorry, and your uncle wanted to talk."

"About?" Nervously, my eyes interrogated my uncle.

"-*Sex.*" I looked at my uncle. He awkwardly steered away. I could tell my uncle was becoming impatient with me. "-Yes, Daya, I specifically asked him to keep his hands off you." My cheeks flared.

"It's okay, Daya. It's not the first time we had this conversation. I gave him my word, but I think you already know I'm not going to touch you either way." Great, here we go; the same old song and dance. Whatever. I already concluded that I had to respect his wishes, no matter how unconventional it was.

"Well, I'm glad you're here. I wanted to ask you-"

"-I know. I'll be honored to go with you tonight."

It would help if he acted like he wanted to be here.

"I wish I could be 18 again. I love spirit night. The live music, the storytelling, dancing, and whiskey and girls," We looked at Misa strangely until he finally cleared his throat, "-I mean the candy. And all the different foods. Skylar's Grandmother's street tacos, amazing." He tried very terribly to change the subject.

"-I'll be celebrating with your aunt tonight, but you guys be careful drinking and remember what I said, **NO SEX**." I exhale hard, watching him skip out of the kitchen, content with his message of anti-intercourse. My powers must have still affected him.

I hadn't noticed Landon staring at me, nearly lost, until his eyes were almost burning me. Then, he came in closer.

"-I had no business calling you what I did the other day. You're not a slut, and I'm sorry." I scoffed, unmoved.

"Please come out with me tonight?" Landon reached for my hand. Without thinking, I took his hand and crawled right into his arms. He kissed me softly, his hands gripping my waist's sides, "Let's go, beautiful… Leyla's waiting." But, of course, he didn't notice how my eyes flared green with envy.

The fall festivities were in full swing when we got to the Grey Wolf River, roughly around 7:30. The bonfire flared, music played, and people gathered at the celebration hall for a feast. Yet, my uncle grabbed Landon upon arriving and took him away to a *private meeting* with the elders. A discussion I wasn't allowed to witness. Worried, I watched Landon walk away with Charlotte and Misael. For more than an hour, they were gone. I tried to engage in what was happening around me, but it was hard to concentrate with Landon gone for so long. Finally, Leyla dragged me to the park pavilion, where the teens were having a full-blown rave—drinking and partying—most of us in our ceremonial headdresses. We caught up with Sunny, who was enjoying the effects of the alcohol in her cup. While dancing, I felt hands collide over me. Landon was back and seemed to be more comfortable. Kind of; there was still an underlying nervousness I felt in the tremble of his cold hands. From afar, I saw my aunt Charlotte. I excused myself and chased her down.

"-Hey, what happened in there?" I was curious.

"Everything went well..."

"What did the elders say to him?"

My aunt knew I wasn't going to let this go. Fortunately, she was a lot more forthcoming than my uncle and Landon. She exhaled, "... Exactly what they suspected... Landon has the blood of the Cree; significantly. Now don't go freaking out on me. It might not mean anything; other Cree boys are walking around. But, look, if I say any more, I'll risk everything. Wait till midnight," Charlotte trotted over to my uncle, finding safety from my evasively digging questions, and the evening went on until most of the festivities had died down. Families and children were now in their homes and beds. We were closing in on midnight, and most of us teens stayed out to finish the celebration with more drinks and stories, down by the river waters, around a bonfire. Like Misa had once remembered, we passed around bourbon whiskey and Halloween candy, telling tribe ghost stories and singing songs. In their selective circle,

Charlotte, Misa, and some of their dear close friends were doing the same, except a few of the elders joined them.

While sitting around the bonfire, I had a strange feeling suddenly come over me. My throat clamped. I felt hot, even in this below 50 weather. I pretended to be fine, but deep down inside, I wanted to toss off the layers of clothes I had on. I had to. The fever's timid flaring inside my bones began to spark up again. With Landon and Leyla here, they were sure to make a scene and alert Misael. I didn't want that. My uncle was already watching me like a hawk. Still, the symptoms came rolling in smoothly like a tropical storm, and Landon noticed. Worried, he took my clammy hands, "-Are you okay? You're turning pale," he whispered below the banjo music. I tried my best to focus and nod. He swallowed hard and glared over to my uncle, who kept his eyes viciously on me. "-I feel great." I lied, nearly gasped for air.

A raging migraine washed over my skull, closer to paralyzing me. Everything that echoed sound pounded at my head. My stomach felt like an inferno, and my ears pierced in whistle. Landon leaned in and kissed me. Staring above me, I could see all the white stars glittering in the sky, but my face was numb. Did the music hypnotize me, or was it the fever brewing inside? I wasn't sure as I tried to pull away from Landon's grip. I looked at the elders sitting there with my uncle, aunt, and friends. They all watched from a distance until they became distracted. The yard gates to our little community were suddenly dragged open, headlights lighting their faces. I watched my aunt Charlotte gasp and spring to her feet, running over to three shadowy guests, tall and strong silhouettes. My uncle got up to join my aunt and the 3, still standing in a densely dark spot. We weren't even that far apart, but I couldn't see, especially with the fever blurring my vision. But- I could hear them talk excitedly. -Dean, I thought. The more I tried to look, the cloudier my vision became. I could now only see movement towards me.

It had to be Dean. At that moment, I noticed something different about the last and tallest silhouette left behind in the background.

Sable eyes. Dark. Hungry. Electric. Sable eyes.

He was electrifying me, consuming me.

The electric was needle injecting, the way it excavates through my veins like blistering bolts of lighting, all hot and cold at the same time. Painful, but the pleasurable kind. And it only searched deeper as it broke into my arteries, down into both ventricles soaking into every tiny fiber in my fragile new heart. I will never be able to fully explain the heat and electricity that ran through me at that moment. I couldn't see his face, but I didn't need to; glancing in the path of his eyes revved my heart up like a hammy engine. The minute I locked my eyes to his, my world went changing.

Colliding. Crashing.

Every atom. Molecule. Cell. Stopped.

Floating around in pieces, weightless and uncollected, I felt like an asteroid hit me and obliterated everything I used to be. Then, only moments later, I could feel the air suck back into me. I can breathe again. My eyes held onto the stranger's galaxy eyes. Instantly, everything came back; now all in reverse. Even that felt exasperating; as each part of me stitched back together. Everyone around me was now staring- and I was standing from my seat. The mysterious guests, the elders, Landon, Misa, Charlotte, Leyla, and all our friends; all stared. I swallowed hard. I wanted to evaporate. Emotionally I felt exposed; physically, I wanted to be exposed. My body was still itching with heat. I needed an escape. Behind me, in a short distance, an opening in the forest. I kicked off my boots, tossed the headdress along with it, and sprinted into the woods, running like that stupid nightmare. Beneath me, the ground was wet from the morning rain shower. The adrenaline soared through.

I couldn't shake the image of his dark shape from my mind. The image burned inside my brain. *How dare he?* I chopped up. *For the love of God, get him out of my mind.* What he was doing to me was highly invading. The sexual tension seeping into my body made me aggressive. I kept running through the forest, raging with power. *Faster.* I could hear the owl hooting overhead like in the dream. I was so hot. Hot and turned on. My nipples hardened, my pearl pulsated, an indefinite aching in my lower abs. The juice was coming.

I couldn't make it. I was nearing my backyard. I somehow ran miles through the woods to almost nearly make it to the garden gates in the trail behind the house. But I was off several feet. I fell to the ground, in the exact spot where I had been lying early that morning. Gray clouds rumbled above, hiding the stars above. A crackle of thunder but no lightning. Rain showered down on me as I surrendered to the sexual feeling enslaving me. My legs peeled apart, and I ripped the skirt by the buttons and tore away at my top, ripping the bodysuit into shreds. My bra snapped, and the hard rain pattered on my naked chest. Sexy moans escaped my lips.

I was lying there, nearly completely naked.

My body squirmed on the muddy dirt ground.

Unable to control.

I looked up at the darkness above me. Invisible raindrops all over my body. An overlay of pressure as I gurgled raindrops from my lips. I convulsed violently. I had to focus on something as this fever took over. My cheeks were hot and blotched red, and I was panting recklessly. An owl hooted loudly above me in the tree as I gave into the wicked desire and began to touch myself. My free hand explored every inch of my salt drip body as I masturbated in the mud. I felt relaxed; Simultaneously, I was burning and stinging inside. I felt like I was falling into a sexual abyss of raging hungry insanity. I was intoxicated by sexual euphoria as I fantasized about the **MAN** with the ***sable eyes because*** he was no boy. Not like how Landon was a boy. He felt all real. I felt like I could feel his hands on me. His lips and body towering over me. I needed him. He could heal me, I thought—the antidote to this pain.

I bit my lip until it bled.

I scratched my body until it bled.

I felt so damn good, on a tumbling high. For the first time, I was having a very sweltering orgasm—my body, from bones to limbs, crinkled and melted into unfamiliar convulsions. My body twisted about in the mud. My nails were digging as it intensified. My toes curled, I gasped for oxygen. I couldn't breathe; I was shaking too hard. Here it came, fast and impassioned without restraints. It ripped through me like a tsunami. I moaned loudly, gripping the dirt ground, eyes rolling back, and knees to heavens.

November 1st

I sprang up from my bed with no recollection of the night before. I'm safe, dried, and fully clothed. It wasn't long until I noticed my aunt and uncle sitting at the bedside, praying to their gods in stunning relief. I wasn't dead, so that was a good thing. I felt pretty great, a matter of fact. I sat up in my bed and looked at them, "-She's okay!" My uncle said, clapping and celebrating. I had known something terrible had happened but only by the vibe and looks on their faces. I just didn't know what yet.

"You were out like a light for like 19 hours…. are you okay? How are you feeling?" Misael approached the foot of the bed.

"I feel GREAT… but who is he?" I asked, pointing to the guy in the back. He was a very tall man around my uncle's age, maybe slightly older with dirty blonde hair, a rough five o'clock shadow, and tired eyes. Handsome, I thought, for his age.

"I'm Dean... We *almost* met last night. But you took off."

Suddenly everything came rushing back to me in violent flash-backs. The Festival. Landon. Sunny singing. *Dean and his boys.* His boy with the dark eyes; something did happen. It all came back to me, and now I was hurting. My body ached but in a different way. I was yearning for something, someone. Hungry. Hungry for *love. Lust. Sex.* I felt miserable, confined to a feeling like this. I felt uncontrollable and worse; my thoughts quickly became perverted, even around these three adults. There was no helping myself. My thoughts ran deep in my head nonstop.

"Um- what exactly happened last night?" I questioned.

"You had your first fever. Everything you experienced is very normal, so don't be alarmed." Dean talked like a doctor.

"...Right... when you found me, I had clothes on, right?"

Both Dean and My uncle awkwardly looked away, very telling. I gasped in embarrassment. "You're fucking kidding me,"

"-Don't worry, Charlotte took care of you. Daya, we will lift the curse, but only you can decide how." I looked at Dean, who just seemed to keep talking despite the irritated look on my face.

"-*Dayanara...* my name is Dayanara." I corrected him.

"Right, I apologize, *Dayanara,*" Dean spoke with an easy and soft Northern voice, despite resembling a Western cowboy. Then, with his doctor bag at his side, he began to run a simple exam on me. Checking my pulse. Eyes. Ears. Nose. Throat. Temperature. Blood pressure. "-The fever is starting earlier than it should... the fever wouldn't set in until about 30 to 40 days after her 19th. So I showed up at the right time. Moboyas must want to claim her soul before she's had a chance to fall in love."

"-What are we doing about that?" Misael cut him off.

"What? The thing?"

"Yes, the thing."

"I'm working on it."

Dean and my Uncle exchanged passive but hostile glances.

"-Right now, we need to find a way for the fever to regress. We need to buy time if we want the best outcome. We won't have enough time if it consumes her too soon."

"I don't care how; let's just do it."

"... I've heard that before," Dean was becoming more reserved each time my uncle spoke, "-Misa, I didn't come here to be an asshole. I know you think I only came here because the elders asked me to, but I only came because I promised Anais I would help Dayanara. It's what Daya, I mean *Dayanara,* wants. This situation is not her fault. We all need to be patient and respect that."

Someone finally had my back, I thought.

The two couldn't hide the fact that there was some kind of history. Whatever happened in the past had been buried, but not exactly dead. And the smug way Misael looked at Dean said it all. My uncles' attitude was flaming, getting under my skin. "Dayanara, I need you to be honest with me. I think I can help you. At least that's what they keep telling me. You're just going to have to trust me. Can we learn to trust each other?" His eyes were soft and honest. I nodded at Dean. I had no choice but to agree with him; I sure couldn't trust my uncle. Dean took the stethoscope to my chest. Time to dig, "You could have warned me. I saw all of you last night. Watching. Waiting. That wasn't fair."

"I know, honey, but it was the only way we could validate-"

My eyes darted at Charlotte. She nearly bit her tongue off, trying to stop herself. My uncle might as well have sliced his tongue and sewed his mouth shut; he looked away reluctantly, cursing Charlotte under his breath. "Validate what?"

My eyes ping-ponged between the three.

"-Whose setting off the fever..." Dean said earnestly, retracting himself. My uncle winced to the confession.

"-We don't have to go into every detail Dean."

"-The hell we do. You're messing with *my* life." I snapped.

"She's right, Misa. You're making decisions for her, and that's why the curse backfired. She has the right to make her own decisions. So how exactly do you want to keep the two apart? They'll cross paths regardless. She has to know." Dean turned to my uncle, awaiting an answer. My uncle took a minute to think; Dean gave him that, *You tell her, or I will look.*

"-Okay... fine. Yes, Landon maybe half Cree, but-"

"-He's not the one." I cut him off, and then I hated myself for saying it aloud, making it real. I tried taking it back, "-I'm in love with Landon, but-" I couldn't. It was silent as thoughts of confusion flooded my inner workings. My uncle looked like he was in no mood for this. Dean held onto his heavy, **no-bullshit** eyes. Misa's silence forced Dean into an unapologetic word vomit.

"-I have two boys myself. Jacy and Haven. We've suspected for *a long time* that Haven could be '*your one.*' But now, the elders think Landon could be a possibility. He is confirmed native blood,"

"Haven," The name slipped from my lips accidentally, learning it for the first time. It felt so good to say it. The three caught the shimmer in my eyes as I shamelessly reflected on this stranger.

"Yes, my pain in the neck... We had to leave town quickly after we thought you were 'cured.' It was for the best at the time. But, now, years later, it brings us right back here. Does she know about the garden?" He turned to Misa.

"Yeah, she knows."

"Good, I'm going to go bind that for you now. Then, at the very least, Daya can seek shelter with a *safety net* when the fever hits."

Dean packed up his bag and left my bedside; my uncle and Charlotte were right behind him, closing the door as they went.

Now I felt somewhat unsatisfied. I had more questions, and they left so suddenly. I didn't have a chance to ask. But at the very least, I knew his name. *HAVEN.* I felt better understanding some of the truth. I'm lying. It felt better knowing *his* name and that read. I threw the blanket off of me and realized I was all wet, and so was the bed. I must have come all over the bed, thinking of Haven. Shit, now I had a name. Haven; what an accurate name.

I took a cold shower. Haven was heavy on my mind, even when I tried chanting Landon. Haven wasn't leaving. I must have been dreaming of him all night. Touching myself, pretending it was him —every riveting ache and move. I wasn't ashamed of it anymore. I was becoming comfortable with my sexuality. I had no choice; my body had said so. And what bothered me was that it wasn't Landon who was making me come undone anymore. It was a stranger. The more I thought about it, the more invasive Haven's name felt as I dried my hair and got dressed.

I wanted to see what was going on outside in the garden. I could barely see from the window; only a rusted white gate in the forest, peering behind trees, abandoned. By the time I rushed downstairs, it had been too late. I had barely made it to the bottom when I heard my uncle and Dean talking in the kitchen. I listened in.

"How are the boy's taking the move?"

"We just got here, so I'll guess we'll see. The girls have grown up. Daya looks just like her mother; she's a very passionate one. I can tell by how reserved she is. And she seems to have discovered her powers. Looks like she even knows how to use it-"

"-Yeah, I know. Daya's been using it to keep Charlotte and me at bay. Also throwing influence over her boyfriend Landon, trying to sleep with him-Hey, I'm sorry. I should have told you she's a near-spitting image of Anais. And she is very passionate. A lot more powerful than Anais; it's kinda scary."

"Trust me; I know the feeling."

"How are your boys? I didn't get a chance to talk to them last night; Haven didn't exactly let me talk..."

" Jacy is good. He did his four years in the Air force, got his diplomas, and is now studying for his Master's. Very smart and organized; he's a good kid. But Haven is my headache; he's always out, causing a riot. -I'm sorry about Haven. He's rebellious."

"-Yeah, 20 was a rebellious age, alright." As Dean caught onto the image, he was making out of Haven. My uncle chuckled nervously. "-Don't get me wrong, he's a good kid—Haven's bright, driven, well-spoken, protective. But unfortunately, Haven is also easily bored, and that's when he gets stupid. If he's in town, he's either being followed by the girls or coming home with the sheriff. But when he's traveling, going on his Quests, he's grounded."

"No offense Dean, he sounds like a big problem."

"Misael, a big problem, brother- Haven's fevers are far worse than Daya's. It's the same thing all over again. The two are connected. The more power Daya abstracts, the more he loses as long as she distances herself. He's weak lately, vulnerable. He's lost agility, and he's not eating right. And *angry,* so damn angry. He's never been that way. I've never seen my boy like this."

"There's a change in Daya too. But different. She's more confident. Bold. Risky. Wild. Sexual. I don't like it, honestly."

"The Spirits did warn us that while they're together, we can't force them together or keep the two apart... balance is key, but you saw how that worked out for Anais and me,"

What? Does that mean they were together?

"-With Haven being so special among the Cree tribe and Daya the daughter of Moboyas, the Taino Zeni-God, the pair seems to be a perfect collision in the eyes of the Superior Spirit's. It's written in Heaven and Stars. Two battles in one war. We're not prepared."

"Dean… how long are you planning on staying here?"

"I would have never returned if the elders hadn't called me. I won't lie; this is more about Haven than it is about you and Daya. It's just your luck that I'm here to help."

"I can't fail Daya like I did, my sister."

"Trial and error, brother. Trial and Error."

My heart steeped low—*perfect time to walk in.*

"I'm I interrupting?" I asked as I walked in.

"It depends. Were you already listening?" **Guilty.**

"It's okay. I was going to head back to town anyway- I'm closing in on some land right outside the reserve. So to answer your question, Misael, yes, I'm going to be here a while."

Dean was stern while gathering his jacket and bag.

"Hey! No matter what, we're brothers." Misa reassured him.

"Always. I've already talked to Haven. I told him what the deal was. He'll be out of town for the next couple of weeks. Camping. He's a natural nomad, so it won't be too hard to keep him away."

"-I'll stay away from him."

Although the words punched the wind out of me, I was serious. I need to keep the peace between the two old friends and keep my life as normal as possible. Besides, Landon was still in the picture. So I had to do as they say or pretend that it was my intention.

I was NOT joking when I said I'd figure this out myself.

Landon had been more than enough. I hadn't appreciated him enough. To him, my curse had been the lack of a romantic. Now—a sensory overload of sensually deep emotions over *two* guys. But, I never had another being seep into my soul and see me in proper form until Haven crashed into my atmosphere. Those beautiful eyes had obliterated me from the inside out, and I felt it. I know he felt it too. I know because when he looked into my eyes, we fell together. I watched him fall and hit. He watched me fall and crash. We nearly hit bottom in a dead heat, and neither caught the other. How reckless was this already turning out to be?

6

Dinner Party

By Monday, my life reverted to normal. No fever, no nightmare. Great dreamless sleep. Each night, I was knocked out cold, but only with the help of a particular tea Dean made every night after he and my uncle played dominoes. Dean was around all the time now. I enjoyed his company. So did my uncle. Dean was funny and insightful. Being around him was easy, and he gained my trust fast.

Haven was out of town exploring the *Catskill Mountains,* or maybe up north, deep in the *Great North Woods.* I wasn't sure, so I wondered. Landon wasn't around either. He was also banned from the house; since everyone claimed they weren't sure who was setting off the fever. My heart had set on Haven.

My uncle and Dean needed to be sure. *Landon? Or Haven?* So they gave me the task of inviting Landon and his mother to the annual Managault dinner party. Every first of December, Misael threw a dinner party. This year they were using the dinner party as an excuse to meet Landon's mother. Everything about that made me clench and cringe. Never mind the unexpected interrogation the poor woman was walking into; Landon didn't tell her about the engagement. An awkward dinner conversation was sure to ensue. To make things worse, in the year and a half I've been dating Landon, I've never met the woman. Lucky, my uncle has. He seemed to be fond of her. Fond enough to rattle my aunt a bit.

I wasn't sure if we were still *'engaged.'* Everything was like a cassette player spitting up the tape in a blissfully slow and tangled unwind. There was no stopping nor fixing this just yet. Not until it spit up the entire cassette. With all the restrictions my uncle put in place, it was hard to talk to Landon about anything. I was hoping that he wasn't even interested in marrying me anymore. Haven was all I wanted, and Landon was sure to make that complicated.

When I approached Landon about the dinner party during his early morning practice with the team, my eyes were underlying with uncertain emotion. I couldn't let him see me, so unsure. I forced myself to stare off into bleachers, "Seven?" He repeated while still trying to catch his breath from the suicide sprints. His hands to his hips, sweating. He still looked gorgeous, watching his brown strands fall over his face and curl up. His emerald eyes slowly killed me, "Yup… and make sure you bring your mom…"

"Perfect. We could tell her about the engagement-"

My heart was at my throat now. I wanted to vomit.

"W-we're telling your mom?" My voice was authentically scared.

"Of course, we're telling her… The past few weeks have been weird and rocky, but I love you, Daya." He reached over, gently pulling me in with his sweaty arms. The way he stared at me was precious. It made my heart sink in a way it never had before. Everything was beginning to feel different with Landon. Out of my control. It was hard to detect what was real and what was fake. His cloudy blue-green eyes were blocking me out, but I deserved it, I thought as I swayed into his kiss. He pulled me in closer. I kissed him back harder; Our pelvis's collided.

"-Hey, that's enough, Upton! Back in the game!" His coach blew a whistle and yanked his bald head in the direction of the field. Landon pulled from me, sizing me up and down. Breathless, I nodded and watched as he joined the practice.

A burst of hatred spewed from within me as I left the field. I fucking hated me right now. How could I take advantage of Landon's heart like this? The boy loved me, and I felt that. But I thought of Haven, someone I've never met, talked to, or seen clearly. Someone I didn't know. He could be out to ruin me. What the hell was I getting into? As I began to cry, Leyla crashed into me, and after exchanging strange glances, she pulled me aside. She was concerned but clueless, and that wasn't surprising; Leyla only knew what they wanted her to know. So I told her about Haven and everything that happened after Halloween night. Now Leyla finally understood my unyielding desire for sexual intimacy. An unsuspecting wave of melancholic emotions sparked when Leyla asked how I felt about it all. My parents, and my magic. I never thought about it further than I had to. I gained new abilities each day and meditating inside the garden intensified the powers. I was able to create at a rapid pace. The land was rich, the views were vibrant, and the water was pure. I only wished I could share my sanctity.

"-He can kill you. One-touch, or one kiss." Leyla reminded me.

I. did. Not. Care.

"-Sometimes, I dream of him ravishing me and engulfing me, eating me up inside, out. I can't even explain it, but I want that. I want him, no matter how dangerous." It was a dream to me but washed over Leyla like a nightmare.

"-You better be careful. You're my best friend. I can't lose you."

She held me a moment, squeezing me as if she wasn't already losing me. I pitied her and my aunt and uncle. They didn't know or understand my longing for this stranger, even if it killed me. And if they couldn't save me, they should just let me have him.

"-Hey, Day, what are you doing with Landon?"

Good question. The same one that's weighing on my mind.

I wasn't sure if Misa was home, so I called out to him from the bottom of the kitchen staircase, "-I'm home! In case you're wondering," and flicked the faucet to run.

"-He left with my dad. They went to some market," an unfamiliar voice from behind startled me as I grabbed a glass cup from the drying rack. The glass slipped from my hand and into the sink. I spun around and found a tall, sandy-haired man sitting at the kitchen table reading. He wore a nice vested suit and trendy seeing glasses that glossed his rusty-colored eyes. He was pretty, for a nerd; he resembled a younger Dean, so he had to be one of his boys.

"-Fuck... you scared me."

"Relax, Haven is not here." I rolled my eyes.

"... Jacy, I presume?" He nodded.

"You're not the stunning girl I met the other night, so you must be Daya." He had to be talking about Leyla.

"Sorry to break your heart. A lot of people say we look alike."

"Really? I don't see it." Jacy was an asshole.

"What? Are you now a part of my uncle's secret service?"

"I was hoping to run into Leyla; I must have missed her."

It was silent. I squinted at Jacy, trying to get a vibe underneath his sophisticated 'know-it-all' attitude, perfectly ironed slacks, and new penny loafers. He looked like a lawyer.

"-I don't see the big deal..." He broke the silence.

"What?"

"My brother. I have never seen him so lovesick in my life. I'd expected you to be much prettier." My face drained.

"Well, thanks... You sure like to stare a lot for someone who thinks I'm pretty ugly," I could feel Jacy staring.

"I never said you were ugly. Sorry if I'm being rude. I can be a little harsh, the Dean says. I just never seen Haven this way."

To my delight, I looked at Jacy, realizing he was all too willing to talk about his brother. Everyone around me was getting so good at keeping him a secret. I leaned over, curious. Secretly, I was infecting his mind with a sweet aroma that would serve as a truth serum. He responded with a look of concern and awkwardness.

"How is Haven, by the way? Back in town yet?"

He choked on his cup of tea, not anticipating the question, "Ha-ha. We shouldn't be talking about him; retract your weapon."

He caught me. *Shit.*

"-I've been going through a lot of sketchy shit right now, and I dead ass didn't ask for this." The slang came out when I snapped.

"*Dead ass?* Where did you learn to talk?"

"Listen, you're not on the west coast anymore."

"Clearly," The both of us looked at each other, smiling. I guess we did have a clear understanding of the language of sarcasm. He exhaled long and tired, staring down at the ground.

"I shouldn't be talking about Haven, but I miss him. The rage is splitting him apart, and he says you're the cure; I believe him."

"I think so too, but my uncle would never allow it... he's set on marrying me off to Landon."

"-*Marrying?*" Jacy seemed unhinged. More secrets, I bet. I presented him with my engagement ring. He was lost in thought, then came out of the mouth with, "-They're making you do it..." I asked him what he meant, but he changed tone, apologizing,

"Sorry if I act like an asshole. I'm not used to a girl coming in between my family. I know it's not your fault; it's the curse. But he hasn't stopped thinking about you since we've got here. Now that he's this close, it's eating at him like a virus. You might as well have a gun to his head."

I didn't know what to say. I could never take that pain from him.

"-So it's true… your eyes do change color." I looked away.

Misa popped open the side door and walked in with arms full of shopping bags. Dean followed behind, "Busy day?"

For the next week, things ran smooth. Until the morning of the dinner party, another nightmare, the dream, began in Landon's truck. It seemed forced together, but I guess we were into that because I craved how fucked me, hard with anger and alienation. And he loved it because he shook and quivered the moment I climbed on top to ride him. The way he aggressively took out his resentment on me in the front seat of his truck left me wanting so much more; at his heart's expense. He let me fuck him until he came close to cumming. He was about to pull out; when I awoke to a bright and sunny morning. Another wet dream; I woke up in another damp spot in my bed, with my body quivering post-orgasm.

However, this one felt very real.

An early morning 2-mile sprint turned into 6 miles without realizing it. And even when I returned to the yard, I still had that stinging ache for Landon. So I took a cold shower. An icy shower and a non sexualize horror movie to follow. But, unfortunately, I was still too distracted. I only wanted to think of Landon, and with Misael running about the house, I didn't want to risk rubbing one out. Besides, I had already rubbed out two while on the forest trail.

Early in the evening, I began searching for the perfect outfit for this dinner party. Yes, Haven was still on my mind, but now like an old toy. I switched on and off between both guys was like night and day. But it was because I had become confused with the dream. I grew into the realization that everyone was going to keep me from Haven; I had more accessible access to Landon. Regardless, Landon and I had unfinished business. I know everyone keeps telling me that sex will kill me, but how did they know for sure? I had to test the theory out. I wanted him to break apart in my hands and give in to my heavy desire.

This red dress. Leyla gave it to me for my first date with Landon. It was sure to remind him how rare I was. Yeah, it has gotten much smaller on me. My lean but full-body naturally tweaked it into sexy, making it shorter tighter, and my perfect tits pulled the neckline, showing cleavage. My legs were oiled and bare—my hair, natural and tamed in long-striding waves. I refused to touch my face with makeup because I wanted him to see me, like that night at the drive-in where he first kissed me. Besides, my cheeks and lips were authentically cherry. I was glowing, but my stomach growled; I couldn't wait to eat. Lately, I've had a hunger I never knew existed. I bounced down the stairs, following the sensational smell of home-made food, and found my uncle with Dean upon walking into the kitchen. Straight off the rip, both Dean and Misa looked at me disapprovingly, shaking their heads at me. I looked at them, 'What are you two looking at?'

"-You're coming to dinner dressed like that?" Dean didn't hide the worry in his tone. My uncle was speechless for that moment, debating whether or not he should yell in front of his company.

"Yes. I am."

"No. You're not." Misael began complaining.

"-I wore this dress on my first date with Landon."

Dean rolled his eyes and looked at Misael.

"Don't you think it's a little… overkill?" I looked at him.

"Hey, I'm right here. It's not like my fiance hasn't seen me in this dress before." I whisked around the two.

"-I don't remember it being that low cut-" I ignored them as the side door pulled open, and Charlotte and Leyla walked in, dressed in lovely decent dresses. My aunt nearly dropped the bottles of Merlot when she saw me, "My Goodness Daya...you look... wow." Charlotte also seemed less thrilled about my dress, which wasn't like her. She usually sided with us girls, but she agreed with Misael and Dean this time. The only positive reaction came from Leyla, who screamed in excitement when she saw me.

"-Daya, you look like a total babe!"

My uncle slapped his hands together; shaking his head violently,

"-Please... -please don't encourage her," Misa begged.

"It's just a dress; it's not a big deal."

"Yes, but don't you think it'll be too much? Misa, Dean, you did tell her?" Their look of blind ignorance confirmed Charlotte's suspicion. "-Damn it, guys; The one thing I asked you both to do-"

"-What? What are you guys talking about?" I asked as an overwhelming feeling of cluelessness publicly washed over me.

"-Haven's coming to dinner!"

The adults swarmed and winced at Leyla's words.

I felt sick instantly. I looked at my uncle seriously.

"Why? Why would you do that to me? Did you two nimrods realize Landon and his mother are coming to dinner?"

"Trust me. It wasn't *our* bright idea; it was *Havens*. He insisted he'd be here," The kid must have had some power over the two. I looked at Dean, wondering what Haven could or might have said to make them agree to this. Here I am, scraping for information, and all he had to do was set them straight one time. That wasn't fair.

"Yeah, you should change." My uncle said casually.

No, not if Haven, Dean, and Misa wanted to ambush me, then they could all suffer the consequences; "I'm not changing. I wore this for my fiance," I protested and took a seat at the elegantly decorated table. Crystal wine glasses, good china, and nice silverware for this dinner. I studied my uncle from afar disapprovingly. He stared into his cellphone, pulling off his 'man' apron.

"Landon should be pulling up with his mother… she just texted me." My aunt shot Misael a troubled glance, grabbing the bowls of fried plantains and acapurrias and setting them on the table in front of me. Leyla and I met eyes from across the table.

"Where are the boys?" Charlotte turned to Dean.

"They went out for a run; they'll be here soon. Misael, what did you say Landon's last name was again?"

"Upton…" Misa poured a bunch of glasses of wine.

"Sounds familiar…" Dean was quickly losing himself to his thoughts. He no longer seemed confident or had that look of certainty. He did know the name but didn't want to admit to it.

Again that side door busted open. Jacy came strolling in, dressed to the nines and book at hand. I watched behind him, waiting for Haven to come walking in. No one trail in behind.

"Son… where's the other one?" Dean seemed just as confused as I was when Jacy plowed down next to Leyla. The two exchanged cheeky glances. Jacy reached for some fried plantains, "-He was taking too long getting dressed, so I left him. He'll be here soon,"

Now I was thinking of Haven. Undressed. Naked. Wet after a hot steamy shower. He probably smelled of rich mineral springs and delicate aftershave. I crossed my legs, begging my vagina to keep her shit together and not start. I had to control myself. I was beginning to feel like elastic. The doorbell rang.

"I'll get it," I said timidly, trying not to spark more controversy. I tipped toed down the hallway and to the front door. My uncle followed me before I could open the door. Landon and his mother both ignored me at first glance. They were too busy greeting Misael. Misa hugged Landon, showing their closeness to his mother, a pristine and sharp, thin, tall, professional, black-haired, blue-eyed lady. Her straight hair stopped after her shoulders. She dressed classy because she came from money. Old money. Her energy was a bit intimidating. I printed out a fake smile. I lent my hand out for a shake, and she hesitated. She gave me one hard shake and looked at me like everyone else did disapprovingly. Immediately and solidly written on her face. Welp, there goes that.

My aunt Charlotte walked out into the foyer where we stood, ready to meet Landon's mom, "Miss Upton, it's nice to meet you, finally-" I analyzed how my aunt's face changed when seeing Landon's mother for the first time. She cleared her throat awkwardly, still holding her hand out.

"... Charlotte? Oh my goodness, it's been years," Miss Upton's eyes widen in total surprise, "-I didn't know my son dated your daughter. What a small small world." She said, looking around to our colorful home, trying to hide the disappointment in her face. She wasn't impressed with any of it, and you could tell.

"... Decades actually, and our NIECE." Charlotte corrected her. Now with defense woven into tone.

Dean curved into the foyer to join the meet and greet, "-Mrs. Upton, I'm Dean, Daya's uncle..." but his excitement changed.

"-What the hell is he doing here?" The cold women snapped. I began to dislike Landon's mother.

"-What the hell are you doing here?'

"-I was invited,"

"-You? Are you Landon's mother? Lord, help us all!" Dean chanted to the ceiling, "-out of all the people in the world." Landon, my uncle, and I stood back, watching the three talk until they suddenly stopped.

"...We all went to school together... briefly." Dean chopped it up, and Landon's mother agreed. Landon and I both looked at each other with worry in our eyes. I knew this was not good.

Landon's mother, Caroline, showed off how arrogant, snotty, and entitled the Upton name was throughout dinner. I thought the true definition of a rich bitch as I sat through that immensely awkward dinner. But, all she could do was talk about how much better she was than us all; and how, despite her family's money, she found success as the local Pediatrician in town.

In what deep trench did they pull this lady out from?

I un-apologetically thought.

It was clear that while she loved her son, Caroline disapproved of me. With all due respect to my uncle, whom, amazingly, she still thought highly of him. Landon was embarrassed. No offense to him, but I would be too. How was this witch his mother? So rude and judgemental? Landon was utterly different, so sweet, holding my hand and reassuring me we were okay. Despite him, how could she be like this? And Oh my God- She would be my Monster-in-Law?!

My head pounded as I listened to my aunt and uncle list off all of my achievements as if she needed convincing. Charlotte and Misael both seemed to be trying to prove something to Caroline. They tried to convince Caroline that I was the only match for her son. However, she wasn't buying what they were selling. I had no choice but to sit back into each insult Caroline politely passed at me. The wine helped. I had nothing to prove to this woman, I already had her son, and he made that clear when he kissed me softly in front of everyone at the table. It was like adding water to sizzling oil. Everyone's face nearly crackled at the sight of us. His mother, especially appalled, expressed to Landon that he deserves better.

To make things worse, 10 minutes into dinner, Dean and Caroline couldn't stop exchanging hasty and aggressive eye glances. I tried using my powers to manipulate the mood. Still, my magic wasn't strong enough to tame everyone at once with so many players. Caroline wouldn't let up either, and she wore on me the most. That was until Dean began to defend me. Dean was a stand-up, friendly, decent guy, and now he was a part of my family. Never mind what she said about me; she couldn't be more wrong, but it pissed me off when Caroline decided to degrade Dean. I wasn't the only one; Jacy bit his tongue more than once. Even with some classic tunes and a warm fire crackling in the background, the mood went to shit. Dean tried to soften her up with jokes and compliments, but Caroline Upton was relentless, barking down Dean's throat. It was evident that Dean and Caroline had some history.

By the third bottle of wine, the adults were slowly streaming out of control. Like watching a volcano erupt but in slow motion, I swore it was not only the vino, with the comments ping-ponging back and forth at the dinner table between Dean and Caroline. At the same time, my uncle interjected, trying to fish for answers: all the fake smiles, tons of slick and offensive remarks, and sarcasm on a different level. Someone is sure to snap soon, I feared. Something was going to pop off the bottle. "-Honestly, I don't know what to tell you, mother, but Daya is going to be my wife-"

There it was.

Caroline. Turning red. Tomato red.

My eyes. Turning blue. A cold, dark, deep blue. I retreated to my glass of wine and finished it as I looked over to Landon. "-Over my dead body, will I allow this girl poison you into destroying your perfect future, *Landon Solomon Upton.*"

That was the final straw for her.

Fuck it. Dinner was already a mess.

Landon argued with his mother until Misa chimed in, trying to be the voice of reason. Leyla, Jacy, and I took to passing the remaining wine around; it's not like anyone else noticed; they were still winding down an abyss of anecdote. So the arguing continued, past empty dirty dinner plates, half-empty wine glasses, and burned-out dinner candles. Then the kitchen side door swung open recklessly.

Here comes Haven, walking in like a scene from one of those old romance films I love watching so much. He came forward with a black tee-shirt that could barely contain his bulking chest, blue jeans, and black running shoes. I froze, swallowing the wine in my mouth while passing Jacy the bottle, wiping away the drip from the corner of my lips. I kept my stare down. He was taller up front, and I could feel it as he drew closer to the table. Much taller. Pale too. Dean did say he was half of a half-breed, but I'd expect that he'd be a tad bit tanner even with a tiny bit of Hispanic blood. His upper body covered in tattoos—predominantly tribal tattoos to the chest. I was building the courage to look him in his face, but I couldn't. Not while I had my entire family and his, staring at us obtrusively.

'You're Late." His father reminded him.

"The wine is gone, but you drink beer, right?" My uncle popped one open for him. Charlotte handed him an overloaded dinner plate and offered him a seat to Leyla's other side, right adjacent to me. The temptation to look up at him melted at my face like blistering flames. Everyone's meddling eyes were hungry for a reaction, and I refused to give them one.

"Thank you," Haven spoke deep but earthy, luscious tone.

No damn way. I oozed in my chair.

I tried to be cool about it, attempting to inhale. My chest rose slowly. In the background, Landon continued to argue with this mother passive-aggressively. Eventually, that took from the watching eyes. Everyone seemed like they were in their little worlds now. Maybe it's the wine. Perhaps it's the magic leaking from me, but a boldness came over me. I can steal this moment. I pepped myself up, and I finally looked up at him.

A brooding 1951 Marlon Brando.

Frosty aurora blue eyes. Intrusively Tall and Lean.

The jawline of steel. Jet black hair.

Charming smile and soft blossomed lips;

He came in storming like a vintage heartthrob and looking like one too. My goodness, those eyes. Soft and inviting, contradicting his irritable and messy entrance. They were of Caribbean lagoons—waves of cerulean and pools of emerald and turquoise. Brilliant filters, as if you were looking at them through sun rays in diamond waters. I fell deeper into his stare like I was free diving into a divine pool of richly colorful gems. Home is what I thought of first; Boriken, the enchanted island. I knew for sure as I held onto his stare, waiting for him to speak to me. But, he rudely scoffed and rolled his gaze away crudely. He was broody and heavy. Like he was in no mood for me. Good, I'm not in the air either.

I backed off and crossed my arms and legs, shifting my body towards Landon. That glance did justice for me, and I was content. On the other hand, Haven had trouble refraining from staring at me while eating. And boy, did he have an appetite.

Nonetheless, having Haven right there was like putting dope in front of an addict. I needed his immediate attention, but Mrs. Upton was still going on. And yet, our eyes met again. Haven couldn't resist this time and held his stare very confidently. Finally, he scoffed and shook his head. Still, he looked irresistible when he did it.

My heart was thumping hard; I was sure everyone could hear it. But no one paid any attention to us; they were more interested in Dean and Caroline's back and forth. Like everything else in the background, they seem to fade away for me. I bit my lip, staring at this creation of a man. Squeezing my legs shut in a tiny dress, arms crossed over my lap, trying to keep myself from falling to pieces. Watching me from across the table, Haven frisks me with his eyes, wildly and shamelessly. Although I could faintly hear everyone talking, it felt like we were alone. My fingers twisted about a strand of long hair as I sat back and indulged in his hungry stares. As if he has never eaten at all. He mirrored me, crossing his arms and leaning back into his chair, then smiling at me. It wasn't what you could call a 'smile,' as he tried keeping up with his *I don't want to be here* vibe, but I'll take what I can get. I blatantly ignored my boyfriend, who was seeking advice to stop this war over the dinner table.

"-Dayanara!" Landon snapped me out of my trance.

All eyes were on me, "Sorry … lost in thought."

From the corner of my unsatisfied eyes, I watched Haven relax into his chair, grinning as if he were pleased with himself.

Son of a - His ego was pissing me off.

"-We were just talking about your plans for College."

Said my uncle, confident like a publicist, filling me in on the conversation I had missed while messing around with the Brando look alike. The look on Misael's face said, 'CUT IT OUT-' I shrugged, looking at Caroline. She already hates me. I didn't need to impress her. Besides, I had no real future. The real question was, what are my plans before I die, "I don't know yet..." I leaned my body forward in deep thought, aware of how my breast looked in that solid pose. I just had to lean over enough to reach the freshly ripen Quenepas sitting in a bowl on the table. I slowly took one and brought it to my mouth in deep thought. I knew what I wanted; I wasn't brave enough to say it aloud. He was right across the table. I crossed my legs opposite and sucked the fruit into my mouth, effortlessly peeling it with my teeth. It was a trick I learned as a child. I spat out the peel and tossed it onto my empty plate. Now I had Haven's full attention, along with everyone else. He loved every second of it and did not feel the need to hide it. His grin got bigger, and he chuckled under his easy breath, amused.

"-I want to travel the world and retrace my ancestry."

"I thought you said you were going to study business? So you can take over the family business." My uncle questioned me, hoping I'd get the proper reply.

"Not anymore. I just can't settle right now; I can barely stand the classroom. How do you learn in a box, right? I would rather be out there in the world, learning what I love from people who love doing it. You have to live to do what you love, right?" It was MY truth. And my uncle knew it. He was also, besides Caroline, the only one who disapproved of the answer.

"Why are you being so damn judgemental?" They all, *but Haven*, stared at me oddly. Silence and stares. Caroline abruptly stood up, "She's not the one for you... Come on, Landon..."

At the same time, Haven slid his chair back and stood up, exhaling. Long and over it; "I need a cigarette..." he complained as he reached in his pocket for a nicotine fix and started towards the side kitchen door. Instantly, he was gone. I wanted to murder everyone in the house for ruining my moment with him.

I stood up with everyone else and watched Caroline gather her coat and purse hoarsely. Good riddance- Landon apologized for his mother's rude behavior, unsure of what had gotten into her. I watched Charlotte shoot Dean a look, and Dean rolled it off his shoulders, carelessly shrugging.

Dean is what has gotten into her. Clearly.

"Can I be excused?" I just needed a way out of this entanglement, but they were too busy to pay any attention to me regardless. I convinced myself that this had nothing to do with me as I tipped out the side kitchen door. The side deck was empty. What a tease. How could Haven show up mid-dinner and leave before anyone else did? This guy was messing with me, I thought until I felt his stare burning down my back like the smell of the cigarette slow-burn. I slowly turned around, and there he stood, towering above. Cigarette burning on his lips as he walked over very slowly, looking at me with those piercing sonic blue eyes. Squinting at me, intrigued.

"Are you dating that guy?" His tone was easy, but he sounded skeptical about it all, almost even laughing about it.

"Yeah... Landon is great..."

I couldn't lie; I was strutting around like he didn't make me weak when I walked out here. Now I had shaky knees and shaky hands. He made me nervous. Partly because he was everything, I thought he would be perfect, partly because he wasn't afraid of coming on strong. Haven was sure of himself, like tidal waves in current.

"He wouldn't be able to handle a skirt like you,"

The words rolled off his tongue like a spell. I froze, realizing he was towering over me, ravishing me with his hungry eyes as I always dreamt about, but this felt good; he felt safe. "-And you can?" I faintly said, unaware I was inviting him in. I allowed him to steal my breath as he drew closer. My hands held onto the deck railing. I was leaning back over the edge, looking up at him. One sudden movement, and he'd press up against me. I might even die, but it was worth it for me. He puffed out some smoke and tossed the cigarette butt aside into the dark yard.

"What happened there?" Haven was staring and pointing to the burn on my wrist from the creature in my nightmare. The scar that no one had noticed but him. I brisked my bony fingers over it.

"Oh, this... nothing, it was just the hair iron," I crackled out a response as he looked at me sternly; Haven knew I was lying.

"-Right. Must be a shitty hair straightener- you have perfect waves...." He lightly brushed his fingers over my hair before stepping back and studying me.

"You run track, don't you, Daya?"

I nodded. Speechless. His sultry eyes bounced.

Toes. Legs. Knees.

Thighs. Hips. Waist.

Breasts. Face. Eyes.

"You have an amazing pair of legs on you -I run too. It's my passion. What's yours?" I stood quiet, entertained by him.

"-Hey, Fuck what they think. I think you're right about not wanting to settle in life. You sound sure of yourself. I love that." The way he said that last part made my heart skip.

"… most times," I finally was able to talk again.

He must have liked that because he analyzed me more.

"You're a pretty little thing, huh… My father really should have warned me. Of course, we haven't seen each other since we were kids but damn, do you know what you're doing to me in that dress?"

His hand grappled at his heart, and he fell into a whisper at the end. He stepped back some more to help self-control. Lord knows I barely knew how to, at this point. His eyes never left mine now. Hiding under thick perfect brows, I could feel how bad he wanted me. Innocent old me. Barefooted, messy-haired, flushed red cheeks, standing out in 50-degree weather in a tiny red dress. The wind strays between my warm thighs. He watched me close my eyes and engulf the subtle breeze, lifting my wild hair. He was still staring when I opened my eyes—not expecting him to be so attentive. Haven was nothing like Landon; I could see how he longed to touch my bare shoulders and kiss my pouted lips. He traced me with his eyes sensually. At this point, he was doing more than enough. I needed a distraction. "-Why did you want to come tonight?" I said, turning away from him and staring up at a full moon in the sky. He was so hot; I could feel the heat rise from his body.

"Because I wanted to see you… Because you belong to me,"

I sucked my teeth. He had to ruin it.

"I don't belong to you." I hated it when he said it but loved it after I repeated the words aloud.

"I know you women hate that. Feminism and you want to free, 'liberated,' or whatever, but I can't help myself… I can be over-protective with the people I love."

LOVE? I turned to him. Once again, our eyes were like magnets, unable to catch focus on anything around us. Haven leaned more into me. So very careful not to touch me. My body tingled with intensity because of how close he stood.

"I... I don't belong to you. I'm promised to Landon."

He ripped his eyes off me and stared into the darkness beyond the porch light; the soft wind carried on.

"Fuck Landon... my dad, and your uncle. I don't care what they say. It's not about them. They're all trying to make it about them. None of them has figured out by now that it's about you. You're a Goddess, and you need protection. My protection. My Elders say *The Great Spirit* gave me a special gift so that I could protect you. I'm still trying to figure out what I have done to prove myself worthy of protecting something as unique as you are."

My eyes darted up, and I blushed. I took a moment before,

"What are you getting out of that?"

"You..."

Our eyes met again. The dark determination in his eyes made me feel safe. I knew he wouldn't let anything happen to me. He touched my hair but didn't break into his urge to touch a single strand. Instead, he admired me with his eyes, mirroring my silhouette with his hands. He exhaled through his nose roughly like a bull. His eyes watched me like one too. His eyes groped me again; this time, he admired me in that red dress. "God damn it... I hope your *'boyfriend'* took the time to tell you how beautiful you are."

I thought about it.

"...Landon... barely said anything to me. He's more worried about pleasing my uncle." I was honestly slightly embarrassed by it. Haven pushed both hands through his perfect hair and stared off into the abyss, frustrated by my words.

"-You're wasting your time with that kid, and he's wasting your time. I told them that. I told them this would happen. I can't have you with someone who won't appreciate you or protect you the way I would. I have to make sure you know what you mean to me *all the time,* through him if I can't have you," His eyes seemed almost sad. I wanted to reach out and touch him, but I was stuck when his clouding eyes became all dark and black, like the first time I saw them. So I wasn't dreaming. His eyes do flicker from black to blue, like bruises. I resisted the urge to reach over and touch his face; he quickly pulled away, feeling me weaken under his stare. He must have felt it coming. He paced around the deck. In the distance, I could see my uncle walking Landon and his mother to her car in the parking lot. My uncle flooded Mrs. Upton with apologies. I rolled my eyes. Pathetic. He was so worried about keeping Landon in my life; he would do anything. I exhaled. I was lost, and Haven knew it.

"You still go running?"

He stepped in front of me, purposely cutting off my view of Landon in the driveway. He wanted to be the only thing I saw. I looked up at his amazing herculean body. His perfect jawline clenched. His dark and heavy brows over his dark eyes seemed to be changing in nervousness. Plumbing coral lips pressed together, unsatisfied. Defined arms crossed as he was waiting for me to say something.

"I do, but not so much since the summer."

"We should go on a midnight run together." I laughed at his words, and he smiled, to my surprise.

"Ha, you know they wouldn't let that fly... I highly doubt my uncle and your dad would agree to that."

"Who said they had to know?"

I looked at him. He was stone-cold serious.

He made me more nervous than I had been all night. The adrenaline running through me was pure excitement and adventure. I desperately wanted that. I peered down the yard to my uncle Misa who stood with Landon waving bye to his mother as she pulled off.

Haven stood there waiting for a response. The side door sheered open, and Dean stepped halfway out. Staring at us suspiciously,

"Haven, we have to go... I have to be at Shane's in 15 minutes."

Dean seemed worried that we were out there for some time talking, but he didn't seem intrusive like Misael. Dean and Haven had a brief staring contest until Haven gave in and took a big step back from me. Dean finally exhaled, "I'll wait in the truck." I was surprised by Dean. I did hear him say something about crushing on my mother the day I met him. That made me near to sure that he knew exactly how we felt.

"Hey, Dad, can you tell Hattie to throw that T-bone on the grill?"

Dean smirked at his son and nodded before disappearing behind the screen door. I was shocked he was even going to eat again.

"-Wow, what an appetite." I stared squarely at him.

"You have no idea." His lusty voice sent shivers down my spine. I pinched my fingers, trying to hold the edge of my short dress down. The slightest touch of the breeze skimming through my inner thighs made me wet. I couldn't stop staring at his eyes. They were utterly sable again. He stepped closer to me, "So?"

The midnight run? He's serious, serious? He's watching my chest rise and fall made me sure he was not messing around.

"... I'll think about it," I said in a mousy voice. We watched my uncle and Landon head toward us. He didn't like that answer but shrugged at it, "Okay." He must have been satisfied knowing I was nearly melting before him. He didn't mind. He enjoyed himself, stepping back more to admire me in this sensitive and yearning state. Leaning up against the rail, helplessly doomed by him.

"-I am so sorry about my mother," Landon nearly shouted to get my attention as he and my uncle caught up with us at the side door. I felt Landon's arms slide underneath my breast, across my ribs, as he pulled me close onto his body, peeling me from the railing. Landon pulled my hair aside and kissed my cheek. I couldn't do anything else but look at Haven as he winced. "Don't worry- Everything will work out." Landon sighed.

"-Maybe things aren't meant to work out." Haven recklessly responded. He stayed solemn, even when we looked at him.

"... Who are you again?" Landon straightened his back and stood like a statue next to me; His hands never left my body, and Haven stared at every touch. He scoffed. My heart was dropping. Oh no.

"-You know who I am... We've met." Haven clenched his jaw shut. His words sounded off like a warning; it seemed like Haven knew secrets, and he had no problem resurfacing them. His honest intent towards me was turning me on.

"Harry?"

"-Haven." He looked like he wanted to punch him in the face.

"Right... Haven Tyson. I see you've met *MY fiancee*, Daya."

"*Fiancee?*" Haven mocked him, letting out an intentional taunting scoff, glaring at my uncle, "-You work fast, Misael."

Haven was suspicious of my uncle, and I didn't blame him. Haven gained my trust pretty fast this way. He carried himself with honor and integrity. His fearlessness and lack of concern for everyone and things, all aside from me, made it clear I was the only thing that mattered to him. He didn't care who knew it. He was too confident and intimidating for anyone to oppose him except for maybe Landon. And it was no secret either. Haven did not approve of Landon at all. Haven clearly said Landon didn't deserve me. I watched his reaction render into hate and resentment. He was just as hot-tempered and passionate as how Dean and Jacy described.

Right now, he looked vexed. Barely able to keep himself from exploding. He watched the way Landon held on to me and how his fingertips ran across my skin, brisking the fuzzy hairs on my arm. His hands dug into my hip as he held me close, smiling in Haven's face, all nonchalant. I choked on air, fearing for Landon's not so detachable limbs. In a second, Haven would make sure he left without arms. I was itching for him to let me go. Haven's jealous eyes weren't nearly as sexy as the movies made it out to be. If looks could kill, Landon would be 6 feet under by now.

My uncle couldn't bear to sit around for it either. He looked just as nervous as I did as he tried grasping away Haven's attention, pulling him along slowly. I don't blame Misael's hesitation; Haven was heavenly large. Mounting on him would be like climbing a tree in the Red Wood Forest.

"Hey, Haven, let me walk you to the truck," Misael suggested.

Without taking his eyes off me, he nodded softly in response, "Good night," he said between my uncle babbling and his father's excessive honking. "Good night," I replied, carelessly sappy.

He ignored Landon and gestured to my uncle before he took one last look at me, and his eyes slowly resumed to blue beach water. Those haunting bipolar eyes made my heart chakra ache. I held myself back hopelessly, watching him walk away with my uncle. The rest of the night with Landon, I tried to hold up a fake smile and pretended to be okay. It worked. He didn't know that inside I was falling apart.

7

The Chase

I couldn't stop biting my nails.

Days after Haven crashed the dinner party, Dean had stopped by for lunch, and surprisingly, Haven had come with him. I wasn't sure what his deal was, but he started to act like a dickhead. His attitude was unreasonable and near to careless; between eye rolls and an icy cold shoulder, sitting around the table with Misa and Dean eating, per usual. But, on the other hand, he was all nonchalant, talking sports. I watched him from across the kitchen, hiding behind Shakespeare's, *Taming of the shrew.*

First, he refused to acknowledge me. Then, when I finally forced myself to say 'hey' after dreading it for so long, he pretended not to hear it. Then, after forty-five minutes of indulging himself in conversation with my uncle and his father, he turned to me as I was walking by and said, "What's up," and continued to grope me with his savaged eyes as I walked away. In my head, I threw up two middle fingers and said *Fuck. You.* Who did he think he was?

My uncle and Dean were arguing about some stupid fantasy football crap, and they had retreated to his office to settle it, leaving

Haven and me in the kitchen alone. I continued to ignore him, even after he pulled up alongside me and stared deeply into the side of my face. I buried my face deeper into the book to cover my flushed rosy cheeks, "What's that you're reading?-" He asked annoyingly and didn't wait for me to speak, "-William Shakespeare? Why the hell are you reading that?" I ignored him.

"How far are you into it 'cuz I can tell you, it's fucking trash."

"-Hey, I *love* Shakespeare,"

"Really... Well, that book is stupid. It's an unrealistic attempt to '*tame*' a real woman. It's a fucking stupid concept. Women are most beautiful when they're wild, like you. That energy is true magic. I love it. Men like Shakespeare and your boyfriend wouldn't know what to do with fire like yours. But men like me? Spirit created me to find that fire inside you, and I can see you're aching to be wild. As bad as you want me to set you free, Daya; trust me, I want to watch you blossom," On accident, I looked up at him with rich Lilac eyes. It made him weak. Sitting there all tall but bent over. His black wavy hair fell into his eyes. So, so black, dark, puppy eyes; he wasn't so big and bad when melting for me.

"You must know a lot about blossoming,"

"... I wouldn't say that. I'm just intuitive. Anyway, I know a wild-fire when I see one." He stared steadily, his eyes burning into me.

"Wildfires are dangerous. Destructive." I warned.

"Good thing I'm both... Did you make up your mind about that run with me?" I scoffed and shook my head, keeping my chin anchored to the palm of my hand, refusing to look his way.

"-Hell no." I sounded off, and he sucked his teeth.

"-Why are you playing with me?"

"-I'm playing with you? I've been sitting here waiting to talk to you, and you intentionally ignored me for nearly an hour."

"Listen, I want to make sure that your uncle and me-"

Oh no. The New Daya was taking over,

"-Haven, you're not the *ass-kissing* type. Weren't you the one who said, *'fuck what your uncle thinks?'* You don't care what he thinks..." He seemed triggered, in a rough whisper,

"Hey, fuck you- I'm not kissing ass."

"Sounds like you were," I teased, putting down the book.

"-Well, it looked like you were fantasizing about me for 45 minutes when you should have been thinking about your *'fiancee.'* I saw you squirm in that seat. You could barely keep still. What were you trying to do? Give yourself a-"

"Shut up!" I stood up before I could find myself strangling him.

"Where is he, by the way? He should be here, keeping you busy. What kind of guy would leave his girl alone dry humping a seat?"

Yes, he was indeed playing with my emotions. Even though he was right, I wanted to smack him, but I huffed unevenly and stormed to the side kitchen door. Following behind, he swung his long muscular arm before me, cutting me off from exiting.

"You should be glad he's not; he could have been the seat."

CheckMate. That seemed to start a fire in his eyes. Haven's grin suddenly fades away, but not entirely, "Now wait a minute-"

"-Excuse me, while I go call my MAN." My colorful language warned him; I was dead serious. It surprised me how fast he knew how to tickle my ribs. I was flustered and looking wildly at him.

"Is that what you're going to do? You're going to call him?"

I stared at him with mild intensity, and he dropped his arm.

"Be careful, Daya. He *might* get his ass kicked. And I'm only saying *'might'* because I'm in a good mood."

"Good mood? Yeah, right."

"Why not? Your uncle said he didn't want me anywhere near you for longer than a minute. Bet? I've been in the same room with you for the last hour. I'm happy. And yet, this whole time, you thought I was ignoring you. Are you kidding me? That's crazy, skirt. How can I not see you there? Looking like a sweet melting peanut butter *limbe; y*eah, I know what those are."

He licked his lips, winked at me, gave me his charming smile, and confidently walked away. I could only stare at him with such resentment as he stopped for a moment. "You're a runner Daya. Be prepared to be chased 'cuz; I **run too**." He drove me nuts, but I retreated to my garden.

I didn't call Landon.

Since that day, I've been on edge. I never had anyone make me so angry but so turned on. Jacy says it was all because he wanted to *"protect me,"* whatever the hell that means. My mind, and especially my body, didn't want to give me a choice of whether or not I liked him. I wanted him, and that's it. I can fight it all that I want to, but there will be bending at some point.

Again I am elastic.

Sadly, I anticipated getting into it with him again. Toxic. Maybe. But he was such an asshole. So smug, so confident, so sexy, so intrusive, and so damn sure of himself. Why? His looks alone did a lot of wreckage without the help of that charming attitude and a slick mouth. Everything he does seems to make my clit ache and juice. I knew the next time I saw him would be intense.

Trying to prove something to myself, I forced myself to rely on Landon for validation. It was a terrible solution. The truth was, I didn't realize how much time we *weren't* spending together. Or Landon's lack of concern for it. I thought that the very few hours we saw each other a week was regular. But getting a hold of Landon these past few days was more complicated than I thought. He was always busy, and I must have been careless to realize. Asking Landon for his time was like pulling horse teeth. Very quickly, I was losing patience with Landon. Still, I couldn't let Haven have this over my head. I wanted to prove to him that he was wrong and was only interfering with my relationship with Landon. I did my best to keep Landon around as much as possible, but the plan wasn't successful. He knew how sexually excited I've been, and in fact, avoided m.

Still, I struggled to get closer to Landon.

It was Saturday, and Landon had a game against *Wale Eastside* tonight. Our rivals. It was Landon's biggest game in the season, and I wanted to make tonight special, so I wore something sexy that showed cleavage and threw my hair up in a thick messy bun, the way Landon loves it.

A while later, we were at the school, and my uncle was off to the side, buying out nearly the entire concession stand, as I was sitting in the bleachers, staring up at a cream and stone-colored sky, with Sunny. Honestly, Sunny was the only person I considered a friend, but I've never shared much of my life outside of Grey Wolf River with Sunny; I'm sure she thought I was strange. I didn't invite her to the game; she just threw herself into my plans when she called me that morning. I was sure it was because she wanted to creep on the local boys in town, off the res. When I tried to cut her out, she made me feel bad about her recent breakup with Skylar, and I caved in. It had turned out to be a big mistake; she wouldn't shut up about how lucky I was to be dating Landon and his good looks.

An electrifying stinging guitar sounded from the minimally busy parking lot. Pulling in, Haven and Jacy had just arrived in Jacy's Jeep, blasting *alternative rock* music from the speakers. Haven was jumping; no, *swinging* around in Jacy's Jeep, Lipsyncing shamelessly. Poor Jacy fought with Haven to turn off the radio. Haven pulled him back. I could see Jacy flush from here, about to give up until Dean pulled in his truck along with them. Dean snapped out his truck casually, reached into the Jeep, and slapped Haven in the back of the head. Unfazed, Haven laughed and shut off the radio.

UGHHHH. Here we go.

"Day- that's the guy I was telling you about!"

Sunny jumped, pointing to Haven. When? What?

"What guy?" I finally gave her my full attention.

"That guy right there. I told you earlier; he just moved back to town, and I've had my eye on him..." Her words rattled the fuck out of me, but I couldn't let that show. Not while I was claiming attachment to Landon. I inhaled smooth but long. I needed all the damn zen I could suck in right now without looking envious as we watched the three walk down the sidelines. Haven seemed playful, grabbing up his innocent older brother and brushing his head with his knuckles. Jacy pulled off him, quickly fixing his hair and spiffy vest as they approached the cheerleaders. Dean pointed up in the bleachers and waved. I waved back, but Jacy and Haven were too busy checking out the girls to notice.

Misa and Dean's faces lit up as they emerged into a group in front of me. Out in the field, Landon didn't seem too pleased to see the Tyson boys here. A look of confusion and insecurity bolted into Landon's face when he looked at me. He was now distracted from his warm-up on the field. The cheerleaders also seemed distracted, and honestly, I couldn't blame them. How could they not be? Haven's the finest thing to walk this field after Landon. The girls weren't afraid to unshelve themselves. Most of them were not virgins and in heat. It irritated the shit out of me. Watching them bat and flutter their fake lashes, Haven soaked them in like groupies. Pouncing around with their boobs pushed up together and brilliant white smiles.

"Hey, skirt." Haven lightly bumped his shoulder into Leyla's, flirting with her. He nearly turned her into cream, like right from a scene in *Grease.* She gushed and then turned to her jealous friends. She must have felt me staring because the little bitch had the nerve to turn around after and look at me like a guilty puppy. She shrugged apologetically with her pompoms up. I shook my infamous, *'Are.you.fucking.kidding.me'* glance and rolled with the punches, as my uncle, now standing next to me, asked me to move down the bleachers to make room for Dean and the boys.

Great. Misa and Dean were terrible at keeping Haven away.

I walked to the end of the bleacher, and as I was going to sit, Haven jumped into the seat. I sucked my teeth and tapped Sunny, purposely giving her the seat next to him. She sat down just as quick as it took me to regret it. *Fuck it. He's only here to distract me anyway.* I told myself as I sat down between Sunny and my uncle. Sunny was already working up a conversation with Haven, "I didn't know you two knew each other? I would have asked Daya to introduce me a long time ago. You've come into my job a few times."

Sunny shamelessly stared up into his face. "Right, the book store." Practically brooding already, he looked around unmoved by the conversation. He could care less what she rambled about. He was too preoccupied, slowly trying to enter my world through stolen glances. I kept my eyes away from him.

"Yeah, her uncle's my dad's best friend. We grew up together."

"-Barely... grew up together," I intermixed.

"What was that?" Thirsting to argue with me already.

"I don't even remember you. So you can't say we 'grew up together' if I don't remember it?"

"Don't discredit me because you can't remember. That's not my fault. I moved away a long time ago, but I'm back. You should be more grateful. I only came back so I could profess my love to you."

"-Oh, too bad she's engaged to Landon, huh." Sunny cut in,

Neither Haven nor I could help ourselves as we snapped a dirty look at her. Not a fan of Haven himself, my uncle glared at him to stop whatever bothered me, "Don't let him get you all worked up, Daya. You haven't had a chance to give Landon his good luck charm." I looked down at Landon, who looked adoringly at me before he shot a dirty look at Haven. He blew me a kiss, and I caught it and blew one back. "Corn balls," Haven claimed absurdity. I looked at him as he flattened down on his perfect chest through that imprinted white shirt underneath his vintage jean jacket. Sex. Damn it. He used his sex appeal to mess with me again, knowing how I felt about all that. Knowing I couldn't defend myself from him. It's like he can smell the sweet, pure nectar, begging to burst from inside of me. I hated him, and everyone felt the tension I was holding. Especially my uncle and Dean, they both looked at him disapprovingly.

"-You know what, I'm hungry. Misael, you don't mind if Daya shows me to the concessions, right?" Haven stood up, shooting me a look like, *'RUN and GO GIRL,'* no questions asked. My uncle stuttered at him, "Y-y-you know what, maybe that's not a -" It was too late. Haven and I were hopping off the bleachers and to the concessions. His attitude seemed to get serious now that we walked away from everyone. Stern, more or less, but romantically melancholic. He walked in close distance, steady and in sync, nearly breathing down my neck. I couldn't deny how comfortable that made me,

"How are you?" He asked honestly.

"Just fine." I folded in my arms.

"You look beautiful," crap, why was he being so sweet.

"Thank you," I said as he ordered some food at the window. He was a gentleman and asked me if I wanted anything first. I told him no before he rambled on with the cashier and then paid her. He pulled me aside by the pinch of my jacket to wait with him. The way he looked at me was such a turn-on, burning through my chest. I had to stop him. "What are you doing here, Haven?"

"Your uncle invited my dad to see your loverboy play. They asked us if we wanted to go. Do you think I'd pass on a chance to see you? So what? Haven't you missed me?" He said, sliding his hand down the long white tee he wore for the second time. So tight you could see every built-in bulk of his strength.

Yes, hell yes, I did. But I couldn't let him have that.

"Haven, I like you, but I don't appreciate you trying to get in the way of my relationship with Landon." He cracked a fake smile and shook his head lightly. Like he couldn't believe I would start with him. He looked at me; his blue eyes had a rim of the black color slowly seeping into his pupils, "Don't make me a prisoner just because you're comfortable living a lie."

"Landon could be,"

"-Don't waste your time Daya. Landon is the only one in the way." Haven abruptly cut me off. I refused to give in to his theory.

"You could be wrong." He ignored me.

"Anyway. You want to take that run with me, or not?" He asked while biting into a pretzel. Haven, like my uncle, nearly bought the entire concession stand, "I don't know yet."

"Okay. Bet. But, you're not about to keep me waiting, skirt. I want an answer tonight, so stop holding out on me, or I'll ask Sunny to go with me instead." Petty, I thought. I huffed, knowing it was useless; I would only say yes anyway. He pushed popcorn into my hands, the two of us started back towards the bleachers.

The Varsity game was to start, and the place had filled up tremendously fast. When we got back to our seats, Misael, per usual, was down by the sideline, prepping Landon. I watched the two joke as Misa handed Landon a bottle of the unique 'training' juice he made for him. Their bond was cute. The way Landon looked up to Misa and how Misa wanted nothing more than to help Landon succeed; I loved that about them. I watched as Landon drank down the juice, his teammates to the side of him winding him up. He cracked a smile and hit one of the buddies playfully before looking out into the background. I hadn't realized how adoringly I was looking at him until Haven snapped his fingers in front of me.

"Down girl," he said in a, *'you're making me jealous,'* way.

I ignored him, looking back at Landon as he looked up into the bleachers at me. Haven squeezed into his trail of vision and condescendingly waved at Landon. Landon's expression soured until my uncle whispered to him, and suddenly he smiled. Haven tried stealing my attention, "I don't see the big deal about him," Haven shrugged, brooding in the other direction.

"Me either." Sunny agreed, her eyes stripping Haven down.

Are you kidding me, chick? Weren't you just saying- You know what, never mind. "You haven't seen anything yet," I warned Haven. He hardly seemed in the mood to be here anymore. *Bend. Bend for me, asshole.* I wanted him to turn into elastic. Meanwhile, Landon and my uncle were smiling at someone approaching.

Shit- Caroline.

My stomach rumbled in nervousness. I hoped my uncle wasn't going to invite- *Never mind, he did invite her.* He asked Caroline to come to sit with us. Although she seemed very reluctant when she saw Dean sitting there, my uncle must have somehow convinced her it would be a good idea. I prayed she wouldn't come over preaching the same crap she did at dinner. Dean and I seemed to be awed by my uncle's persistence. Being a semi-smart woman, Caroline chose to sit in the row directly behind us to keep up her conversation with Misa while avoiding the rest of us. He seemed to be the only one she liked, but that didn't surprise me much.

Landon sent a hollowing whistle my way from the sidelines. I, nervously knowing Haven was watching, went down the bleachers and to Landon. He squirted more of Misa's special green liquid in his mouth and bounced about. His eyes glowed with intensity, "-I can't start a game without my good luck charm," I came close enough for him to pull me in. I couldn't deny that Landon looked extremely tempting in his football gear. His eyes were glowing, pulling me in so fast our hips collided. He brushed the waves falling from my updo out of my eyes, "You look so sexy," Immediately, I noticed Landon was unusually not himself; his paws were all over me, and he didn't care who saw. Landon was always a romantic but did PDA casually like everyone else. Not so passion-aggressively and showy like right now. *Whatever,* I thought. He's showing me he cares, and that was the point I was trying to get across to myself and Haven.

"-Why did them two show up?" His voice with deep loath, Landon glanced out to the bleachers, questioning the Tyson boys. Haven wasn't paying us any mind, keeping himself busy, talking up Sunny pretty good. I could see her flip her hair and giggle; her hands lavished all over his arms.

I pulled away from gawking; I would deal with the two in a minute. Landon seemed more irritated with Jacy, who was down the sidelines, complimenting Leyla on her cheer skills. What seemed like a normal conversation was a nervous Jacy trying to flirt. As if he needed to; the law boy suits were fitting for Jacy and did his lean body justice. Leyla particularly loved a man in a suit, and he only wanted Leyla's attention. *"What the hell is he doing?"* Landon whispered, thinking to himself. Something rattled him, staring at the two. I tried to steal back his attention,

"-You know Misael, he's always bragging about Mr. Grey Wolf High. They came to see you play." I played with his jersey as he cracked a confident smirk. Then, ripping his eyes from Leyla, he looked at me as if I were a sugar treat. His fingers swiped across my bottom lip, "Hector's tonight, babe?" His hands now reached for my hair strands, softly touching my tousled hair. Finally, he looked into my eyes. His eyes were hitting mine differently with some unyielding superpower. They were amazing.

"Yeah," I said in a near faint whisper.

"You'll be my lucky charm and my victory prize," he pulled me closer for all to see, and then he kissed me hard. I fell to his whim and let him lay passion on me. I could feel my eyes glowing, even after he pulled himself off me. I squeezed my eyes shut and buried my face in his chest. I felt too vulnerable to move, yet, Landon slowly peeled me from his body, looking down at me while caressing my jawline. His teammates and the cheerleaders cheered, and his fans in the rumbling bleachers. But I wanted to disappear when I looked up and saw Haven with a dropped head between his knees that rolled into his hands and Sunny leaning over him as if she was trying to block me out of sight for him. What was Haven going to say when I sat back down? I stumbled away from Landon, but not before he slapped my ass. My cheeks flushed more;

Why was he acting like a chad?

When I got back up the bleachers, Sunny and Haven were gone. A part of me was relieved, but another part was also thinking the worst and dreading it. Haven had to have lost faith in me and put his bets on Sunny instead. I'm sure she already clarified what her talents included, and he wouldn't have to worry about her holding back because she was not a virgin. Dang, it. I was beginning to like Haven. It's my fault. Now I felt awful that I pushed away like that. A pit settled in me that made it hard to pay attention to the game. I hated myself for secretly wanting to make him jealous. Even more for being so careless, knowing how I truly felt about him. Oh, new reckless Daya.

At the start of the fourth quarter, Sunny and Haven had come back from a very long '*smoke break*,' which seemed believable with the dank smell of pot and cigarettes they carried. Even though on the inside, I was cheering that I might have a slight chance to reverse the damage, Haven wasn't thrilled to be back. Nonetheless, he made sure he got to sit next to me. He **ordered** Sunny to the corner so he could sit between us. Sunny didn't seem too thrilled about that, but who cares? They're back, and that's all I cared for, so I can keep the two in clear view. We were all pretty quiet except for Misa and Caroline, who went on and on to Dean about Landon's achievements and skills.

"I told you, the kid is fast, like a stallion." Misael boasted.

"Landon does have a great pair of legs on him,"

Dean agreed, despite the dismay of both his sons. I felt Haven's arms stretch behind me and settle on the rim of my chair. I could feel his warmth radiate behind me like an embrace. He was getting comfortable, lost in thought while watching Landon running across the field. "He's not bad," Haven agreed. Jaw-dropping, he gave me another charming smirk. This time I couldn't deny how good he made me feel. I hoped he wouldn't notice me, slowly edging towards him, catching the feel of his aura, but he did. He didn't mind and also edged closer. I was about to look up at him when Jacy interrupted.

"Hey- what do you guys do after the game?"

"Hector's," Misael murmured without looking away.

"Hector's? They still do that?" Dean asked,

"Hector's?" Caroline chimed in appalled, gripping on her pearls for dear life. She didn't surprise me.

"Hector's? What is that?" Haven chimed in.

"-Well, in the early '80s, our local, wholesome haggard bum, Sam, lost an uncle named Hector- or something like that and ended up inheriting a fortune. Sam was kind and humble and not persuaded by a lavish lifestyle. So Sam decided to buy a shabby old cabin on that huge land off the state route. He couldn't let go of the place he used to call home, so Sam mounted that old school bus he used to sleep in onto the field." Misael finished his little storytelling without an accurate answer. Sunny, Jacy, and Haven all looked at me, agitated. I shrugged at my uncle's half-ass response.

"-Since then, Hector has allowed the kids to safely party on the field. It's inevitable after games, especially one like tonight."

"They still have the Lucky Charm bus?" Dean elbowed Misael.

"-For the love of God, when is that going to die down?" Caroline complained.

"Awe, it's not that bad. Teens will be teens, Caroline. Besides, I remember every moment of our Lucky Charm pull up," Dean teased, "-Or out," My uncle and Dean chuckled hard like the stupid men they were, while Caroline slapped my uncle's shoulder in disbelief. Haven nearly choked on his popcorn to his solicited remark.

"What- what are they talking about? What's that lucky charm thing?" Haven was just as curious as Jacy and Sunny.

"After the game, all the kids follow the MVP and his *lucky charm* for the victory ride to Hector's. They all parade around, causing havoc for Fifteen minutes around town, while the MVP and his lady head over to the lucky charm bus at Hector's."

"Fifteen minutes?" Sunny rolled her eyes impatiently.

"How much longer do you need?" Jacy was unsuccessfully trying to help Sunny figure it out without spelling it out.

"-Daya, you're not doing that." Haven calmly protested at me.

"It wouldn't be my first time," I was honest.

He looked at me with melancholy horror.

"Relax, no rules say she has to give it up. You can do whatever for the fifteen minutes." Dean and my uncle agreed.

"What kind of uncle would I be? I trust Landon."

Haven could care less about my uncle's opinion. He pulled at my jacket a little, "-Are you okay with this?" He sounded genuinely concerned about how I felt. The truth was, **NO,** I wasn't okay with it. I never was. It was degrading. Last year, I cried to Landon because I didn't want to give up my panties, the *'lucky token.'* Everyone knew Landon wasn't a virgin before our track meets, so they expected something. When he came back empty-handed, he lied to his buddies about running bases with me and told them I was too prude to give up the 'proof.' Needless to say; his buddies took his word for it. This year I would expect the same, but as long as I didn't need to prove anything, I was okay with running bases. I shrugged at Haven's question, and he didn't like that, so he melted hatred into Misa, "She shouldn't have to do that,"

"Don't worry, bud. As I said, I trust Landon. With my life and *my* girls." My uncle condescendingly reassured Haven.

"-Although panties were a good token to show the boys, right Caroline? I bet yours is still hanging in the bus with all the others." Dean continued to tease her as she shifted, appalled in her seat. Dean and I exchanged winning glances.

"You're going to let Landon degrade you like that? In front of his friends. **For** his friends?" Haven was now unable to let it go.

"Don't see it that way. And before you get all huffy and puffy, I've been through this whole routine with him."

"**Nah,** I'm taking you to Hector's myself," Anger brewing in his words, I ignored him and watched the game swoon down. *He was bluffing.* Four more minutes to uphold. *He **had** to be bluffing.* We were in the lead, but not by far. I got lost in my thoughts about what would happen after the game for a moment. It was becoming harder to pull away from Haven's grips. He cared too much, and it was such a turn-on until I glanced at him again. His hungry sable eyes were all over Leyla, cheering. Eyes of desire, Leyla had noticed, and she was 'cheer fucking' him right back, with no remorse. She enjoyed the attention from his unique brooding eyes. *This night has been unfairly out of control already, I* thought while snapping Leyla's attention off Haven and backhanding his stomach.

"-Don't you dare use my cousin against me," I whispered.

"I'm trying my best; it's been a weird day. Truce?" I nodded, and he seemed to adore me at that moment, biting the corner of his lip while looking down at me with sparkling, softened dark eyes. I was breathless and crawling into him, amazed at how he flipped me on like this. I wanted him, but the jealousy was now pumping.

"-Where did you go earlier?" I whispered, and he rolled his eyes.

"Did you think I would sit here for that bull shit? I said what I said about Sunny, and I meant it, so don't worry about it."

"DON'T WORRY ABOUT IT?" I murmured, *double* worried about it. I moved anxiously around in my seat for a moment.

"Stop." He murmured back, annoyed.

"-How about you both stop," Misael scolded us as the crowd cheered and counted down to less than a minute. Leyla tossed and split while the coach cussed and squabbled at Landon's sideline as he was jetting down the field. He was focused as he passed the line just as the buzzard went off, and the stance went crazy—everyone jumping and cheering, here and there.

Yet, I was eye to eye with Haven, unable to get along for more than a minute but completely seduced by Haven's dark eyes. I could see into his beautiful soul like no one else; we both knew it. And poor Landon searched for me, only to find me consumed with this stranger he seriously disliked. At this point, Landon was revved up by more than just adrenaline. Jealousy was beginning to set. When I looked down at Landon, he sported the disappointment on his face, which made me dread the Victory Ride to Hector's.

I was freaking out in the girls' locker room. It was the only place I could hide from the guys before heading to Hector's. Out in the parking lot, Landon, the Tyson boys, and Sunny waited, along with the rest of the class. The game ended 15 minutes ago, and I was stuck, asking Leyla for advice. "-He's in love, Daya."

"Leyla, you're not helping. I'm still engaged."

"But what if Haven is not wrong? Come on. You two have some magical connection; you can't deny that,"

"Right, like what you two had out there?" She rolled her eyes,

"Please spare me; he's so gullied over you. He only did that to make you jealous. All he talks about is you, and how smart you are, and pretty, and how your scent makes his heart skip." Leyla threw her gym bag over her shoulders. My heart melted to her words,

"*Really?* Ley- Haven is insisting that he drives me to Hectors."

Leyla's face grew brighter as that, for sure, was a melodrama.

"How? Landon **has** to drive you."

"I don't know, but I'm pretty sure Haven will punch him in the eye if he makes me go with him."

"Shit- I hope Dad and Dean are still outside." I followed her out the locker room and down the nearly empty school halls.

Dean and Caroline were near the parking lot as we exited the building, passively arguing. They seemed to fall into a faint whisper, and I tried to catch pieces of the conversation as we drew closer, "It's not that easy, Caroline. I can't just spring this on them. If I tell them now, they'll be upset. Haven already dislikes Landon-" I looked at him suspiciously, and he returned the look, "-Hey, Misael took off. He had left some documents from his office and told me that he will see you in the morning, and don't stay out too late." We nodded at him as it grew quiet and awkward. Finally, Dean cleared his throat and turned to Caroline. "Let me walk you to your car." They gave us a parting look and walked away.

In the Parking Lot, Landon and his pal's were super hyped up, celebrating. The entire student body crowded into the parking lot. There was a riot with loud music, classmen cheering, and the *'pretty and popular* at the center. Most of the class were in their cars, waiting for Landon to *'mount his lucky charm'* on the bed of his truck. *'Lucky charm';* meaning me. I hated this part. I was always so bashful about these school traditions, but, despite my timidness, I was determined to do it again. I needed to prove to myself that I still loved him, despite the growing pit in my throat.

Everyone took one look at me before roaring in cheer. Landon and his buddies were sitting on the edge of Landon's truck, waiting for me. My heart sank nervously, and I found myself searching for Haven. I needed his sanctuary, and my heart wouldn't deny it any longer. Thankfully Haven wasn't far; Jacy's had unknowingly parked next to Landon's truck. "Here's the lucky charm!" Landon saw me coming and slowly rolled up from sitting. Immediately, he was trying to make a show. Landon sucked me into his arms as soon as I was close enough to grab. He was rough, and my discomfort showed. I tried pulling away, and his friends continued to cheer on as he glanced over at Haven to make sure he was watching. I hated the attention Landon was forcing on me. I was embarrassed by its weak and translucent disguise. He was only trying to piss Haven off, and it showed. I refused to be a chest piece. Besides, Haven was not the one to start a fight. I tried to push Landon away softly, but Landon continued the show. He fist-bumped his buddy and bluntly ignored my comments as he continued,

"-Come on, let's get that sexy ass up there." Landon evasively smacked my ass while four of his friends caved in on me. They picked me up by my arms and legs. In the distance, I could see Haven hop off the Jeep as if a match was lit under his feet. I felt my body mid-air, and I fell into their catching arms while my heart nearly continued to drop. They tossed me onto the bed of the truck. I looked at Landon and his friends. **Assholes.** Just as they tried to pull up the tailgate, Haven slammed it back down harshly, warning.

"-The Fuck are you doing? You're making her uncomfortable."

Haven yelled, with a look that read, *'I dare you to.'* Landon wouldn't test him and waved at me to get down. I anxiously crawled over and took Haven's firm, rustled, big hand as he helped me hop down from the truck bed. Easily predicted, Haven was a pleasing rumble of thunder, making the girls bat their lashes, and boys became guarded. "Bruh, she's coming with me," Landon said calmly.

"Is that how you treat your girl? Tossing her around like some piece of meat just to entertain your *boys*?" Landon looked at me, waiting to hear me disagree, but I couldn't "-Landon, this is stupid. I'm not doing this," Haven smiled until he realized I was still heading towards the truck door. *All of this, and I'm taking the ride with Landon?* Of course, I wore his ring. "What are you doing? You're not riding with him," Haven followed behind as I went to open the door, and he slammed it shut before me. Landon and his goons watched as Haven shamelessly vied for my affection and didn't care who knew. "I *have to* ride with him. He's my boyfriend." It came out stinging. I only hoped Haven understood that I was only trying to be loyal; I had rightfully belonged to Landon in the first place. I couldn't deny Landon in front of the entire school.

Haven didn't care. He was pissed.

"Fuck that. I don't trust him. Let me take you." Haven begged.

"-Can you get off of my girlfriend? It's fucking pathetic."

Landon was also losing patience as he steered closer. When the words came out, Leyla and I immediately looked at each other while Jacy lifted his jaw from the floor.

Where the hell was my uncle Misa?

Where the hell was Dean?

Those were fighting words, and the two were would start swinging like baseball season any minute. Haven huffed a long huff. He was probably trying to keep his shit together in front of me because he didn't care about what everyone else thought.

"I think you need to mind your fucking business. What Daya and I have, is between us and has nothing to do with you. But since you can't seem to mind your own fucking business, let me enlighten you. Daya belongs with me, but she's stuck with you. You don't pay nearly enough attention to Daya. She's a gift, not a damn trophy. She isn't yours to showcase. You don't even appreciate her *all of the time.* Daya is a Goddess, and only a *real* God can give her what she desires. Her DNA is just begging for **MY** attention, and guess what; I'm right here. You get that, right?"

Haven punched his shoulder *lightly,* but that light hit was pretty heavy. Hence, most who watched on gasped, looking at Landon for a dramatic reaction. Landon calmly giggled. Raising his hand to him, he says, "Harry, *relax.* I can't *blame you* for infatuating yourself with my girl. She's smart, beautiful, a good girl, but this Queen already has a King. I'm all the king she needs. I would know; from how wet she gets for me when we're making out in my truck. She isn't afraid to tell me how bad she wants me. In. Her."

Shots fired.

My head fell into my hands. My eyes grew vast and wild.

Fuck. Why are they throwing me in the middle of it? Everyone looked at me, and even though I cleared my throat, nothing came out. Why did I have to fall in love with two dumb asses? Haven's eyes were changing again. Rapidly now, and it's not because of Jack Daniels rushing in his bloodstream. He finished his whiskey and hit Jacy in the chest with the flask. A flash in his eyes made Jacy so nervous he shot up to interject, "Now Haven, hold on-"

"Shut up." Logan pushed him aside roughly as two other friends co-signed. It only lifted the flames in Haven's eyes as he saw his older brother pushed into a corner. "-You don't have that kind of power on her," Haven tried to reassure himself.

Unfortunately, they both held power over my sacral chakra.

Or maybe I had that over them, "-Maybe neither of you is worthy of my yoni. I could always leave with Logan," The seriousness in my eyes shook them both. They both looked at Logan hex-lusted as Logan nervously swallowed hard and looked at me. In an instant, he was chasing the crimson sway in my eyes. Haven was over it. He knew what I was doing and snapped in the middle of it.

"Stop playing around, Daya." Haven's shoulder pushed mine softly as he tried moving me along towards the Jeep.

"Daya-" Landon whined, "-don't you love me, Daya?" My knees buckled underneath me. I refuse to look disloyal, yet I couldn't bring myself to say so in front of Haven, and now Landon was freaking out, "-Daya! Get in God damn the truck!" Landon snapped, opening the passenger door open for me. His tone was like a whip, and it immediately scared me into the truck. He slammed the door.

"Don't talk to her like that!" Haven snapped. I could see Leyla and Jacy getting in between them in the side-view mirror just as they would start and swing.

"My girl doesn't want you. You see where she's sitting."

"Because you yelled at her like that dickhead."

"I don't know who you think you are, Haven, but I'm not going to let some random loner loser obsessive over my chick and check me in front of my boys unless you're looking to get your ass beat."

Haven wouldn't have it any other way.

"For Daya? Let's go!" Haven could easily trample over Landon, but Jacy refused to allow it, so Logan and a couple of the stronger players also got in between now. It was like putting a rickety shotty gate between two pissed-off bulls in heat.

"Seriously guys, can't we just-" Jacy intervened again.

"Shut up, Jace!"

"Please, guys, no fighting!!" Leyla uselessly pranced around trying to stop the fight. Puffed stiff, I was stuck watching from the side view. Landon's buddies pulled him aside and began to whisper to him. Slowly, the expression on his face softened until he was smiling. He nodded at his friends, and they clapped as if they were still huddling at the game. Then, Landon approached with an idea.

"You wanna prove your love to her so bad? Fine- I challenge you to a foot race for the first dance at Hector's."

A foot race? Was he serious? I poked my head out the window.

"I am not a game, Landon!" He ignored me, and Haven could see the distress in my eyes. I was impressed how Haven seemed to let his concern for me give him a double-take. He had a lot of pride, but not enough to make him embarrass me in front of everyone. He and Landon met at a middle, "I'm not doing this if it bothers her."

"Come on, Loverboy, don't you want that dance? Or how about a lucky token? Daya is particularly sweeter than the other girls. Rare. But no man knows that but me. I get to taste, touch, and smell her every night. You have no idea how mouth-watering she is," Haven pushed him hard enough to get him off balance. I could care less. Landon deserved it. "-The winner gets a dance and her token,"

"-What the fuck, guys!" I bitched from a cracked open window. Haven's desire to protect me from Landon only made him cave into the idea. He looked at me with helter-skelter eyes, hungry to rip Landon apart. "-Foot race? Sprint? You and me? Say less. Let's do it." Haven chuckled proudly. Sure to have this in the bag, Haven threw his jacket to Jacy, then pulled off his white long-sleeved shirt, tossing it on Jacy. The girls whistled wildly in a sex-crazed frenzy upon Haven. Even I got a little wide-eyed for a moment.

"A race? That's stupid. How will that be fair if Landon's been running around all day?" *Leyla just had to open her useless mouth.*

"Easy-" Landon said while running to the truck's driver's side. His buddies revolted to their in-park cars. Everyone scattered, hopping into cars, trucks, and ATVs. Haven looked around confused, as Landon got in and revved his truck, pulling down the windows simultaneously, "You have to get to Hector's first!"

8

Hector's

Staring at Haven from across the way, Landon aggressively forced a kiss on my lips. Livid, Haven was already bolting towards the woods. Landon revved his truck engine, then skidded out the parking lot while everyone followed behind, including Jacy's jeep. The school parking lot was a ghost town in less than a minute.

Landon whispered angrily to himself, questioning Haven and his authority. His eyes were glowing green, brighter than before. Landon was super pissed off; I've never seen him this angry. I knew I wasn't a very convincing girlfriend, but Landon didn't have to be so mean. He drove like a mad man. I tried reasoning with Landon, but Haven had gotten deep inside Landon's head. Behind us, Sunny and Leyla clinging on to dear life, as Jacy tried keeping up. I didn't see the point. We all knew there was no possible way Haven would make it to Hector's in 15 minutes or less; it was across town.

In the woods outlining the roadway, there were glimpses of Haven through the dark slots of the trees. The street lights hit him clearly when he passed them. Haven ran like a beast; I had never seen anyone run so fluid and perfect without a glimpse of distraction. He said he ran track but damn, Haven was relentless. Impressive, nonetheless, and when Landon saw the glitz in my eyes, it made him even madder.

And then an intersection.

Landon hit a hard right, nearly sending me flying. Haven caught the terror in my eyes. I watched him run faster, and he almost surpassed the truck until Landon hit a hard left. "Landon, stop!" But he only drove faster. The rest of the parade of cars and trucks kept forward into the town. A flood of honking horns and whistles called out. A flare was ignited and thrown.

15 minutes.

Even after everyone disappeared, Landon raced through the back roads, and Haven was no longer visible in the woods. He hit 70-80 MPH. I gripped his arm. He looked at me and suddenly was flushed with regret; he slowed down...75..60..45...30 MPH.

We were nearing Hector's field. I could see the sparks of a massive bonfire in the middle of the dark grassy clearing ahead. Landon didn't stop the truck until he pulled deep into the field and drove down to where the mounted Lucky charm bus and fire pit stood. Hector, a 49-year-old, thin, haggard 'bum' with wild salt and pepper hair under a ragged winter hat, pushed around an empty barrel. He looked at Landon and smiled, "-Dude! They just called 15 minutes. Fastest one yet, Upton!" Proud and sticking up his thumb. Landon laughed a little to himself in achievement. He glittered pride in his eyes. I looked at him with hexed eyes, and he wiped away all the smiling when he noticed. "-How dare you!" I cried, slapping him across the face. He ate it like the man he was.

"Daya- babe, I'm sorry." He rubbed his flaming cheek.

"What the hell Landon? Bidding on dance is one thing, but my panties? That was the most embarrassing thing to ever happen to me. You had no right. Why?"

"Because he pushed me."

"Why would you let him push you into treating me this way?"

"Because I see the way he looks at you. I see the way you look at him. I can feel him ripping you from me, and I don't like it." His eyes were now raging upon reflection—guilt sunk deep into my veins.

"Landon I-"

"Don't explain yourself, Daya. I don't want to hear it. I only want to hear you say you're still mine."

"I am..."

"So prove it. Don't make me look stupid anymore."

I could see the hurt in his eyes. He meant it, and he was right. Haven was clouding my better judgment. Landon loves me, and we're kind of engaged, so why was I turning on him? Yeah, he drove recklessly with no regard to my livelihood and bet my underwear on a dumb foot race in front of the entire school, but Haven provoked him. Right? God, I was seriously confused. "You're my girl, right?" softly rolling his head in my direction, Landon looked at me.

My eyes fluttered doubts of color, "...Of course," My insides cringed. I couldn't ignore the fact that I didn't mean the words as they came out. "-Come here, babe," He reached for me. Hesitating, I moved into him as his arms collapsed over me, pulling me in. His once-raging eyes were now soft and calm again. He even chuckled.

"What a rush, right? Look, I'm sorry, I didn't mean to scare you. I got scared of losing you and got carried away. Maybe Harry is right; I haven't been paying much attention to you. I've been distant for a long time. Maybe a little distracted too."

His hands were now stroking my hair. He leaned in to kiss me, and I kissed him back, hoping to see a flame ignite. Nothing. It was just hollowness like the wind in an old empty trunk, which pissed me off. Haven didn't need to touch or kiss me to spark the passion dancing in me. My mind was stuck on Haven's whereabouts. He'd probably get here after Hector's was already in full swing. Right now, it was just us and Hector, voyaging around the corner.

"Do you love me?" Landon asked.

"Y-yes." I stuttered.

"-Good... Panties. I need them."

"Are you kidding me?" I revolted, pulling away from him.

"I wouldn't just ask Daya. It's the only way he'll back off."

"I am not doing that for you,"

"You want to prove to him you're mine, right?"

"I don't need to prove anything to anyone. That's degrading, don't you think?"

"You were willing to do more with me not too long ago. I held back in the past because of Misa, but we can play around if you keep it between us. Daya, I'll go down on you for the panties."

My jaw dropped; I was so disgusted with him. "You're an asshole," I snapped, but he looked at me sternly. Landon wasn't about to back down. Haven's immediate arrival saved me from further discussing it. He came running at full force towards the truck from the abyss of the woods and collided with Landon's driver-side door, severely indenting it. The truck shook with violence.

"Get out!" Haven paced around the truck. Even Landon had to admit he was shaken by how worked up Haven seemed. Landon sighed with exhaustion and looked at me one last time with begging eyes, but I rolled my eyes at him and popped the door open.

By the time I walked around the truck, Haven had Landon flatlined on the hood, choking him as he pushed him into an indented imprint. Landon's new truck was now a 3D crime scene, Haven was about to kill him, and we were all alone. "Haven! Stop it!" I meaninglessly yelled. At the same time, all the trucks and cars started piling into Hector's field, with their bright headlights and erratic honking. Finally, Haven released his grip on Landon's neck upon everyone's arrival, coming to his senses. I exhaled in relief.

"You almost got her killed, dummy." Haven barked at Landon, pressing him into the truck's metal before backing off. Landon coughed, trying to regain his vision and breathing as he sat up. I wanted to help him, but he flagged me away aggressively.

Whatever. I was just trying to help.

"You okay?" Haven asked as the crowd began to spill around us. I nodded, trying not to look at him. I envisioned that his piercing, sable eyes would be angry with me for taking the ride, but they weren't angry when I looked up. They were worried. I could almost feel his blood rush through his veins. And, damn it, he looked so good, huffing and puffing. Shirtless, like a Calvin Klein model. Sweat dripping off the curves of his chest, I dug my nails into my palms, knowing how much trouble I'd get in if Landon caught me looking. Fuck it. I didn't care. I was already looking.

"Y'all ready!" Logan's words pulled at everyone.

From the starting edge of Hector's property-

At the first touch of the *Lucky Charm* bus, the finish line.

That was the race. I posted against the lucky charm bus, and the crowd formed two solid lines down the invisible track.

"-I can't believe they're going to run for you?" Sunny moaned.

"-Landon is so stupid." Leyla also complained.

Haven surprised everyone after making it across town before the 15 minutes. Flexing how much of a talented runner he was, he didn't have to say it. It was pretty straightforward; don't underestimate him. I was anxious for them to get this pissing contest over with, "Can we just get on with it?" I leaned against the graffiti bus.

In a pulse, the crowd became still and quiet. Nothing sounded but a truck horn, blurting solo. All you heard and felt after were rumbling footsteps. I was their destination, right in front of their path. But I couldn't see much from a distance. You could only hear the kids cheer as they passed each meter. They footed closer to me with each passing second. Rattled, I honestly wanted Haven to win this. I was so bothered by how Landon had treated me that I only wanted to go home to my bed and not with him.

The uproars approached. I could see them now, toe to toe, as they neared. The two swapped enduring fiery glances. It sounded like horses hurdling towards me; I could feel the frozen ground melt and shake underneath. My heart twitched when I realized neither one would stop as they got closer. I closed my eyes tight, preparing for an epic collision. I took a deep breath,

BANG! The bus shook and even inched back. I felt the wind past the sides of me, and energy burst into my Merkaba atmosphere, igniting my heart chakra. My hair fluttered. Nothing touched me, but I could feel my chest radiating the energy in return. An elevated pressure over me told me it could only be Haven. I opened my eyes, and no surprise, Haven was smiling down at me, breathing loosely, nearly inches from my lips, staring into my eyes with ice blue eyes. I smiled back, relief draining into my face. His arms bridged above my shoulders, his hands dented into the old bus. Two literal handprints. Damn, he was strong, damaging everything he came across. "He's not getting that token," Haven whispered to himself in achievement. We both looked back at Landon several feet away, crouched over, nearly wheezing.

"You love running, huh?" Running had never been more of a turn-on until now. His face got closer to mine.

"Not as much as the way you're looking at me right now. You owe me a dance and your Lucky token." Wait, what? What a dick.

Every time I was beginning to accept him, he had to open his big mouth. "-No, I do not. Landon's lying, by the way," Haven pulled away from me and faced everyone else, doused by adrenaline and excitement, "Oh, I believe you, but I want what I earned."

"Well, you can just forget about it," I said as he sized me up.

"Bet- I'll get them, eventually." I kicked myself off the lean of the bus and stepped closer to him, "Bet-"

"TRUCE!" Haven and Landon smacked their tallboy cans together and then threw them back like frat boys around the bonfire. Landon's teammates pounced and growled like apes, hauling in their tipsy ladies, celebrating the winding down of well, in my opinion, a crazy fucking night. Music was blaring from the bus surround sound. Everyone was partying and getting wasted, high, and even 'lucky' behind the block backs of a bus seat. The two idiots called a truce, 'FOR NOW,' and agreed to enjoy the rest of the night. Landon didn't admit it, but he was impressed by Haven. Landon was also not a sore loser, and he showed, "Good sportsmen ship makes the player, Misa always says." Landon sucked down his beer.

It was a group of us, sitting around Landon's truck by the open fire. Leyla was already drunk in her little world, dancing on the truck bed to the music playing, beer at hand, and stripped off her sweater. All the while, Landon just wanted to kick back, get wasted, relax, soak in the energy of his peers and catch fire watching Leyla dance on his truck. He wasn't alone. Jacy watched her too. Landon had a thing for Ley; although he could deny it all day if he had to, for some reason, he refused to act on it. I thought the two made a better pair, and it would make things easier for me. But Landon made it apparent that he wasn't just going to hand me over to Haven. But for now, he was off my back, and that's all I needed; A second to appreciate Haven before me as I sat up on the now dented hood of Landon's truck. My uncle will kill both of them when he sees this damage.

Haven leaned onto the truck from the side of me, inches away. My heart fluttered in gratitude for saving me when he did. He was now wearing his long sleeve, but my eyes wandered his body.

"-What cha' looking at skirt?" I blushed as his elbow frisked my jacket. How could he not see the way he turned my guts into knots. I could practically unfold before his eyes, and he wouldn't know it.

"-Why do you like me so much? You barely know me."

I had been curious to understand for some time.

"Is that how you feel? I feel like I've known you all my life."

He confessed while his weight shifted the truck.

"I barely remember anything from my childhood," I confessed.

"I wish you did. You wouldn't hate me so much."

"I don't hate you. I'm just confused."

We were silent until he broke it, "Can I say something without you holding out on that dance?"

I looked at him strangely, "Sure, shoot your shot."

"-There are details of your 'curse' your uncle hasn't told you about because he's trying to manipulate you into choosing Landon over me. I know he thinks that I'm going to hurt you, but I think he's the one who's going to hurt you. No one understands that hurting you goes against my nature, but I can't shake off this feeling, so I want you to be careful around him."

Coming into my life and wedging himself between Landon and I was one thing, but Misa was my family, and I wouldn't tolerate it. "Shut up; my uncle would never hurt me," I had grown pretty irritated with his words and hopped off the truck, walking away into the dark of Hector's field. Haven followed me out a distance from everyone partying, and everything seemed to blur on me.

"-Look, Daya, I have one strange desire, and that's to protect you at all costs. Even from the people you love most, even from myself. So if I'm the dangerous one, I can accept that. I'll turn away and leave you alone for good, to keep you safe; I'd let you try to be happy with someone else you will never love if that's what you want. But if I'm being honest here, I love you too much to consider the possibility of being dangerous." What? He what? Maybe he spoke too soon because you don't say words like 'love' to strangers.

I chuckled in almost disbelief.

"You can't use words like that, Haven."

"What? **LOVE**? Does that scare you? Are you philophobic?"

He came in closer to me.

"Maybe I'm not ready to feel that."

"Well, maybe don't dwell on it much, Daya. I'm not trying to force you to feel anything; you already feel it. I want you to embrace how you feel. Ain't nothing to be ashamed over; you're allowed to embrace it. It won't hurt you, but I think holding back might."

"What do you want me to do? Say it back? Even if I feel some stupid attachment to you, I don't throw those words around."

"-I want you to stop punishing yourself for feeling the way you do. You're allowed to love. You're holding back like you don't deserve it, which kills me. Let yourself feel what's true." His words tickled my insides a bit. It felt like the crisp blowing wind weaseled itself deep into the nooks of my bones and cells.

"How?" A shiver cracked down my spine as I said it.

"Like I've been telling you- drop your weapons."

Haven had utterly stripped me of my being without using his hands. Yet, in the bitter cold dark, he looked solid. "You want me to be sorry about how I feel, and I can't. I'm not sorry. I don't owe anyone a damn apology for how I feel about you. Neither do you. I spent too much time feeling sorry for us both. I don't know what Landon thinks when he looks at you; frankly, I don't give a shit. I see much more than a timid virgin girl Daya. That's not you at all. I see your power, and I want to live in it. You're a Goddess. You're kind and sweet and clever. A little nerdy- but who am I to judge?"

We both laughed; my eyes slipped away to the grass.

"-I'm just being honest here. I see so much more than anyone else. The possibility of your potential is endless, like mine. We are purposely made for each other, and when everything fades away, we'll only have each other. That's what I'm trying to protect. You and me, beyond this world. You'll only have to trust me."

I didn't want to look at him. If I did, I'd probably kiss him and test the theory there and then, all because I wanted a taste of his delicately rare candor lips. So I kept my back to him, refusing to turn and be sucked into his eyes,

"Are you done chasing me?" I whispered.

"... Depends. Are you done running?"

I watched Landon wrap his arms around Leyla's waist, giggling as he swung her about, feet away from his truck. His eyes lit up like fireworks burning across a summer night sky. Elation fought with guilt on his face. Forgiving, of course. I couldn't hate Landon for how Leyla made him feel. I would be a hypocrite. It was exactly how Haven made me feel. And that pleasurably numbing sting, armoring me from the heartbreak I suddenly felt; that was Haven radiating pitied sorrow. It was dumb for me to ignore it for so long. Haven was right. Landon could never love me as deep as Haven could.

"Where they go?" Landon asked that very moment, anxiously looking around. That was my cue to break the silence. The boys were beer bottles deep into the night, no reason to cause a brawl. "You owe me a dance, Haven Tyson," I said, running back towards the truck. Haven smiled and chased after me.

Everyone was dancing around the bonfire when we reeled back into the crowd. Leyla danced with Landon, and even Jacy seemed to find his drunken woes satisfied in some sleazy classmate of ours. Haven and I were the only ones standing still, surrounded by electric frenzied bodies. Awkwardly, we cracked a smile at each other. When our sappy eyes met, all I could think about was, *'finally, I get to touch him,*' and I threw my hands over his bulked shoulders, but he flinched away. Insecurity rang through me like a Church bell. Why was he stepping away from me?

"-Everyone warned me... my touch could kill you. Daya, I-I don't want to hurt you." Haven was crumbling into dust earnestly. Was he serious? The big bad wolf, falling weak to the whim of a scarlet hood runner. Scared to 'hurt' me, like Landon was. I was pissed. This confident, bad attitude, terrible habit having, sky-scraping, majestic being of a 'man'; nearly begged to have me, and now was too afraid to touch me? "All that for what? 6 feet apart?" I was sarcastic, but it wasn't a joke. It was a warning; he was not about to treat me like Landon did. Haven hovered closer. So close, we were nearly touching. Still, it wasn't good enough, which read in my bratty stare. I unzipped my thick jacket and let it fall to the ground. Haven's wild eyes invaded my body immediately.

"Jesus, relax... Let me warm you up first..." He promised as he moved his hips. Haven rocked his body into movement like the wind. Damn, he was good at that. So long and tall, but Haven had more control of his dangerous body than anyone else, and his sexually charged dancing seduced me. Unsuspectingly, Haven was a great dancer, and everyone else noticed too, as he soaked in the music and passed on contagious energy that made it irresistible for me to chime my body with his. My body sizzled up underneath the layers; he was highly distracted. To my satisfaction, we were dangerously close, but nowhere near to touching, yet. I realized that the energy we were harvesting from each other was healing, despite my body slowly overheating and smoking like a car motor, breaking down with every *almost touch* of his.

"You're a great dancer. How?" My lady parts were pulsing.

"This might come off surprising, but I'm a lover, not a fighter."

"You keep moving like that, and I might have to find out."

I was so faint it was near to whisper, but he heard it.

"Easy there, Goddess..." he whispered back. His eyes met mine, and I caught all the sexual emotions he was bottling up. The lilacs and pink posies grew from my eyes, illuminating into his. It made him nervous, "Don't- don't look at me like that." He snapped subtly.

I gleamed more of my anticipation. "Like what? I'll jump you right here," I warned him as my body reacted with intent, reaching to touch him. "-You wouldn't be so stupid." He whispered back.

"You wanna bet?" I challenged him.

I went to jump into Haven's arms, and Landon came swooping me in from behind, pulling me into his embrace. Landon's hands smoothed over my rib cage under my already stimulated breasts. The tingle of his breath on my neck turned me more. Fuck. This was all Haven's fault and how he moved his hips near mine. I had to close my eyes to keep my thoughts a secret. "You got your dance-" Landon pulled me farther away, and his drunk and irritated voice made me settle into a bittersweet emotion. I opened my eyes, and Haven was now several long feet away, staring painfully. It looked like I had shattered the sapphires in his eyes into obsidian with a meat cleaver. I no longer was aroused, but the sexually induced reggaeton song coming thru the noise wave was no help in cooling me down either. Landon kept me close, slowly grinding on me to the music. His hands grappled at my hips, and I closed my eyes again in ruptured pleasure. I dared to open my eyes, but I had to.

He was gone. He was walking away. Deeper into the crowd. Very quickly, he was disappearing right before me. No. No. Not yet. I called after Haven, but he didn't care. I pushed Landon off of me and didn't think twice before I took off running. It was like Halloween night all over again. This time I didn't run from him; I ran after him. And he was fast. *So fast.*

I had to keep up. I knew I couldn't just let Haven go, so I chased him out into Hector's empty field. But he was gone, even in the dark. He disappeared from my view several times, but I did what I could to keep up with his energy. I was halfway down the field when I saw that he had disappeared into the forest. I used my intuition and some magic to find his path.

I didn't want to go back to the party. I couldn't face Landon. I made my decision when I took off, and even so, I don't regret it. Why should I? I knew that I already loved Haven, no matter how 'new' he felt. I knew I needed to be with him. Now I just regret being stubborn about everything he said to me. I didn't mean to hurt him, and seeing that hurt in his eyes was causing the pain that sliced inside me now. I had to fix it. No. I wasn't going back.

3:52 a.m.

I was exhausted and cold, and the nippy wind dried my cheeks of regretful tears. I was ready to fall asleep, dreading every step. I had to see Haven once more before the sun came up, but it all felt useless after a couple of hours. He was gone. I wasn't sure where he was, only that he ran along the path where I was heading because I could still smell him in the northern air, heading up the mountain.

I prayed that the break into the yard was coming up. I knew I was close when I started to recognize the path, and I tried to focus on that, but a ruffling in the bushes startled me. I stopped and turned around. *A HUGE fucking bear,* slowly creeping towards me from the darkness. I stopped, but my heart began to race. The bear wouldn't stop coming close until it was nearly over me. I stepped back, tripping over hidden logs, practically twisting my wrist when I fell to the ground, and the bear growled over me. Angry. So angry. It roared in my face, and stood up on two feet. I couldn't scream, especially after it slammed back onto all 4's over me.

Hovering over me, his teeth gleamed in the moonlight. I was sure it was going to bite me. I squeezed my eyes shut and turned away as he leaned in and- *licked* me? From chest to ear. Surprised, I opened my eyes to find this strange, colorful resin left behind by its tongue; as its dark sable radiated through me, it glittered silver in the moonlight. It was weird but warming as it tingled through my skin and sank deep into my being. Maybe I've been fighting with my lusty half all day, but I felt so sensually surreal. I closed my eyes and took in the night air. Every fiber in me felt dopamine. In another world, all I could hear was my unsteady breathing, and when I opened my eyes, nothing. And when I pulled myself up to sit, it was true; the bear was gone in the near distance. That bear almost ate me for sure but seemed to back off. Maybe I didn't taste good. I didn't care why. I stood up and shook off the mystic animal's hazy effect over me. I ran until I found my white garden gates creaking against the soft wind. The backyard was just right there.

I don't know why, but I was pretty surprised to see Haven sitting in the shadows of Misael's back deck. I hesitated when I saw him at first. I still had the jitters coming out of the woods, and he caught me off guard, but I nervously walked on over to him. I searched for the words to say, afraid to look him in the eye; mine was the deliverance of deep rust, the color of shame and regret. When I did finally surrender to him, Haven was smiling. Our eyes met; nothing but clear sky blue eyes.

"Took you long enough..." He stood up to tower over me.

"-I was coming,"

He thought a moment very carefully before saying, "-I don't want him touching you anymore. I don't give a fuck if he's your boyfriend, Daya. I don't. He's reckless with you. He will get you hurt, and I don't want to kill him. But I won't have any control of it if he fucks up." I swallowed hard.

"Okay- He won't... ever again." He scoffed, circling me.

"Don't promise me, promise yourself. You deserve better."

Myself? "These days, I barely trust myself," I whispered truthfully. I pulled away and leaned up against a tree. Haven mirrored me like a reflection. His energy was trying to heal me, but I didn't need to recover from anything.

"After all that?" He sounded confused.

"-What are you trying to prove to me, Haven? That Landon was an illusion? Haven, I always knew that. I'm sorry that I fought back, but I don't care about Landon and Leyla. I care about us. That's why I'm here- I'm dropping my weapons," It's what he's been dying to hear, judging by the way he rolled his eyes back when he exhaled. He wanted to touch me but held back. I hated that, "-You're nearly begging for me to let go, but you're holding back. If you want me so much, why don't you just touch me, Haven? I'm all yours." I fell back into his stare, so yummy; I could entwine myself in him.

"... I can't. I am not Landon, Daya. I won't be able to stop. I'll ravage *the fuck* out of you." My lips trembled. His words sent a shiver down my spine. My clit throbbed excitedly.

"Good- ravage me. I want you to."

I never recovered my jacket at Hector's or my wool cardigan I had aced during the chase across the field, but I wasn't cold anymore. He made me hot whenever he looked at me like that. I tossed my head to one side revealing my neck. My fingertips pulled at the straps of my bodysuit, a little off my shoulders.

The sight of my soft skin enticed him.

The big bad wolf swarmed in place, "Daya-" He whispered.

I closed my eyes the moment I felt his body crash into mine. Tiny sparks ignited when he pressed his long body against mine. His large hands held mine above my head against the tree's bark. His lips were so close to the skin on my neck it made me quiver and nearly cum as he held me down in place with his pelvis pressed against mine. I shifted about underneath his strength, causing more sparks and friction wherever our bodies met. He felt so good, so liquidating like a temporary drug overdose. My heart was lost, simultaneously, against his. I felt his warm tongue on my neck.

Ohhhh hhhmmm~ I couldn't take it. A faint whimper of pleasure and inclination from my breathless lips was enough to send Haven hurting. He mimicked my tone back to me, moaning faintly before fighting it all off. He struggled to pull himself together, "-I can't! Not right now. I have to -uh- make sure Jacy is okay. I left him at that party alone," I was still stuck on stupid even after he moved away, but he continued to babble, "-Even though you didn't like what I said earlier, I think you should consider asking your uncle for the truth." I nodded, in sexual aftershock from his touch, but trying to listen to his words as he was right. Haven has been right about everything. He looked back at me with his hands to hips; He, too, was still in awe, "-Y-you saw what I saw, right?"

Haven reflected on the impact our bodies made. All the vibrant and colorful sparks of electric orgasm. Electricity spitting every-where. He still seemed to be learning how to breathe after it, just as I was. "Fuck. I want to so damn bad-" Anxious, he gently embraced me, touching my cheek. Finally, he pulled from me and was about to take off into the woods until he stopped and looked back at me, "Are you going on that run with me or not?" Haven was jittery on a reckless love high, waiting for my answer so he could run off with the gratification.

"Yes," I agreed.

Excited, he took off into the creeping sun-rise.

9

Midnight Runs

I was at war all of the time now.

With my uncle. With Landon.

But not with my heart, not anymore.

That night changed everything, and I was a mess. After watching Haven take off that night at Hector's, I swore I wouldn't play any more games with my heart or his. Despite all my efforts to fight it away, I never expected to fall so deeply in love so quickly.

I retreated to my bedroom and wasn't surprised to find my uncle waiting for me, sitting near the window. It had been a stage; where he had watched Haven woo me only moments before. All my uncle wanted to do was argue and tell me how naive I was, but I couldn't feel bad about it. Intuition brought me to my knees; I trusted Haven, and my uncle didn't tell me the whole truth. It seemed like the perfect time to ask for the truth, so my uncle began to talk. He was putting in pieces where there were no memories. My life was suddenly in shambles. Nothing hurt more than finding out that my uncle had staged my entire existence.

When the nightmares began, he freaked out and turned to magic. He didn't know that having Haven and me together as children would cause the monster to animate and attempt to consume me so young. That fueled an obsession with keeping Haven and me apart. And he knew what he had to do. Misael stopped the curse from engulfing my soul; at least he had convinced Charlotte and Dean of that, and all I had to do was an 'innocent' Tribal dance. And when the nightmares vanished, they thought the tribal dance worked. It only temporarily worked because my uncle had a far greater plan. A plan he thought was foolproof. But, of course, he didn't know much about Haven and is his heavy obsession.

Adding gas to the fire;

Landon knew about *everything.*

From the very moment Landon walked onto that track top, Landon knew everything about me. And so, once upon a time, my uncle trusted Leyla to find a suitor that would keep me from ever finding and falling for Haven. It was to keep the curse from returning. When my uncle met Landon, he saw his potential as my perfect match. Over time, they bonded, and he trusted him enough to confront Landon with the truth about me, the curse, and even Haven. And so he asked, '*Protect and marry my niece.*' And this idiot went along with it. Soon after, my uncle started the love magic over us.

Landon cared for my uncle so much that he found it hard to refuse Misael, and so he consented to the magical love influence Misael had over us. As long as he went along with everything, he got to keep the good relationship with my uncle, along with college money, a guaranteed inheritance to the Mangualt's lumber dynasty, and a beautiful virgin wife; all too good for Landon to pass up. Later on, Landon would argue that the money and other perks were never a part of the deal, but fuck, I didn't trust him either way.

I didn't feel heartbroken. Instead, I found it easy to use it as the casting stone. My uncle's manipulation hurt more, and I made sure he knew it. We got into a screaming match. It was so bad that Leyla called Charlotte over so early in the morning. I pleaded with Charlotte to stop my uncle from interfering. I wanted my uncle to back off, but he stuck to his claims that our love was *forbidden.* REAL love, how could they oppose it?

"He's too dangerous. He'll get you killed,"

My uncle wouldn't give up either. He blackmailed me into going through with his original plan of sabotage; I would continue my relationship with Landon and come to summer, Landon and I would marry. Dean would bind the garden so that Landon could visit me, and we could be intimate, but all in all, I'd be confined to the Garden realm forever, and Haven diminishes forever. All I had left of freedom was the next three seasons— and I was to spend it all with Landon against my will. The garden would be a prison, a shameful hideaway for a wild, sex-driven Queen. My uncle should've felt shame for forcing this unwanted life on me.

I would gladly die to be with Haven. I'd spend every last moment I had with him. But *NOOO,* forget Haven. Forget being happy, true love, and truly living. That's what I heard, but not how I felt, and it was **not** what *we* were going to do at all.

That following week Haven was on a mission. He was old school, so he wrote short love notes, and Jacy and Leyla became messengers. Of course, they weren't pleased about it, but what other choice did they have? Haven and I were persistent. Leyla was more willing to help if her father never found out. She seemed to like spending that extra time around Jacy, which surprised us. Jacy, on the other hand, was paranoid all of the time. 'There's *another way,*' he always complained but found himself helping regardless of what he protested. Jacy loved his brother and wanted to keep him happy, and of course, there was the whole thing with getting to see Leyla.

On Wednesday morning, I got another note from Leyla, "*To-night at midnight, meet me on the trail.*" The thought of being alone with Haven again gave me butterflies, and I knew he needed to be near me just as bad. He needed to be close, so close that he could touch me. He needed that fix tonight, and I was determined to make it happen. So I made Leyla do the honors, and during breakfast, she asked permission to camp outside. The urgent reason; Winter was coming, and it would be the last time until the spring. Seeing me mope around for three days didn't make my uncle any happier- "She feels like a prisoner, and you're the guard, dad. One harmless night under the stars would be great for her. Don't you want to gain her trust back?" She could have been a lawyer. He agreed.

The plan was to have Jacy stay behind with Leyla in the tent, and if my uncle came out to check in, Jacy could easily pretend to be me, sleeping soundlessly under a pile of blankets. Okay, so it wasn't foolproof, but it was a plan. On a lucid love high, I let the day go on stress-free, not letting anything, no matter how big, ruin this mood for me. I faked happiness for Landon all day. He even thought I was over being mad at him. *Yeah, fucking right.* He lied for over two years. I was nowhere over it, but I let him think that I was.

That afternoon, Leyla and I started setting up camp, ensuring the tent wasn't visible from my uncle's bedroom window or the living room window. We also made sure it wasn't suspiciously close to the woodsy trail, where my uncle could easily peer out my window and spy, like the last time I was alone with Haven. When my uncle walked in around 6, he surprised us with occasional news. He was going out tonight with Dean. The two buddies had been invited to the sheriff's 40th Birthday party and had initially declined to go. But for some 'odd' reason, Dean convinced Misael to go with him. Dean didn't seem too fond of Sheriff Ruiz, but they planned to be home sometime after midnight. We said goodbye to Dean and Misa, ordered pizza, and restocked on Red Bull and junk food. Terrible for my run tonight, but these days I burned right through it. Besides, Haven wasn't going to make me run, right? I showered and dried my hair. Spritz some delectable perfume and wore only a sports bra, short black dolphin shorts, and a black cropped sweater. I cleaned my room and grabbed my running sneakers.

12:07 midnight, Charlotte peered in the tent and tossed me something. **BEAR REPELLENT**. I looked at her pretending to be clueless. "Just in case you run into bears when you go on your *midnight run*," she winked at me. I was confused. I looked at Leyla, thinking she had spilled the beans, but she threw her hands up defensively and shook her head. She mouthed the words, 'NOT ME,' and Charlotte explained. "Your uncle is probably not going to be back till morning; Dean is getting him pretty hammered. So you can relax, he won't find out. Dean and I talked, and you're both right, Daya. There's no reason for your uncle to push you and Landon together when you and Haven love each other. I can't sit back and watch you kids hurt and suffer. I've seen it once before. But please understand, I trust you to be responsible?" I silently jumped into her arms and hugged her. Charlotte knew I appreciated it more than anything, and I didn't have to say a word.

"This was a bad idea."

Leyla was beginning to sound a lot like Jacy. It was a quarter to one, and Leyla and I had been roaming the outskirts of the forest before starting down this forest trail, looking for Haven and Jacy. Leyla hated the woods. She hated the dark even more, and she was fearful of what may lurk beyond the shadows. "Can we just wait for them by the tent?" She begged for the 100th time. I looked at her, hiding under the warmth of her quilt in her cute pink Pj's. She looked so adorable, and I couldn't help but laugh at her. Annoyed, she rolled her eyes at me. An owl hooted, and she jumped.

"What was that?" In distress, she picked up her pace.

"Calm down, campsite Barbie, it's only an owl."

"Was mom serious about the bear repellent?" Leyla went on.

"Of course she was Ley, we live in the mountains… We shouldn't use it, though; it will harm the bear," I suddenly stopped. Mid-conversation, deep out in the cold Late-November forest, I was indeed looking at a bear. That same *giant bear*. Even from where I stood, it seemed unusually big, and when it began to come closer, I knew for sure it *was* the same bear I encountered the other night. It snapped twigs and branches as it came forward, revealing itself to Leyla when the silver moonlight hit its brown fur.

"Oh-My-God…" Leyla slowly whispered, fear at her throat. She grabbed on my shoulder and pinched hard, "Daya, let's go,"

Standing in silence, I watched the bear get closer. I knew the bear wouldn't hurt me. Those strangely familiar sable eyes were like a lighthouse, illuminating safety. I let him get closer until I could nearly touch him. "Daya, what the fuck?" Leyla whispered, tugging at me. I ignored her, slowly reaching out to touch his thick brown fur. It was soft like silk, and I ran my fingers down the side of him. The friction from the bear's hair caused neon sparks of electricity, all to my entertainment, just like Haven's touch. It must have been something new with my powers. Its eyes were magnetic and affectionate. "You're not so scary, huh… it's beautiful, Leyla, look at it," As my fist kneaded gently down its muzzle, I turned to Leyla, and she was fumbling with the can of repellent.

"Bitch, you better not," I warned in a whisper.

"-What the hell are you two doing?" Jacy echoed from the abyss. He stood several feet behind us, dressed differently than usual, in a well-fitted tracksuit and running sneakers. I was sure it was Jacy's rude, interrupting tone that scared away the bear, but it headed straight out into the dark woodland. "Great, you scared him." I broke my whisper. "Thank God," Leyla said, finding a perfect reason to weave her arm into Jacy's. She was looking for protection, and Jacy didn't mind at all, smirking down at her sweet smile.

"What are you doing out here approaching wild bears?" Jacy unzipped his jacket and threw it over Leyla's shoulders.

"We were waiting for you… Where's Haven?"

"Who?" In no mood for his sarcastic shit, I crossed my arms.

"Don't act dumb, your brother… where is he?"

"For all I know, he's on a run with your buddy Sunny,"

I rolled my eyes and sucked my teeth with jealousy.

"-Come on, Jacy, leave her alone…" Finally, Haven climbed out of the shadows, scolding his older brother. He was shirtless; he must have been running for a while. He dripped with sweat, standing in classically revealing running shorts and muddy running shoes. The moonlight hit his face, sucking me into his wild sapphire eyes. "-Wow." Leyla caught us all off guard as she eye fucked Haven. I calmly laughed and looked at her, biting down on my teeth, "Can you be any more of a spaz right now?" I chopped at her. Haven chuckled before walking closer to me, hypnotizing me with his eyes. I could say nothing. He slowly walked around me, inspecting me, admiring my bare legs.

"You're not cold?" No. I was a few moments ago, but not any-more. I was hot. Overheating. I swallowed hard and said nothing. He stared down at me—butterflies in my stomach, my legs felt like jello, and I hoped he didn't notice, but with his eyes so attentive to my legs, I knew he could see me tremble. His desire was unruly enough to get borderline close to me. His face almost touched mine as he dug his nose into my hair, shamelessly inhaling my scent, "You smell like coconuts, sea salt, and flowers..." His tongue flipped into a closed mouth. He could almost taste me."-Okay, we'll be back in a couple of hours." Haven pulled on my hand, urgent to be alone.

"Haven, don't you think this is enough?" Jacy tensed, objecting to the thought of leaving us alone.

"Relax, big bro. Think about Leyla. You have to walk her back. Make sure she's safe and makes it home?" The three of us looked at Leyla. A jacket and quilt, and her teeth still chattered innocently. As expected, Jacy caved immediately. Haven was clever to use her. She squeezed Jacy's arm before saying, "Come on, sir, you can keep me company..." Jacy threw his hands in the air like a white flag. She pulled him towards the house, and they were gone off the trail within moments. Now we were alone again. Haven grinned at me scandalously before he took off, sprinting, "Try and keep up."

In the early morning hours, Haven and I were innocently chasing each other through the still forest. He was a fast runner, but I kept up, mostly. In a game of tag, we teased each other through the woods, hiding behind dried maples and pines. When I was close enough to touch him, he ran off. I played along, and just as he thought he had me where he wanted me, I took off into the darkness. Burning through the distance, we found ourselves coming to a clearing ahead, near the edge of the river waters. I was tired. My legs were tingling and ready to give out just as we broke out of the forest, nearing closer to the sound of rushing river water. Standing there, we quickly realized that the meadow clearing was in a rare heart shape. Lighten bugs in the tall, flower-ridden grass, under a navy star-ridden sky, "I feel so fucking alive," he confessed. My eyes brighten to his elation and endurance. He felt so energizing; it was contagious. I climbed onto a boulder, admiring the way his body glistened the subtle moonlight, giggling and watching as he fearlessly splashed freezing water over his face. I melted, watching him smile in his thoughts, "-I feel naked with you, all of the time."

My unsuspecting words shocked him. I watched his adam's apple flex as he turned away, "Well... same, skirt. But you also make me feel protective, possessive, sometimes dangerous. Concupiscent-"

It only took a second, but I unwillingly whispered, *"Hypersexual?"* and Our eyes met again. This time by accident. "-It's a feeling I can't describe because I never had it with anyone else... some ungraspable superior emotion." His eyes flashed like heavy headlights. **Caution.**

He changed the subject, but that didn't stop me from staring at his perfect statue. I wanted to be inside of his mind, soul, and heart. Haven was all that I wanted to explore. "-If we could go off-grid, as far North as I can, and build us a home, would you come with me?" He stood right in front of me, my knees far apart as I sat there, and my hands holding my lean behind me; he planted himself between them, careful not to touch me too much, but his hands frisking my inner thighs. "-I'll go anywhere with you," As suggestive as it came out, I meant it. He admired me with his wild black and blue eyes.

"You're not going to marry him, right?"

I grinned nervously at him. He cracked a fake smile, "Seriously, Daya. I know what your uncle is up to." He tugged at Landon's ring on my finger, and I pulled my hand away shamefully.

"... I know what *I* want. *I want you.*"

"-But you still wear **his** ring."

I could say nothing. Haven paced around anxiously before standing in front of me again. He pulled out a cigarette carton from his pocket and slid out a Marijuana joint. I watched the lighter flame reflect on his structured face, puffing. He snapped the Zippo shut and returned the lighter and carton to his pocket. He inhaled the Northern Lights deeply before pulling the joint away from his luscious lips, "For someone who smokes a lot, you run like you haven't smoked a day in your life." I bagged on his grotesque habit.

"Eh- perks of being me, I guess… How was your day?"

"It was okay. Dragged mostly."

"Yeah, mines too. I've been thinking about you all day."

He searched for my eyes, but I hid from him. I don't know what he loved so much about being lost in them, but he didn't mind the pull. He took his time to finish the joint and tossed it to the ground, urgently crushing it. He inched back closer to me, closer than before. This time he was prepared. "Don't be afraid… Okay." I trusted him. He came closer. I could smell the essence of the danky Northern lights rolling off him. Slowly he reached for me.

If it were dangerous, neither of us cared. The surrounding world seemed to blow away into pixels, and all I could see was Haven. He sat me better on the boulder with one arm before his rough hand very slowly caressed my soft cheek. Sparks of electricity flickered at instant skin-on-skin contact. His long body came closer, and his thumbs traced my lips. My knees rose as our pelvis collided. My body tingled in a way I had never felt before, quivering violently under his simple touch. His hand wandered my body before he fixated on my pulse—feeling every bump my heart made. My fingertips found his jaw. I went to trace his lips with my tongue, but the tease licked me. His tongue felt so good. So warm. So addicting. Very suddenly, he pulled me closer into his body, his chest and pelvis rubbed against mine. He sucked on my fingers and licked my neck. We frolicked about for several long minutes but never kissed. In the still air, whimpers of pleasure. Unable to handle the erotic torment, Haven pulled away, "-I don't know what I'm going to do with you… with us. I don't know how I'm going to stay away." His alluring voice was low and surprisingly calm, unlike his nerves. I bit my lip and reached to kiss him finally, but he pulled from me again.

"-Then don't," I sounded scared because I was.

"I want you to understand me, Daya. You're my superpower and my kryptonite. I can sprint but only with broken legs; you're the only thing that could *break* me, and that scares me. So if you can't leave, Landon, I'm going to have to stay away from you."

The cloud of pain in his eyes said he was serious,

"I need you to understand me. I can't sprint. I have to walk. With my uncle and Landon, I made a promise that I'm obligated to keep. But I can't deny that I'm falling in love with you. So please don't stay away." I nearly broke out in tears. Empathy induced, he pulled me into his arms but looked away, biting his lower lip. He didn't want to say anything he didn't mean, but he kept me in his arms. The feeling of him never wanting to let go was euphoric, and I lived in it long enough to keep us quiet. He combed my black hair in his fingers and smiled when I forced his eyes into my path.

"Come on. I have to get you back." I interlaced my fingers with his before he pulled me into his warm arms, and we strolled into the forest trail and held a lighter conversation the rest of the way.

Haven was, beyond doubt, a beast. I was in trouble.

Temperamental. Jealous. Most annoyingly, stubborn.

Haven wore his bad-boy attitude like a badge of honor. I learned so much about him in the darkness of the midnight hours. He came looking for me every night. With the help of Leyla, Jacy, and Charlotte, it was possible. He showed up every night and always sent Leyla and Jacy away as he lured me into the dark. Haven always stayed an arm and a leg away from me. We only ran together and talked, and for hours sometimes. Under the sky, over the twigs and logs, across streams and tall cricket hiding grass. Sometimes we would stay silent. Our breathing apart from one another is all that sounded the quiet around us. And sometimes, we couldn't shut up, laughing and talking in between the long strides our long legs took.

He was honest and always forthcoming, never afraid to reveal what thoughts ran through his mind, even if it was sure to piss me off. He never apologized, even if it was over something stupid. Before or even after, the runs were only pillow talks but without the bed or sex. But it was just as intimate. He was willing to let me into his world as long as I gave him access to mine. As if he needed to ask, I was an open book for him, and he took advantage of it more nights than some. My uncle never suspected. He was the only one. Dean pretended to be blind and deaf. And as long as I pretended to be happy with my uncle's rules, there was nothing to suspect, and I played that well over the next few weeks, despite Haven's no contact rule with Landon. Haven's jealous flares over Landon were heavy, but I did what I could to reassure him, except give back Landon's ring. I feared it would be too telling, and I was afraid my uncle would find out. He very badly pretended to understand that. So I forced myself not to react and just deal with the mood swings. We were okay as long as he appeared at the garden gates every night.

Day's swiftly turned into weeks.

One day, during study hall in the library, I was staring off, eyes fluttering lilac-orange, thinking about my last argument with Haven when Landon caught me off guard. "-You're thinking about him again, aren't you?" Landon was seriously annoyed; it hadn't been the first time I had been distracted by memories of Haven. Hiding behind a textbook, I pretended not to hear him.

"You make it harder to pretend every day." Landon was now the one who sounded worn down. Yet I didn't feel so terrible, knowing he pretended for so long. I peered at him over the rim of the book, and his eyes followed mine. I put the book down finally and caved into the argument, "I'm sorry. I literally can't help it. I've told you all; I'm in love with Haven." Landon refused to look me in my tantalizing eyes. Instead, he sighed hard and long. "It's not your fault...

I knew what Misael was asking me to do when he asked. I shouldn't have agreed to it. Then again, no one knew *Harry* was going to show up and ruin it." I rolled my eyes. Landon knew his name.

Landon was good at pretending. Today he seemed to be beating himself up pretty bad for something we no longer had control over; for Landon, there was no turning back. Landon didn't deserve this, as much as I didn't deserve it. "We have to talk to my uncle."

"-I can't. Daya, despite what you think, I still love you. Yeah, it's weird now with Harry in the way, but I am a man of my word. Your uncle chose me to protect you. I take pride in that." I shook my head in frustration. Misael had brainwashed him.

"Misael can't do anything if I break up with you."

"-Stop Dayanara! Things were going smoothly until Dean, and his boys showed up. You can't tell me you weren't in love with me a few weeks ago before this guy came walking onto the reservation."

"Ya-yeah, I was starting to fall for you, but you were never in love with me. Are you even in love now? Can you tell?" He looked down to the back of his hand where Leyla had written a note on him and left hearts, and he blushed. His face and eyes said everything I needed to know. I was unruly, sitting back into my seat, looking at him victoriously, waiting for him to counter-attack. But, instead, he said nothing, just ripped through his face miserably.

"-Exactly my point Landon. I know what sits in the back of your mind, Leyla, as it had always been. While I'm wasting away in a Garden, you'll be out here, with her. Don't act like you didn't see her that way. The way you look at her. The way you crumble under her every demand. How do you feel about her, Landon? That's how I feel about him. Are you honestly willing to give up your happiness, along with mine? Do you want to drag us **ALL** through the mud for Misael? Haven won't allow it, and if you do this, you'll always have to worry about him." Landon knew I was right.

"-If I had never met Haven, I would have lived a lie while you all got what you wanted. At least now, all you can hope for is that I die right after my birthday so that you can be with Leyla-"

"-You need help. I'd never wish that on you it's the only reason I agreed to help in the first fucking place, Daya. Besides, Leyla doesn't even like me. She's sweet on the Tyson brother." Landon was disturbed, putting away his books. The bell rang, and I took my book bag over my shoulders and stormed out of the library. Landon chased after me. He stopped me and pulled me off into a corner of the corridor,"-Give me back the ring."

"Landon, what are you doing?"

"I think it's pretty obvious. We're breaking up."

I suddenly began to cry. It stung like ripping a stubborn piece of my heart. Landon wiped my tears from my cheeks as they came down, and I pulled off his engagement ring and dropped it in his hands. "I wish he never showed up. We could have been happy," Landon whispered before he kissed my lips, passionate and hard for the last time. It felt seemingly different. I couldn't deny feeling something, but he managed to pull away before it consumed me. This time I was not numb. This time it hurt. I watched him walk away, and I sank into a strange sorrow. My 'first love' was walking away from me. I let it happen. It wasn't easy to let go, but I did. By the time I got home, all of that melodrama was far behind me.

Later that night, I found myself once again running with Haven through the forest. It was a quiet night. I tried to concentrate on the cracking of brittle branches and dried leaves underneath my shoes rather than my already irritated running partner.

Sounds of the night; owls and crickets and slithers and breaks; zooming past my feet. Haven was out of sight. I had no idea where he had run off to. I crashed into a tree, my palms scratched by the bark as I gathered my thoughts and caught my breath. Where was he? I flipped over, my back against the bark. Haven abruptly appeared in front of me, running at full force. He nearly crashed into me like that night at Hector's. His breath steamed down my neck when we stared at each other, our bodies becoming synchronized when his hands took my hips. The sparks flew like fire and ash, swaying into the wind, and his eyes searched mine, squinting as his face came closer. Was he finally going to kiss me? I waited for it, but he held back. He found a strand of my hair in the wind and twirled it before he tucked it behind my ear slowly. His fingers slid down my jawline, and without a word, he took off running again.

I ran after him.

I followed him down the remaining woodsy trail until we broke out into the grassy heart-shaped field, and we were back at the same boulder we've been coming to every night—the place where we safely buried our secrets in each other's souls. I finally caught up to him, but I could barely contain my breathing. I nearly collapsed onto the boulder, pushing aside the hiking bag of snacks Haven carried around. He was always eating. I pulled myself up to sit on the boulder while shirtless Haven drank from the river. I pulled the book bag close to me and pulled out a ziplock bag of apple slices. I chewed on apple slices as I watched as Haven washed off the sweat from his overheated body. Something was different about him tonight. He was quieter than usual, more broody, and had low and depressing energy. Not as eccentric and go-lucky as he usually was. He was in no natural mood to flirt and maybe even distant. Dripping wet, he was drying off with the flannel shirt he once had tied around his waist. "I don't know how you don't get sick doing that in this cold weather." I scolded him. He finally smiled.

"I'll be fine. I'm just glad you stop coming out in spanks. You have no idea how crazy it made me." He pinched at my kneecap.

"What's wrong?" Finally, I found the courage to ask. His eyes took cover to the night sky, trying to keep from becoming lava at my fingertips.

"-You already know me so well." He said before eating an apple slice from my fingertips. The way he stared at me while he did it was dangerous, but I knew he only did it to distract me, and so I looked the other way. Then, exhaling, he nudged me over before sitting next to me. The wind blew, and my lips trembled. Haven wrapped his warm arms around me as he got comfortable.

"...I keep thinking about the winter. When the snow hits, our runs are going to have to stop. That could be any day now." His words troubled me. What was he thinking? He stared down at the tiny sparks from our innocent body contact and said nothing more.

So I pleaded, "Why?" The look in his unconvinced eyes said it all. I didn't want to talk anymore. I was afraid of what would come out of his mouth. I leaned my head on his shoulder and looked up at the sky above. Only puffy pink in cream night skies. Bleak but beautiful.

"-I trust in *The Great Spirit*. But when the snow falls Daya, the new season will come, and so will change. I *need* to know that no matter what changes, your feelings for me won't." Insecurity wasn't a typical trait of Haven, but his words didn't surprise me. I could see he was still terrified of losing me—more than I had first realized.

" If my love ever changes, it would only be to love you better... you saved me. I'll never be able to repay you for that, but if I can love you forever, I always will. You don't have to worry. "

As the wind blew around us, Haven peeled from the boulder, leaving me to fend off the cold alone. "Coming here wasn't easy, Daya, but my intuition led me here. I had some fucked up feelings coming back. It opened up wounds and all the bullshit I had to deal with growing up; the responsibility of who I'm becoming—

protecting the elders and the tribe. I never asked to be responsible for so much, so young. It was too much, and my father had no choice but to take me away from here. But as I grew into a man, I had to find my own path, and it led me right to you *again.* You are the only thing that makes all the bad in me disappear. When I'm around you, nothing else matters to me. I want to give you my entire heart Daya, but please, I'm begging you, don't let me down."

"-I love you, but exactly are you asking me? Because-"

"Can I be honest with you?" He cut me off and said that. I hated when he said that. It was always something I didn't want to hear. His hands had gone up the sides of my leggings until he stopped at my hips. He gripped me, and I braced myself for his brutal honesty.

"I can't stop thinking about you with Landon." His once sea-colored eyes turned to sable ice crystals. He let me go and walked away.

I, too, stood up from the boulder.

"Why would you be thinking about that?"

"-Because Daya, you're uncle is determined to make the union happen, and I can't do anything about it. That shit hurts. When I'm not with you, I wonder if he is. Then I get the thinking, wondering if you let him touch you the way I do? Wondering if you talk to him the way you talk to me? If you're looking at him the way, you look at me? Do you tell him your secrets? Do you love it when he puts his lips on you? It kills me to know you have to be around him. I tell you everything effortlessly, and I never connected with anyone like this, but I can't have you. It's fucked. And it's turning me into something that I'm not. I don't like walking around like the bad guy. I barely know Landon, and he seems like a good guy, but as long as I know you wear his ring-" His raving voice suddenly became faint. One glance stopped a world of doubt from clouding his mind. **No ring.** I dug my face into his bare chest, and I could feel his thundering heart slow. "No -to everything. He never will be you. I thought you'd notice by now, and I was trying to tell you, but your attitude... I can't marry him." My words were like lithium, more so when he confirmed, there was no ring on my finger. And just as he lowered his lips near mine, snow flurries intercepted. We stared up at the snowflake magenta sky. The snow came down beautifully and peacefully, each flake softly kissing our faces. We smiled at each other, "You should come out on a date with me." I laughed,

"My uncle would never let that fly." He laughed back,

"Who said he had to know?"

10

First Date

For days, a thick winter snowstorm invaded our town of Grey Wolf Hollow. Our small town became a beautiful tiny winter wonderland and flooded with Christmas, seemingly overnight. Cars drove around plowed streets with giant blue spruces attached to the roofs, and colorful lights twinkled everywhere.

On Friday afternoon, I walked into the kitchen where my uncle and Charlotte waited for me. The two sat uncomfortably and awkward. Misael has been on a rampage since the day Landon and I broke up, and the two haven't been able to stand the sight of each other lately. It surprised me that Charlotte was even here. I walked in with caution. I could still feel the argument roaring in the room. Something was up, I could tell. Maybe my uncle found out about my secret midnight runs with Haven. I've been sneaking out every night for weeks now. It would be inevitable. "Daya, we need to talk to you-" I nodded before sitting across the table.

"Charlotte and I signed the divorce papers."

Divorce? Yikes- not what I expected. I wasn't sure what to say. The topic of *divorce* was like Groundhogs day in this house. Every year, it determined the flow of our family for the following months. Cold or hot. I've felt the heaviness in their relationship for a while but tried to ignore it. Granted, they spent years trying to repair the damage, but all was lost, and not even I could deny that. And I knew better than anyone else you can't force two people to love each other. "Are you sure you two want to do that?"

The silence yanked at my heart; this conversation hurt more than I expected. I looked down and inhaled. If I cried about how much the change would hurt and desolate our family, I'd be just like my uncle, trying to control something I shouldn't. It wouldn't be fair. Everyone deserves to be happy, not just me. But I couldn't shake the fear that poured from me, thinking of my aunt Charlotte abandoning me up on this mountain with my uncle, who wasn't my uncle anymore. Since I broke up with Landon, he's grown distant and mean. His behavior change made me cautious.

"-Your uncle has been sleeping with someone else... and he wants this divorce, which is fine. But, frankly, it's been years, and we need to go through with it. " As the words left her coral lips, he glanced her way. Guilty, he put his head in his hands in shame. I couldn't believe it, my uncle and his damn lies. Like a tattoo gun, I felt every stab of betrayal. We were a family. How could he ruin such a valuable thing? "With who?" I wanted to know.

"Do you want to tell her who, or should I?" My aunt warned.

A feeling burned inside my chest; I knew who my uncle would mention. "-Caroline and I have been spending time together. I don't see the problem, so what if she's Landon's mother? You and I haven't been intimate in a long time. I'm human, and I have basic needs, like love." I scoffed and rolled my eyes. He had a lot of nerves using that language. I had never seen my aunt filled with so much angst, and who could blame her? She was kind, beautiful, selfless, and patient. And yet, my uncle hadn't been very attentive or friendly to her. My uncle has been cold and had no remorse for the pain he instilled in our family, and that infuriated me more than his sad attempt to keep me from Haven. Who was this man? I didn't recognize the man sitting before me. My uncle Misael, the one that tucked me in, told me bedtime stories, took care of me when I was sick, fed and clothed me for 18 years. Although I tried to deny it, my uncle has turned into a monster ever since my birthday, and now I struggle to face him. My curse has made him angry and filled with disillusion and ruthlessness. I wanted to blame myself, but how could I have known about any of it? My given fate wasn't my fault, and I had no time to hate myself for my uncle's mistakes. He was now distant from everyone, and that included Landon.

Misael lived for the power he secretly harvested from me. *MY powers* were slowly dwindling, and I hadn't noticed much, but Haven restored my energy balance daily, and it was Haven's suspicions that quickly grew on me. My distrust has turned into a steel shield. I worried more about Charlotte and Leyla, but it seems Charlotte has grown tired of my uncle's pressure. "- I just wanted to tell you myself and let you know that nothing will change. I'll be here for you as I always have been and we both think it would be a good idea if you start spending the weekends at the cabin with me, like when you were younger. Your room still has your things in it, and I just put fresh sheets on the bed. We spoke with Leyla, and she's not taking it well. She's a mess and won't leave her room. So we figured you can cheer her up with a girl's night?"

"Okay," I agreed before silence climbed the walls.

"-Daya, just one more thing-" My eyes unruly shot at my uncle, "-this situation made me realize that manipulating you and Landon together was a big mistake. We know about you and Haven sneaking around, and I want to say that I'm okay with it, as long as you two are careful. I have no right to tell you what to do with your life. I love you like a daughter Daya, and I only want to see you happy and alive. So as long as he does the right thing, I'm okay with you dating Haven." Inside I was thrilled, but I still didn't trust my uncle.

"Go get your things, and I'll wait for you in the car," Charlotte said, heading towards the door and taking her purse from the kitchen counter. My uncle and aunt briefly had a staring match before I ran upstairs to gather my things. I pounded all that I could into a weekender bag and ran back down the stairs. The kitchen side door looked like a clean break, but just as I made it to the doorknob, Misael called out to me. He stood still at the frame of the kitchen door, "Daya, I'm serious. I want you to be careful with Haven. If he messes up one time, I promise he'll regret it..."

My aunt Charlotte had some intriguing things to say about my uncle Misael on that drive down the mountain. She confirmed that Misael harvested my magic and used it to make his magical influence as potent as possible. My 18th birthday was a meteor colliding and crashing, setting off more events than just the one inside me. The night my fever set, Misael's harmful tricks dissolved, and everyone awoke; Dean, Charlotte, Landon, Leyla, and the Tyson boys. We were all under Misael's spell. Everyone agreed that a terrible feeling had awoken when the Tyson clan came to Grey Wolf.

I expected Leyla in bed, obliterated from the news of her parent's divorce. Instead, she was pleasantly only 'kind of' angry, as she snipped off her father's head from the majority of her family photos. Leyla was especially disgusted with the other woman's identity, as should. It was more so about how fucking arrogant the woman was. I agreed. We spent a great deal bashing my uncle's name.

That night in the living room, after Charlotte got a fire going, she pulled out a magical suitcase, and when I opened the bag, I uncovered all of my mother's sacred things. The old bag illuminated in her magical essence. Old photos, jewelry, and precious jewels.

Seashells and pearls. Sundresses and love letters from Dean Tyson. I admired it all as I sat on the carpet floor,

"How come I never saw any of this?"

"Misael made me hide it-" Charlotte shamefully replied. "-I hope you two can forgive me for my decisions under his influence. You two are my world, and I won't allow him to ruin your lives. He doesn't realize he has a chance to do things differently than what he did with Anais. Your mother was my best friend and soul sister, so I admired her. On her death bed, I promised her that I would always protect and guide you, even if it meant going against Misael. What he was doing was wrong and not what Anais wanted."

"Can I keep this?" I asked.

"Yes, of course; you should know more about your mother." Charlotte reached into the suitcase and took a small velvet sack that had been knot-tied at the end. She took the mystery sack and went back into the kitchen without a single explanation. Seconds later, she approached me with the ancient Taino book I got on my birthday, my notes on loose-leaf paper plastered between the pages.

"-It's a birthday gift from Salome. It seems to be a collection of different spells, potions, and dances that other tribe Princesses conjured up to help break the curse. Most will disable the curse, but none of the solutions end with true love, only keep from dying. I decided life was meaningless without Haven, so I need to find a cure that will allow him to live inside my Garden."

"Sounds great but be careful, these books of magic can be powerful-" With the mysterious way my aunt spoke, a simple tapping at the window jolted us. Leyla pulled back the tan curtain, and Haven stood out in the snow. My aunt smiled, nodding approvingly. It felt surreal that I was allowed to be around him finally. It's been several long days since the snow departed us, and I had missed Haven, so I jumped him at the doorway. He wrapped one of his large arms around me and lifted me from the ground. Setting me down on his snowy black boots, I hinged onto his heavy coat as he walked in.

"I didn't come to see you, skirt," he said regretfully, admiring how my eyes flexed for his viewing pleasure. Haven only came to pick up a wellness basket for Dean, but it was the only excuse he needed. I bit my lip, admiring him back, and his eyes weakened under my longing stare. Then, finally, he softly pulled me off, setting me on the ground. "Hey Charlotte," he greeted my aunt, who admired our young love from her stance in the kitchen. She waved him to come into the kitchen, and I followed him across the living room. Charlotte handed him a basket filled with harvested corn, squash, apples, and jars of herbs.

"Thanks… we appreciate it, Charlotte."

"Anytime, are you staying for tea?" My aunt asked.

"Sorry, I can't. The Dean's waiting." My heart sank. We spent hours together most nights, and now that we had the freedom, he wouldn't stay for more than one. The disappointment read on my face, and so Haven nipped at my chin as he studied my subtle reaction, "Wanna talk for a minute?" He cocked his head toward the front door. I nodded and rushed to get my boots and coat. I met him at the door and followed him out to his father's truck. He put the basket down on the passenger seat before facing me.

"Your aunt is great." He leaned against the truck,

"She's the best actually… why are you leaving so soon?"

"Guy stuff. I have to take care of something with my dad," Staring into his chilling eyes, I melted as his fingers traced my face. "-So, tomorrow night, you'll be here?" He was hopeful.

"I'm here all weekend-" Relief melted over his face.

"You wanna go on that date?" I cracked a crushing, girly smile.

"Yes, I'd love to." His thumb traced my lips.

"Hey, don't say anything, but I love you," My heart stopped. I couldn't say anything, contradicting enough, because I felt the same way, but also because I thought he'd finally kiss me, but Haven only gave me a satisfying glance and let me go. His teasing was killing me, and he knew it. Haven doesn't mean to, but he was determined not to cross any line. He fought daily to keep from touching me, which frustrated me down to my atoms. The feeling of being left aroused stung and ached like a car light left on, just wasting battery. But I had no desire to control him. I was free-falling, and I was okay with it. As for Haven, it was just knowing that he *could* have his paws all over me without harming me that was enough.

"Nine, okay?" He hopped into the truck.

"Why so late?" I backed away as he started it.

"-Skirts man. I'm giving you an extra two hours to get ready."

Winking at me, he pulled off.

I stood in my robe, "It's gorgeous!" Leyla's keen rainforest eyes shot at me from the sewing machine. Leyla became inspired with one white lace dress while going through my mother's things with me. I let her hack it into something sexier for my date. She washed it, restored the bright white color, cut and sewed it. Leyla's design was short but flowy, with a deep skin teasing keyhole neckline and long flounce sleeves. She embroidered a beautiful Taino design on the collar and cuffs with golden thread and buttons.

Combs and brushes, mousse and gel. Bobby pins and extra-strength hair ties. I had created the perfect high ponytail by the end of all the twisting and pulling. My natural waves flowed down my back. Strawberry was the shade of lipgloss Leyla whisked over my softly scrubbed lips, and she finished my face with a sexy retro eyeliner wing. Charlotte walked in just as I slipped on the dress. I immediately fell in love with the new version, especially how she tailored it to hug my shape to perfection. Leyla adored how it looked on me, but my aunt Charlotte said it was short because of my lengthy legs. I didn't care. Haven will bend to my whim when he sees me in this dress and black knee-high boots. I wore a scarf, hat, and a heavy winter coat because it was snowy and blistering out.

Haven showed up at precisely nine at night, with a bouquet of cherry-colored hibiscus and white lilies, a bottle of wine for Charlotte, and chocolate-covered strawberries for Leyla to share with her mom during their movie. As if he needed any of it to be charming. Haven's eyes were periwinkle, damn it. He hasn't even seen me out of this coat yet, and he was *still* looking at me, in the way that made me quiver. "-Haven, please keep her safe..."

"-Yes, of course, ma'am.

A beautiful view of the masking navy sky glittered above a tiny diner right outside Grey Wolf Hollow. Placed in the middle of nowhere with a rickety green structure of an old greenhouse, it had a cozy name; *Star's Blanket Inn & Diner.* I never noticed this place until tonight, but it carried a magical feel. Most businesses were closing, but this diner was a lively, cozy, and inviting little place. Delicious homemade dishes filled the air, and a glittering Christmas tree and lights set a festive mood. The occupied jukebox played, and families, pal's, and lovers filled the booths, bar, and tables for two. Haven pushed through, pulling me along.

"-My Uncle Shane and his wife Hattie bought this place years ago and renovated it into a restaurant. The Dean told them a greenhouse was a terrible idea, yet here we are." I agreed, looking around the whimsical place. "-Now it's The Star's blanket. They left parts of the Greenhouse intact. Hattie says it would be shameful to destroy all of its beauty. They also run a small Inn, upstairs." So, of course, my mind thought salaciously. He ignored my immediate sexual innuendos as we neared the kitchen. Finally, Shane snapped for his attention. Hattie, a tiny, salt and pepper-haired woman, popped out from behind the bar back and stood before me, with wide excited eyes and a tomato smile, "It's nice to meet you, Daya,"

"-He legit talks about you all the time." Shane chimed in.

"No- I don't. Don't mind my aunt and uncle," I giggled at the teasing and looked around to the charming place; couples were dancing on the dance floor, the hanging plants, glowing lights, mistletoe, and music. Hattie and Shane Tyson entertained us a minute with Tyler, Haven's cousin, until a thin, pretty, olive-skinned waitress walked into us. Immediately she looked into my eyes, gasping in total shock. *Fuck.* I think my passionate eyes scared the girl, her eyes shot down, and she apologized, trying to avoid Haven's thick stare. No. It wasn't about my eyes.

It was about Haven. They must have known each other.

"Seneca, can you show them to their table?"

The waitress, unhinged, folded a tray and menu underneath her arm and brought us over to a secluded corner of the restaurant. The hidden space was behind a half wall, away from the crowd, and never restored, remaining its natural greenhouse form. There were glowing candles in mason jars and Christmas lights. Boxes and crates were neatly stacked aside, and the walls and ceiling were all panels of greenhouse glass. Flowers and vines tangled around the corners from hanging baskets of living plants.

The waitress rudely gestured toward the romantic table.

"It's perfect... thank you, Seneca." Her name flowed out of his mouth as if he had said it so many times before. The two stared at each other awkwardly as he took his coat off and tossed it aside onto a dusty, broken table. With eyes of bright forests, I watched the two suspiciously. Why was he looking at her like that? I tossed away my hat, scarf, and coat onto the same side table and restlessly distracted myself with the decorations until Haven's eyes set on my gaze. Like a magnet, his eyes ravished me. The look on his face said he was pressed on, and I left him speechless. The way he stared at me ripped the waitress's breath away. She looked down nervously now that Haven spoke without looking at her, "Uh- Seneca, can you bring us some of Hattie's cider. But can you like- bring me some ice- lots of it?" Haven was turning beat red, and he could barely talk with his throat so dry. His eyes were still too busy, groping me down. Finally, he pulled his eyes from me and apologetically looked at the pretty brown-eyed waitress. She walked away immediately.

From the glow of the candles, I could see the romantic old paintings mounted on the walls above. The mood felt intimate and cozy, and outside the windows, flurries danced in the winter wind. Haven looked at me and then pulled out my chair. As I sat down, I could not shake the genuine tension between the two. "-You know her?"

The question got his attitude going. He rolled his brooding eyes and cleared his throat through the soft folk music. He didn't seem like he wanted to talk about it, but he knew from my jealous eyes that I wouldn't let it go. He explained so casually, "You know how you had *Landon* before me? Well, I had *Seneca* before you," as if he didn't care. I squinted at him awkwardly.

"She's your Ex? You should have told me,"

"-We broke it off years ago, and we're still friends. She's cool."

That honesty of his was something else. Great. Haven's *Ex* was our waitress. Even though my mind began to flood with harmful waves of his ghosting girlfriends' past, I kept quiet. Did they still care about each other? What does she know about me? Does he miss her? Do they still hang out? Why did he look at her like that? And then, "-Have you had sex with her?" I blamed my paranoia.

First, he squinted at me, unsure if it was a serious question. Then, he rolled his eyes, seethed, and sat back in his chair,

"-Daya, what are you asking me? Because I'm not a virgin if that's what you want to know." Suddenly my insides crawled with the thought of Haven's body on another girl. A pit hit my stomach.

"Haven, this is weird-" I snapped in a low tone.

"-Welcome to my world… and before you go there, we died the day I found out about you." And so I was curious,

"How long have you known about me?"

"I don't remember… my sixteenth birthday," Haven has known about me for the past six years, and here I am, just finding out about him. I was more jealous of his honest relationship with Dean than Seneca. Haven has had time to soak and be somber over his fate, which is why he was already so comfortable with it. He lived his life knowing where it led. I would never get the chance. Without my knowledge, too much time had been wasted, which made me sad in more ways than I anticipated. Splitting the silence, my eye roll gathered up my attitude, and posture and I slammed the silly conversation to the side, "I don't remember much. My uncle wiped away all of my memories." Haven scoffed and looked away.

"Yup… they're good for that. Look, Daya, I don't want you to be pissed with me over this. I know how I feel about you, and it's dif-ferent." He said faintly, fallen victim to venerability. He stared away but not before I caught the same hurt in his eyes. It infected his once blue eyes with ebony ink. As always, his eyes were ever-changing like his chemical imbalance, sapphire to sable. I reached over and touched his hand. The hairs on his arm stood up, his eyes softened, "Misael came to talk to me today, or rather ruin my day. Besides the point, come to find out, there are things Dean never told me,"

"I trust Dean more than I trust my uncle. You were right about the energy imbalance. Every day, I uncover a new lie or truth about myself or who I thought I was. There's not much that I can do about that, but I have to make it my business to take control of my life now. You can't let Misael keep you from trusting your father."

"-You're right," He pulled my hand and gave it a soft kiss.

The night went on over a delicious meal. We laughed, and flares between our eyes ignited as we explored the depths of each other more thoroughly and delicately. There was no rushing or fear of getting caught. By then, his chair had come closer to mine. His fingertips caressed over my kneecap. I had naturally drawn closer to him, my elbows shaking on the table, body leaning into him as I admired the way he talked with strength and confidence. We both knew since the beginning, even before our midnight runs, that we blended well together. But being there with him, in his element, made our chemistry so apparent; it was undeniable. From the patrons to the splinters hanging from the old split wood, the whole place could feel what we felt. "-I'm sorry I'm stalling here... I don't want to be alone with you yet." We stood up from the empty table.

"Why not?" I asked as he threw my coat over my shoulders.

"Because I don't trust myself alone with you. Being around you is like edging insanity, and I want you to be yourself around me. I don't want you to feel pressured to go crazy *with me; folie à deux*-"

Haven was right. The more time I spent time with him, the more I wanted to push the edge of my innocence. He made me feel wild and confident. Each day the limits I set are snipped free like ribbon, and I keep inching towards a new doom I had no control but lust after. His efforts were telling. He was trying to slow me down only to save me. "-Dancing? You want to go somewhere and dance?" He was timid when he asked but looked at me adoringly,

Haven had his mindset to get close, but not **too close,** so he took me to a blue, seedy, windowless bar not far down the road from the diner. A pit-stop for Americana bikers and their lady friends, *Pick em' up Jack* was a gold mine for live rock music, whatever the flavor.

As we walked to the door, Haven pulled me deep into his embrace. Inside was nothing more than a typical raging rock bar of the young and the old, having a good time listening to live music. It seemed crowded, but Haven's size was helpful. He also knew everyone from the moment we got through the door. The bar had to be a regular hangout for him. He gave a fist bump to the owner, who stood behind the bar serving up beers and shots. The music was so loud I could barely hear his greeting. I shook his hand briefly before we sat at the only reserved stools in the corner of the bar, and there was a view of the occupied stage. Haven stood before me with his arms at my sides, holding me up against the bar ledge, admiring me a moment after tossing our coats. "Come on," he pulled me off my seat. I fell into him, dancing as we gravitated into the hyperactive crowd. It was very different from our first dance, we were comfortable with each other, and there were no restrictions. No limitations. His hands were all over me, and this time he didn't hesitate to push, collide or pull into me. Stuck in bliss, our movements felt like sex. It gave us a high-induced rush that made the time pass too quickly. And so hours passed and dancing wasn't good enough.

By three that morning, we searched for any reason to seclude ourselves further. We hadn't realized the frenzy we entangled ourselves into on the dance floor, and we were both riding seriously high on sexual anticipation. Haven pulled me from the dance floor, hoping we would bring down the energy. Instead, while drinking a bottle of water, Haven's eyes were stag, savoring every inch of my legs in shameless captivating. Then, without a word, Haven scooped me into his arms and carried me out of the bar. Neither one of us wanted to waste another minute in that crowd.

Haven surprised me when we found ourselves parked in the middle of that hidden, snowy heart-shaped meadow. We stripped out of our winter cover-ups, and it was all recklessly thrown about, despite his relentless resistance to lock lips with me. For a while, we only had been silent. Windows fogged, lights dimmed, and warmth blew from the vents. The windshield showcased a natural icy silver screen of pure winter enchantment; at its most serene and delicate state. Most animals were going into hibernation, and everything was so quiet, aside from *The Killers* album that softly echoed angelically through the speakers. I sat across Haven's lap barefoot in his arms, his fingers caressed over the scar on my wrist as I sat staring into the outside world. It had looked just as enchanting as it did when he and I had our final run, but now a thick blanket of sparkling white snow. My chin rested on high knees, and my frozen toes dug into his jeans. No words, only emotion. It's been driving us both down a hole, but we only sat there innocently. He cared too much, I thought. Feeling the way his chest rose against mine, the smell of his aftershave, the spearmint lingering on his breath as he annoyingly chewed his gum, nearly seconds apart from my lips. He watched me as I watched him, with abrasively energizing soul searchers, until he broke his daze, "I have something for you,"

Haven handed me the velvet sack from Anais's suitcase. I opened the bag and snaked out an enchanting pearl necklace. In the moonlight, it glittered magically. I recognized the pearls from my mother's photos. The smooth conch pearls were of pure ivory gold. Beautiful and rare, together we admired them. "They weren't easy to restore, but I hope you love them," Haven slipped them around my neck and locked them in place. He didn't need to say anything to melt a love-sick fool like me, he only stared vicariously with eyes of turquoise waves, and I was mesmerized. "I've done some wild shit since I've got here. I'll risk everything for you, but never out of recklessness. If I hadn't made this clear enough, I want you, in every life that we exist together, I want you. I love you, Daya."

Early morning and he was finally breaking, but he wasn't alone,

"-I love you too," My hands pulled him in harshly, and now he was too close, but I never wanted to bury myself so deep into someone EVER. He let me hold him that long moment, soaking in his energy. His fingers dug into my ribs, fighting the urge to completely devour my body as I fell apart in his hands. Our thriving hearts were so loud and clashing like a thundering hurricane; so vivid, I could hear the rumbling of the waves above us. The truck was heating up. Sweating from the humidity, it felt like everything around was on fire. The way we looked at each other was dangerous, but my lush eyes should have been a warning sign. I caved into his lips, and all I could feel was this extreme magnetic pull right from my heart chakra, crushing me into his. As if I didn't come willingly enough, his arms drew me in like blood, and he pulled me in deeper. He held his grip, kissing me right back. It was getting unbelievably hot.

Steam dripped from the windows. It smelled like salt, sun, and ocean; dirt and musk. Haven didn't let me go, and I didn't want him to. His touch made trembled like a bunny, but the electricity running through my veins felt like adrenaline sugar-high. I didn't care about the consequences of our souls colliding and catching fire. From that moment on, nothing but recklessness, and I couldn't get enough. We tussled and rowed around the front seat, back and forth, until I found an opportunity to get on top of him. He didn't want to fight it in that split moment, so he gave up control.

-This strange color dust followed my every move. First, appearing, then twinkling in the thick air like glitter, pulling at Haven's curiosity. He seemed to be mystified, staring in wonder. I felt like I was in one of my sex dreams. I sat down right on his shocking erection, bulging from tight blue jeans. It only made sense; he was a big man. He anxiously pulled up my dress, his hands cupping my bare ass, gripping me hard enough to mark me. He felt so good, and I threw my head back in his comfort. His fingertips played with the rim of my lacy panties, his tongue sliding down the middle of my chest. I was beginning to get off, rubbing deeper into him. Our bodies could have quickly started a flame. Instead, I could smell smoke and fire as his fingernails pierced deeper into my delicate skin, helping me push my body into waves over his hard-on. Haven slowly sank into his fingers into the warm wet folds of my clit for a slick moment, as his other hand belligerently pulled my hair back and licked me savagely, from my neck to my chin. Each love bite was like sugar nectar, ripping through me in adrenaline high.

The euphoria on my face set a fire in him, and the anticipation dragged out the primal within. He ravished me like an animal. He pushed me into the passengers' seat into missionary position and leaped on top of me. The truck shook. His face mirrored mine, and his hands gripped the sides of me. My long legs draped over his arms; my bare feet dangled in the air. His tongue reached for my exposed ankles, kissing and sucking. My eyes rolled back, and I nearly ripped his shirt as my fist gripped his collar, and my other hand sank deep into the back of his neck. I licked him back, from his neck to his earlobe. His hand was holding my hands down. Haven couldn't hide how excited he was to see how wet he made me, staring down between my thighs while licking his lips. His hands lifted my dress further, and he went down to kiss my bare navel. I gave him a melting look, unable to help myself. I was still hot. **Too hot.**

We looked at each other, but our eyes didn't exactly meet. Instead, we were both caught in awe to see electric heatwaves forming in the air. The once enchanting color dust now sizzled into fading pale ashes. Haven retracted from me out of fear and fell back into his seat. I sat back, and as he kept his distance, everything seemed to simmer down quickly. Haven rolled down the windows, and steam poured out like boiling water. He shifted in his seat uncomfortably, "-We can never do this again, Daya. I want you so bad, but not for the price of your life." He was serious. Maybe even upset.

"-But that was nothing." I felt like we didn't go far enough.

Haven scoffed in deep internal thought for a moment, "Are you that desperate to knock boots?" Haven wouldn't back down, "-Daya, "I don't trust the curse. Your uncle told me about what the desire does to you. You don't even notice from your high horse, but your scent intoxicates every guy around you to fall to their knees, and it's not just me. Not like you need that kind of magic. You're fucking beautiful. I came to see you on your birthday Daya. I saw you with Landon in his truck that night. The guys warned me of those lilac eyes you hide so much, but nothing compares to seeing it up close." -I wanted to scream. But, instead, my eyes flared flames of deep yellow, red, and orange. How can I be held accountable for that?- "I need to know that if I leave tomorrow, you will stay loyal to me. You're mine. Do you understand that? Something about you cures my soul. I never wanted anything more in my life. I won't sit here and gamble with your life, so don't play with mine either. I can't give you what you want, and if I'm being honest with you, I don't know if I could trust you, no have no self-control. Winter's are lonely as fuck, and you're on a high rise, darling. You're so careless about it, and it pisses me off. -" Was he fucking with me?

He thought I had no control of my body. It was easy to contradict me for the most part, but I was still a virgin. I was afraid to have sex, but not with Haven. He made me so comfortable that I didn't think twice about losing myself in him. Now I just felt embarrassed.

"Okay… how dare you ruin this moment for me? First, do you know how long I've waited for you to kiss me? And what do you mean *if you leave tomorrow?* What the hell is that supposed to mean? I've done nothing but prove my loyalty to you. I gave Landon back his ring, and I've disobeyed my uncle, went out looking for you, chased you, risk my life every time to be this close to you, and you have the nerve to think I'm just going to do it with anyone? I know

I make it seem like I don't care about my life on earth because I don't, Haven. I know what I'm after, and that is a whole new world with YOU. But if you're so worried about it, Haven, we could end it all now. I can only give one person the power to take away all of my existence, and here I am with you."

My legs dangled about, still shaking from adrenaline. Then, looking at me defenseless, Haven sulked into his seat, "Not like this."

"-Fine, take me home," I demanded.

"-Not while we are both mad. Sit your pretty ass back because we're not leaving here until we're good again." He was ridiculous. He wouldn't let this go; his stern glare said so. I pulled myself together, sitting up and fixing my hair. Then, crossing my legs, I fixed my dress and shifted my body towards the door.

"SO, you're just going to believe everything my uncle tells you?" My fingertips traced the melted snow droplets on the window, "Everything between Landon and I was before I knew you."

"That's bull shit. That night at Hector's, when Landon pulled you away from me, you wanted him. I saw it in your eyes." I had been guilty of things that were beyond my control, and yet, I only wanted to make love to one man, And he was a fucking idiot.

"-Are you fucking kidding? My uncle has suppressed my emotions for years Haven, of course, I'm feeling crazy right now. And I'm still a virgin! If I was was weak, I would have let Landon go down on me that night at Hector's. He nearly begged me. No one has ever touched me the way I let you tonight. Please don't act like you know how I feel. You've never been romantically suppressed."

He scoffed, "Suppressed? Sweetheart, you have no fucking idea. -Wait till I see Landon. I can't believe him." He was so hurt reflecting on it, but I refused to let him make me feel bad.

"You think you're so innocent. How about we talk about *your* *'EX.'* You said you broke it off a long time ago, but that's not what

YOUR eyes said when you looked at her tonight. You're so obsessed with me but is that really what *you* want? I'm just this young, boring, nerdy virgin girl you're not allowed to fuck, but obsessive over. I know you crave what's between my legs. Tell me, what does a guy like you do after fooling around with a tease like me? Do you see other girls? Use them like medicine balls? Where did you go that night after the dinner party?" In a slight bitter silence, he chuckled,

"You know nothing about me, skirt,"

"-You went to high school in the San Francisco Bay, and you played three varsity sports. You played in a popular grunge band and ran with a motorcycle gang. I know about the endless train of girls that hung around you. You told me you weren't a virgin yourself. So how many were there, Haven? I hear those groupies treat you like a God out there. That's just some of the things MY UNCLE told me about you and *your brother* validated for me. I came out with you tonight because I trust that after all that, you only want me."

"You don't see girls hanging around my neck. I don't pay them any mind because I'm always preoccupied with your dumbass. But I've had to watch Landon put his hands all over you, more than once, more than I cared to watch, and I've watched you enjoy it."

"-I was under a damn Spell."

"-Because you're easily manipulated."

Haven's words sank like a ball and chain, "Listen up, skirt, Landon will never be me," the way he said it made my heart race. I dared to gaze into his eyes—his lips apart and jaw solid. Sultry obscured eyes. He looked so damn sexy in the dark. It was just a shame that we were squabbling. He caught me biting my lips and scoffed in utter disbelief. He gave himself a minute before plunging back into me, seducing me again. He kissed me so *slowly*, his full mint lips traced away from my lips, and he kissed deeply into my neck, and his hands slipped underneath my thighs. Grasping the cuffs of my cheeks, Haven pulled me closer to him. The way I let him take me in was too submissive. Why was he doing this?

"He can't touch you like this," He whispered in my ear. His fingers raked across my bare skin as Haven soaked in all of my magic energy with his raging jealous eyes. His hands wandered my body, pulling up my dress once again. I let him touch me, even though it made him mad. "He can never make you feel like I do," Haven spoke the truth as he laid down a clash of kisses on my heart and sent violent shivers down my spine. The air was leaving my body, second by second. He brushed his hands up my inner thigh until his knuckles purposely rubbed into my love button, right at my middle. My core pulled into me like a black hole. He teased me over the lacy fabric, tickling around the folds of my lips and clit until his fingertips dragged across the panty fabric, closing in on the middle of my swollen lips. I was so wet and burning up a toxic fever.

"Fuck me," I whispered. I closed my eyes, attentive to the pleasure he gave me and not his emotional pain. He was so close to breaking into me that we could nearly taste my doom in the air. I couldn't help but look at him sharply in his intimidating, sable soul. His eyes roared at me to concede, but I refused. I was too drugged by intent. So instead, I gave an honest moan, sexier than I had intended. My head fell back, indulging in the suicide, and then he suddenly stopped. I felt his fingers hook onto my panties, sliding them down my airborne legs until they hinged at my toes, and then I watched him savagely pull the panties off with his teeth. He dropped them in his hands and urgently put them away in his pocket as he kissed at the weak spot behind my knees. He was trying to distract me while pulling away completely.

He finally got his '*Lucky token*' and was deeply satisfied as he sat back in his seat. Calmly, he licked at my juice on his fingers, like fresh honey, and he continued to ignore me, turning up the music and looking out the window. He lit a cigarette after I halfheartedly kicked his shoulder. I sat up straight, fixing my dress. Haven disengaged, smoking down that disgusting cancer stick, and I began to beg, "Why are you leaving? Where are you going?"

"For fucks sake, Daya, can you stop with the questions? I have no say over this, and I worked hard to wake you up; if it means that much to you, catch your cheap thrills, but not with me."

"-Why don't you want me anymore-" I began to cry.

My sadness quickly weighed heavy, and Haven softened. He reached to touch me, but I smacked his hand away. Finally, my coldness made him snap, "Fine, you win, Daya. Do you want to know why I can't let it go? Because -Landon is my blood brother."

As the words left his pressed lips, it slowly hit me, word for word, like one of those tennis ball launchers, "I beg your pardon?"

"Caroline couldn't handle raising a family, so she left us. Jacy and I have no memories of her, but that doesn't mean we didn't have suspicions. At the dinner party, I was too invested in you to realize, but I noticed something was familiar about Caroline at Landon's game. They told us the truth right before I went to pick you up."

"How is this possible?"

"Caroline left, and Anais showed up. Dean fell stuck on stupid in love with her until one day she went missing. Do you think Dean trusted Anais when she went missing? With all that desire from her curse? How do you think you *and* Landon got here? Her disappearance ruined Dean, and he was hurt enough to reconcile with Caroline until Anais returned. Dean felt so bad after discovering what Anais went through with Moboyas; he never gave my brother a chance. Dean is the most loyal man I know, so if Dean couldn't trust Anais, how am I supposed to trust you? And from what Misael claims, no one knows which Tyson brother set off your fever."

Lies; designed to rip us apart & obliterate us into weightless dust.

"In a world where I can't trust anything, there's one thing I unconditionally trust, and that's the way I feel about you. I do not need to convince anyone. I'm more worried about where you're going."

"I'm a warrior, and I have responsibilities to my Native blood. I *have to* leave, and I'll be gone for months while you're here with him. You and I, we are not our parents. I am not level-headed; you are not controlled. It was easy for them to fix what they broke, but Dean is forever haunted by his disloyalty, especially after discovering the truth about Landon. Misael had so much time to push you two together. Landon had all the time to learn your every need and desire. I just came out of nowhere from the woodworks demanding you be with me. You were going to marry him, and I intercepted that. What if I'm wrong? I can have anything I want in this world except you. Maybe it's a learned habit to want you the way I do. I've waited years for that moment we were face-to-face in your dining room. All you want is to sleep with someone. Either me or him." He quietly pleaded his case. His eyes raged in sorrow as he flicked the cigarette butt out the window, the smoke snaking behind it.

"You set that fire in me, Haven. And I love you more than you know for it. I'm sorry you let everyone mess with your head, but I am not weak. I think you're just mad because you allow your insecurities to let other people convince you otherwise. If you can't trust me, I don't know what else to do but to show you."

"Fine," was all he said. My choice of words came off so heedless. Haven looked at me, defeated. It was true. What else could I say? He's going to learn how to trust me, whether he liked it not. I returned my glance outside. He sat there quietly for a second before pulling his seat belt. I, too, reached for my seat belt as Haven started the engine. It was quiet and dull. Haven drove the truck through the now tainted meadow and back onto the main road. He turned the music up, and it was a relief. I could cry without him listening.

Haven couldn't focus on driving with my heartbreaking next to him, so he pulled his attention away from the road. Then, drying the tears from my cheek, he pulled me closer.

Suddenly a haunting *crunch* obstructively rang.

Haven pulled his arm away abruptly and grabbed hold of his left side; his ribs were in stinging pain, and I knew because his eyes lit up like fireworks. He growled harshly in excruciating pain, and then we heard the subsequent cracking and crumbling sound. Haven yelped again. He was now gripping at his abdomen. Those sounds, of what could be the sound of crushing bones, echoed out. It reminded me of my nightmare and the sounds the monster made as it broke its limbs to attack me. "Haven?!" He coughed up thick dark blood, spitting it right on the dash. His hand uncontrollably twisted the wheel, and the truck went skidding on the quiet back road. I yelped, grabbing hold of the safety handle above. The truck continued to spin out of control down the vacant winter road until it smacked right into a telephone pole, stopping on impact. The hit wasn't as bad as it sounded; Haven and I were both okay when the smoke cleared. His hands were shaking, but he managed to cock the shift into the park with all his reluctant strength.

"-Daya, I need my dad," Wincing, he snapped the seat belt and released himself. He cried out and spat more blood. I couldn't watch him suffer; he was crushing from the inside, out. I rushed to take the wheel without causing any more pain to him. It wasn't easy, but I got into the driver's seat. I was barefoot with little driving experience, but there was nothing that could stop me from saving Haven.

11

Winter Hibernation: Daya

Was Haven was alive or dead? I didn't know. I had recklessly driven into Dean's driveway at dawn that morning, crashing into their rotted-out porch steps. Haven, in harrowing pain, spewing out blood and black ink. I tried holding him together but, **"GO! GET OUT!"** Haven roared. Dean came running outside, jaw-dropping at the sight of his truck, wrecked; more so, worried when he came to face with Haven, who was slowly but surely turning into a monster.

Haven and I ruined any chance to be together. Dean made that clear when he sent me home with Jacy. I cried in the shower as I washed off the blood, and I cried until I fell asleep. I wasn't sure what daybreak would bring, so I hadn't left my bed since. Charlotte asked no questions, so I was left to wonder, was he okay?

When I heard Dean's truck later that evening, it was the first time I had gotten out from under the quilts. I looked through the shades; no Haven. But I walked into the kitchen anyway. Charlotte was brewing tea when he walked in, exhausted and worn down but smiling, "Hey, kid. Long night?" He joked as he hung his coat by the door. I was near to bursting into tears. Dean looked at me regretfully before shaking his head, "-Sit down, we need to talk." Ugh. I hated that. Every time I hear that, I find out about some *crazy shit,* so I braced myself. I didn't want to hear *crazier shit.* I still had to process the news that Dean was also Landon's father; and that Haven and Landon were brothers. Now I had to deal with that crazy shit Haven did in the truck. Like, *form shifting?* Nonetheless, it terrified me.

"-Where's Haven?"

"Haven's very sick, and he needs rest, so it's best if you left him alone until winter blows over."

"Winter? What are you talking about?" I was skeptical.

"Daya, there are things you won't understand about us."

"Well, help me understand," He sighed.

"-What happened this morning resulted from Haven's jealousy and possessiveness. Haven's convinced that you're in love with Landon and only blinded by his lust. Your uncle told Haven that you lusted after him because Landon refused your advances. He made him believe that you carry no value to your human form as long as you get what you want from any Tyson. Haven has spent his entire life running away from his fate. It took him a long time to accept his destiny, and now he's been told it was all for nothing."

"Why does Haven suddenly feel so threatened?"

"Because Landon is a Spirit Warrior, like Haven. It was the only thing that split them apart. I knew the minute I met Landon, he was special, like Haven and Jacy, but Misael ambushed me; he knew Landon was mine and waited until he reintroduced me to Caroline to tell me that our DNA was a match. I've known Caroline for a long time, and she hasn't changed. I'm not surprised she kept Landon from me. I might hate her forever because of it. My boys are my world, and that now includes Landon. We told Landon right away when we got the results back. He wasn't happy, but he seems to be warming up to me now. I wanted to wait until *this* morning to tell Haven, but your uncle felt the need to tell him before he took you out. That wasn't fair." My uncle's meddling was going to be the death of us. The built-up rage for my uncle was beginning to overload and spew; I was sick from the lies.

"-I'm going to kill my uncle." My eyes flickered crimson.

"We can't stop him as long as he has this close bond with Landon. Landon knows Misael can manipulate him, and he's okay with that because Misael has been there when he needed a father. Misael and Landon both hate Haven, just like they both hate me. But I'm his father, and he's Tyson blood. I have a responsibility for him, and I won't allow Misael to hurt any of my kids. The Tyson blood; we weren't expecting to fall in love with a Managualt-"

"You need to tell me what happened with you and my mother."

"Fine- Going back a couple of years before you were born; I had been a single father for a while. Caroline had left us to live at the University. It tore our family apart, and her absence broke us more nights than some. When I saw Anais for the first time, I knew it was fate. She was the most beautiful thing I laid eyes on; something took control of me that day. Her beauty haunted me because something much more profound was going on. An undeniable connection, fate. Your mother had healing abilities, and she healed us from so much pain. She was always helping and so kind and great with the boys; they loved her. I couldn't imagine losing her. Your uncle and I were close despite my infatuation. I trusted him because Anais trusted him. Unfortunately, Misael never found me worthy of Anais. I was also older, broke, and a single father of two, struggling to get through school. He's always worn a poker face, but he couldn't trust us to break the curse, so he turned to the spirit of Guaybana, who said, destroy the union. He did what he could to separate us, but we loved too much and too fast. We were reck-less and crazy, and we loved pushing boundaries, just like you and Haven. It drove Misael straight off the deep end, but only because he wanted to protect his sister. Anais trusted him, but he sold us out. He lured her into the garden and told us she had run away, but I searched for months before giving up. I was with Caroline when Charlotte finally called me with the news. We don't know why, but weeks later, you were in the picture-

You were a blessing, and despite circumstances, Anais and I were going to find a way to lift the curse before she delivered you. But it was too late, and you were born too soon. Anais had diffi-culty during the birthing process. Your ancestral mother, *Atabey,* blessed your birth 1000 times in pity of Anais. To have a divine spirit reborn into this realm was a high calling. Your delivery was so rare, many spirit tribes of the world offered their blessings. The Great Spirit also offered its blessing; Haven. A protector. A shield. Another divine ancestral spirit from the North winds protects you from the ancestors who wanted harm to come to you. Haven has always been your ONE and ONLY *true* protector-

At birth, the elders who had witnessed Haven knew he had a unique fate. Now it was manifesting before us all. So your uncle and I knew for a very long time that Haven was to protect you-and when your nightmares came, we found out you two were star-crossed. The Spirits and Zeni's warned that you two should never be pulled apart or together by force. Your energy should always balance his. Misael convinced us that the tribal dance was the only cure. I believed him because I no longer had Anais and needed a way out. It was an opportunity to run from it, and I selfishly took the chance. If we successfully break the bond between you two, we can go on with our lives. We thought it worked when the night-mares didn't return, and I left with the boys. Throughout the years,

Haven gave me enough reasons to be suspicious. Haven is rough, but he's a good kid, so I wasn't upset when the elders tracked me down to tell me Haven confronted them. Moboyas has conjured an unholy force within him to come in between your union. The wendigo inside must be killed, and only Haven can do that."

"-You have to help him." Desperation basking intone.

"I can only help if Haven is willing to kill the demons that keep him bound to the wendigo, and I honestly don't think he's strong enough. However, your mother's brilliant plan I think could work. She called the Zenis and asked for a challenge to restore her fate. In the beginning, the Zenis refused to help because they said it was the will of Moboyas and that they didn't interfere with the affairs of Moboyas. However, Atabey and her sons Yucahu and Guakar were impressed by Anais's resilience and strength. So they allowed us to challenge Moboyas for one chance to break the curse before her next birthday. Then, if she could rebirth her garden successfully, we were allowed to be together. The idea was perfect, but you came as we were preparing for the war." Dean drew silent. I watched as he went into a melancholy stare and inhaled deeply, "-Your uncle blamed us for her death. He was so sure that if she had only married Ruiz, she would still be alive."

"Married Ruiz? Like an arranged marriage?"

It wasn't Misael's first time conjuring up an elaborate plan.

"In the beginning, Misael chimed in with a popular spell. An arranged loveless marriage to someone of Taino blood, but she was against the idea. I had to beg her for the sake of her life. The day of the wedding ceremony was when she took off and disappeared. I didn't see her until she washed up ashore. Anais had a choice. I supported her regardless. Unlike Haven, I approved of her suitor, Sheriff Ruiz, who treated her well. In the end, Anais chose me, which started the war with Misael. So he chose a new suitor. Moboyas incarnate. Our love was more powerful than Moboyas. Anais and I learned to forgive and love again, but we never got to win our war. You and Haven have one chance, and I have warned Haven; Misael doesn't play fair. This love must be tangible, unconditional. I advise you not to jump into anything and give Haven time to find himself. In the meantime, do what your mother did."

"How can I master the power of Atabey?"

"You already have the power of Atabey. You, like all your Taino brothers and sisters, were born with it-"

Not another moment passed when Misael came storming into the house. He swung the front door violently, "-What the hell are YOU doing here!?" he asked Dean upon walking into the kitchen.

"Came over for tea. Are you joining us?" Dean played the good guy, as grounded as someone in his shoes can be.

"NO- Crazy story; I bumped into *Landon* this morning, and Landon had a fascinating story to tell me about Haven and Daya's date last night. I told you, Dean, this was all a terrible idea! Are you guys trying to kill her? I can only imagine how last night could have played out had she not driven to your house. I expected this from Charlotte, but I had to sit there and think, Dean? My best friend put one of my daughters in danger? I told you, nothing good would come from this. I want Haven to stay the hell away from Daya-"

My uncle tossed all of Haven's stuff he found in my room; an Aerosmith vinyl, a concert T-shirt that smelled just like him, a stack of love letters, and *The Alchemist by Paulo Coelho,* he let me borrow. I rushed to recover everything, but my uncle slapped it all out of my grips, and it all went crashing to the floor. That's when he noticed the pearls around my neck and ripped them off. The pearls scatter to the floor. My pure light magic began to defend me, but I was no match for my uncle's vile energy. I crumbled underneath him, crying in defeat when Dean suddenly stood before me with a stern glare. He was ready to fight, and his body glowed a noticeably blue aura. Misael eased up off me, pulled his jacket straight,

"Get up, Daya; you're coming home." My eyes of crimson roses refused. He took my wrists, pulling me up to my feet. Charlotte tried pleading and pulling me from his grips, but it was useless. Dean pushed her aside, giving my uncle the right to snatch me up. Although hurt, I knew this wasn't over. My uncle hauled me out of Charlotte's cabin, nearly by my hair and nails.

I was in the dark for days, withering away. I stayed a prisoner in my bedroom. It was like sticking a slug into a box of salt rocks. I could feel the energy drain from me. Physically sick, I was vulnerable under his control. I grew weak until I could barely feel my powers. I counted stars, trapped, and I was sure to die.

Endless days and I wasted away until Misael finally came and checked on me. He walked in with my survival book in hand as I read *King Lear*. Gray-faced and soiled with revenge, he brought in an eerie aura. I sat up as he sat down on the edge of my bed, "Look, I don't want to be the bad guy here, okay? I'm only doing this to protect you. Our people have faced thousands of years of oppression at the hands of the akani. Our ancestors didn't want this for you. You'll be safe here on this mountain. Here's your book; there are good ideas here. I'm sure you'll find one that suits you."

"None of the spells end up with Haven, so I don't want your fake happy endings." I forced my words down his mouth.

"I see your pain, and it's not what I wanted for you. I just wanted you to live and be happy with Landon. You were always so happy. But, you're young, and you don't know what you want. Haven is not what you want; he's selfish, temperamental, and his ancestral roots aren't pure. He'll lose control one day and hurt you. True love can be spiteful, hateful, and jealous. Don't you want to be happy? I know the magic that can make dreams come true on Earth."

"Landon isn't in love with me. He never will be, not like Haven."

"We can change that... you see how my spells work. They're potent, especially with your magic in the mix. And you have to admit what you saw in Haven the other night was brutal and terrifying. The mental torture that poor kid is going through; turning into that thing in your nightmares. You saw how much pain he was in. Don't you want to heal him from that pain? Give him back his easy life with Seneca? Don't you think that's what he deserves? He never asked for this, but you have the power to heal him. So you can still have your life and make everyone happy again."

I hated the fact that my uncle was making so much sense. All the pain in Haven's eyes has haunted me repeatedly since. All his torment. In my mind, the decision was as clear as day. I almost considered what my uncle was implying. I was the reason Haven was hurting so much, and I wanted to cure him of it all. I should disappear from his life. "You can always stay in the garden realm, you would be free from the nightmares, and you will live forever. You'll always be able to see the Zenis and your mother."

"But I *love* Haven. My loyalty lies with him."

From that moment on, I ignored him.

Days passed. It was hard to remember the days of the week, but I can recall it was a Wednesday because my uncle left the protection spell over the house half-assed so I could get the mail and take out the garbage. My uncle was at work, so I hoped to conjure my powers for those few minutes and break free from the property. At 2:10 pm, I felt the energy dull and the kitchen side door unlock. I put on my coat and my snow boots and walked outside. I had only ten minutes. I threw the garbage bag in the trash as the mail carrier stuck the mail in the mailbox and drove away, casually waving at me. I smiled, marching to the mailbox. I didn't hesitate when my hand easily penetrated the force field. I pushed through effortlessly like jello and took off running towards the woods. I hated running in the snow. Granted, I was a runner, but this terrain was trash. Slushy and wet. Icy and unstable. Cold. Still, I pushed myself.

As I came close to the woods, I heard Haven's voice. Echoing in the woods, "Daya!" He cried for me. I nearly twisted my ankle twice, running towards Haven's voice. I ran until I couldn't hear him calling anymore. I tried to remember which trail, in what direction, would lead to Dean's house. It was all different in the winter, and I could only trust my gut as I trampled through the snow. I hadn't gone too far from the yard. I just passed the garden gates.

"Daya, where are you going?" Something unusual echoed in the stillness of the winter afternoon. At first, it sounded like a tree branch, cracking under the pressure of the wind. But when I looked clearly in front of me, I saw that creature from my nightmares—just standing there several feet away, blending in with the dead bushes in the background. It watched me, dripping with black hot poison goo, steaming off its skeletal body. Teeth sharp and skin tearing; foam glistening. Sharp nails, ready to rip me into shreds. A fire sparked underneath its hooves. I couldn't breathe. More so when I watched it come running towards me, but it wasn't a dream.

I had no choice but to run back to Misael's. I tried running as fast as possible, sprinting like I was at a track meet. I had a good pace, until I slipped on ice and fell to the ground. My ankle sprained, and that thing was still coming for me. I could see the break into the yard just ahead, and I began to crawl through the slush and mud. The thing was still gaining on me as I gained on the break. I was almost free from the woods, but any minute, that monster was going to trample over and engorge me. Suddenly its sharp crawls burned into me, digging into my left thigh. It burned through my jeans and skin, leaving my thigh in shreds. I thought this was the end, watching as it crawled over me—flames from within its inner skull workings. I closed my eyes and took what I thought was my last breath.

Nothing happened at first. Then I felt myself getting lifted.

Before passing out from the pain, I managed to look up. *Misael.*

I woke up in front of the crackling fireplace in our living room. A warm sea of blankets over me and my wounds patched up. It was dark out, but I could see it snowing through the windows. My uncle watched the snowfall from the corner of the room, lightly playing his banjo. The melody reminded me of when I was a girl, and I danced to his songs. Misael was up to something, withdrawing bitter-sweet memories. I cleared my throat, and he stopped playing, "You okay?" A worry in tone jolted my bones.

"... Yes." I shifted back into the sofa.

"Good. You have to be careful when you leave the house. That thing that's after you comes from the Tyson curse; when loose, it flourishes in the winter. It knows your scent. It will come looking for you every time you're out there. That's why I tried to keep you here, where you'll be safe from that monster," When my uncle spoke, he instilled a strange comfort in me that left me vulnerable. When I looked at him, I couldn't resist feeling sympathetic and sorry for him. He wasn't the evil villain as everyone made him out to be. He only wanted the best for me. Misael handed me a fresh cup of tea. It smelled of buttermilk. Lavender. Northern Lights. Spearmint. *Cigarettes & Sex.* It smelled like Haven. My heart fluttered at the aroma, "Thank you." I sipped the warm tea.

My uncle continued to play his banjo.

I woke up in shutters. When the tea knocked me out, Misael had carried me to the garden and locked me up using his magic. I had become my uncle's prisoner. I hated myself for becoming weak under his influence. I was powerless. No one would ever hear me, lost in a realm no one knew. I would never know if anyone was looking for me. Days passed, I cried relentlessly. I only had the picture of my mother for comfort. That was it. All that I had of Haven's was gone but his memory, and it was killing me. I couldn't stop thinking of the way the pearl necklace spewed onto the floor. I'd never see it again. But I did my best to keep him every day. I painted pictures of his forever-changing eyes, and I wrote to him every day.

Weeks passed, and I had grown accustomed to the long days and tender short nights here in the garden. I made friends with all the creatures. From the turtles, frogs, bats, and birds; to the flowers, lagoons, mountaintop, and forests; all the caves, waterfalls, and rivers. I tried to make peace with myself with the help of the ocean-blown rain. Every death and rebirth of the Taino sun made it easier to cope, but nothing cured the heartache and boredom that my adventurous heart suffered. Very soon, I had grown impatient.

Atabey would take some pity on me. After all, I was one of them. I checked the time with the twilight sky. The moon was overhead of the glistening lagoon, silver shining into its glowing hypnotic waters. Most of my day creatures were falling asleep, but the coqui's were just starting their nightly symphony. I took out my ancient Taino spellbook. I harvested from my garden all the necessary ingredients I needed to summon my Ancestors,

Natural sea salt. Coconut milk.

Nectar from a fully ripened Guava. Yuca & seashells

Cemi's; Atabey, Yocahu, Guakar and Maroya.

In the salted sea lagoon, I stood knee-deep before the cemi statues that only touched the water waves. Guava smeared on my stomach and bare chest; I drenched my hair with coconut milk.

Lips of sea salt. Underneath a mysterious Taino moon and count-less pretty stars to witness, I chanted to the amethyst night sky with tributes of Yuca, Guava, seashells, and pearls;

"Supreme spirit Yocahu, mother spirit Atabey, brother spirit Guakar, have mercy on my broken heart, hear my plea, let my fate go free!" It didn't take long for the magic to set in. The night sky reflected off my skin like glass. A universe danced down my shoulder. I looked up, a holy light deep within the cosmos ahead, a lunar light escaping a cave and coming straight towards me. Maroya, the *Diosa Luna.* My eyes widen and then shut suddenly. And then I slept. I could see my majestic soul leave my human body.

The Taino Moon Goddess, Maroya, took my weightless hand, and I followed her into the dark nothingness. Barefooted, with violet and silver strides painted on her delicate skin. She had a crown of twinkling blue stars and wore a gown of purple, blue, and silver silks. Long black silk hair. Her neck, arms, and fingers of gold and jewels. Her thin and flexed body danced before me, leading the way with her lanterns through a dark wet cave, face hidden behind a Taino crescent moon mask that glowed white underneath. Her everlasting beauty unmasked. I followed her up to a place that resembled *El Morro* at Fort Cristobal. There we met Boinael. Black haired, thin, and lean like his twin. His skin bared gold and orange stripes of paint. His crown only shined bright yellow rays. Blinding and breath-taking, he wore silks of yellow, orange, and gold and wore an elegant mask of the Taino sun. He led us out from the Sentry box and into a hurricane-sicken Sea. Like an invisible stone brick path, we walked out into the ocean, up and beyond. Together they led me right to the realm of *Peace & Reward,* where the *Opiel Guabiron* had waited for us. Half Jaguar, half-human; the *Opiel Guab-iron* was the watcher between the realm of the dead and the *Land of Eternal Peace & reward.* Only the worthy entered.

A Jungle kingdom built over the Caribbean islands, made of glass and clouds. Golden rainforests and vines. Caves, rivers, streams, and fruit. Glistening silver. Although the ground was of glass, the world was a natural world that glowed gold vigorously—a dramatic contrast from the darkness and rain underneath in the realm of the recent dead. I could see lighting rip through the gloomy sky through the ice and frost flooring beneath me. I stepped into *the Land of the Divine Spirits.* God of the Sun made it clear; walk forward and say nothing. Then, right at the center before everyone and everything was a dozen enchanting steps that led to the thrones of the Divine Superior Zeni's Earth Mother *Atabey,* with her sons; the superior spirit of light *Yocahu,* and trickster twin and guardian of harsh lessons, *Guakar.* And lastly, the grandfather's wise nature, *Bayamanaco.*

I walked up those golden steps until The Zeni's before me. My ancestors were sitting classic and divine in their Golden thrones.

Yocahu. Supreme God of all Taino Deities. Protector. Creator. The Great spirit of the Taino people. He was bulky, huge, and handsome. He had thick black locks that fell to his abominable chest. His headdress was gold-dripped, and he wore white, blue, and red feathers to match his apron. His chest was bare, and he wore a cloak of only green and white silk, still dripping in gold—feathers, grass, and gold on his wrists and shins. Red face paint with a golden staff, a bat sitting on the top of it. He was intimidating and fearless. Holy and majestic.

His counterpart brother sat at the opposite end. **Guakar** was the distinguished opposite; his headdress was thrown aside, and he was seated erratically on his throne. Guakar wore no cloak and only gold jewels and a white apron with gold stitching. His face red with face paint, he smiled with the boldness of a jester. His handsome face cracked a smile at me first. It was enough to make me nervous, but he wasn't nearly as intimidating as his Queen.

There were no words to describe the everlasting beauty **Atabey** had. With a baby face so fresh and young, the Queen Goddess had locks of heavenly black coal hair that flowed like waves beyond her feet. Her perfectly etched body was in a provocative and revealing white and red silk gown. Her headdress was mainly of red hibiscus, green peacock, some red parrot, also dripping gold. Her skin gleamed in the holy light, and it looked like her body was a universe of its own. I could see the births of every stream, river, and waterfall. Her breasts were like sunrises and her eyes of night skies. Her legs are like a rainforest, and her womb is like an ocean. She had a precious smile that could slow downtime.

Lastly was Grandfather **Bayamanaco**, who sat at Guakar's end. With a long silver beard and a massive Headdress of white parrot and peacock. He wore all white with a thick white cloak and golden stitches. His staff was of flame and fire and flickered in time. His lips scowled and eyes of judgment. He made me think of the turtle woman Caguama, but then I realized that Caguama sat on a throne of her own, off the side. She, too, had a unique beauty that stood out from the others. She was gorgeous, with shiny and long black hair. With only a headdress of seashells and red parrot, she was seemingly naked with red paint stokes all over—nursing at her chest, two twins of her own.

"Princess Dayanara… Spawn of the Moboyas and his Taino Queen concubine." The servants announced my arrival.

"*Seneko kakona* divine mother spirit Atabey, I come with gifts…" I threw down the tributes I held onto at their feet nervously. Atabey cracked a whimsical smile.

"How precious, *Seneko kakona! Mabrinka!* Isn't she gorgeous?"

"Indeed, she is one of the most beautiful I've seen; fair Queen of the Antilles, Ocean, and sand." Yocahu greeted me with a kiss on my hand in a quick grasp upon searching my nervous eyes. It was apparent; I took them. Immediately intrigued, "Dayanara? Such a funny name for such a romantic Queen."

"-*Husband killer*... seems to be a fitting name. She *is* the daughter of all that is Moboyas." Guakar patronized his twin, laughing at his joke before Bayamanaco smacked his head with intention. He rolled his beautiful dark eyes as he carelessy bit into a yuca.

"-I remember now. *Anais.* We couldn't save her mortal life, but I blessed your birth a thousand times. Only, you have now inherited her fate. How? You are only a child, just as your mother was."

"My uncle, he has interfered with my fate, and now he won't allow me to break the curse. Moboyas will come for my soul-"

Atabey looked at me with compassion, while Guakar seemed bored and careless. Finally, he looked at me ruthlessly.

"Inaru... is that why you came to thee? For a cure from this love disease? That is barely a problem at all. We've already weakened the curse of Moboyas. So many princesses have successfully kept their lives. You can too."

"Guakar! -" "His name came out endearing but pulling from Atabey'slips. He looked like a shameful puppy.

"We can make an exception. This one is special." Atabey took my hand but felt no power. Exasperated, confusion invaded her perfect face. I could see an alarming flicker in her calm eyes.

"**EXPLAIN,**" Atabey's revoltingly sassy voice made me tremble.

"My uncle stole my magic and locked me inside my Garden."

Atabey was calm despite the rage that fumed within her. How dare someone disrespects her given power? She was enraged, and it showed as she looked around to her court. Digging her fingernails into the sides of her throne, Atabey looked at Yocahu.

He rolled his eyes,

"Nope, Nah. I refuse to, yet again, intercept in the affairs of the mortal realm, and I'm tired of dealing with Moboyas. We help but never hear a thank you or see a tribute from our earthly tribes. And more than half of our kin refuse to acknowledge their glorious inheritance. We gave Princess Anais the opportunity and looked at how that turned out. Besides, the curse is just, Jan katu." He stomped down his staff. Atabey looked at me and smiled before glancing over to Grandfather's spirit.

"The boy has a point, Queen mother. The curse was to keep the bloodline pure, to keep the akani from seizing our kin through blood. Punish she who betrays her blood, taking the side of the colonist and a blasphemer against their ancestors. By the laws of the Taino peoples, no Inaru should ever fall for a pale face akani. It is their choice, their chosen fate."

"The way of the Taino is not, nor will it ever be, to live with hate or anger in our sacred hearts. We are people of compassion, gratitude. Have I not taught compassion and understanding to our people? Have we not ascended into a divine power much higher than the hatred we had for the akani? We rely on pure hearts like Dayanara's to teach our living kin who live with hatred in their hearts. We are not dead, nor will ever be. That is because we love. Hate is poison. The hate within them will poison the most admirable part of them; their babies and what's left of the Taino spirit. Our people do not carry hate beyond the realm of the living. We will never forget, but we will forgive. It's in our nature, for **WE ARE NOT** the akani. **Daca, Taino!**"

"**Taino, Daca!**" The ancestors around cheered.

"Perhaps, Mama, there is a lesson to learn within all of this chaos," Guakar admitted, winking at me from afar. My eyes darted once again, for he was too beautiful to consider flirting.

"I will Summon Moboyas myself."

Guakar clapped his hands. Immediately the mystical world around us seemed to go dark, and the thunderstorm clouds and winds that once below us now formed around us.

A clack of destructive lightens enthralled. At the center appeared my rightful father; *Moboyas*, the spirit of nightmares and fear. Spirit of Death, Darkness, and Destruction. He bought along with him the fear you felt as a child, hindering from the darkness under your blanket after a nightmare. The dark creatures of the nighttime, crawling from underneath his cloak. Pale, gray, rough-skinned, with black wavy lengths similar to mine. Tall and ominous, with a bleeding scar over his right eye. Apart from his superiors, he instilled fear and terror in all those around him, including me. He felt dangerous and wild but beautiful, like chaos.

He came forward with an extravagant black and green head-dress. His eyes were of intense honey yellow, and his cloak flowed over his large sharp shoulder blades, green and black. His finger-nails were long and yellow, like his cat-like eyes. He wore a jewelry collection of primarily bones and gold and a green amulet pinned at his chest. He carried a long black staff with a sharpened hook tip in his hand. Sickened, I looked to the ground.

"Why do you call upon me, Supreme elders?" As he tantrum, the rest of his court stood behind him. They were of harsh lessons, sad truths, and fears of unknowing. It was of resentment, mis-fortune, pity, and depression. Emotions that were very natural and real but that were suppressed and abused.

Yocahu suddenly took on a harsh and heavy, hair raising tone,

"It looks like we have something that belongs to you," Moboyas's trailed across the way and fixated on me. *Blood recognizes blood.* I could feel my energy string away from my being. He knew who

I was. There was no resentment. No anger. He smiled at me, all nonchalant. Inviting me in, he softened to my presence.

"Muneca… My broken doll, your beauty has exceeded all in the cosmic universe; never seen in all worlds." It wasn't the reaction I had pictured. I figured he would be more chagrin, hateful, evil. He wasn't violent or frustrated. Yet. Moboyas reached to touch me, but I flinched away from his toxicity. He reeked of death.

"Little bat, why do you come? Is it your birthday already? Was it the wendigo who has brought you?" He patronized me.

"I've come on my own," I admitted faintly.

"Moboyas, our young princess wishes to be with the Tyson boy, and I shall grant her my everlasting blessing." Atabey intercepted.

"What? But it is forbidden. Any union between Taino and akani is an abomination in the eyes of our people. I won't allow history to repeat with my seedling. It would be a dishonor, and it is why I've cursed the Tyson name with the conjured wendigo."

"I love him. I won't let you stop us."

"How could you allow this Queen mother, Atabey? Do you not care of what the Taino people will think?"

"I am the Taino people, and I do so as I want. Their love is unconditional, written in stars, and should be respected more than they hate you carry in your heart for the Akani. Forget that the boy runs blood with the Akani. He also runs blood with one of the oldest tribes we've shared bread with. The Tyson clan has been, for centuries, allies to our peoples. Their ancestors banded to protect and uplift what's left of our kin in this land and beyond. The nothingness has chosen them. Those who can love, appreciate, and respect the Taino spirit have a place among our people, just as other natives have done for us in times of support."

"Dayanara is **MY** creation! She is far too good for a weak Akani spirit warrior. She belongs in this world with us, and I refuse to undo my curse over her living life. It will end, and she will be Zeni." My father was a mirror stimulation of Misael. Hungry for control over me. But I was no one's broken doll, and Atabey would make sure of it. The darkness got thicker. His blood shot eyes reached an explosive red, and the thundering became too loud, terrorizing all who stood around. I tried not looking at him, but Yocahu and Atabey seemed unmoved. Yocahu seemed bored and Atabey impatient. But it was Guakar who arose,

"I've heard enough. It's confession time, so it was I who tricked Cacique Guaybana into sacrificing his sister, just as I tricked Misael into handing over Anais before she had the chance to break her spell. But in my defense, atiao had no business interfering, not to mention the black magic and worship. We honor, not worship. As a result, your seed takes that same fate. But- I have a perfect plan that will fix this. Dayanara **will** have a fair chance to prove her unconditional love. And it will be with me."

"-Excuse me?" Guakar smiled at me and went on,

"Upon returning to the realm of the living, I will follow along and test the lovers. I will try to woe the princess with my charms as she tries to seduce the Cree warrior and revive what's broken. If I deem successful, she will return to this place of peace and reward and be one of my Queens. If she keeps resilient and revives the broken love, her written destiny will alter as she sees fit within her garden with her betrothed, and they shall also have my blessing."

"This sounds too easy." My father complained.

"You will have one chance to challenge the union, after the hour of the taken virginity. If they fail, she becomes my wife."

"I always liked you, Guakar." Moboyas showed gratitude. Stares of mutual agreement locked in a covenant.

"I'll be seeing you soon, my broken doll. Real soon," Moboyas took one harsh glance at me and disappeared into thin air.

"-Look for me in your sweet daydreams..." Guakar blew a condescending kiss my way before he disappeared into nothing. Standing there, Atabey turned to me. She took my hands and closed her eyes as she began to chant in whisper Taino Tongue. Atabey's magic began to pour into my hands like a waterfall. My body soaked in all of her magic. Whatever that I couldn't absorb turned into a solid Pink Larimar amulet, glittering in my hand. Petite like a flower bulb, but with power and protection.

"Take my magic, learn to harness it, and use it wisely. Beware of my alter ego, Guabancex, the spirit of the hurricane. With wraths of infidelity and jealousy, the two will stop at nothing to interfere. Good luck, princess." She kissed me, and I Slept.

Engulfed back into the lagoon, I gasped as I resurfaced. I pulled myself onto the sandy beach and sat for a moment. In my hand, I tightly held onto the glowing pink Larimar amulet. Excited, I looked at my reflection in the water. My eyes glowed rainbow colors of emotion, and my heart sank with relief. For weeks I was frustrated with relearning my gifted magic of Atabey. All the Chronicles and ancient books were no use to me. I studied all day and sometimes all night, but it seemed like I was going nowhere. Lacking progression and achievement, I was beginning to doubt myself.

As I sat by the river, I heard a melody coming from the lagoon one day. I tossed my book aside and followed the pretty song until I found myself staring at my reflection. There seemed to be something in the water. It shined rays like gold. I reached in, and suddenly something pulled me into the water. SPLASH! I swam until I resurfaced, but I was no longer in *my* Garden realm. Honestly, I didn't know where I was, but it felt warm and safe—inviting pink clouds over a magical tropical garden of bright hue colors. Mostly yellow. I was calmly floating in a pond and staring up at a near carbon copy of myself. Only it wasn't me. It was her, *Anais.* She was nearly unconvinced. Confused, I let her help me out of the shallow pond—all around me, a pristine, bright, and mystical rain forest.

"Where am I?"

"You're in *my* garden, and I'm your mother," Young and time-less, she was more beautiful in person. She dressed in red silks, her wrists in chains. I choked up but tried to be as poised as possible. Her hands were soft as she caressed my cheek. Despite the chains, she hugged me tightly, "How is this happening?" I whispered.

"The Zeni's told me that you came to them. Atabey asked me to help you remaster the gifted Magic of Atabey. Don't worry, this place will be safe for now. It was the only way I could see you. Now that you're here, I wish you could stay forever. But I understand how important it is to get back to the living realm. So you will come to me through the lagoon waters every rise of the Taino sun. I will teach you all that I know." I was thankful that my mother had been watching over me this entire time. Every day at noon, I went to her garden through the waters. All she wanted to do was talk, which was okay with me. We had a lifetime to catch up on. All the while, the outside world was passing along.

Winter into Spring.

Anais wanted to know everything about me. So I told her every-thing. My studies. My favorite books, my favorite songs. My love for Shakespeare and track. I told her about everything she missed. We talked about Haven. She told me her side of her love story with Dean and went in-depth about how my uncle betrayed them. I told her about Landon and Haven and how Misael condemned me to my garden. It was after those conversations that she showed me the magic. My mother spent so much time studying and mastering the power of Atabey. I watched my abilities flourish and thrive within my being once again with patience. Better than ever. I felt stronger. I had relearned all the things I used to know and much more. I relearned to grow flowers, trees, fruits, and plants. I learned to create rivers and waterfalls and calm seas and oceans. Make them still. I learned to multiply my creations and help them thrive. She taught me how to create dusk and dawn, rain and winds. I was now an artist. The more I practiced, the better I became. It was not easy, but now I have *ALMOST* mastered it all. But, I had to learn one last thing. And it would be the hardest lesson to learn.

That last day of lessons, my mother brought me a lifeless parrot. My mother laid it before me and whispered, *"revive."* Then, concentrating on her trick, she blew life back into the bird, and it took a breath before it flew off. Amazing. My heart almost stopped at the magic. I needed to learn it. Again she brought another dead parrot and gave me a look to go. I tried and tried, but I couldn't do it. I couldn't concentrate enough and bring forth that energy. Something was pulling my attention from the magic,

"Somethings wrong," Her pond was rippling.

"Atiao…" She said, rushing over to me.

"Atiao… he's looking for you. You have to go-"

"But I haven't mastered the gift of life-"

My mother took my hand and caressed my cheek.

"Meditate, eat well, be thankful, and let your heart guide your powers into a miraculous intention. Dean can help. Don't let Misael or anyone else gets in the way. And don't give up on Haven. Instead, find it within yourself to trust and love each other. Use that love to help bring forth your powers, little one. Tell Dean that I still love him very much. Remind him of my magic Daya."

"I promise." In tears, she hugged me one last time. I kissed her cheek before entering the pond, sinking back into my lagoon.

I jumped out from the lagoon, scaring my uncle half to death. He was searching around the garden for me. Upon meeting his gaze, he looked pretty nervous. God only knows, how many days it's been since the last I've seen him. "-*Jesus*, Daya, there you are. I thought you were lost or worse, dead." My hand slid clear down my face as I climbed out of the lagoon. My uncle was notably looking rough.

"I was just taking a swim." I was all *calm*, walking around with a new poker face. I remembered what my mother had warned, so I played along. My powers were more vital than ever before, and I could do anything I wanted. Of course, I could use my rage to repay my uncle for all he has done, but that would be an easy mistake. I didn't want him to know that I had my powers back.

"What are you doing here?" He looked like he had gotten into a fight. I assumed because of the black eye, cut lip, and broken nose.

"I had to check on you, make sure you were okay. And- it seems like your aunt Charlotte went to the family court and got some papers signed off- I can't keep you hidden anymore. You under-stand that I didn't want to do this to you, right? I had no choice. You wouldn't have survived the winter. You could have put your-self in danger," More or less, he was trying to convince himself.

"Of course. I was out of control. How's Landon?"

"Landon? Well, good. Are you okay?"

Of course, he was all a part of my plan to get out of here.

"-Yeah, just miss him, that's all."

"You're free to see him, that's if you're ready to get out of here?"

I was more than ready to get *the fuck* out of the garden.

And I *ONLY* planned to see Haven.

12

Winter Hibernation: Haven

UNTOUCHED.

The fucking gate was still untouched. It was the 2nd time I checked that morning in this rain. This girl was going to be the death of me. It's been 92 days since Daya disappeared. In more ways than one, her absents has been non-stop gnawing at my brain. I'm going fucking crazy; I can't eat, I can't sleep. Not with her gone. Damn it, Daya, where the hell are you?

I can't get my mind to stop running like a crazy train. How can I? Unfairly for me, my world revolves around Daya. Her delicious magic. What a fucking high. As if I wasn't already off the deep end from the start. Now, I was losing it—a super withdrawal. It felt like falling into a shatter of endless broken mirrors into fucking insanity. I've now hit the edgy bottom, but I still feel like I'm falling into a black hole. Daya was both the antidote and the kryptonite. A contradicting standard but so was her curse. She radiated sex appeal for someone so pure and sweet. Regardless, I needed her more than anything. And that skirt went running off on me. Now I'm constantly anxious as if there were a ticking time bomb over my shoulders. Time was running out. I have to find out where she'd gone to, and I've devoted every waking moment into doing so; after finally waking up from that long ass winter hibernation.

No one ever thinks of one's soul of being a damn prison, but for me, that's how it felt. A place so intimately private, it's the only place you could keep your secrets, your fears, your anxiety. A place you harbor everything you love and cherish. Your memories, and what you hate about yourself. Your ego and inner child. The one place you could hide from the world. The only place that you, and *only you* could ever go. But for me, that wasn't true. Daya had the power to see deep inside me. A scary thought, but I had gotten used to it after that night on her uncle's porch. My dad and the elders warned me of her miraculous powers. They said I'd lose myself in her. Not me, I laughed at them; there's no way she was strong enough to crash into my atmosphere. But she did.

Daya's the most beautiful woman I've ever laid eyes on, and I've traveled to many exotic parts of the world. Jamaica. Cuba. Columbia. Ibiza. Brazil. Bangladesh. Shanghai. I spent summers traveling, and my nomad lifestyle was very fast-paced. I've already been with a handful of beautiful ladies, but nothing impressed me about the female and what they harbored between their legs. Sex. Enticing, of course. But sex never had *true power* over me. I was too powerful, and not one doll was good enough to make me cum. I couldn't fully let IT go. I suppose they were all beautiful but broken; none of them was my other half, so I've never been satisfied. After years of looking for some *superior* emotion, the appetite I had worked up had taken me to some dark places. After a while, I stopped trying to find that. Blue balls are as painful as they say. I learned to enjoy the unsatisfactorily, and I ignored the rest. It gave me a rep, **Hold Up**

Johnny. 'Cuz they always assumed I was a sex addict border lining the edge, or a literal addict, too high and unable to release. I got used to it. I thought, *Fuck it, I'm a man*; I still loved knocking boots.

Daya is a different story. First, the nerves of her, breaking into me like that. I tried to ignore the fact that she was the only girl who could bring me so close without doing much; that night in Dean's truck gave me all the reassurance. Despite that, I honestly loved the girl. Our chemistry was undeniable; She had become my best friend, lover, and teacher. Before her, I knew little about romantic emotions. Spending time with her allowed me to learn to feel love in-depth; I had fallen for everything odd and extraordinary about her unconditionally. I couldn't get enough. I loved watching her, but her perfect ass and tits weren't what turned me on the most; it was her smart mouth. I get turned on by the way she speaks to me. She's so intelligent. So classic. So passionate. I knew she'd do something to me, but I didn't think it would be this bad.

Secondly, when Landon appeared in my visions, I'd thought she made it easy for me to disregard her. I've known about him, and I had to stand by and allow them to fall in love. I partly did it to prove that she meant nothing to me. After all, the elders and Dean claimed they had cured her. Regardless, I'd protect her no matter what. THAT was in MY blood. Not long after, I realized I was secretly falling in love with her—everything from her snoring to her lighthearted chuckles to the beautiful rising morning sparkle in her eyes. I'd be the only one with the power to protect that. Only my father could see how my heart quaked the morning of her birthday. He knew I had one thing in mind. I *had* to check on her.

When Dean hauled us back to Grey Wolf Hollow, my atmosphere was 'annoyingly' reinforced. Extra strength with walls of rude and heedlessness. She wasn't getting into my world. I didn't know Daya yet in real life, and if anyone were doing any worldly penetration, it would be me. Haven Tyson doesn't *'fall in love.'* I'm everything that frustrates a skirt; too proud, sailor's mouth, good looking, demanding. Too headstrong, too stubborn. Too possessive. Too mean. Wild. I was a fucking animal she wouldn't be able to tame.

Lastly, I had no idea there was some fall festival Pow Wow going on that Halloween night. I wasn't aware she'd even be there, especially with Landon's dumb ass. I walked into a trap. This girl stood up, looked me dead into my eyes, and came walking, **NO**- running, deep inside my soul, and she saw *everything*. I haven't had complete control of myself since. She makes me so uneasy. Especially now. I'm sure to hit the brink of murder soon, starting with her damn uncle, who I stalked every day since waking up from hibernation.

I'd been hibernating all winter, and it was long as fuck. So when Dean came to wake me up that first spring morning, he was rightfully pissed the fuck off. Groggy and confused, I rolled over and awoke to my father yelling. At first, I had no idea why he was so mad, but I slowly recalled everything. Charlotte's serum knocked me out the moment Dean injected it. It put me out for months after that date with Daya. Now, she was the first thing on my mind that morning. I felt terrible about what I had done. I scared the living shit out of her, and there Dean was, tearing a new hole in my ass about it: *'Son, you have a hell of a thundering war heading your way. Boy- You need your rest. Boy- You need to mediate. Boy- You better read and eat clean. You better take care of yourself. Drink water. Run.'*

Yeah, fucking right. Beers. Cigarettes. Endless fat Joints.

Pizza. Burgers. Fries. Chemically induced TV dinners. I was stressed. He even found out about the times I skipped out to the strip club; not that it helped me forget the missing Taino Queen, but come on now boobs? Still one of the best things created in life.

I've been a prisoner every winter to my gifts. Even as a cub, hibernation wasn't exactly my favorite thing to do, but it is a crucial part of balancing my power and strength. Hibernating also helped rid the Wendigo spirit inside me. It couldn't attach or host while I was in such a holy slumber. So in the winter, it ran free into the world beyond, and I was free from it. Now that I'm awake, it could come and infect me at any given moment. So I had to keep myself in control. I've been trying to keep myself level-headed, but this particular early spring has been a harsh one. It's bad enough; I'm roaming around stag since Daya. Fucking Daya. I thought she'd fight harder for us, but all she could say was, "*If you can't trust me, I don't know what else to do but to show you,*" Wow. So how I felt didn't matter?

Truthfully, her words hurt, but I wasn't about to force her to love me back. If she wanted Landon, she could be with him as long as she cut me out for good and says it to my face. I can't be angry with her either. I nearly shifted into that fucking thing again and almost killed her in the process. The look in her eyes. It haunts me twice a day. When I wake up and when I go to bed. Regret is a poisonous thing. Regardless, her protection was my sworn duty. It only took two minutes to let the jealousy and rage take control. Still, the effects of my actions continued to linger, and Summer was slowly creeping up on me. If I couldn't pull myself together, the Wendigo could attach its slithering locks around my spine and weigh on my back like a ball and chain until it could consume me.

It was what I had to protect her from; myself. I couldn't fully wrap around the concept because I truly loved her and believed I'd never hurt her. How could I? She gave me purpose. But one ignorant slip from me scarred her for life. What made shit worst was that it was the very last time I had seen her. They told me she disappeared when I woke up. Despite Dean's warning, I went looking until I couldn't anymore. I should have known by the look on Dean's face, but it took me all that first day to realize she was gone. For now, Daya's essence was like the wind, barely here but not completely invisible. For a while, it was enough to lure me back home.

I was losing it. I tried working out my issues at the beginning of spring and jumping into intense exercise programs, but all that energy still couldn't eat through all the anger and despair inside me. I'd run on the treadmill, but then I'd get lost for hours binge running and wear myself out till I'm out like a light. I slept and ate. Charlotte's secret tea recipe kept me somewhat grounded, although it did seem to lift me. It was like a crackhead's melatonin. I didn't care. Without Daya, I had nothing better to do than somber around. Summer was approaching, and still no trace of her.

For now, the garden gates are my favorite place to stalk. Daya's presence radiated there the most. I heard of the Garden's magic. What carries beyond that old white gate. A paradise made from Daya's magic. That wasn't a paradise to me; that was **Heaven**. The elders say I'd never be able to live in that magic because I'm a shifter unless Daya found a way. I could only imagine; naked in a lagoon paradise with the girl of my dreams. I lived in too much envy of what I had but couldn't keep. But it was true what they say; you can't just walk into the Garden Realm, I've tried. So instead, I guarded the gates. I've been here everyday checking, even though my dad specifically warned me to stay away from the Managualt place. Misael had made it clear that he didn't want a fight with Dean or me. *Good idea.*

I always felt like I had to protect Daya from Misael. The Quests always had warnings against him. Misael was a threat to our love, but more importantly, he was a threat to Daya's divine Taino magic given to her by her ancestors. Somehow I got the honor of protecting that divinity within her. I took pride in that, and I saw right through him. The way he looked at me, you just knew he hated me with all the energy inside of him. I knew he would do all that he could to blind her from me. I couldn't let that happen.

It was hard opening her eyes at first. I never put so much effort into wooing a skirt. Usually, they came to me and wilted at my touch, but Daya was excellent at resisting me. Misael did a shit load of damage, especially with his fucking lies. And between his magic and their solid relationship, I could never tell who she truly loved between my brother and me. I had plenty of reasons to hate Misael, but putting me against my blood was a good one. Landon. Misael. I knew one of the two had something to do with her disappearing, but I had no choice but to give them the benefit of the doubt.

When I woke up and left my cave, I was unpleasantly surprised to find Landon upstairs in his *'room'* in *our* house. I know, Fucking ridiculous. Dad's way of welcoming him into the Tyson clan, with bonding time, praises, and gifts. Quite frankly, I was over the bull shit. Seeing Landon **all the time;** now that he moved in with us, it was like seeing red all the fucking time. I hadn't even had a chance to voice an opinion about it when my father made it clear that he wanted to keep the peace in the house. We were *'brothers'* now; no use in fighting over a missing girl. FUCK. THAT.

Daya isn't just some girl; she's my soulmate, and talking to Dean and Jacy about it now was useless. They wouldn't hide how much they loved having Landon around. Dean had always been a fantastic mentor and father; pulling in Landon was easy. With the time lost between the two, it was something they both desperately wanted. But unfortunately for Dean, Misael still has power over Landon, a heavy *fatherly* influence. And even that was evasive because I can't imagine a life without Dean, so I see why Landon held onto Misael. However, there's no comparison; Dean's my hero.

Jacy, on the other hand, was a pure act of betrayal. My big brother was my best friend, my *only* friend. Jacy was the first person I drained my soul to about Daya. The moment I found out about her was the most challenging moment of my life. I was scared, but he was there with me. Jacy, way before Daya, had been the only one to see me lose control, and I nearly killed him too. But, he's forgiven me for my recklessness. I wasn't used to begging him to occupy me.

It was 11 in the morning, and I had run up the mountain twice to check the gate. I've been on a rampage and needed some restraining. So, after another hot shower, I walked into the dark kitchen in a fresh dry pair of running shoes. I was still getting used to the new polished black marble countertops and brand new black appliances. Dean's renovations were fresh and modern but dark and depressing as fuck, like today. Before hibernation, this house was in shambles, but I knew Dean wouldn't stand leaving the house a wreck.

Dean glanced my way as he was brewing a new pot of coffee. Unsurprisingly, Jacy and Landon sat at the table. I couldn't stand the sight of Landon; eating *MY* food, sitting in *MY* chair, and possibly sleeping with *MY* girl. Fuck, I was mad already. *Don't look at him. Just don't.* I snatched a water bottle from the fridge before sitting at the round black table with my brothers. Dad grabbed his newspaper as he sat down with me; he looked like shit, like he had been out all night, again. He was up to something. Weary eyes, and yet they were bright, per usual. I tried to block Landon's stupid ass out.

"So, my precious son, what are your plans today?" I shrugged at his sarcasm. These days Dean disapproved of my daily activities.

"-Because I was thinking, we can go down into your man cave and start the renovations." *Renovations?* What the hell was he talking about? I had no desire to change my bedroom down in the stone basement. Yeah, there was a giant solid hole through the foundation, and I could see the fucking woods. Moss and grass grew like fungus inside, and I slept on an oversized sediment boulder that I, myself, brought in from the woods through the hole. I was used to the outdoors, and I had no desire to change a damn thing about it until Dean joked that I wouldn't be able to get a girl to spend one night with me down there. Dean could have meant Daya. I knew her people found caves sacred, but Daya was too classy for a boulder. It might be all too much for her with the bugs.

"-Ion know-" I said, thinking about it now. Damn it, Daya, why can't you leave my mind alone for five fucking minutes? Why did it even matter what she thought? She wasn't here anyway. It would all be useless if she were just messing with my head. Hiding somewhere that only Landon and Misael know. That would be a special kind of fucked up. I'd never forgiven her, "-Nah fuck it. Leave it how it is. I have plans today anyway. But this kitchen can use some color."

My stomach growled. I reached over and stole two pieces of bacon and some toast off of Landon's plate. We both stared at each other for a moment until he conceded his look. He couldn't size up to me, and he knew it. I was older and bigger than him.

"Plans doing what? Are you stalking Misael Managualt again? Haven, I told you, *please* back off. I'm handling it. You'll fuck it up."

Upon hearing Misael's name, Landon and I exchanged hasty glances. I looked at him, almost begging, 'G*o ahead, baby brother, say something. Please give me a reason to knock that perfect condescending smile,* "If I could, I would. But no one wants to tell me anything." Again I studied my 'brother.' I was looking for clues, but Landon was always solid. So quiet. He almost pitied me in a way.

"She'll turn up; until then, Haven, **DROP IT**." My father closed the newspaper and stood to his feet. Dean was in no mood for my shit today. He made that clear as he left the kitchen, warning me to mind my business and keep away from the Managualt residence.

A couple of hours later, I watched Dean's truck pull out the muddy driveway. Every Tuesday and Thursday afternoon, he was on his way up that mountain to play nice and smile in the enemy's face. I couldn't understand why or even how Dean could keep up the friendship charade for so long, but I had no choice to trust Dean and what he was doing. Besides, I found the loyalty to his old friend beneficial. While they were together, now was the perfect time to search the Managualt house. I turned to Jacy, who was still talking to Landon about video games, "Jace, you're coming with me-"

"Can't- I have things to do, Haven. The Dean needs me to look at some commercial space. But, you know, you should come with us. It will help keep your mind off Daya."

"No, thank you. I need help getting inside Misael's-"

"Haven- I'm not helping you with your teenage obsession."

Teenage obsession? I scoffed at him, "Funny, you never com-plained before, with all the time you spend with Leyla-"

"-What about Leyla?" Landon interfered.

Look at us, a bunch of lapdogs jumping to the Managualt name. The fuck was wrong with us? I couldn't tell you because a moment later, "-Jace, I need your help. I know Misael has her locked up," I was desperate, and I knew Jacy understood how I felt deep down inside. Then, just as he was going to agree, "-Have you ever considered the possibility that maybe all she wanted was to get away from YOU?" Landon just had to open his *damn* mouth. I turned to him, and a frustration rattled inside, knowing I couldn't rightfully toss him across this room without getting in trouble later. Best save Dean the aggravation for a reason worthwhile, despite the sinking feeling I got when his words came out the way they did. Was he telling me to give it up? Maybe they *were* back together.

"If that's the case, how come someone won't just fucking tell me? Are you two back together? What do you know that I don't?"

I grilled Landon in his face. I knew he had to know. Landon and Misael were still two thieving peas in a pod. Yes, Landon is my brother, but I couldn't trust Landon as far as I could throw him.

"For the 10th time *NO*. But Misa says that the last time he saw Daya, she claimed you attacked her in the woods. So, maybe she's just afraid of *YOU, BRO*."

Would it be so terrible if I hit him once?

"-I don't believe that shit. And Daya didn't see me shift, *YOU* dummy. I've been asleep this entire time. There's no way that was me. But she probably hates me. I yelled at her and made her cry," My mind went on reflecting the last few minutes with her in that truck. Her words echoed in my head again. She begged me to trust her. I knew she loved me, but I couldn't trust her. Between her uncle's hexes and that ruthless desire, she was fucking poison for any man that crossed her path. It was easy to distrust her. Even if she was such a good girl, she was always innocent until I came around.

Jacy turned his back to me for the first time. But, of course, this was all Landon's fault. Jacy spent all winter with the enemy, probably listening to him talk about *my girl*. I know I'm annoying, being the younger brother and constantly messing with him, dragging him along on my adventures as my sidekick. Still, I never saw the day he'd turned his back on me, but today, I was on my own.

Dad dragged Misael to *Star's Blanket* for lunch, as I had suspected. Better for me. I'd have more time. I paid Hattie to stall on their lunch for as long as possible as uncle Shane pulled my *Thunderbird* from the garage. I didn't use her much because she was too valuable for me to wear down; Dean helped me fully restore her over the summer. But I needed her to race to the Managualt place. I drove up the mountain as the radio played a song that reminded me of Daya.

Breaking into the Managualt house was a piece of cake. When I was 15, I ended up in Nashville for two weeks, where I learned to pick Motel room locks, so it only took me a few seconds to pop the kitchen side lock open. I slithered my way into the Managualt house. It always smelled so homey here, like cookies and fresh windblown lining. The Managualt's were a neat family, and everything seemed up to par, cleaned, but placed too fucking perfectly. Although these halls felt like they hadn't had much to see lately, it had to be a setup. I couldn't feel Daya running down the hallway or sitting at the kitchen table reading. I couldn't feel her yelling at the bottom of the kitchen steps or gorging on grapes by the fridge. There was no residue of her anywhere. Everything untouched was only collecting dust. The more I felt the absence of her presence, the more it worried me.

Everything's in order, except for the blankets on the couch. And that dusty teacup on the fireplace ledge. I glanced it over. Inside had dried, unknown herbs. When I got closer to the couch, I swear I could almost smell her. Sitting right there, wrapped up in blankets. Crazy how her scent can kick-start my fucking heart. I didn't intend on touching anything, but I grabbed the top blanket and took in her essences; sea salt, coconuts, sweet red hibiscus; I had to find Daya.

I immediately checked the first two doors to the top of the steps. A closet. A Bathroom. The 3rd door on the right just happened to be Misael's room. It wreaked evil and havoc and wallowed in misery and envy. A toxic glow radiated, and not one shred of daylight streamed in. Everything was emerald, satin, and illuminated on an altar. I knew nothing of it except that it radiated wickedness. In the middle was a mason jar. It was tightly closed and had a cloud of thick black dust, seemingly mixed with sparkling ivory glitter. The kind of dust that dead flesh and bones would make with magic. It glowed and sparked a bit. Something wasn't right about it, and that feeling sank in my stomach like an anchor. *WHAT THE FUCK- is going on?* Caught off guard, I stepped back and noticed the book. Pages left exposed; I knew my phone would come in handy at some point. So I started snapping pictures of everything.

FRANTICALLY SWIPES ALL NOTIFICATIONS~
The books. (SNAP SNAP)
The offerings. (SNAP SNAP)
The weird jar. (SNAP SNAP)

All of this felt wrong. Thinking of what harm Misael could have brought to Daya made me too angry to stand there any longer. I slammed his bedroom door, purposely taking it off the hinges. The second door on the right had LEYLA on it, so I skipped it. But the last door on the left had Daya's name on it. If I'm lucky enough, I might find her safely on the other side. I prayed for it as I swiftly popped the lock, but I found nothing but a bright baby blue room.

I shut the door behind me because I wanted to privately wallow in Daya's essence. Instead, it sent shivers that rang from my spine and into my core, as heavy as cathedral bells. I could feel my heart get antsy, provoked like a bear in a cage. My fingers stubbed over her books, dusty but sitting neatly on her neat desk. *King Lear.* A picture of her at a track meet pinned to her busy schedule. I smiled when I came across her history notebook and saw hearts over my name. She was such a skirt; I was proud of her. I proceeded to search every part of the room for clues. I didn't want to get caught up in my girl's underwear drawer, so I avoided it. I had no reason to be curious because I kept my 'lucky token' underneath my pillow. I felt like such an asshole that I stole them right off of her—premeditated because my stupid ego couldn't bear to leave her without them, as if it proved anything. I let Landon get inside my head. She hated that.

I finally stumbled over her most private of things, her bed. Messy and undone, as if she had gotten out of bed only hours ago, I gave in and found myself trying to fit into the small imprint that her body left behind. My long legs hung off the bed at the knees, and I had no room to turn over entirely, or I'd be on the floor. Still, I stretched my arms out over my head, and I could almost feel her tossing and turning on top of me. I missed her. And I was too angry to admit that I was hurting heavily for the skirt. I closed my eyes, pretending she was still there with me. I induced myself to where her body once laid. Her essence left sparks that flicked off my skin. I thought of her and hoped she'd come back.

'Where the fuck are you, Daya?'

As I had laid there, I conjured up a childhood memory of her at Charlotte's cabin. Daya opened the back fly door, giggling before she ran off inside. "-Come out and play Daya," I said before I chased her around like an incompetent kitten. I scooped her under my arm and carried her right out that door, "Show me a trick!" I demanded. She didn't smile at me, but instead, she rolled her eyes. She's always had that sharpness in her eyes. It was clear she didn't want to play. Daya complained, so I teased her. I ripped a dandelion from the ground and put it up to her face like a hostage, "-Mama had a baby, and its head popped off." My thumb flicked the dandelion head, detaching the flower from its stem. It shimmers to the ground in two. Unsurprisingly, she wept right before she knocked me to the ground. For me, it was worth the fall. I watched her as she picked up the broken stem and its flower bud, and she mended the flower back to life in her magical hands. She poetically stuck the flower back into the ground, and it grew, along with new budding flowers. *"-I won't ever play with you if you hurt another flower,"* she warned.

My heart was healing from the thought of how we affixed so perfectly until the screeching halt of a truck ripped my thoughts away. **FUCK.** My eyes widened, and I jumped up from the bed and to the window; Misael was home. I was too big to sneak through these tiny halls; the Managualt's were small people. I'll get caught for sure. The window was my only escape, and it had to be now, so I popped the window open and stretched it as far as it could open. I did my best to squeeze through that small window. I made so much damn noise; I was cringing on the inside. My heart was in my throat, and I almost broke out, cussing from the anxiety of trying to fit myself through that tiny ass window. I had no time to close it either; I could see the doorknob turn. I pulled away from the window and skidded down the roof. I hopped down to the ground effortlessly and looked for cover in nearby bushes. For a few long seconds, I could feel Misael staring out the window from above me.

I gave it a minute before darting into the woods. I ran behind the bushes and shrubs where I had left the Thunderbird. I sped out that, *not so useless,* back road, smoothly skimming down the curves of the mountain, and yet, I happened to pass Dean driving UP the hill.

The look on his face said everything—**cold-busted.**

"What did I tell you? Why don't you listen? You're going to get killed!" At least I'm prepared for it. Dean knew better than anyone else; I DON'T CARE. Daya is my purpose. I'll follow where she goes.

Charlotte's place was the only place I could go to from there. Charlotte and Dean grew up together, and our families were close. I've always known Charlotte as my aunt, and she was always there to help—most times, more willingly than Dean. So I busted into her house without even thinking and ran right into Leyla. Her gorgeous eyes jumped me, "-Where's your mom?" I shouted.

"Calm down," *SPIT IT OUT, but don't sound crazy;*

"-I broke into your house, and I think your dad hurt Daya-"

I said it too crazy. I was freaking the fuck out, and it came out too fast, too paranoid, too weird. Leyla stared at me, confused, and could only say, *"You broke into my house?"* ~That was all she could say? Knowing Daya is missing? Daya could be trapped, dead, hurt somewhere, and that's ALL Leyla could say?

"FUCK-" I steamed, trapped in frustration.

"-I don't care if you did, Haven. I want Daya home just as much as you, but I haven't been allowed to my dad's. What did you find?"

"-How Taino are you?" She crossed her arms, offended.

"I'm very Puertorican and very proud; I know my stuff."

"Fucking A... tell me what's going on here?" Unlocking my phone, I began to show her a slide show of all the pictures I took at the house. Leyla took the phone and analyzed the photos. I watched her solid pretty face wrinkle up. She seemed horrified as she sat down on the couch. I followed her, "My father must have convinced her to drink it. See, the tea was a love potion used to destroy soul connections. And that jar has her Zeni powers."

I've grown impatient. But not soon enough.

Daya could be gone for good. Daya could be dead. I was pushed into a vexation beyond passionate rage, into oblivion of psychosis, and I wasn't sure who I should hate more—Misael or myself. Yes, I was that vexed. One thing was for sure; Misael was going to die. I didn't say two words to Leyla before storming into the rain. I drove up the mountain again. Coincidentally, I passed my father a second time while speeding up there. This time I didn't look at him. I couldn't stand for any *'outside influence.'* Not while there's one thing on my mind. But all that rushing was for nothing. Misael was gone. But that was alright because I knew where he would go hiding.

I whipped my car into the Managualt Lumber Co. Warehouse, screeching and skidding my tires recklessly like a warning alarm. No more fucking games. I was ultimately out of thought when my body started to convulse. In comes that bone-breaking sound. My body was trying to shift but couldn't. It's never happened this way. Probably because I never tried forcing out so much pain and sorrow. I couldn't willingly turn into the Wendigo. It had to be because of Daya. Her voice ringing in my ears, asking me to be kind; here she goes intercepting again. Her love was constantly fueling this passion within me. I could control it, but I didn't want to. I wanted it to run free, despite the pressuring pain holding me hostage. I tried to let the allusive beast inside consume me. I felt powerful. I slammed the metal door at the loading dock, leaving a loud echo. I knew he could hear me coming, and I found him in his office, rummaging through his desk. "Misael? Where is Daya?" I harbored in the shadows.

"Haven-" I immediately took him into my hands and tossed him against the wall without warning. His body crashed into his desk; papers and some other shit went flying. I drew close to him as he was cowardly defenseless in the corner, "-You have this wrong."

I took him with one hand, "Where is she, Misael?"

"-I don't know, I swear. I-I found her right outside the garden trail in bad shape, claiming you were trying to kill her. By the morning, she was gone. No explanation. I haven't seen her since. I swear." He was trembling under my grip. I didn't want to believe it, but it was all beginning to make sense now. The Wendigo might have gone after Daya while hibernating. It flourished in the winter and could have been lurking. Yet, there were some unanswered questions. So, I pinned him up against the wall like a butterfly,

"What was the tea for?"

"I'm not sure," I growled, unsatisfied with that answer. "-She wanted her old life back; She threatened to give up her powers and run away. It was the last thing she talked about before asking about Landon. She was wearing his ring."

"-Bull shit, I saw Landon this morning. He wouldn't lie."

"You think so, Haven? Because I'm not so sure. He spent two great years with her and only a few months shy of getting that chastity key until you ruined it. They were supposed to get married;

would you give that up?" Fuck. Misael was right. Was this all a game to them? Could Dayanara be more or less angry with me to the point of fucking with my head? As I held Misael by the throat, her voice echoed, *"I won't play with you if you hurt another flower!"*

Shit- she's in my headspace again. My power began to fade, and Misael felt heavy in my hands. An agitated growl warned me from behind. I looked over my shoulder, and sure enough, a giant gray wolf stood at the door frame, snarling at me. Great. I dropped Misael to the ground; I had to get home before Dean.

I busted into his room swinging like a Louie slugger, destroying all of his mounted trophies and awards. Landon had a severe death wish lying to my face. Finally, I have had enough of fighting my urges to kick his ass. I grabbed him from his bed and tossed him to one side of the room. Everything was in chaos in the corner, except Landon. You could tell he was a Tyson; he was gleaming heavy. Poised, he stood up, undamaged and ready to fight. Hesitating to hit him, I noticed Daya's ring dangling from his gold chain.

"-What the hell is your problem?"

"... He lied to me." Suddenly I was locked into my father's arms. I thought I had gained enough time between Dean. It didn't matter how much power the Great Spirits gave me. My father was no match for me in any life. **"-GO TO YOUR ROOM, HAVEN!"**

I couldn't stop staring at her now. Confined to my den, I was stuck on stupid admiring the picture of her on my phone. I wanted to erase the image, but I couldn't get myself to do it. No wonder people hated these things. Finally, I tossed the phone aside; I couldn't deny the erection I got from staring. Looking up at my collection of Fender and Gibson mounted across the wall, I wanted my mind to get away from the idea of Daya somehow. I had no choice. My Taino Queen wanted nothing to do with me. I had to accept it. Damn, it's all my fault. I was rude, reckless, possessive, and jealous. I should have left my mouth shut, but the talk with Misael left me insecure. I should have trusted her. My thoughts dispersed when Dean came trampling down the steps. I couldn't bring myself to look at him, "Look, dad- I'm sorry-"

"-Haven, please, you're not helping the situation. I told you Charlotte is handling it. You're going to ruin everything by not laying low. Daya could be in danger now that you're out here breaking into Misael's house, attacking him at his workplace, and attacking your brother."

"He's not my brother."

"Like it or not, Haven, he's your blood-"

"He will never be a Tyson."

"Landon is a Tyson. More than you're acting right the hell now. What the hell is it with you? Why are you so threatened, Haven? Everyone knows Daya doesn't love Landon."

"She can if she decides to change that."

"You're overthinking this. You can trust Daya. -Haven, you can't let Misael trick you against your brother. All this drama is going to distract you, and soon enough, you'll be going against your instincts," He rambled on, but I didn't hear a thing.

"-Dad... where is she?" I clenched onto my throbbing heart. How could this pain be more severe than any physical pain I've ever had? The cracking of bone marrow couldn't compare to the despair of snapping heartstrings. Daya was the antidote. I was hopeless. I haven't cried many times in my life, but I was crumbling under pressure. Dean knew it. He sighed long and hard, unsure of what to say.

"- Haven, trust me. I've asked the same questions. Misael is the only one who knows, and there's no way we will get her back showing up at his place of business like that. It will help if you rein yourself in a little. It's spring Haven; camping season. The weather will be nice for the next few weeks, why don't you get out of town for a week or two? Go on a Quest so you can get some answers." I hated how he always made sense. He was right; I was able to see Daya through Quests. Maybe my father was on to something.

I packed up my Thunderbird, I needed to see *her* again. I needed an explanation, even if it was from a vivid illusion. I'm an asshole for yelling; I'm a douche for stealing her lucky token; and fucking stupid for breaking up with her. I don't care. I still needed a reason why. Daya could be with Landon if she wanted, but I wouldn't make it easy for her. I wasn't about to let her walk away from me either. Not before explaining herself. She wasn't about to abandon me; I was going to find her. I was gone for three weeks. I indulged myself in that Quest, and when I came out of it, I was still confused about **"us,"** but I was confident that she was safe and sound.

The "*Welcome to Grey Wolf Hollow*" sign was like a revolving door, as I returned to town. It felt different. It was scorching hot and smelled of bloomed flowers, fresh rain, and enriched forest soil. My senses immediately high lighting on a forest trail; I already had a good feeling about this. I could feel her again and even smell her. She was home, and that was the motivation behind my smile as I drove through the absorbed village. The town was steadily rocking, with many locals doing their daily business. Girls in skirts every-where made me think of Daya in a dress. Fuck, I'm not prepared. It's so hot, and here I am, catching a rise from my perverted thoughts. I was practically stuck on stupid with a hard-on at a red light on my way to Dean's. As the light turned green, I noticed the book store Daya goes into countless times. Daya loved Shakespeare. *Huh.* Trash, but fuck it. *My Queen* needs a welcome home gift.

13

Where have YOU been?

It was a different season;
There are no banks of snow or icicles, no icy roads. It was warm outside, and flowers had already bloomed. Trees were full of green leaves and blooming buds. Spring vegetables swooned the backyard; everything was colorful once again. At night the moon was different, and so was the taste of the air. I had missed this so much, and Summer Solace was indeed upon us. I could feel it in my blood.

Charlotte told everyone I was *'missing.'* The Family courts ultimately scared Misael enough to release me, and he had to prove I was still alive. Now I was free to do as I pleased, as long as I kept quiet about the *'held against my will'* part. Misael had no choice but to comply with my wishes. Yet, he continued to play the nice guy, and I was beginning to see why, as Leyla rambled on. "-Girl, your man Haven came busting in the warehouse, and he broke dad's nose. Anyway, we figured out you were in the garden."

"-Where is he?" I asked right away.

"Honey, Haven left town for a couple of weeks. Dean wants his family together, so he invited Landon to move in, and well, you know, Haven. He can be a little precarious. He's still struggling with the same issues he had when you disappeared. So Dean sent him out of the house to clear his mind. He needs to drain that out of his system before you two can reunite. For your sake, you get that right?"

Are you kidding me? Hell no, I don't get it. Nearly months apart and he was still acting immaturely. Haven always seemed to get me frustrated when I couldn't just confront him. And in all honesty, I missed him. Now he was gone, doing God knows what. I crossed my arms and looked out the window. Just wait till he comes home.

Slowly things began to fall back into place, and soon, it was all routine again—even the nightmares. At first, it was brutal, even with all the shaman care from Dean and Charlotte. I had forgotten how exhilarating and painful the fevers were, but each night they had simmered down more, and now they were lacking. Bearable. I spent all my time with Leyla. I needed to keep my mind off Haven, and she was a great distraction. It was during these times that I noticed the change in her. Leyla seemed different, in a good way. She was happier, glowing, almost in a world of her own. She was always perfectly groomed and tailored, and now she was careless of all that. She let go of that standard and allowed herself to glow naturally. She was much more gorgeous this way. I knew a guy had something to do with it because she was also disappearing a lot more often. After dinner, she'd usually use the forest trails as an excuse. I knew better. Leyla doesn't jog regularly, and she dislikes the woods, especially when nearing nighttime.

Her eyes glowed with a new craving for the world. I suspected that with her birthday coming, so was the same burst of love, sex, and desire, like I had. Leyla carried the bloodline, so she had to be cursed. She was always a lot more into dating but never had any luck. No one's ever stuck around after realizing that she isn't going to give up the goods. She walked around like a hopeless romantic, monotone zombie, just like I was before my 18 birthday. Now things were slowly changing inside her, and I could see it. It made me nervous for her summer birthday, which she often raved about now as if she had some secret plan for that day. When I looked at Charlotte, I saw the same nervousness.

As for school, there was only a couple of weeks left before finals and Graduation. I've missed everything else in between, and that included Prom and track season. To make it worse, everyone had heard that I 'ran away, and I was all that everyone could talk about for the first few days. It's been a week and, I haven't bumped into Landon or any Tyson brother. Maybe they were avoiding me.

I hadn't expected to see Landon in the library on Tuesday, but there he stood. He was sitting at *our* corner table. He saw me the minute I walked in as if he was expecting me to walk through that door. But, something was wildly different about him too. The way he was carrying himself. Landon has always been confident and charming in his own right. In a *teen dream; popular jock,* kind of way. But *this* was very different—a bad boy. A go-getter, *'bow down to me,* spirit. He was nearly glowing in front of me with his perfect smile. Eyes wild, checking me out. Ignore him, I thought.

Charlotte says that since Landon moved in with Dean, Dean and Misael have been in a passive-aggressive war over him. I knew Landon must have felt some kind of unyielding power. He's always had such mixed feelings about lacking a father figure in this life. Now he had two fighting for him. Misael was all that Landon knew up until Dean came in the picture. I'd hope for Landon's sake that he would come to see who Misael was, a master manipulator. But from what I understood, Misael was still Landon's favorite. It was dumb even to consider. Leyla says Dean favored Haven too much, which wasn't acceptable for Landon. Unfortunately, it looked like Landon was still hanging on to Misael's bullshit. A spell. I know one when I see one. I could tell he was in deep by how he watched me from afar. It was reckless, and he seemed like he was ready for a go-again. He didn't wait long to approach me.

"-Too good to hang out with us?"

I slowly looked up at him. I wasn't expecting him to grasp my attention so suddenly. His eyes were different. Not like the emerald that he radiated under Misael. No way. They were a clash of aubergine and azure skies, with ivory clouds and bits of heliotrope. They were so sexy. Sexy enough to make me squirm around a bit, and he noticed. And then he smirked and winked at me like he never smirked before, and it stung me. 'G.U.A.K.A.R.?' I said so faintly. He smiled, confirming my suspicions as he winked and bit his lip. It was true—Guakar in Landon's body. Poor Landon was just everyone's G.O.A.T. mule. I looked down fast, tucked my hair behind my ear, and glanced away. "Why him? Out of all the people?"

"I couldn't resist myself. Besides, I wouldn't be who I am if I didn't. I know it's not the same sexy Taino physique you've got to know in *Turey,* my love, but this body will do til WE get back. You seem attracted to it anyway, for some odd reason."

Odd was right. And I couldn't stop staring either. He was muscular, and his entire aura yelled seduction, but those eyes were indeed hypnotizing. Finally, he smiled slyly, "I think I'm turning you on."

"- I'd rather be alone." I swallowed the lie.

"Don't you think you've done enough of that?"

He pulled out a chair and spun it 180 before taking a seat.

"I-I have a Government exam tomorrow."

"You're so smart. It's so sexy. It wouldn't hurt to get to know me, Daya." My cheeks rushed rose, and my eyes wandered.

"I rather not." I was honest. He sucked his teeth.

"What can I do to make you reconsider? Anything, I'll *do* it."

He needed to be tamed before I slipped into the same emotions.

"Gua- Landon, we've been over this. You know I love your brother. We shouldn't even be having this conversation."

"I know. But I'm in love with you, Daya. I know you ended things last fall but, I don't know. I still want you, and I'm willing to prove it." He reached over and lightly pinched my arm as I restrained the urge to look at him. I was nearly choking. How could he be this brilliant? I still loved Haven, but he was making me think twice. Despite him, I found the will to cut it off.

"I don't know what to tell you, Landon? I Love Haven."

My words made *Landon's* eyes light up.

"Why are you chasing that loser? Granted, he has Tyson blood, but he is still part akani. He has nothing good to offer you. You're too good for him. A woman like you deserve to be with a real nitayno, a true Cacique. Instead, he's going to destroy you and get you killed if he's not careful, princess."

"-Haven loves me. He won't give up. He'll be back." I tried forcing myself to believe the words. Landon dropped his head condescendingly and let out a small laugh. When he looked at me, his eyes were intense. He sucked me right into them.

"I wouldn't be too sure, Daya. When he left, he was over it. He said, *'messy ass curse,'* in his own words. He claims to be going camping, but I think he's just running away, Daya. Haven is doing what Misael said he would do; coward and run away. Why? Because he can't deal with the pressure. He's scared, and he can't handle being overpowered by something as beautiful and wild as you, just like akani. Nothing, not even fear, could ever make me abandon you, Daya. You are my land; you mean that much to me. Haven is just an immature kid. It's that same immaturity that will ruin whatever future you choose. He's selfish, and he only cares about himself and how he feels. I don't think I have to remind you how large his appetite can be. I wouldn't be surprised if he went off with one of his *'skirts'* on some Quest to find a way to relinquish his ties with you-"

"-Shut the fuck up!" I snapped, right in the middle of the library, "He's coming back," I looked at him sternly, and my heart cracked. Damn it. He made so much sense. With all the insecurities Haven has, not to mention that we were still technically broken up, I wouldn't run the idea past him. He was super mad that last night we were together. Add that to whatever pissed him off enough to leave in the first place. Maybe he has given up completely. But I couldn't trust that from 'Landon.' And I couldn't let 'Landon' know he was getting to me. So I pushed the negative aside and looked at him rudely. Landon nodded and withdrew, standing up from his seat.

"-But if he doesn't? I can give you all that you desire too." I looked away from him. He was trying to hypnotize me.

"I rather take my chances." I gathered my books.

"I'll be here waiting, beautiful... You should come over to Dean's. You know I'm staying there now. Dean seems cool. Anyway, I'll be home if you want to hang."

"Sorry, I have plans. But thanks anyway."

"-Daya, I'd hate to see Haven break your heart,"

I stood up at his eye level, and we stared intensely. The sexual tension between us was ridiculously thick, and I began to blame myself for it. I looked away from him. Feeling the way he was yearning for me. "-I'll see you around, Landon," and I left.

I still had those lusty nightmares. And it was those confusing lusty dreams that fed my treacherous desires. The new magic that grew in me was much more potent, enticing, and incredibly rich. I was vibrant, but I was also very sexually unhinged and frustrated. Not to mention that growing desire in my pit to engulf Guakar's wandering soul. I was near to starving, waiting for Haven to show.

Things weren't any easier with 'Landon' trying to hang around me all the time. Thanks to Misael, he always knew where to find me. He followed me to the book store enough times to get the *'they're back together'* rumor flying. I found myself constantly denying him. Guakar's personality with Landon's physique was tempting. I was worried about how long I would last, knowing Haven was out there and could do whatever he desired. I was beginning to lose hope. Where the hell was he? Haven was wasting *OUR* time. Now I'm getting impatient. Is he coming home soon? I needed to find out. I needed to go to the source.

On Saturday, I got invited to Dean's house. He came over asking to borrow me that afternoon for a home decorating project. I didn't mind. I loved hearing the stories about my mother and how they fell in love. I thought spending time at his house would be great, especially since I'd hoped to find Haven there. So, with a brutal sun shining, I made my way to the Tyson home, not too far from the Res. It was a beautiful day to show off my powers. It was hot, so I wore cutoff shorts with hiking boots and a white bandeau crop top, showcasing a pink Larimar set of waist beads.

The Tyson's fort hid deep in the back forests of Grey Wolf Hollow. When I was nearly only down the dirt road from it, I was startled by something lurking in the woods. That same colossal bear that always seems to be lurking around. Even though it almost ate my face off, it was always friendly. But this time, strangely, it stared at me from a distance, startled. It watched me for a long moment before he went hauling in the other direction as fast as he could. By the time I tried to run and catch up to the bear, he was gone.

"-You wouldn't believe what I saw," I walked into the living room at the Tyson house, where Dean and Jacy were sitting around reading. The Tyson home was huge and newly renovated, large enough for four grown athletes. Aside from the beautiful displays of their Native culture, it was a man's cave—a hunting cabin. A girl can never possibly come in here and think it's *cute.* Except I loved it.

"Trust me, can't be half as bad as the things I've seen living with three boys... what did you see?"

"Well, I keep bumping into this bear. But like, gigantic."

Dean was curious, closing his book and leaning forward.

"What kind of bear?"

"Brown bear, I think... but with its size, it could easily be a brown-colored polar bear." Dean chuckled at me in disbelief.

"Maybe you should stop approaching that bear and get some bear repellent." Jacy joked.

"... Funny. You shouldn't harm animals. The bear never hurt me at all. Not once in our many encounters."

"Many encounters?" Dean shot an under glare at his son.

Dean wouldn't wallow in the mystery of the bear but instead brushed it off and offered a tour of their new home, which I agreed to as I paced around the space of their living room. Pictures of Jacy and Haven everywhere. Certificates and achievement awards. Trophies and cute class photos. There were even some of Landon now. It seemed like Dean was trying to catch up on Landon's life, showcasing pictures and certificates he must have got from Caroline. It would be my favorite room in the house. It's the only room I could see Haven, even if it was only photos.

Dean never showed me Haven's room during the grand tour, but I had gotten familiar with all the other parts of their house. Jacy loved up high, so his room was on the 2nd floor across Dean's bedroom. It was nearly a library with a bed, I thought. Books ruled the walls, and his ceiling was all retractable glass windows so you could see perfectly into the forest, and you felt like you were outside when the windows were open. Jacy had been in the army. He bared the metals of a veteran, his bed made neatly, and tags dangled from his dresser. His decor was wood and green. It was beautiful.

Landon, as I have always known him, has always liked bottom. His room was 1st floor, right across from the living room. Even though it was his room at Dean's house, it wasn't far off from his old bedroom at Caroline's. All blue, clean and neat. So neat, I used to think he was O.C.D. It smelled of his expensive cologne, musk, and pure linen. Sports medals and achievement certificates crowded the walls. He could be so vain sometimes. He even kept the same blue blankets and lining stretched over his bed that I had spent many make-out sessions rolling around on; in the past. His room was the only one that had a side door that led right out to the horse barn Dean was beginning to build. Funny, I didn't know they had horses.

I wanted to see Haven's room, but I didn't want to push my luck asking. Although it would be great if I could smell one of his tee shirts, or see what book he's reading, and check out his annoying playlist. Lay down in his bed, where his body has been, and feel his essence. But, for now, all I had was his photo's on the wall that I stared despairingly at until Dean cleared his throat, pulling my attention away from Haven's most recent picture on a motorcycle.

"-He's incredibly foolish," I couldn't agree more, "But I know my son… he'll come back when he's ready."

We worked in the kitchen for hours, painting the pale, lifeless walls to sunshine yellow. A little bright for my taste, but Dean stuck by it. Dean reflected on the love he and Anais once had and told many kitchen stories. From her delicious recipes to stories of kitchen experiments with medicinal herbs. You could tell he was still so madly in love with her. The way he talked about her was as if he had met her for the first time, passionate and excited. He wasn't afraid to admit how much he cared for her. That was honesty that Haven lacked with me. But per usual, Dean had Haven's back, "-I know what it's like for him... Haven never expected to fall in love. Neither did I; Nor do I ever expect to ever again."

"-Anais made me promise to tell you that she still loves you, and she wanted me to remind you of her magic." Dean looked at me with attentiveness in his eyes. Then, for a moment, he stood quietly, taking it in. He seemed to be relieved but sad at the same time, "Show me what you got, kid." I smiled.

Pulling away from them, I stole a token leaf from a flower soaked in a vase on the island counter. I pinned the leaf on the wall before me with my boney finger and concentrated. Slowly, roots sprouted from the leaf-ling. The seeds grew more vines, climbing all over the freshly painted walls, perfect and natural. Then, like a barrel of snakes, bright yellow Canaria buds and thick green vines ravished the walls and ceiling above. Hanging plants formed. Moss grew. Critters were born. Ladybugs and butterflies. The kitchen was now a beautiful, lively greenhouse. Dean and Jacy were both impressed.

"This is amazing. You should continue to practice and harness the power. Trust me. You're going to need all the support to master revival." Dean's melancholic energy caused Jacy and me to look at each other apprehensively. At the same time, Dean's cell phone went off. He answered it with wary caution, slowly stepping away from Jacy and me, despite how suspicious it already seemed.

"Hey kid, you're feeling better? -What? Now- don't go jumping to conclusions, do you think that's- of course, he has to stay -" Dean's tone was reaching a faint whisper when he left the kitchen, pulling along that sadness. As always, Jacy didn't look too happy about getting stuck with me. I helped him with the mess, and even so, the silence was stinging, and I couldn't stand through it,

"-I'm sorry." Jacy looked with tired eyes.

"My father is still in love with Anais. With that comes a lot of regrets. Regrets he reflects onto Haven. Regret is a fucked feeling to carry all your life, Daya. I know it's not easy for him to be back here. All he wants is for Haven to do the right thing. Clearly, as always, Haven is doing his '*own*' thing. Look, I know it's not your fault. I can't blame you. But please don't keep dragging my family." Jacy walked out of the kitchen before I could respond.

Left alone, I stood there over the sink, rinsing away bright yellow paint. I didn't realize how invested Dean seemed to be in helping Haven; or how much more he was doing it for Anais. Dean needed this not only for his son but for himself too. So many hearts at play. Everyone else seemed to grow tired, waiting on Haven.

My thoughts suddenly dispersed. 'Landon' was posing at the door frame shirtless. Sweat storming down his steamed body, he stood there huffing and puffing, strolling in wholly elevated.

HERE WE GO, I thought. I dried my hands with a kitchen towel, looking for a quick exit. I haven't been able to stand 2 minutes alone with the kid in his condition. That glittering in his eyes was too strong; I knew he was here to mess with me.

"Waiting for me, beautiful?"

Already he made me giggle, "Yeah, right… you wish."

He came in close with the heartthrob vibe in his eyes. Now I was nervously avoiding his stare. His sex appeal has been relentless, biting away at me like piranhas. I've been trying to keep my distance, but he was sure to show up anywhere I was with the same intentions. His over-flirtatiousness has been getting on my last nerve.

"Looks like summers here, babe. Soon you and I will be nearly *naked*, swimming in the river, down by the launch again. Remember those hot summer days tubing? That summer night up Wolf Cliff, I held you under the stars, rolling around on a blanket. Remember how I kissed you in the grass? Can you imagine how *ALL* of that is going to feel now?" I can feel the rise he was pulling from my bones, tingling inside me. I didn't mean it, but my eyes closed, and the memories rolled in. Fuck. I rolled my eyes and shook it all out of my head, trying to keep the memories in the closet. Inside I had wished he would just give it up already. *Instead,* he checked himself a smile and came closer. "Last day of school is on Monday. Let's skip the party at Hector's and go somewhere we can be *alone.*"

"-Sorry, Landon, but I'm **still** not interested."

"I think your lying,"

"Trust me. I wish I weren't. I can't stand the way I'm feeling."

It was truthful enough to get Landon to huff a frustrated exhale.

"Tell me, Inaru, what's so special about him? Why not me?"

"Why not you? Because I barely know you for one. And you're super charming, but you're smug and self-absorbed. You're more like the Tyson brothers than I realized, and honestly, there's a feeling I get that keeps me on my toes with you. Anxiety. Like I can't be myself. -Haven is comforting. Euphoric. I can be who I am and never have to question whether or not he loves me. He might be reckless, but he's honest and passionate. He has a good heart and good intentions. I feel it in his aura. For a girl whose heart has always felt numb, that feel's real enough for me."

"You're an innocent young one. You trust blindly and forgive loosely. But it's driven by ruthless desires. How careless are you willing to be for the akani? Would you risk it all?"

'Landon' turned around and walked out the kitchen, making his way to the front deck. I stood there until finally, I gave in to the urge to check on him. I followed him to where he sat swinging in a patio love seat. Sipping on a cold bottle of water, he didn't even look at me when I sat down next to him.

"You're right. I'm not thinking about the consequences if anyone else gets hurt. But love is reckless, and I trust in Haven, and he makes me trust myself. My whole life, the closest people to me, have lied and hurt me the most. So what's the risk of trusting a stranger whose only ulterior motive is to love me?"

"Because Daya, it will never be enough. The akani wants more. You're a woman. Sacred, beautiful, and loved by all creation because you are a source of creation. The akani doesn't understand that concept. They disgraced themselves, treating our women so horrifically after killing us off like animals; how can you forgive?"

"It's the only way our people can heal. It's up to the nothingness and time to cast judgment, not I. We heal and learn to understand so that the akani will learn and understand how terrible it was to act out of fear, lust, and greed. That is our karma. Maybe our only job is to forgive and find the peace within ourselves to let go. What we can fix and heal right now is our priority. Our peoples are still here, living within us, and that's important." I kicked my legs up onto the deck railing in front of us. He stared at me with hungry honey eyes.

"I'm mesmerized by you Daya, can't say I don't like it."

My lips curled. Suddenly I wasn't prepared to feel this way. I inhaled slowly, and he looked into my eyes. Those daunting skies appeared again like crashing amethyst and violet waves. I was yet again lost in them for a moment.

"You should think about being my Queen, Dayanara."

He reached over and touched my knee. I was falling into his will.

In the clearing distance, I could hear a buzzing sound of a car engine approaching. While hypnotized by ' Landon, 'I wasn't paying much attention to it until it turned into the riffing sound of *Ozzy Osbourne's 'Crazy Train.'* Landon and I looked at the car coming in fast into the driveway between Dean's new truck and Jacy's jeep. A beautiful black 1962 Thunder Bird, restored with a fresh coat of gleaming black paint and illegally dark tinted windows. The driver's door swung open, and HE climbed out. ***Haven.*** Like a ghost from one of my wet dreams, his eyes fixated on me so suddenly. Gasped in awe, I lunged forward in my seat, nearly falling over my clumsy knees. But, of course, Haven was livid. Super mad, and I can see it in his body language. Landon and I stood up, watching Haven walk to the tinted passenger door. It was a chick. He was opening the door for another FUCKING female. Was he crazy? Who the hell was this girl? I felt my blood rush like river water after a storm underneath my hot skin, and I think Landon had to help me keep my balance when I realized that the female was *Seneca.* That bitch.

"-What the hell are you doing here? I didn't know you were back in town-" Landon had addressed Haven first, even before he came near the deck steps. Haven wasn't at all intimidated by his younger brother. He was more worried about me standing there;

"-You thought I had left for good? Is that why she's here? What are you doing here, Daya?" Haven addressed me, his eyes grazing past mine. I choked up on the words I would use to argue and had nothing to say. I was still confused that Seneca had come out from his car with him. MY man. But there wasn't much I could do. He technically broke up with me. Now he was with *her,* and she came out of the car so happy and bubbly. As if she didn't even know I dated him. The jealously crawled under my skin like how frogs pop from the ground during a storm.

"Why? I know Landon lives here now, but I didn't know you two would be hanging out *here-* of all places." Haven complained more. I took a deep breath that everyone noticed. ***Do I hit him now? Or give it a second?*** I thought. As I flexed to swing, Landon grabbed a firm hold of my arm and pulled me back. The eye contact was vicious and unruly when Haven neared the top of the steps.

Seneca had a fire in her eyes of ruby and coral and looked so damn cute in a blue romper and white platforms, hanging her tiny body from Haven's sexy fit arms. Not to mention the new bold energy she had. I hated the shit out of her right now. It was torture, and they all knew it. Dean came bursting from the front door, just in time. "Dinner is on the stove. Come in," Dean rejoiced in conversation, pulling both Haven and Seneca in the house. I couldn't move, I was still in shock, and I couldn't feel my heart cringe anymore. Haven gave me one last disapproving look before disappearing into the house. *What the fuck? Why the fuck?*

I couldn't wrap my head around it. The severe effect was so evident that Landon stood there staring at me, asking if I were okay. His eyes weren't crazy like before. Now he just honestly looked sad for me. I couldn't say a word. Tears just came pouring down, just like the unexpected rainfall that suddenly poured down on Grey Wolf Hollow. Landon reached out and took my shoulder, pulling me into him hard like some war hero, holding me calm during a treacherous storm. He didn't have to, but he held me while I cried. And even though I had him, I still wanted Haven. Very badly.

Dean had made Haven's favorite for dinner; fried fish and wild rice with avocado salad. Dinner was colorful and awkward. Hung up on Haven across the table, and of course, he didn't care about how he was tearing out my guts. I hated how highly I spoke of him to Guakar, just for him to treat me as so in front of him.

Seneca and Jacy were non-stop talking, and it annoyed me. Even Jacy seemed to like the idea of her better than me. I had to block them out and her little story of how she ended up hanging out with Haven. It all reminded me of the last dinner party. This time I was at the other end of the table. It was better to block it out, going off into a daydream. All the flowers that had blossomed around the bright kitchen clammed shut, unwilling to flourish. Ironically, Haven was the one who pointed them out, despite knowing the vines and flowers were all of my doing. I let his stares burn into me.

Haven has been back in Grey Wolf Hollow for a couple of days now. Who knew? Huh? *No* one but Seneca. He had been hanging out with Seneca the last day and a half. She lives next door. How did I not know? So no one even thought about warning me, at least? He did not care. Nor did Seneca care. I could tell by how she boasted about Haven in front of me. She was praising him like a young *god* or something. She was obsessing over him, and it all made me want to strangle them both to death. I did my best to hold it together and pretend that everything was fine. I decided to focus my attention elsewhere. I looked at Landon and forced a smile. Shifting his attention to me, I tried picking up our conversation from earlier,

"-Do you still want to hang out Monday? I was thinking about that ATV trail that leads to the blue hole… is it opened?" 'Landon' was wide-eyed, completely surprised but excited. It was easy to sway him, and he was confident and overzealous enough to grab Haven's attention. *Fuck it,* I thought.

"-It sure is, Queen. Funny you say that Daya, **(gives a contemptuous smile)** Logan and I was just talkin' bout going camping. Are you trying to go with me? So we can set up camp at that spot you love. You know, that spot we used to watch the sun come up," The way he eye fucked me in front of everyone was rattling. *What did I start?* Haven's eyes of poison sap glanced my way, and I swallowed hard. The memory was making my heart flutter again. I couldn't feel it with Landon, but with Guakar's charm, I couldn't resist.

"Yeah, I remember… **(sexy eye roll)** you used to trick me into going up there with you all the time… we never did look for that buried treasure," Landon sat there feverishly, remembering.

"Well, I'm sorry- **(giggles)** it was the only place your uncle didn't go looking for us. The offer is still there; we can skip Hector's." Guakar certainly had his ways. I could have honestly reined it in a little, but Haven ultimately had me fucked up. The memories were meaningless, but to the *new Daya,* they were not. Landon whispered some salacious shit I only half-heard, but his words rattled me, sending me into a frozen frenzy.

Across the table, Haven's eyes were of dark heavy forests. All moss green. A color I had never seen in his eyes. So livid, he was drowning out of misery. *Good.* So was I. Landon cleared his throat nervously and straightened himself up. The color in his eyes also swam around in a frenzy, "-You sure you want to go up there, beautiful? The things we'll get into up there might change how you feel right now," I glanced at Haven; The jerk was playing with her hair—staring at her adoringly, actively ignoring me. His eyes and hands were on Seneca, who carried on a friendly conversation with Dean and Jacy, pretending to be all sweet and innocent.

"-I've been locked up for months. I could use a night underneath the stars." I meant that. I desperately needed to heal and be with nature. Sleeping on dewy grass under sweet spring skies was the only remedy. But I wanted that with Haven, not with Landon.

I watched in total sadness as Haven touched Seneca's face softly and joked with her. He wanted me to see him pull his chair in closer to her, put his hands on her skin, and brag about her 'classic' beauty. I tried telling myself it wasn't worth getting upset over; he had the right to do what he pleased. And so I thought about Atabey and her warnings and Guakar's opened invitation to be his Queen. It had to be the Zenis interception because all this was just way too crazy. And maybe Guakar was the answer to all this craziness.

"-Hello? Are you listening?"

Haven impatiently snapped his fingers at me.

"What?" It was too late to reel in the attitude.

"Where have you been? What have you been up to?"

"Wouldn't you like to know?" I snapped from across the table.

"-Yes, Daya, I would like to know." Haven snapped back.

"It's not *your* business."

"Daya, please don't-" Jacy coughed out a plea.

"Please don't what? You're kidding. I've been- isolated for months alone. I'm not okay. However, my *good friend* Landon just invited me camping, which is *so sweet* of him because I've been *dying* to sleep under the stars since I've been back, and he knows just the spot." I tried to sound as positive as possible, but I lost it.

"Where? Maybe I can meet you two there." Haven stared at Landon like he wanted to rip his head off that very moment. The new' Landon'; needless to say, and quite frankly,

"-*Don't give a flying fuck. Sure, it's fine. Bring your chick.*"

"-That's a terrible idea!" Dean intercepted nervously, hoping we weren't as serious as we sounded.

"Do you two want to do this now?" Jacy tried helping.

Haven and I both snapped at him together,

"Shut up, Jacy!" Our voices clashed as Dean clapped,

The silence after was inevitable. *What have I been doing?*

"-This is stupid," I whispered under a short breath. I could feel my eyes swish in color and cheeks flush soft rose under the scope of five pairs of eyes that drilled into me, "I should leave."

As I was getting ready to stand, Landon grabbed my hand.

"Hey, don't go," Landon's eyes were killing me today. Rushing and rolling tropical waters in bleeding sunset. He looked like the perfect knight in shining armor, but to me, that wasn't what I wanted. I wanted Haven. All tall and dark. Black and gray. Dis-armored and scarred. Mysterious and sexually cannibalistic. I wanted him, and everyone knew it. It was dumb to pretend. I could feel Haven's jealous stare, realizing that his resentment and stubbornness were only going to fire back at him, as it did. He was giving Landon a reason to comfort me.

"It's pouring out there. Wait till it calms down, and I'll take you home." Dean insisted. I stood there in pure indecisiveness, unsure if I wanted to start this dangerous game with Haven. But Landon had all the time in the world to convince me, and so he pleaded his case with a perfect smile and wink until I melted right back into him.

Dean carried on the weight of the conversation after that for a while. I simmered in the heat of Haven's eyes' watching 'Landon' and how he hung his arm over my chair, leaning into me. "I was going through some boxes, and I found that copy of Pocahontas we rented. We should watch it while the rain settles." I nodded at Landon's plan. It was better than going home crying.

"I was thinking us, alone in my room? Like old times." Landon's eyes seem to wander over me again. His remark was slick and ballsy enough to get him smacked in the mouth by Haven, who bounced frustrated in his chair but bit his tongue as Dean intervened.

"-*Everyone* can watch it in the Den."

"I guess, but honestly, *dad*, I don't see what the big deal is... Daya and I have been alone in my room plenty of times before-" Haven gave a judgemental grunt; unable to keep to himself anymore, he stood up, "-Can I talk to you, Daya? Alone?"

I was pretty surprised to hear Haven say those words. It was what I wanted, but I didn't bring my hopes up for a good outcome. Dean permitted us to use his office. Funny, he wouldn't leave me alone with Landon but gladly left me alone with Haven. Haven closed the door behind us. I leaned up against the desk as he approached me, "Where have you been? You owe me that much." I thought about it for a long moment. I didn't want to start any trouble for my uncle that could interfere with this reconciliation, so I didn't want to throw the blame on him and tell the truth.

"I was in the garden. I needed some time to think."

"Daya- How the fuck am I going to say this to you nicely? The Fucking Garden? Do you know how many times I've gone past those Garden gates, looking for you? And not once did it occur to you to stick your big ass head through the gate and let me know you were alive and well. Skipping out like that was bullshit, and you know it. Don't ever take off like that again without talking to me first. All the shit I went through, tearing myself apart, wondering if you're okay, for nothing? You can be with Landon all you want, but we need to be okay with each other. Together or not, I'm supposed to protect you." As I stood there quiet, I understood everything said to me, but I had to address one tiny part of the equation,

"-Except, I don't want to be with Landon,"

"Weren't you making plans to go camping with him? Look, Daya, I was wrong about us. You were never mine, and I'm sorry if I made you believe so." His words burned through me like acid. I wanted to cry, but I couldn't let him see me break down. So, I took a deep breath and convinced myself he didn't mean it,

"Sure. I'm cool with it."

"-Are you joshing right now?"

"No, I agree. Are we done now?" I pulled to my feet from my lean and started toward the door. Haven suddenly grabbed my arm.

"-Wait, what's that?" He reached over, pulled me into him, and brisked his fingers over the deep scars on my leg. I slapped his hand away. Why was he touching me? As if he couldn't be more dis-respectful? What the hell is his malfunction?

"This? I was attacked, in the woods, but I'm sure you already know since you know so much-"

"So it's true? It attacked you?" He stepped closer to me. My heart began to pound. I've missed staring up at his perfect face and figure. I fought with the urge to jump his bones. Even when consumed in anger, I was falling for him again.

"Seriously, Daya, I was fucking worried."

"I'm sorry... I didn't think you would care."

"Of course, I care, Daya."

"Well, are you okay? I heard you went crazy..." He cracked a chuckle and looked away adoringly.

"Yeah... never better..." His dark eyes quickly seized my body in rapture, as if he couldn't believe I stood there in the flesh. I smiled back at him when he reached to touch the waist beads over my belly button. His fingers brisked over my skin, "-Daya, I can't lie to you, I still love you," His honesty took me in, and I couldn't hold back any longer, I pulled him into me, and we began to kiss. He shoved me wildly into the desk, ready to devour my body. His aura felt so good, I caught myself moaning, and when I did, the office door flung open, and there Seneca stood.

"-I hope he told you that he slept at my house last night. I thought this time would be different." She didn't wait to exit.

Five more seconds, and Haven and I would have been dry humping on the desk, back together. Now it felt like we were seas away. I glanced up at him, hurting. Before he could say a word, I found myself banging the front swing door open to the unsettling storm-ridden night. Still pouring, I tried to take in the breeze with spring rain. Heartbreaking. Thinking of him kissing her the way he kissed me made me sick. My uncle had been right. Love is fucking hurtful. The door swung open behind me, and I braced myself to look at him. I had been crying recklessly, and now I couldn't stop. I could feel the sorrow in his energy. But why? He knew how to hurt me, and now he felt ashamed about it? He probably thought he could come out here and charm me with an apology and make himself feel less of an asshole. Well, too bad. I wasn't going to let him,

"All this time, you were worried about me being unfaithful when it was you the entire time. I'd never trust you again," I shoved Haven again and again until I was explosively taking my anger out on him. I pounded at his chest, screaming. He pulled me into his arms, trying to get me to stop crying.

"I was with her last night, but not romantically, I swear." I was devastated and weak. The warmth of his hands holding me up was so comforting. I've missed him and found myself innocently holding onto him. I hated how right he felt. But when he tried to kiss me, I couldn't help but push him away aggressively, slapping him clean across his face. Unfazed, I wanted to release myself from his grip, but he was too strong. Now he wouldn't let me go. As I dug my nails into him, his grip only got tighter. Finally, at the perfect timing, Dean came out, "Everything okay?"

"Please, Dean, take me home!" I snatched my wrists from Haven as he unwillingly released me at the glance of his father, and I ran off the deck crying into the rainy abyss. Haven tried running into the rain, but Dean stopped him with one firm hand to the shoulder.

I was silent, crying the ride home, and tried concentrating on getting to my bed. I knew Dean felt tremendously bad, but it's not like he can force Haven to act accordingly. I was just a girl, blinded by love. "My son will come to his senses Daya." I rolled my eyes. I expected that from Dean, "I don't want you to give up on Haven. I know he loves you. Haven's going through a lot. Now, I don't know why my son does half the dumb shit he does, but you know they're *just friends*. I'm sure Seneca said it out of context to make you mad. He cares about you, Daya, which is probably the most conspicuous thing I ever said about Haven with anyone. Very few things in this world drive that boy's passion. I know what he feels for you is genuine, but he doesn't know how to be vulnerable. He's just learning how to love. Like you, Haven's never truly tasted *'love'* 'til now. I'm not ready for what you two might get into if you continue to fight and have these petty, meaningless battles. You're supposed to be a team. You get that, right?" I nodded as if I understood. '*You get that, right?*' seemed to be the adult's go-to words.

I hated that.

14

The Trails

The ATV camping trip was now a 'GO' for Monday. I was surprised when Charlotte told me about it, thinking Dean wouldn't allow it to happen after rejecting the idea in the first place. I was on the fence about going but truthfully, the thought of not going made me anxious. I couldn't stand not knowing what Haven was doing.

I decided to meet with Landon and Leyla late that Monday morning when classes ended. I felt a bittersweetness rushing to leave school, but I was too distracted by my future to care more or less; I was looking forward to the camping trip. Although I still wanted to punch Haven in the face, I was deep over my head with him and just knowing he was walking about in town made me crave him more. Call it toxic, but I wanted him.

After the bell, I sprinted to Landon's truck, and when I reached it, I realized Leyla wasn't there immediately. Confused, I hoped that Leyla hadn't ditched on me and left me alone with Landon. I've been avoiding him since that night. However, 'Landon' was acting super strange. Not like the *'Guakar'* Landon at all; although, I knew he was in there. *Guakar* seemed super thoughtful today. His vibe stuck to disappointment, and I tried catching his glare as I got in the truck, but he just hid from me. He never does that, so I blurted out,

"Landon, I *love* Haven, and I *still want* to be with him. I'm sorry if it seems like I'm-" Landon sped out of the parking lot,

"-I know, but that's neither here nor there. I wanted to ask you something?" My face stiffens in the horror of another proposal, "How long has Misael been using black magic on Landon?" It was a random question, but Guakar was serious. He looked rightfully pissed off, and I was a bit intimidated, if truth be told.

"I guess for a while now... I tried telling you. I did." Irritated, he cleared his throat and rolled his eyes off the side.

"-Misael believes he has us all fooled, especially Landon. Granted, Landon's a dummy and an easy target, but he's a talented kid with lots of potentials. He carries strong native blood, but he's young and too weak to defend himself from Misael. The magic Misael is doing is not Taino magic. He's broken another law, and Queen Atabey is infuriated. That just can not be tolerated. When I spoke to Dean last night, he was pretty pissed off at Haven and me over the whole showdown at dinner the other night. Dean warned me about Misael's black magic. They told me about how he had been using dark foreign magic to mess with our fate and steal your gifted power. I refuse to allow him to use Landon to distract you. Dean said I had to get clean from all the years of poison. I wasn't sure what he meant, so I stuck around to find out. I am Zeni, but that was the most painful experience. Even as Zeni, I could feel the pain Landon endured, but he took it with grace. Landon's finally sober from the magic. Despite their unfortunate ties to Cristobal, the Tyson clan has always shown strength, courage, leadership, and wisdom. They have felt the same crimes against our kind and held their ancestors' pain. Dean, especially, has done a good job of honoring and upholding his Native blood without Akani influence for decades, as taught and passed down from his ancestors. It's why we resonate well with them. Landon's most important relationship will be with his father, parents, and ancestors, regardless of origins, as long as they're good people, with goodness in their hearts. I'm having a good time being Landon, but Landon isn't a toy gun, and he's not the one I have to teach a lesson. I'm staying out of this game. I just want to give him a chance to build a bond with Dean and learn his people's ways through his father. But I won't be far off because we all had a deal."

There was a severe but pleasant change in 'Landon.' It was clear, he was over it. I was glowing, and I purposely wore a super-thin, peach-toned bodysuit, bra-less, with some short shorts that would catch Haven's attention. I smelled like berries and vanilla, and the sharpness in my eyes was enchanting. I honestly expected Guakar to start up with his shit the minute he saw me, henceforth the snappy attitude about not wanting to lead him on. But, no, this Landon wasn't mesmerized by me at all. Honestly, he looked pretty bored as he drove. "...Everyone deserves to know their roots and grow from it... but I still think Landon is the better Tyson brother for you." We both laughed a bit. It was refreshing to see the caring side of Guakar. He could feel Landon and how unheard and insignificant he truly felt. Guakar found genuine empathy for Landon within him. I let him keep the silence as we drove.

Old Airport Road;

Old airport road was a dead-end road with a clearing near the forest land. However, it was easy to access all the ATV trails near Grey Wolf cliff, a beautiful mountain top cliff hidden in the forest's depths. A clear view of the night sky and the always fresh swimming hole hidden underneath the pines made it an ideal romantic camping spot. It was a place Landon and I often went to last summer.

But it was a new day, and neither one of us felt much nostalgic that morning; Guakar had a new mission.

Landon pulled into Old Airport Road as Leyla waved us down. He parked in between Haven's Thunderbird and Jacy's Jeep. With Dean and Jacy, Leyla stood near 3 ATVs in a neat row. Haven was sitting on the edge of the red one at the end. As always, he was pumping out massive sex appeal, smoldering at me as Landon helped me out of the truck. My outfit indeed pressed on him quickly. He raised his eyebrow and cracked a dirty smirk as I shamelessly walked past him. I could see him force his arms in a fold as he resisted the temptation to grab and pull me in. My face flushed like cherry Kool-aid, walking over to Leyla.

"Today would have been a nice day for a spirit quest, right?"

A shock at first, but Haven spoke to me directly. I looked over, and I smiled at him. He checked me a smile back and fought with himself to behave. He's trying to be a gentleman; I pretended not to notice his solicitous glance. It was the first time I had sincerely smiled at him since he's barged back into my life nearly 72 hrs ago. It was only a split second, but it was enough to make his jaw drop a little, and I only smiled because Seneca hadn't come along.

"Yeah, I guess." I shrugged.

"Well, you're a girl. I'm sure you can get away without one."

"Girls like me tend to get away with a lot."

"Oh yeah, like what?

"Sleeping in the garden all afternoon, swimming at night, eating fruit right off the tree-" Dean looked at me disapprovingly before saying, "-Kid, that's terrible. You always wash your fruits first. Speaking of fruits, we're having lunch before we head up; sandwiches and snacks are in the cooler..."

Dean had packed a massive picnic for the trip; the boys would eat all day if they could. We ended up sitting around for the first 30 minutes eating, and it was peaceful at first. I sat on Landon's ATV, watching everyone from my throne. Dean with Landon sitting across Jacy and Leyla, arguing about a rare bird they spotted; she was giggling her cute laugh, taking Jacy's side in his argument.

A couple of feet away, Haven was leaning on his ATV, now smoking a disgusting cigarette after eating through what seemed like four courses. He did a great job of keeping quiet with his lips but not so much with his eyes. Like a bad habit, he has been watching me like that the moment I showed up, watching me soak in all of my majestic power, energized by the sun ablaze. That gleam in his eyes of pride was always there, no matter how mad I made him. He made me feel wanted, cared for, and safe every moment with me. I wanted to hate him for making me want him back, but his attention was too good to ignore, and as I sat there seemingly alone with him, I was reminded of that early winter night, how happy I was dancing with him. How alive we felt in Dean's truck all before he ruined it.

Haven tossed away his cigarette and slid into my headspace so I could see him. I gave him a severe look. No matter how deeply in love with him I was, I wasn't going to let him get away with spending the night at Seneca's. I couldn't just forget it. He needed to apologize. We studied each other from afar briefly until he decided to open his cocky mouth, "-You sit on it like a pro..."

He chuckled, but I was in no mood for his sexual innuendos.

"-Funny, that's what your brother said-"

I smiled, and he nearly made it bounce back as he gave me a severe look in return. Regardless, he continued with his antics.

"-Well, if you get bored, you can come to sit on me. My lap or my face, I'm not picky."

"Is that all I am to you? Sex with legs? You white boys are something else." I shook my head disapprovingly and leaned back into the ATV, my breasts perked up and legs dangling in a split.

"A little contradicting. All you do is sexualize Landon and me. And I'd use that term loosely; I'm not full pale face, miss. And there's plenty of sex with legs out there, **trust me.** Although your legs," He winced in utter fake pain after groping me with his sharp eyes. I rolled my eyes at his theatrics.

"Remind me to put more clothes on next time I come around."

"Will do because I can see your nipples… you have a killer rack."

Appalled, I crossed my arms before my full and erected breasts and scowled at him. My cheeks flushed a deep red, and all he could do was laugh at me. "Awe, babe, I'm just kidding. I'll stop. I can't help it. Can you blame me… 'cuz **BOOBS** right…" He stepped closer to pull me into his arms, but I flinched at his touch.

"Shut up, Haven. You're starting to piss me off, you know."

He had the nerve to scoff before saying, "What's your problem?"

Was he for real? "**You.** You're my problem."

"Listen, if you didn't want me bothering you, then maybe you shouldn't have agreed to come out here, let alone, looking like that. You don't even try, and you're still goddamn gorgeous. You can't even blame me. I melt for you, and you know it."

"I blame lust…" He chuckled hard immediately.

"Lust? Yeah, Daya, okay. We both know our connection is far beyond that. Sex is just what's getting in the way. I've accepted that we haven't had sex, nor will we be anytime soon, but I still want your crazy ass around. For, you know, comfort." His timid eyes shot to the ground, kicking about pebbles in the dirt.

"Comfort?"

"Yeah. You're familiar, like a childhood blanket. You remind me that things can never be too bad when I have you. I want you around Daya, all the time if I could." It was evident that Haven was running hot and on the make. He was a wild stag in heat. I twisted my body around to face him, and it was down to business.

"...Why didn't she come along?" I questioned him about Seneca.

"Because I used her to piss you off that day. She agreed to help me make you jealous, but we took it too far, and I don't want to hurt you both with lies. If I had brought her, she'd get in the way, and I only came up here to woo you again." I hated how honest he always had to be and how good he made it look.

"That's rich... Haven what you did, hurt."

"Look, I know you're *kind of* mad at me, but I was only trying to prove a point... you still love me... and I love you. And, in my defense, you provoked me. You didn't make the situation any better, letting Landon talk to you like that. So it's not entirely my fault."

"You're not fair. You're always using sex against me."

"You're the one to talk, Daya. You're so worried about whether or not I'm having sex, but I think you're being dramatic. I want to make this clear, Daya. You're my wife, and there's only one pair of legs my face wants to be in between, and it's yours. But I think you already know that." His hand slowly rolled up my thigh.

"Ugh, shut up!" I squeezed my knees shut. I didn't want him to know how much his words were getting me wet. I was pretending to be more annoyed than I was pressed. Somehow he still noticed; his fingerprints graze my inner thigh again. I couldn't hide my periwinkle eyes anymore. Huffing slowly, he said, "Let it go. Not everyone gets to recognize their soulmate in the Flesh."

"That's ironic to say, considering your lack of recognition."

He pulled away, pissed off. "-Here's a cheat code Daya, I'd be more romantic if I didn't catch you under my brother's belt every 5 minutes. You want me to apologize, but I'm not going to. I never asked for an apology; I accepted it. So I won't apologize for my mistakes because I'm learning from them, which is more than I could say for you. You deserved it."

"Beg your pardon, sir?" I smacked his shoulder. He was being so insensitive and stubborn right now.

"-You heard me, skirt."

"Why are you so mean?"

"Because I have been steadily losing it, looking everywhere for you, trying to find you, and when I come home, I find you chopping it up with my brother. You have no fucking idea how crazy that made me. All I wanted to do was come home and find you sitting in **MY** bed waiting for **ME**. Not slung over Landon."

"I *been* waiting on you, idiot, before and after I left that garden. Your house was the only place I hadn't gone looking for you till that day. And oh, how much I regret it now. Maybe if you weren't so quick to replace me, I could have told you how much I missed you too," I confessed, and he finally eased up on me; setting both hands to the side of me, he leaned in close and found my frantic eyes.

"Daya, I promise, no one can replace you… not nobody. Put that in your beautiful thick brain."

"Why should I trust you?"

"Wow. How the tables have turned."

"You know what..." LIVID, I kicked off the ATV and walked over to the others. He followed behind me,

"I wasn't there for Landon; I was there hoping I'd find **YOU**. But you showed up out of the woodwork, pissy and already spazzing, with Seneca dangling from your arm all nonchalant. I couldn't say two words to you. You know how bad that hurt?"

"And now you know how it feels. So let's move on."

"Why do you want to hurt me back so bad."

"I'm not doing it on purpose, Daya."

"So why would you bring her home? To meet your dad?" He was laughing, completely taunting me with his hands in pockets,

"Meet my dad? You're crazy, babe. Dean wanted me home for dinner, so I came home. She just happened to be with me. We were hanging out *as friends*. **That's all**. I saw YOU letting Landon put the moves on YOU. I wanted to piss you off. Now I wish I hadn't..."

"You two hang out a lot?" Shimmering from anger, I kept my jealous eyes to the ground with my arms folded.

"Since I been home recently, yes-"

"Why? Are you sleeping with her?-" He scoffed, rolling his eyes, "That's a stupid question."

"Well, you have to take your frustration out somewhere, right? I'm just curious, where."

"If I were having sex with her or any other female, you'd know it. Trust me; there's not nearly enough time in the day for me to let out that kind of frustration." His indirect answer and smug attitude continued to infuriate me, "That's bullshit."

"Well, you ask bull shit questions, you get bullshit answers-"

The others watched on steadily up until that moment. Leyla, peachy as always, quickly pulled me aside to collect myself as the guys prepared the ATVs. Landon insisted I share his ATV with him, but that wouldn't save me from making this situation worse. So I confessed to Landon that I'd instead share Haven's and walked straight over to Haven's ATV. They all watched as I did.

"Are you sure? You're safer with me." They all seemed confused, but both brothers stood there waiting for a response.

"I'm riding with Haven..."

As if he had already forgotten the bickering, Haven held onto a gratifying glare as he walked over to me excitedly, "-Say fucking less -and watch ya mouth; she's more than safe with her true mate."

As he put a helmet on my head, he couldn't contain the smile that ripped through his gloating face. A smile so charming, it reflected on me, and we both were giggling with glistening eyes.

Haven made it clear; I was exactly where I was supposed to be. His fingertips caressed my lips and chin amorously before he hopped onto the ATV, and I climbed on behind him.

"-Landon, you can ride with me in the truck; have some father-son bonding time..." Dean gave Landon an offer he couldn't refuse. He immediately accepted. Miraculously, today, the boys seemed level-headed, and we all wanted to keep that peace. Dean must have laid into them last night or something.

As the ATVs started up, my arms wrapped around his waist, and my diamond-hard nipples pressed against his back. I could feel his blood rush upon feeling my embrace. He exhaled softly, and his one hand traced at my arm across his belt.

"Maybe you should get up here in the front, princess..."

So he could press himself against *ME* and assert his manliness.

OH PLEASE. I melted my face into Haven's back and inhaled his delectable scent. Having him this close, to where I can feel the rips of his contoured abs and the steady collapsing of his shaky breathing, felt like the home I've been yearning to find. I knew he felt it, too, once his heart stopped cartwheeling. He took my hand, interlaced it with his, and kissed my knuckles. My grip became tighter. His eyes shot back at me, but I only grazed them over his shoulder.

"Don't let go..." He faintly expressed.

"I don't plan to," He took off beyond the herds of evergreen into the forest. We spent the early afternoon blazing through endless trails up the forest hills. Haven's subtle but hedonistic nudges, strokes, and grasps were hard to ignore. I couldn't fight the way I was feeling with him, so I indulged in it for his viewing pleasure. The afternoon melted away perfectly.

The sun was still flaming when we reached the top of Grey Wolf cliff. Jacy steered his ATV into the campgrounds while Haven hit left and headed straight towards the edge of the cliff, skipping out behind trees and bushes and stopping just before the mists of the dropping ledge. We were secluded here. He turned the ATV off, and for a moment, we stayed quiet. I held onto him. I wasn't ready to let him go. I never felt more simplistic as I did with him. His heart was already beating irregularly, but now I could hear it like turbulence on a plane. My touch was easing his frightful heart. My fingertips continue to dance on his now shivering skin. He fidgeted around and began to smack the bubble gum in his mouth so loudly.

"Can you be any more annoying?" I released my grip on him.

"I dunno... what annoys you?" He says in a sarcastic tongue. He got off the ATV, stretched out his long body, and then took off his soaked in sweat tee and tossed it onto the ATV. A body like a warrior; those blue eyes crashed into mine. He reached over to lend me a hand, but I hopped off, and he caught my hips and brought me to my feet, my breasts brisking against his face.

"-You look amazing, by the way." Breathless, trying to keep straight, my eyes whirled in exotic hot colors. Scarlet. Rich Tangerine. Sultry Red. Flame Flicker Yellow. Haven was as captivated as I was of him. Standing before me, he traced my face with his pretty blue eyes. Then, satisfied with the masterpiece in memory, he pulled away from my gaze and explored my body with his eyes.

"You know I was only kidding... about covering up." His hand touched the thin straps of the bodysuit. His fingers danced along my shoulder, teasing the straps. Inside my mind was a collapsing bridge, and in my shorts, a broken dam of rushing waters. I had to keep strong and keep holding the Dam up, so I didn't drown in my lusty love puddle. I turned away from him. He wanted me to be all over him. I could feel him get impatient with my lack of words and affection. My actions were speaking for me, so he let his actions speak for him. His lips brisked over my neck.

OH MY. *Shivers.*

I closed my eyes and took in his essence. It took everything inside to keep from jumping his bones on that ATV. We were hot, aroused, and bothered. I opened my eyes, hoping to catch his eyes, but no. He was too busy eyeballing his cell phone screen from his free arm, in the reaching distance.

What the hell? Haven hated technology. What was he doing letting his phone distract him from me so much today? It's the 3rd time I caught him checking out his phone. I shifted my back towards him, facing Landon in the far distance. That wasn't on purpose but worked. I began to twirl my hair and walked towards the view before us. His eyes followed me because I was intensely glowing. I lightly bit my lip and sighed, long and soft.

"-Okay, Day, what's the deal? Quit messing with me."

"I'm not messing with you." He stepped in front of me and stopped me with his hands. He slithered his arms around me and pulled me into him. I was content with the touch of our bodies. I think his eyes even rolled back, but he maintained a firm stance.

"Your eyes look like an Andes sunset; it reminds me of the second night I was there in the mountains... The color looks great on you, but what the hell? And that glow. I've never seen it."

"It's because I love you," When the words left my mouth, a weight lifted from his chest. He finally had it.

"I love you too, skirt," This big tough guy faintly lost his breath, his thumb brushing my chin, smiling. He made me mad, but he made my heart flutter so much more. I couldn't deny it as I felt myself beginning to crack. Lost in his eyes, and he was quickly coming in for a kiss I wasn't ready to give him. My hand caught his lips immediately. I stopped him from stealing one.

"What? I thought we were doing good?" He complained.

"That doesn't mean I'm just going to let you kiss me. I can't trust where your lips have been." Haven melted like lava. Frustration increased on his face, "I can tell you where they want to be."

"-Apologize-"

"Seriously?" He scoffed.

"Don't touch me-" I pushed him away.

"Okay, bet. You won't be able to keep this up."

I rolled my eyes from him and climbed onto the ATV. I sat there waiting for him to hop on, but just as he exhaled, strangely, his cell phone went off. The both of us exchanged strange glances before he checked the caller ID. The look on his face only became more suspicious when he said he had to take the call, and he walked off, closer to the cliff edge and further away from me. I rolled my eyes, wondering who was interfering with our time and why he would need privacy from me. I watched him from the ATV but could hear nothing. Finally, after 5 minutes, he returned with a request.

"Go on a run with me tonight?"

"No... Is everything okay? I mean with your phone call..."

"Yeah- weird. I didn't know you could get reception up here."

It was quiet as we awkwardly looked around at the beauty of nature, trying to string away from the phone conversation.

"This place is beautiful... Romantic and secluded, I can see why Landon brought you here." I rolled my eyes. Of course, he's making this about *Landon.* "It's gorgeous..." I admitted.

"-I can't compete with him, Daya..."

Frustrated, I tossed his shirt at him, hitting him in the face.

"No, you can't; he has nothing on you."

"He knows you, Daya. Everything about you; your favorite foods, your favorite books, your favorite place."

"So do you, Haven. You know me so much more. So much deeper. Did I tell you this was my favorite place? Because neither of you has a damn clue." Haven said nothing, but his eyes rolled.

"-This isn't my favorite place Haven. This view doesn't compare to my favorite place. Do you want to know where my favorite place is? It's the heart-shaped meadow by the river. The place where *WE* fell in love... I doubt you'd remember. December feels so long ago,"

"I run through there every day; I live in those memories of us."

I couldn't deny the fact that his words were breaking down the walls I'd built the past few days. I had to be clear with him. "Listen, Haven. You have to get over the whole Landon thing if you want us to work. I grew up with him. He's one of my best friends."

"No- *you and I* grew up together. *We're supposed* to be best friends. Landon was there to replace me when I left. Just 'cuz you can't remember doesn't mean you can write it off..."

"You're right, Haven, and I'm sorry."

"Don't apologize. I'm used to it." He was brooding again. But underneath his anger was an underlying sadness. I sighed.

"I can't change my past with him. But I can change my future, and I want that with *YOU*. Spend the rest of the day with me."

"I already planned to... you're my Queen."

He lifted my chin, and my eyes timidly met his. An invisible white flag went up. He took the opportunity to move in close, climbing onto the ATV, but sitting right behind me. He pulled me into his collapsing arms, too close for the heat that was coming down. Despite it, I felt comfortable in his embrace. He got even more comfortable behind me, etching his body closer to me until his erection was poking my left butt cheek with a hook. I gulped before I told him, "... You're psycho-obsessed,"

"You have no idea, baby. So, go running with me tonight?"

I laughed at him, looking back, "Hell no."

"You wanna go back to chasing?" I was resilient. Unmoved.

"Apologize, and I'll give you whatever you want."

"Haven Tyson doesn't do apologies, so don't hold your breath-"

"Don't hold your breath for that run-." I rubbed up against him, teasing; our eyes had a space war standoff. Battleships collided, shooting lasers and a black sinkhole tornado between us. The hair on my arms stood up, and I shivered, shifting. He smirked devilishly underneath his thick brows and rolled his eyes away. I didn't want to admit it, but his closeness set a fire in me as it always had. Theoretically, he was a 'cold man' but radiated with warmth and coziness. Alleviation; that was what I felt, despite being angry with him. He couldn't know how bad I wanted to keep him around.

I went to stand and hop off the ATV, but his large hands took hold of my hip, and his right hand grabbed my pelvic before pulling me back down to sitting. He sucked me into him, his large biceps over mine and readjusting his erection behind me while still holding onto my crotch. He teased me over the jean shorts. The thought of turning around to face him pressed on my chest. I longed to feel the extent of his bones. That's when my plan to frustrate the shit out of him sexually slipped into motion. Yeah, I was already doing that, but I was also letting him feed off my magic energy like a bear to a helpless submissive Goldilocks. He made me into goo every time he came around, and that just wasn't fair. I had to turn the table on him. I was going to push him with my charm until he craved my touch. I'll tease him until he's bent for me, but I wasn't going to satisfy his hunger with my power. The only way this plan wasn't going to backfire on me is if I made him believe he's already won.

" Truce?" He begged, still pushing against me.

"Okay, Haven. Truce. I'll go running with you tonight, but only if you're kind, and only if I get to sleep in *YOUR* tent with you.

"At first, I thought he'd make a big deal about it, but he smiled and hugged me from behind. I closed my eyes; I appreciated his embrace. I needed it for so long, I couldn't imagine him letting go.

"I'll be kind," He says...

<h1 style="text-align:center">15</h1>

The Emerald hole

Haven and I made it to camp on the other half of the Wolf cliff by mid-afternoon. First, it was a rocky drop, submerging into rich forestland, under a clear view of endless blue skies, *Turey (Heaven)*. Then, behind trees, bushes, and shrubs, rushed a deep freshwater creek that ran into an emerald swimming hole—outlined by rocks and boulders, hanging moss, and boarding trees. It was vast and trench-like deep and stretched halfway down the mountain. It was simplistic, clean, colorful, but sometimes brutal and stubborn.

"-It's 103 degrees, and that water looks great right now,"

Haven parked the ATV and turned it off. He rose to stand, but I pulled him back down, using his face for stability as I hopped off the ATV. He rolled his eyes of salvo before slapping my ass. I looked at him ignited but couldn't say anything because I secretly loved the way it stung, warm, and sent currents through my inner thighs.

I passed aunt Charlotte, basking in the sun, as I walked over to Leyla and Jacy, who watched Dean, trying to get the barbacoa in full swing. The cooking scent of fish, burgers, and hotdogs puffed into the air. My senses were on 1000, and I was feeling unruly. The scarlet in my eyes gleamed like my glowing skin. Haven seemed to notice, brisking his lips over my shoulder while shadowing behind me, until he saw Landon, eyes closed and knee-deep in the creek.

"-I'm teaching him how to fish, like how I taught you," Dean explained before Haven immediately began to taunt him, laughing at his stance on an uneasy rock. Distracted, Landon lost his balance and fell into the water. I looked at Haven,

"You promised to be kind."

"I'm trying, babe, honestly. He's not going to catch anything like that." Landon cussed in the near distance and flipped him off.

"You think you're so great at it? Why don't YOU teach him..." Dean challenged his son. Haven gave a nervous laugh and looked off. When Dean and Haven's eyes met again, Haven scoffed and raised his shoulders; finally agreeing, like he had a choice,

Haven walked in knee-deep into the creek. He pushed Landon aside and took a natural stance, slowly closing his eyes. He concentrated as if trying to talk to the wind and spirits. I watched him with arousal. He was annoyingly hot but complacent. Maybe he was a God; humans are not that beautiful. Even so, he had no business existing on this plane. Haven was created for *MY* world, and the thought enticed and pulsed my cervix like a boombox. Dean caught me staring and cleared his throat. I nervously looked away for a moment before Haven lunged forward in the water. He didn't fully immerse himself, but he had several fishes in his arms when he stood up. He casually tossed them in a bucket beside him excitedly with a grin from ear to ear, "That's how a real man does it..." Haven roared.

Landon checked him with a look of contempt. Then, he cupped some freshwater into his hands and splashed his face, tracing back his hair and puffing up his chest. His eyes quickly found me, and by that perfect smile and a wink, I knew that Guakar had come to play.

"Every fish I catch is a symbol of my love for Daya."

Wrong words, Guakar! Wrong words.

"-Oh no, that's alright, *Landon!*" I tried waving at him, but it was too late. He jumped into the water. But, of course, Landon's choice of words got me into trouble. Haven glanced at me, shaking his head with disapproval. I shrugged my shoulders; this wasn't my fault. Like Haven, I couldn't appreciate *Landon's* grand gesture. We were finally beginning to get along, and a stirring competition between the two will ruin what I've fought so hard to achieve.

"He ain't guna catch anything anyway," Haven teased out of nervousness. He gave an arrogant chuckle but immediately stopped when Landon resurfaced with an armload of trout. It was too much to count, and as he dropped them into the bucket, his gleaming eyes strayed to me. Dean and Jacy were instantly amused.

"Hey, that's a bucket load!" Jacy hooted at Haven. Frustrated, Haven kicked the bucket of fishes, and they dispersed back into the creek. He drew in the empty bucket and set it back on the emerged rock. "Boy's, don't," their father begged, but Haven jumped in and went underwater. *I had to distract him from this pissing contest.*

As Haven emerged from the water, he wouldn't look at me until he dropped all the trout he caught in the bucket. He turned around and stopped mid-sentence when he noticed me pulling off my shorts. His eyes came waving into mine like brilliant blue currents from a distance, and his face completely lit up. His peachy cheeks were flushed watermelon pink. His cove eyes sparkled, and I waved him over. In a split second, Haven was standing in front of me, dripping wet and nearly falling to his knees in praise. He said nothing as he took a seat and pulled me onto his damp lap.

We watched Leyla and Jacy awkwardly flirt while sharing fresh guava. So consumed in *my* love story, I didn't notice how close the pair had become until now. I've always known that Jacy was in love with Leyla, so he didn't surprise me, but Leyla seemed wholeheartedly indulged in Jacy, and she melted for him. Who could blame her? You could tell he was a Tyson, regardless of his dirty blonde hair and pretty russet eyes. Unlike Haven and Landon, Jacy looked more like Dean. He had thinner lips and dressed bookish. He was also the more emotionally tamed and well-spoken out of the boys. We could see how that made it hard to express to Leyla how he felt about her. Leyla, however, turned from dust to mud around Jace.

Jacy paced around, looking at the rushing creek before walking over to Leyla, and pulling off his shirt. Leyla watched shamelessly as her cheeks reddened. Modestly old-fashioned, book boy Jacy had been holding out on her. Underneath that loose tee and oversized flannel, Jacy in natural muscle. And he had a few tattoos. He had the Tyson name on his back, and on one shoulder blade, a condor, and on the other, an eagle. Roses and native tribals. Leyla was lost at the sight of him but managed to choke up the words, *"Chacho nene."*

"What?" He looked utterly startled by the words.

"-Just something that our cousin Salome used to say. We visited them every summer in Puerto Rico. Until uncle Juno and my dad got into it a few years ago. I miss them. "

"Yeah, we know the Managualts from the homeland... I'm also good friends with Juno." Dean mentioned.

"-Another Managualt girl? LORD protect us." Landon was sarcastic, but I'm sure he meant it. The Other two brothers agreed.

It was true. Another Managualt girl was running around. Salome was the youngest, a few days off Leyla at 17; she was bossy, jungle smart, and exotically beautiful. Salome was island-born, so she was more adventurous, fierce, and wild. Super headstrong, Salome had a sharp tongue that could cut any Ivy League Lawyer. She is a beauty, and her beauty is deceptive because she's a genius. Salome is also the youngest and most temperamental. Still, she could study anything she wanted with her academic credentials. "-You think Daya is a brat? Wait till you meet Salome." Leyla joked, and the boys all laughed. Leyla took off her sundress, showing off her top-notch cheer body. Both Landon and Jacy awkwardly admired her as she reflected on family trips to Puerto Rico. Leyla bounced her wavy, lux, shoulder-length hair and charmed the two with her smile. "We should take a trip together," she suggested to Jacy.

Meanwhile, I knew Haven wanted me in the water with him. We were nearly half-naked, and the thought weighed in his mind as he kept eyeing the water and gesturing to the creek. Now that I was short-less, Haven became agitated with me in this tiny, ridiculously thin bodysuit. I was glowing, but in the sunlight, I sparkled and shined, and he was becoming weak as I felt him pitch up between my thighs. When I looked back at him, there was something different about his sharp eyes. They were bright royal blue with a glimmering tint of ivory that gleamed a lecherous fascination. He wore a showstopping smile that nearly knocked out my defenses like a magnetic pulse. I quaked in my skin. Somehow he caught on to my plan, and now it was outright war. He held me in his arms as he stood up, and our bodies met close-knit. His breath fogged over my lips, and his fingertips flowed down the curvy length of my body. I was nearly naked, and he was *very* aware of that.

"You two ARE being responsible, right?" Dean interrupted.

"-Of course!" In conjunction, nevertheless. It was apparent that we needed privacy, and Haven had the perfect spot in mind. Taking my hand, he tried pulling me along, but my heels scraped the ground to a halt. I yanked Haven's arm back, and the strength of it was powerful enough to jolt him back violently. Horror in my eyes.

"What? What's wrong?"

"I don't cliff jump."

"Queen of the Lagoon, and you don't cliff dive?" In disbelief, he tried pulling me along, But still, I didn't move. I was honestly afraid. The fear was great, and I was nearly in a terror dome trance.

"I… I hit the side of a cliff once. I broke my shoulder blade."

"Trust me. I'll protect you." I looked at him skeptically. He looked at me long and disappointed before he exhaled hard,

Tossing me over his shoulder, he carried me to the diving point. My fear made me react by sinking deep into him, like a soft, cozy security blanket. He adjusted me into his arms as I straddled him. I wrapped my arms and legs around him tightly and dug my face into his chest. Shaking and trembling, I couldn't stare down at the rapid waters. Haven and all of his useless fears. *"Don't be nervous,"* he says as his thumb dances along my jawline. His touch, so innocent but ached with intention. He kissed my shoulders and neck. His lips were like a stamp, marking every part of me as much as he could. Releasing my nervous grip, I could feel that I was no longer afraid,

Without warning, Haven pushed off the ledge. It was an unsettling drop. I didn't seem to have a heartbeat as the wind swam through my hair. Haven's eyes caught my eyes, and I could feel all of my fears disappear with the wind. It was only Haven's power that could do that; pull apart my weakness and give me strength.

I jolted him with energy because I loved him so much.

Our bodies crashed into the ice-cold water, engulfed into an abyss of bubbles and rushing blue and green waters, dispersing all around. For a moment, our bodies floated apart, but I soon felt his hands find me. His fingertips gripped my hips, and we shot up from the trench waters, both our bodies breaking the surface in double time. Our eyes met again as all became still. Haven smiled, and the feeling was contagious because I smiled back. We danced in a current swirl, and I knew he was thinking of kissing me. *Not yet, buddy.*

He jumped towards me, but I swam back. He smirked at my childish grin before I took off swimming. All that time spent in the lagoon, and all the knowledge I have of oceans, seas, and waters from my ancestors, made me an Olympic swimmer. If he weren't to apologize, I would make him chase me till he gave in. Instead, he followed me down the deep creek with no problem. He was an expert swimmer, too, with unyielding energy. So I used a little magic and cheated. I swirled the current in the opposite direction behind me. Still, he swam against the powerful current. He wasn't going to give up. He stretched the current back as far as he could pull.

Far from lurking souls, Haven and I wandered into a secluded pool. A natural dam of large submerged boulders formed a barricading wall. I was trapped. I had nowhere to go as Haven drew close. I looked around for a quick escape. Another boulder was large enough to hide behind, so I took refuge there. I pulled up to the surface and leaned back against the boulder, trying to keep still. He was making me anxious, as I anticipated him surprising me. I soon felt a handlock at my ankle. My heart dropped as I could feel Haven's head suddenly push in between my knees. *OH MY GOD*, what was he doing? I held onto the boulder. My fingernails scraped deep into the sediment as Haven brushed his face against my inner thigh and kissed my love button through the thin fabric. He used my body to pull himself up and broke the surface before me. He trapped me, grabbing me by my wrists and pinning me up against the boulder, like butterfly wings. I pretend to struggle, absolutely loving every minute of him demanding my love from me. He melted me with the charm in his eyes. I had no choice but to concede—partial white flag. *Fine. I'll play your game.* I latched onto Haven and straddled him as I made the current push him deeper into me.

In the middle of nature, all alone, "Do you trust me?"

I pretended to be hopeless, biting my lip and thrusting on him.

"I trust you," I whispered breathlessly; my slow thrusting was surely letting me get off, and he was beginning to notice. His eyes ignited. I felt his river monster grow suddenly, pressing up against my clit. Rolling my hips over his, he watched my body flex over him. His fingers gently tugged against my waist-beads.

"Don't. I won't be able to hold back."

I wasn't afraid. I was falling in love with the rush of pushing the boundaries. I danced on him slower, and we both got the shivers. You could see the hunger in his eyes. He wanted me so bad.

"You're not touching me once we get out this creek."

"We had a truce. So I have the whole day."

"Yeah, the whole day to apologize."

Now he was trying to create some distance between our hooked hips. He was harnessing self-control. He did what he could not to look down at my breast, and I tried to cast them in his view, but he ignored them. Instead, he stared me in the eye. Then, without warning, he sincerely *hugged* me. Like I've never felt before. Somewhat stunned, I kept quiet as he held me in his warm arms, "I missed you," he said after he rested his heavy jaw on my shoulder and kept me close, innocently twirling my falling curls. I absorbed his waves of superior emotion. That valuable feeling I seem to get from only him. His eyes dramatically searched me, and I pushed into Haven with a passionate kiss, and this time, we wouldn't stop.

Our lips collided in cohesiveness with the motions of the surrounding water. Haven became weak, like the river. I settled my toes on him, his hand tingling against the back of my neck, his other hand gliding down the side of my breasts. He pushed his pelvic into mine, and a stream of love gush came out of me. My powers were causing a fit, rippling currents of color and parrots singing above on palms. *What was he doing to me?* He nipped at my earlobe as his hand slipped between my thighs. He began to *touch* my clit so softly and in-depth; my eyes rolled closed. Now, all I could hear was the chirping of more exotic tropical birds; hummingbirds and spindalis. My eyes opened up to foreign turtles and frogs swarming around; so exotically colorful, and the birds were singing. Even the air had a different taste to it. It was sweeter, wetter, richer. It was hotter and more humid—the smell of musk and sweet honey. Everything reflected off the sun. Everything shined bright, like in Boriken.

Haven and I continued to marvel in a frenzy, trying to restrain ourselves but also wanting to let go. He kissed my neck hard, then licked me—a familiar tingling feeling all over my tainted skin. I've missed *this* feeling. My arms drew him closer as he kept licking and sucking on me. God, he felt so good. My heart was pumping, and my lungs kept rising and colliding too fast, refusing me to breathe. I moaned breathlessly when his lips left my neck, and he found the strength to pull away from me. He gave me one last aggressive kiss. The kind that steals your breath away, the kind you want to be angry about but can't because it makes you feel so desired.

We were enchanted by my powers; I had transformed our surroundings into a river in *El Yunque Rainforest*. From the birds to the frogs and trees. Stunned, we looked around mystified. Then, his hands reached for me and pulled me back in. He sat me on his arms and lifted me over his waist, breaking free from my trap.

"-Thank God this water is like 40 degrees-" he joked, fixing his shorts in the water. "-I love you." He said firmly.

"So, then why do you ignore my feelings, Haven?"

"I'm not. Haven't you noticed you're hard to ignore,"

"Yet, you seem to be so good at it." I peeled away from his grip.

"Trust me. I hear *everything* you say."

"-So don't ignore my simple request."

"-*Request?* For what? An apology? First, off Daya, I'm your Guard, not your lap dog. How about you apologize to me?"

Our bickering broke the magic, and the tropical rain forest quickly faded into the dark Northern creek again. No longer were we bobbing in a tropical river in the tropics. Instead, all we could hear now was Leyla and the others calling out for us.

"-You kissed Landon in front of the entire school at that game. I think about that all the time. I think you could let this one go."

We could see Leyla with Landon and Jacy swimming over.

"-I wasn't your girl at the time."

"-You weren't my girl when I came home," I scoffed.

"Are you trying to be funny?"

"No, Daya, I'm not. So forget about that damn apology, okay."

"-I rather marry Landon,"

Haven's bloodshot eyes narrowed in on me, "-*Watch your fucking mouth!*" Haven snapped as the others approached. His anger didn't scare me so much, as it hurt. At a loss with him, I abruptly splashed his face and took off swimming, and this time, he wouldn't keep up.

Eventually, they all followed me back to camp. I stormed into the center, where Dean and Charlotte were lounging. They could see how crossed I was even before I approached them. I snatched a towel and blew past as my aunt followed me over to the camp makeshift shower. While Dean grilled, Haven was coming from behind, several feet away. Haven didn't say anything as he walked over to his camping chair and angrily got dressed over his wet swim shorts. I slipped behind the tarp and stripped, starting a cold shower. I wanted to drown in it.

"It's useless to talk to him! He just doesn't understand-"

"What, honey?" Charlotte wondered.

"It was the first time *he* broke *my heart*. I could feel that." I started to cry, and I knew everyone could hear me at this point. I was embarrassed, but I couldn't hold it in any longer. I've grown used to being stripped down by Haven. I held myself together as my head bowed under the cold, weak shower. "I've apologized so many times for things I had no control over. He had control over this, and he let me down on purpose. He won't even own up to it." Tears came down, and so did my body. I buried my face into my knees.

"-I don't want to be judged for my past."

"No one's judging you. The curse and fevers are a natural but terrible reality for you, and we take that seriously."

I scoffed miserably, "I wouldn't be too sure with this hothead."

Charlotte smiled, handing me a long robe. "He's a boy in love. They act up when they're in love, especially the Tyson men-" I expected her to say that. It was ludicrous to think that Haven didn't want to apologize. I loved Haven but hated how worked up he made me. Either I'm over the moon hot and heavy for him, or flustered and angry, hanging to my last branched nerve. "-You and Haven are not a common collision. You two are very different, yet so much the same. Of course, it doesn't help that you both are feisty and stubborn, especially about each other. It's quite beautiful to watch. The spark of true love before your eyes."

"Is it just a spark? I feel like I'm in a forest fire."

"Haven can be a little harsh. But, sometimes you forget that Haven's been through a lot, growing up without a mother, traveling all the time, not always having Dean and Jacy around. Haven had time to make mistakes and learn from them, and we all know he lives by that motto. Haven fought his battles alone and is more than comfortable with his battle scars. That's what sets him apart from the other ones, especially for you. You and Haven are powerful enough to heal each other from those wounds. You want something honest, and he needs someone understanding; you both need something real. And here it is." I watched him from afar, smoking his gross cigarette and glancing at me as his father laid into him.

I knew nothing of the deep stuff that haunted him,

"-Don't try to compare your sheltered life to the torment that Haven lived through. Dean's a great dad, but some things you can't do for your kids. Dean forbade him to make contact because he knew the danger of Misael's spells, but some pain you can't take away. Haven was never supposed to know about you, yet Haven found his way here. He was okay with a meaningless life, but no one understood him. More so when the Great Spirits showed him his true purpose. They warned him and even gave him a chance to relinquish the given gift as your sole protector. He took that vow without knowing who you were but also knowing it would indefinitely cost his heart's freedom. In the end, you were more important. It was painful for him to watch the girl of his dreams fall for someone who turned out to be his blood. Sometimes it's okay to be blissfully ignorant. I think you should consider all that still runs deep within him. Have some patience. I don't want you to live with regret. A broken heart is most painful when you realize nothing else makes you happy but him, even when he's being impossible."

"You're right, but I won't allow infidelity. I don't know what else to do, and there's no taming Haven Tyson."

"Daya, I know coming to your womanhood is an awkward stage, but don't focus on the writing in between. You're a good girl. All you have to do is be your mesmerizing self. There's no shame in being sexy—even a tad submissive. Remind him why you're *his Queen.*"

Haven was gone by the end of my shower, so I planned to keep to myself until he returned. Dusk came, and the sky was seeping sundown colors. Dean had hauled us in around the fire for dinner. Burgers and BBQ chicken skewers with grilled veggies. I kept my distance from everyone and barely ate. In my mind, I was stuck. I couldn't understand how I'd already started to miss Haven.

As Charlotte and Dean cleaned and packed up for an early leave in the morning, Landon, Leyla, and Jacy sat around the campfire, drinking whiskey from the bottle, listening to the radio, and talking. Leyla waved me over, "-Stop acting like a stick in the mud." So I walked over and sat down at an empty camping chair. Leyla gave me the liquor bottle, and I took a big gulp.

"-That true love is serious; I saw that river magic."

Leyla confessed, and I rolled my eyes, "Haven and I are doomed,"

"No- You two are perfect for each other." Jacy cut in,

"-I know Haven better than anyone else. He's an ass, but I don't need to convince you that he loves you, Daya. Haven only opens up when *you're* around. Don't you ever wonder why we all are so intrigued to see you two together? He's never like that. And you, all flushed and irritated all the time. You two use your defenses on each other, and it's a fucking train wreck. But, at the same time, you can see **it** between you two. It's undeniable, despite how stupid my brother is. Haven never apologies. It's a part of some practice, or whatever. If I were you, I'd just let it go and sit pretty."

"I'm not just going to '*sit pretty*. I have Taino blood. I can't. My ancestors didn't even bother with men. They were content living separately and only needed them around for one thing."

"Damn, but it's true." Landon's border personality agreed.

"Regardless, you should stop dwelling on his bull shit."

"Even if it hurts?"

"Love hurts, Daya. Welcome to your *real* life."

"-And they'll both continue to hurt if they don't learn to trust each other. It would help if you focused on your powers," Dean chimed in as he joined us around the fire. I took one more sip of whiskey before Dean snatched it away.

"Yeah, show us something cool," Leyla begged.

I put my hands out before them, cupped like I held something. Very quickly, my magic began to materialize before me, hovering over my palms. Lights of color, floating in my hands, a glowing orb appeared, golden. It swirled like a planet in the solar system, and pollen from the world around swooned into the orb. I showed them the dandelion's pollination, birth, and life cycle through the globe. In the end, I was holding the flower in my hand. I handed Landon the flower, "I never knew you could do that..."

"-I know, right..." I hiccuped, realizing I was sinking into my intoxication quicker like quicksand. I tried hiding it.

The quietness in the air was slowly passing when headlights appeared from the ATV trail. Haven was back. We all watched as he parked the ATV with the others and slowly walked over. His head hung low like he wasn't ready to face me after making me cry, but he had no other choice. He stopped before me, "Are you okay?" He softly reached for a strand of my hair. I looked away from his sad eyes, "-Yeah, I'm okay." I was only okay because I was drunk. Alcohol gives you heart, the courage to stand in the face of awkwardness. Haven bent over and softly kissed my cheek. He felt calm and friendly, but I didn't say anything as he studied me a moment, then pulled up a chair next to mine. He sat down comfortably and asked, "What's everyone doing?" stretching his arm over my shoulders.

"-Daya was showing us a trick," Landon held up the dandelion.

"Where did you get that?" Haven asked, near to amazed. It glittered and sparkled a bit, but it was only a crummy dandelion; the way he looked at it, like the akani to gold. Landon handed Haven the flower, still glowing from its manifestation, "Show me." He was stuck, twirling the flower by its stem. I scoffed and sat back, thinking, he didn't deserve to see my magic. He stared on, and I hiccuped again, so casually. But then Charlotte's advice rang in my head. I softened and looked at him differently. Intrigued. He checked the look right back. I shifted my body towards him, on a make, and then softly took his hands into mine, and I didn't hesitate to start over again, over his nervous hands, staring at him in his struck eyes.

I did the trick a second time. This time the pollination and life cycle of red hibiscus. After the flower was in bloom in the orb, I tossed the globe up in the air, and suddenly a hummingbird broke free from the glowing sphere. The hummingbird flew and dropped the flower in Haven's lap before taking off. Haven was captivated, completely awed, and turned on. The look he gave me was dangerous enough to ignite an erotic fire within. I quickly stood up and urged away from everyone, stumbling away from the campfire, giggling. "-Hey, where are you going? Come back,"

Haven followed me towards the cliff ledges and stopped when I stopped, meters from the drop. In the silence, we admired the northern night sky. Stars twinkled, and the sound of clouds passed. My easy spill magic lured in the angelical sound of rain frogs out in a northern forest. My power radiated, and it lured in lightning bugs and crickets. I shooed them away, and he laughed at me.

"Please leave me alone. I'm too drunk to deal with you."

"I didn't mean to leave like that. What are you thinking?"

"I think you're mean to me because you're angry that you had to watch me live a lie, and maybe you hate me for it."

"Yeah, I'm pissed off, so this 'apology' thing seems stupid. But I love you, and I can't tell you enough. Especially your magic."

"My magic is special. I can't share it with just anybody."

"I'm not just anybody, Daya-"

"-That's how you make me feel."

For a moment, he was quiet, in deep thought, "Okay, I've been reckless. I regret the times I've been harsh towards you, but I've been a hostage of your love for so long. You're my Queen. Stop the attitude. You have more of me than you know," He pulled me into the warmth and security of his arms, closing in on me. "-I swore to protect and love you. Life and death, ever after. Do you want to continue to fight? Or can we communicate? And before you ask, I told Seneca to back off. She knows how I feel about you, and she won't be in the mix. That's done, so don't bring it up anymore. You have my loyalty-I swear on my divine soul; you're the only one-"

The next thing I know, Haven and I are somewhere off in the woods. Completely alone and entirely in the dark. The night obscured our crashing bodies, as innocent as possible, but we were going at it against a tree—only kissing, but his lips were on me and mine on him. Haven held me against the tree, sucking in all my delectable energy. The air blew, but it felt so still and quiet, like nothing else existed but the pounding of our inevitably tainted hearts. His hands touched with such intention. Who could imagine wanting someone so dangerous and not having the control, nor the urge to keep away? He must have felt what I felt cuz he moaned between his smearing kisses, "I'm sorry, baby, I'm so sorry, " I smiled in the moonlight, as his vicious kissing slowed on my navel, but as he reached to kiss me more, I pulled away and vomited.

Early morning,

I felt the sunrise hours before it even came up. It would be a hot day, and I felt it in my bones. I had passed out in Haven's tent, but he wasn't here with me. I searched in the dark to find Haven's cell phone and used the light to look around the dark tent. He was gone, and it was still dark out. I checked the time. **4:50 am.** I tossed aside his phone and saw a text from my friend Sunny. *Hell. No.* How did *she* have *his* number? I swiped the screen; no passcode, and surprisingly, I was his background photo. *Cute,* I briefly thought, before I wondered how he had gotten this photo of me. Finally, I clicked on her message— So, it reads:

"I have what you're looking for."

In which he responded,

"On my way."

I couldn't help it. I had to text back,

"This is Daya, fuck off."

The messages rebirthed jealousy in my mind. I tossed the phone aside. I'm too fucking hungover to deal with this kind of reality check. Was Haven now hanging out with Sunny behind my back? Haven swore on his divinely wretched soul. I could feel my weak powers rush with anger. I slipped my shoes on before taking off into the dark trails. Storm winds formed, and my eyes were gleaming bloodstone. Thunder rolled, and rain began to pour. I kept running. My head filled with damaging thoughts. *Is he on his way to see her?* Lightening zapping and winds broke branches and blew leaves. I had to find a safe place from the rain, I thought. As I took cover from the storm in a cave, so did the colossal bear I always seem to meet. I didn't fear the old friend. He was calm, as always, when he appeared. He snuggled his extensive body up to me, and I collapsed onto him. Devastated and broken, I lay there crying, holding onto the bear for comfort. The bear's loving energy alleviated me from the heartache. His aura rocked me until I fell into a peaceful sleep.

I was no longer in the cave with the bear in the morning. Instead, I found myself back in Haven's tent, as if none of it had happened. As if it were all a dream. But I knew it had happened. I didn't need my muddy clothes to tell me that. I sat back up just like I did earlier that morning. Again Haven wasn't in the tent. *Déjà vu.* The storm had passed, and only blue skies greeted the mid-morning. I crawled out of the tent and stormed over to where Dean and Haven sat poking at the morning fire. Holding the red hibiscus I gifted him, Haven tried to intercept me, but I stopped him,

"Daya, we have our revival lesson today."

"Dean, I don't want to break the curse. I give up."

"Hey, stop talking like that," Haven demanded, "-you forgave me last night," his face was in a frenzy of confusion, "Do you know how fucking hard it was to apologize?"

"Real *hard;* give me the flower back,"

I firmly held my hand out. But, instead of giving it back, he held out the flower and popped the flower's head off with his thumb.

"You are just like the *conquistador!*"

We were meteors crashing. I picked up the flowerhead.

"Are you going to tell me what the hell I did now?"

"Why were you texting Sunny?"

"*Are you fucking kidding me, Daya?!*" Haven was so loud that Landon came out of his tent. When he walked over, I stupidly ran into his arms. Landon was so concerned, he caught me and immediately absorbed me. "How can he be the one?" I stupidly questioned.

Landon's hands slid to my hips, "One way to find out," he pulled my body into him. Excitement pulsed through Guakar's human veins. "No-wait!" I pleaded, but it was too late; his lips were on mine. I tried to pull away, nearly tripping over a rock, but he pulled me in against my will. Haven lunged forward to hit him. For that moment, they wrestled, but Guakar was a lot stronger. 'Landon' held Haven to the ground until Dean pulled him off.

"-I don't want anything else to do with you, skirt!"

Haven's words added fire between our quarreling eyes.

16

Lesson

DAYA-

Dean didn't care about what Haven and I wanted during a moment of 'madness.' He took me on a detour to learn a lesson anyway. The drive was long enough to force me into reflecting. I couldn't stop thinking of the words exchanged between Haven and me. Were we officially done? I wanted nothing more than to be with the Haven I fell in love with, but I couldn't fix this alone. By tonight, Haven would relinquish me and be consoling himself with Sunny. He'd have his arms around her, and they'd rejoice because Haven will have a future on earth, now that he wasn't with me, a living ghost. Dean couldn't silence his disappointment in us,

"I don't think you mean any of that, Daya. I think you're angry, and you have every right to be. Believe me, when I tell you, Misael's games had your mom and me at our breaking point too. When Ana disappeared, Misael made me think she was gone for good, and somehow, as fate would have it, I got tangled up with Caroline again. When your mother returned, Misael had a field day with the drama between her sudden pregnancy and my affair. That's when she chased me with that sandal,"

"Well, what happened? How did you fix it?"

"Honesty, patience, and communication. And mostly understanding. But your mother and I, we are not you and Haven. I'm not a loose cannon, your mother wasn't so uptight, and our love affair wasn't so complicated. Ana, for some reason, took a liking to sheriff Ruiz. He brought her flowers every day, and she used to mount them on the window ledges to piss me off, and I actually would take them down. I hated him. But, our situation wasn't nearly as bad as this. Misael turned my boys against each other, using you, and I have to say, that trick back there; I never want to see you do that again using Landon. My boys can be idiots, but they're kind. They don't deserve it. As for Haven, his heart is in terrible shape. You have no idea what kind of mess I have to clean up,"

"I'm sorry, Dean, I was just so angry. All these emotions are new to me. I never had to feel any of these feelings before, let alone control them. Anger and jealousy are a lot to deal with when you've been a loveless girl. What I did was immature, and I feel terrible."

"Your magic will wear off on Landon as it has done in the past. But, unfortunately, Haven saw you make your decision. He's always been insecure about your history with Landon, more so because you accepted Landon's engagement ring when he asked you to marry him, and you accepted at free will after the curse broke. He feels like he's forcing you to pick him, and he wants you to want him back. It's no secret that my boys are all different. This whole, 'do as I say. I'm your queen', makes Haven feel like your trying to change him into Landon. Does that make sense?"

To be ignorantly blissful again,

"I suppose so." Dean was right. I've been harsh on Haven.

"-How did this start anyway? You two were desperate to find each other just a few weeks ago and now look at you two."

"-It doesn't matter anymore, Dean. I've made my mind up. I'll give my soul to my garden and give everything up. And, I'll have my father release your family from the Managualt curse. You can all live a normal happy life." The truck came to a halt on the side of the road near the forest edges. He looked at me skeptically.

Dean and I got out of his truck. He grabbed a camping chair and a large lunch box and led me into the woods. We walked for some time until we approached a devastating clearing. It was all freshly burned down and destroyed. Horrific, dark, and still steaming. "What happened?" I walked further into the damage.

"We don't exactly know... Haven came across it one night while on the run and called me down to check it out. It took the firefighters nearly 17 hours to put it out. As you can see, it was pretty bad."

I looked around. It reminded me of the damage the fire in my dreams would leave behind. My magic was strong, but I wasn't sure if I had it to revive this much space with this much damage, "Dean, no offense, but are you loco? This forest is in serious shape, and I'm not powerful enough to fix this."

"Of course your not. Not while you and Haven keep fighting. You two need to realize that you two feed off each other. Whether positive or negative, he gets his power from you; you get your power from him. Connected, you share more than just emotions and dreams. You share power. If your weak, he's weak. If he's weak, so are you. I don't expect you to clean this up right now in your condition. I expect you to sit here all day and think about it."

I felt like a kid again when my uncle forced us to do *Bomba* class, and all I wanted to do was play outside. I sucked my teeth and stormed in more, collapsing to my knees and recharging my magic. Dean put down the lunch box and took a seat in the camping chair only meters from me. He expected to be here all day but prepared to be here all night. I sat down and meditated as he guided me through for nearly 7 hours. Even though we were there all day, I didn't get much done after clearing away the negative energy. The damage was pretty bad, but I could whisk away the smoke, ashes, and damaged plants and trees. I purified the tainted soil and cleared out the harmful stuff. I multiplied all that was good, organic, and rich earth. I had a new slate and stripped the land into nothing but fresh, new soil, which was better than how we found it. It was late when we finally left the clearing. All that was left now was nothing but clean soil, an empty canvas for the next time. Dean dropped me off, and as always, I thanked him for an honest day.

It was a rough night, and I had another nightmare. I saw the wendigo causing the wildfire. It was hungry, searching for me. It burned down most of the forest in a rampage until that colossal bear appeared and stopped it. I woke up, and the scars left from the creature, felt as if they were on fire. I woke the house with my screams. I was too nervous to sleep, so I waited for the dawn so that Misael could take me home to the garden. I needed my garden and all of the natural remedies. My uncle never questioned it. He had been waiting for this to happen. Even if I was dying inside, at least I had my life, and he still had some control of it. Misael took the opportunity to make amends. He was spoiling me with takeout, books, and boasting about the graduation gifts. I didn't care about any of it. The melodrama with Haven and me was enough to keep me from the *world* for a couple of days. Then, finally, I went to the one place I could hide out in safety from my untrusting uncle, the heartbreaker, the fevers, and the wendigo, *my garden*. I needed to heal in the comfort of my beautiful, magical garden.

But mostly, I needed my mother.

Upon going in, my Garden world was naturally in turmoil. A low-level hurricane had ravaged my rain forest, and it poured for days straight. The cure to my broken world was reiki healing magic. With my garden stuck in a compromising state, I left to the tropics garden of Anais; and indulged in pineapple juice and coconut cocktails, flower crowns, and dancing on the beach under a Taino moon. Meditation, night and day, and Reiki daily. The natural coconut macaroons were a plus, and I loved talking to my mother. Anais was wildly entertained with our antics, just as everyone else was. But unlike everyone else, she also had great motherly advice as a mother should, and she laid into me about my toxicity. She was right. Anais knew what to say to make me feel better. She reminded me that evil forces were out there to destroy us, and it sounded like I was helping those forces win. My weakness to such possession infuriated Anais, in which she inflicted a protection spell against these evil, jealous, and belligerent forces.

"You are my child, of the ocean, sand, and salt," As we sat on her beach, she soaked her hand in the ocean and splashed the saltwater on my forehead. She took the warm sand and painted a Taino symbol on my forehead. She spoke in her native language, *"Guava will heal the heart. Soursop will keep you together. The mango juice will open the flow of communication. The salt will make barriers and boundaries to ease the fighting. Palm will add relief, while the Coqui tear will strengthen your heart. Lastly, the bite of the Puerto Rican racer snake will restore faith in this union and help you carry on."*

I was pleasantly surprised to find a rainbow over a clear, bright sky and the sun shining again in my garden. The storm was gone in my garden, and as if not thought possible, it was stronger than before. And so I finally left the garden. When I got back to the Earth realm, I realized that pulling Haven back into my graces wouldn't be much of a challenge. He's already missed me as much as I missed him. Misael's front porch flooded with gifts. Not even my uncle magic could get rid of the flowers, love letters, teddy bears, coconut water, grapefruit, and shiny crystals and gems, sitting around like offerings. I magically sent it all into my garden, except his last note. I read the apology he wrote, and it made me cry. I didn't wish to change the man Haven was. I only wish he had been kinder. He was honestly sorry for what he did. There was no need to beg for my forgiveness, and I intended to do so.

HAVEN-

Finally.

Daya has left her garden. I don't like stalking her from the woods, but what else choice do I have? She doesn't want me anywhere near her. As if I'm going to stand around and let her do that to us. She's fucking nuts. Christ, she looks stunning as always, in tiny red romper lingerie and that color on her perfect olive skin. Her angelic face blushed. How the fuck is it possible for someone so heavenly to exist on this earthly plane? It should be considered a damn sin. That face. Those legs. All killer. Damn, it was hot this morning. But, on the other hand, it could be Daya's powers. The morning had been diligently pushing along, and I haven't been able to take my eyes off her since I've noticed her out here reading my letters. I wasn't sure, but it seemed as though she was crying. Curiosity kills me, and I have to get closer to confirm. Dean wanted to move me as far as Hawaii so that I wouldn't show up at Misael's door. Yet, here I am, stalking his precious niece from the woods religiously.

The first time she disappeared, I didn't know why or how. But this time, I knew she was only trying to avoid me, which turned out to be more frustrating than the fear of her just being taken. I wouldn't say I liked every minute of it. It pissed me off how content she was just staying away from me, and I couldn't help but notice that she was in good graces with her uncle once again. Dean tried to warn me. All I've done to open those classic eyes, but she always chose to see the good. And because I was acting like a fucking dummy, my dumb ass just pushed away. So now, she willingly reports back to her dangerous uncle. Dean had been right, and I resisted apologizing to Daya for nothing because, at the end of it all, I was still looking for Daya.

Yeah, I was upset for sure. Once again, she was acting childish over a stupid text, and then she kissed Landon and threatened to disappear from my life. Like I don't already have trust issues. It hit me hard. I've been aggressive and possessive, and all she ever tried to do was love me with all my flaws. Daya was a Goddess, but a fragile one. I had been careless that I *was* her *first love, her first heartbreak* **ever**. I've already known how it felt, so I should have been cautious. But, instead, I was too familiar with it, and I mishandled her tender heart. I hated myself for making her cry like that. I had to leave that very second. I couldn't face her eyes.

So I did what any man would do, and I went home for a couple of hours to give her space. I fished in the pond in the back for a while, sprinted suicides down the front lawn, ate some food, listened to songs that reminded me of her, manually exercised in the shower. Okay, so I couldn't help but rub one out; can you blame me? I couldn't get that early day in the creek out of my mind and how tempting Daya looked almost naked. She knew what she was doing, and this wasn't like in the past, where I'd sleep with a babe, knowing she wouldn't get me to climax. I'd end up there all night knocking boots till she's all tired and taps out, sending me on my way unsatisfied. No. *Daya* was so different.

I've had Daya encrypted in my mind, and I've imagined how she would look like taking in my entire dick from under me. What a powerful thought that would nearly cap me in my knees in the shower. Dean just renovated my bathroom, but I pushed one hand clear through the new shower tile after making myself cum for the first time, severely, I'd say. I only hoped no one would ask about what happened to the tile as I tried cleaning my mess.

When I was getting dressed I started to cry. Not a silent cry either. Don't judge me. I was going through it. Hearing Daya cry made me feel bad, and I had decided I would apologize. Randomly using Seneca to make Daya jealous was a massive mistake. I created a love triangle that I didn't want to be in, and I felt terrible knowing Seneca would catch the shit end of the stick, but I had to be honest about it, I only cared about Daya and this whole platonic friendship with Seneca bothered her. Seneca would eventually get over it. Daya might never will. I needed Daya to know that the only person I wanted around was her. But, as I learned from memories emerging from the abyss of my mind, her magic was unmatched, and I wanted to see it all the time. Even if I had to force her to do the spell for me, that wasn't fair for her. I should have known that as an adult, Daya wouldn't stand to be pushed into doing **'tricks.'** Especially if I had to hurt her to do it.

I expected her to be mad but not drunk when I returned to Wolf Cliff that night. Daya wasn't much of a drinker. But, unfortunately, that text with Sunny, she wasn't going to let go. Her hiccups and slurring were cute but being drunk wasn't a good look on her. She seems always to be the only one who could ever get a rise from me like that. I hated how easy it was for her to make me weak. I talked to Daya that night about **everything;** I gave her the *real* apology she wanted from me when we were in my tent after throwing up all over me. I was her man, whether she wanted to believe it, and I'll prove it if I have to. I'd thought it would be weird apologizing. Not with her. I felt better. For a minute, I thought we would be okay after she told me she loved me before passing out.

It wasn't until my usual nightly run that I knew something serious harbored her mind. I saw her running completely focused and knew she was tripping. After chasing her to the cave and calming her down, I carried her back to the tent. As she slept peacefully, I had realized; she had replied to Sunny's text. I couldn't help but chuckle, *(This is Daya, Fuck off,)*

I loved her passion. I was entirely in my feelings about her. That's when Dean pulled me from my tent, and per usual, he wanted to talk about how much of a fuck up I was. I explained to him that I would cool it and apologized, but she woke up flying off the handle with those creepy green eyes, talking about how I lied to her. Daya must have taken the text out of context. Of course, she was assuming shit because females tend to do that.

My heart has always belonged to Daya since the first day I've roamed these parts, and Sunny knows it. Seneca knows it. Every female I came across, I made sure, knew it. They all wanted me to fall for them, but I didn't fall. I've done that already with Daya, and I'd only do it once. Seneca was my last sexual conquest with no success, and I have been abstinent since. I only asked Sunny to text me when the books I ordered were delivered to the bookshop. I should have gone through the manager; he wouldn't have texted me at such an awkward time. If only Daya knew she was beginning to break me without knowing it. My thoughts of her alone were powerful enough to help me push along on my own, and I only hungered for more. No girl could ever distract me from her magic. As I learned from my memories emerging from the abyss of my mind, her magic was unmatched, and I wanted to see it all the time. I should have known that as an adult, Daya wouldn't stand to be pushed into doing **'tricks,'** especially if I had to hurt her to do it. But I figured I'd keep the stem in my wallet.

When dad took Daya, unwillingly, for her lesson, Jacy, Landon, and I separated into our bedrooms, and I took to working out; with actual weights this time. There was so much tension in that house I'm surprised Dean didn't find us chewing at each other like rabid dogs. The truth was, messing around with Daya, I've grown more patient and resilient, stronger, and sharper. I knew Landon didn't mean to cut in the way. With his magic drugs, Landon had been pulled into this by Misael, and Landon was only temporarily under Daya's spell that she says *I* provoked her to do. I was livid when they locked lips, watching her give in to his arms that way.

I knew Dean wasn't happy with my decisions ever since coming into town. I wasn't making him proud, but still, I felt like I didn't do anything wrong; if Daya kept shut for 2 minutes, I'd explain. Her intent with Landon made me say those horrible last words, and it's been weighing heavier than the weight I was lifting for a while now. In the dark, Dean finally flicked on my bedroom lights. Blinded, I looked for a time—**9:28 pm**. Dean's been out all damn day with Daya, probably listening to her talking crap about me, and now he came storming down my bedroom steps. I sat up on the bench press and looked at his rusty brown eyes as he stood at the steps. I tried to be casual about things, although there was nothing ordinary about how Dean came down here. "It's a damn mess, kid," **Fucking Great.** It was already nerve-racking, catching on to my father's anxiety about it. In all my years of life, nothing made Dean nervous. He always has a solution. So this look on his face jolted me, "She'll calm down, right? It's just a misunderstanding."

"No kid, it's not. She's just learning how to deal with her emotions, and you more than likely traumatized her. Don't you remember how hurt you felt the first time you saw Landon kiss Daya?"

Dean was turning me into venom. I shot up from the bench,

"-Christ sake's Dad, I'll go talk to her in the morning,"

"It's too late, Haven." The air was too hollow. Dean was too quiet. "Haven, she's going to reconcile with her uncle and willingly ask him to spellbind her to the garden."

"She wouldn't do that." I was getting mad again.

"Do you know what the last thing she said was? She wants to free the Tyson family from the curse, and you can live a 'normal' life. You, Jacy, Landon, will never see a Manigault again. So if anything can slap the sense into you, let it be the thought of spending a lifetime without her love. For centuries we helped protect the Manigault bloodline. That was our honor. Misael has been waiting for you to mess up so he could convince her to accept Landon again. So that bullshit with Landon; you have to let it go, son. Her past has always been a lie. You have to trust Daya." Not many words were exchanged after that because I knew Dean was right. I planned to go to Charlotte's during my early morning run to talk to Daya and get her to stop the bullshit; she wasn't going to leave me. But when I broke free from the woods, I hadn't come soon enough.

That was a couple of days ago, and ever since, I've been sleeplessly stalking the garden since she retreated beyond the gates. I'd wait day and night until I saw her again. Everything I wanted to say, I wrote in letters. Any extra money I made went to gifts, flooding Misael's front deck with my infinite love. I had put a spell over each gift, so Misael couldn't destroy any of it. Each morning when I circled the perimeter, I rejoiced in pride. I had used Misael's house as a dumping ground for all my excess love. Every day I waited, and she will know it. Finally, that Sunday morning during that early lap, I stopped and watched her leave the garden. Her perfect glowing skin sparkled in the morning sun. As always, she was radiant. It was all that I needed. Now that she's out, I couldn't waste another minute.

17

Hidden Talents

It was ablaze outside.

Early Saturday morning, and it was insultingly humid out. Hot enough to pull the aggravation right out of me, except I couldn't be angry with the front steps flooded with gifts from Haven. In silky tiny shorts, bralette, and my hair a mess in wild slumbered waves, I sat in the morning sun, thinking about how bad I wanted to fix things with Haven, but my day was already causing such a headache. I could hear Leyla and Misael arguing so early this morning, and that feeling was in the air again, so I kept my distance and moved all of Haven's gifts into my garden.

On the steps, another love letter appeared. I cracked a smile, picked it up, and then noticed the gigantic bear watching me from the shadows of the woods. I met the friendly bear halfway and caressed his big head as he gave out a slight growl of appreciation; familiar blue eyes. I giggled at how soft and nurturing the big scary animal had become with me. Then, suddenly, I heard my uncle screech from behind me, "Step away from the bear before it attacks!" He scared the bear off, and it hauled into the woodland. I sucked my teeth. My uncle was determined to ruin everything.

"He wasn't going to attack..." I argued.

"It's a wild bear Daya. I'll have to buy some bear traps." My uncle trotted back through the swing of the fly door to finish what he started with Leyla, who had been crying over his new rule; **NO JACY**. I felt terrible for her because I knew how she felt.

Unfolding Haven's love note, I blocked out the verbal war between Leyla and my uncle. Unlike the romantic and honest love letters, this letter was a very detailed letter of all the sexual things Haven thought of doing to me, the more I've ignored him. He loved how I teased him. I squeezed my knees together and glanced around not so innocently. I swallowed hard, dancing about my stance to please my yoni. His written words turned me on, and soon enough, I wouldn't be able to hide it. My hand slowly slid between my thighs, brisking over my soft skin, just before Haven tapped my shoulder. Haven stood before me in the flesh, looking great and shirtless, per usual; all too entertained with my body language,

"Catching a high-rise Goddess," He wore a smug smile.

"Maybe?" I checked a smile back.

"-Well, let me help you." His arms flew open so quickly.

"Not a chance Haven Tyson." He dropped to his knees,

"I'M **SORRY.** Please forgive me. I've been such an asshole, and I shouldn't have used Seneca to get back at you, and you really should have waited for me to explain the text to Sunny. It was all stupid, and I don't want to lose you. Say you'll work with me and stay. Tell me you still love me," He demanded. I wanted to bury him inside me. It took strength, but I was in control.

He had nothing to apologize for,

"Haven-" His solid face became stiff as he slowly raised from kneeling. Our eyes squared off a moment, "-I've been a royal bitch. I'm the one who should be sorry."

"Eh, stop that shit right now. I'm supposed to be apologizing. Don't fuck this up for me. Accept my apology."

"No, I'm the asshole here. You're right, I assumed. I should have asked about the text first before going crazy."

"You got to be fucking kidding me," Haven expressed. It seemed neither could win nor lose, and it was too hot to argue. He looked at me with seizing eyes, and I knew what lingered on his mind. *I'd make a run for it,* I thought. But something told me he wouldn't be letting me walk away this time. Still, I bolted down the yard, and he chased me until he found the perfect moment to pounce on me like a lion on a gazelle. We rolled in the grass until his hands held me down. He glanced at my revealing skin, and I smiled shamelessly at him, "Let me go," I warned.

"What are you going to do? Call your uncle? Not until you tell me you forgive me." I pushed my hips into him. "Please. I love you..." I huffed over his lips, and he shivered, digging his hard cock into my pelvic. I moaned at the teasing. "Hmmm, tell me again,"

Haven was melting fast into me, kissing and groping me wherever he could. We hadn't even spoken about what happened between us, and we were falling down a hole of fake make-up sex too fast. Not to mention that my uncle would be walking out here soon enough. I used my strength to throw him airborne across the lawn. He landed on his back, several feet away. The shock of my power awakened a lusty beast within him. He could do nothing but blindly smile at me, completely turned on. I dusted my knees off, fixed my hair, and trailed over to where he laid happily in the dirt.

"I'll always love you," He threw his head back and closed his eyes. Smiling, despite the pain I had inflicted, he was satisfied.

"Damn, you're glowing... Come to the river with me tonight?"

"No-duh, I'm glowing; I spent the last few days basking under a Taino sun crying over you. But I can't, tonight. Tomorrow's Leyla's birthday, so we're doing Misael's storytelling."

"Fuck it to hell, Daya, we can all skip out, like old times. There's a bed of flowers with your name on it." The words he said were just as tempting as the look on his face. I would love that, but Misael was already starting with his crap. I could tell by how Leyla flung the front door open and trotted angrily over to us, near to tears, "Tell Jacy I can't see him tonight. My father is going to ruin my life!" Haven and I exchanged knowing glances,

"-What the hell are you doing here? Shouldn't you be somewhere? Hunting?" Misael trotted over, looking down at Haven, who lay drilled into the ground. "I'm just doing my morning rounds, sir. Making sure my *WIFE* is alive and well," Haven was bold today, and I lived for every moment. As I was melting for him, he winked at me, "-Which reminds me, Daya, the Dean wanted me to remind you; you have a lesson tomorrow, at noon." I agreed.

"A lesson, huh. What are you doing down in the dirt? Did you do that, Daya?" My uncle praised me, patting my shoulder. I smiled proudly. "I sure did. Mom taught me that. She said Dean used to love it, revved his heart right up." I winked back at Haven, then took Leyla's hand, and we started back to the house. I looked back at Misael helping Haven to his feet and smiled.

I didn't know much of what had blossomed between Jacy and Leyla over the winter. But since I've been home, Leyla's been surging in details about her secret romance. Only in secret did Jacy and Leyla have the freedom to fall in love. They met every day in the forest. They were great at keeping it a secret, but the pressure pulled and tugged on their growing love. Leyla's problem was that she loved her father and was comfortable pretending to be blind to her father's evil schemes. Everything weighed down on her, and Misael couldn't poke at Jacy enough. Jacy grew impatient and recklessly. Leyla was breaking under the control of her father. Her pretty forest eyes were tired, and she was pale, quiet, and nervous. She was beginning to pull further away now that her birthday was here.

Leyla was a mess, thrown over the corner of her bed, crying, as she tried justifying her father's brutal interception of our love lives. I could see how she was losing all hope. I couldn't allow Leyla to believe her father's lies. There was an off spark in her eyes. My uncle's magic clouded everything else, but come morning, and she will feel the extremity of the curse. "Something happened between Jacy and me the night we met. I can feel it ready to burst. I don't want to live without him." She was so nervous she could barely speak. Her magic rushed in her blood like coastal waves; her heart chakra was set ablaze by unconditional love for her father and lover, burning like wildfire. Jacy was already here, and Leyla was catching flames.

"-My dad's been stressing him out. What if he abandon's me?"

"Trust me, Leyla, Tyson men might act up when they're in love, but abandoning someone they love is not in their DNA."

"Die by the hand of true love, or die by the hand of fate? Daya-True love is too great to pass up. Is this our only truth? Nothing more, nothing less?" I looked at her eyes gleamed romantically. "I don't even know what's my curse," And a bulb lit up, and I ran out of the room, returning with a birthday gift."-Maybe this could be a clue," I handed her the gift; a pretty maroon and emerald hummingbird with a red hibiscus flower carved into a wooden music box. "Oh, Daya, I love it. It's perfect," she winded up the box, and the sparkling music poured out.

"I'm scared, Daya. I don't want to hate my father, but this war with the Tyson's is stupid." Leyla was right. There was no fighting this without emotions, toxic family versus honest love. We knew my uncle wouldn't give us a chance unless we took it ourselves, and Misael wasn't going to be easy with letting us go,

"-I would do anything to see Jacy. But how?"

Leyla and I were **determined** to live our lives.

So, it wasn't too hard to get away. At sunset were waiting outside aunt Charlotte's for the Tyson brothers. Although the sun was setting, I was melting in the heat, and I wore a super short, olive-floral summer dress that tucked tightly into my curves, but I left my thick hair wild. Haven's thunderbird appeared, coming a mile away, blaring a song he played during our first date. He pulled up to us, glaring at me through the passenger window. That stellar face of a god killed me with ease. His heavily anchored eyebrows shadowed the outlines of his perfectly chiseled face through the darkness, and I wasn't only melting, I was boiling. He left the car, watching me the whole time as he walked over. *Damn* the way his basic tee complimented every nook and cranny; his blue eyes were sparkling in the sun like Virgin Island waters; his wild black hair falling in his face. I prepared myself for him as he drew closer,

"You look... delicious. I'm glad you didn't take my comment seriously about covering up," Puckering up my lips in disbelief, I shifted away as he tried finding my eyes, opening the car door for me, "-Okay, I'm sorry. I don't want you all mad at me while you're looking like that," *Right*, a reminder that my body was the best weapon against him. When he got back into the driver's seat, I slowly crossed over my coconut oiled legs, caressing my fingertips over my exposed neck. His tongue nearly on the ground, hungry, I gave him a sexy smirk and pumped my cleavage at him. **Check-mate**. It made him nervous. His eyes bounced from my knees to my breasts, to my neck. He licked his lips, and it was enough for me to nearly jump him. Finally, he jetted out, "BET. You can't keep this up, I know you want me, and I want you too." And he turned to Jacy. Haven and Jacy chopped it up, plotting the destination, and not long after, we found ourselves running through the summer flowers in that heart-shaped meadow. Charming, we danced to the music underneath the stars. It was a stunning vibration, I had never been happier as I danced with Leyla, and she took my hand and twirled me. I let go of her hand and did my little curvy twist, my skirt lifting just a bit.

Haven's diamond eyes were watching me for some time. Something about my happiness brought him happiness, and that gave me peace. As I caught him glaring leaned up against a familiar boulder, along with Jacy, he couldn't wait any longer; taking the opportunity to pull me from Leyla, we giggled as he pulled me into him, and suddenly, we were alone. The smell of his cologne dripping from his overpowering body made me hungry for his lips. My knees trembled from how he watched my chest rise with every inhale, sizing me with his sharp eyes. Things were aligning then,

"Let's talk about December and all the other dumb shit we've done?" He mumbled, distracted by my dress as I knew he would. He gently took my hand, the river glowing in the distance as the Summer wind laid over, frisking my hair into the warm air. There was only water, land, and sky. It felt like the first night we were out there. The river was still, but the warm breeze pushed. I could feel the heat from Haven's body, hovering over me, dangerously close. His lips trembling,

"I need to know, honestly, do you love me?"

"Yes, Haven, I love you," and he would cut me off too, as his lips crashed into me, and hands pulled me into him. He lifted me off my bare feet, and I laced his crown. The feeling of being in his arms again was not like any other high I've ever induced. This time was much more powerful, like a serotonin socket, electrifying. My powers crashed like tide waves into him, like he's never felt before.

He seemed to hesitate. Almost afraid that he would completely engulf me, as he used all his strength to pull his lips from me. Haven released me from his hold, stepped back, and took another long look at me. But I couldn't look at him. Not with that look on his face. Not with his eyes eating me up the way he always did, so I turned to the water. There were still a lot of unanswered questions.

"Why did you break up with me? Why did you have to leave in December? Where did you go?" pacing behind me.

"I had no choice. You've seen what I can turn into if I can't control myself. I didn't want to hurt you. I couldn't bear it if you hurt me back. Your uncle put everything in my head about Landon, and when I woke up, you were gone. What was I supposed to think?"

"The obvious, Misael locked me in the garden. Well, you found me, right? Listen, Haven, despite what you and everyone else think, I know who I am, and I could never go back to Landon after finding *you.* When my uncle released me, I waited for you. I went to your house that day was because of Dean, not Landon. I hoped, at some point, you would show up, but not with Seneca. But I never once was afraid of you or your love. I know it might hurt me, but I'm here with you again, and I might be foolish, but I don't care. You make me want to be courageous and fucking dumb too." He gave a reserved chuckled, taking a moment to gather his thoughts.

"I'm sorry. The thought of you and Landon turns me green, and it might always will. I've never fallen so deep, and I was afraid Landon would take you from me. It took a while to see the way that you fight for me. It's funny, you always say you don't know, but you're always so sure of me, you're exactly what I knew you would be, and the way you make me feel, Daya; is why I never want to hurt you again. I owe you more than just respect, Daya. I owe you the love I promised you," His hands framed my body, huffing his warm sweet breath over my lips. His energy healing every broken part of me, as I did in return. "-You feel that?" Haven interlaced his hands with mine. I felt his gravitational pull on my heartstrings—the synchronization of our thundering hearts. Rubatosis settled in. It was provocative and perhaps even a little abrasive but stimulating. I could feel his energy crawl into the depths of my being, bringing light to the darkest places in me, like a lantern.

In the meadow, the two of us stood captivated by each other. For a moment, all you heard was our weak but tangible breathing. His eyes were melting of cigar tar, and I could see all the pain and torture he's been hiding from the world diminish. The ambiguous intensity of my implored stare gave him Opia, but he had nowhere else to go. Seeing the world inside of him was such an unparalleled but superior emotion. Haven must have felt that *'Oh shit'* moment because we were both stuck in place.

"You're going to master revival, and we're getting out of here. I love you," his face was inflected with his scattered emotions, but I felt safe in Haven's eyes. Safer than I ever had, my entire life. I was ready to let him ravish me in this dark, but then, "Do you want to dance?" he cracked a sexy smile, his eyes smoldering under heavy brows. I took his hand and danced with him.

The summer night smelled like sweetgrass. Sweet and earthy; pine resin, damp cedar & dew drop warm air. It was dark, but the dull orange streetlights led down the rural road, from Dean's house to Charlotte's cabin. It was perfect for walking. The walk was quiet as we let our innuendoes do all the talking. I thought I would have to relearn everything with Haven, but it all came back naturally. It was easy to be me around him. Swinging my long legs in front of me, I was giddy and blushed. Haven's side smiled at me as we neared Charlotte's cabin. I stepped in front of him at the door, admiring the way the shadows and tiger-shaded path light turned him into a piece of invaluable mosaic art. "Daya, you trust me?" He broke the immediate silence, but for a brief moment he was quiet, but hesitated, "About the text from Sunny," He rolled his eyes, "-She was helping me find *this* for your collection," and so he pulled out a book, flipped through the pages, and began to read:

'Let me not to the marriage of true minds,
Admit impediments; love is not love
Which alters when it alteration finds,
Or bends with the remover to remove.
O no, it is an ever-fixed mark
That looks on tempest and is never shaken;
It is the star to ever wandering bark,
Whose worth's unknown, although his height be taken.
Love's not time's fool, though rosy lips and cheeks
Within his bending sickle's compass come;
Love alters not with his brief hours and weeks,
But bears it out even to the edge of doom.
If this be error, and upon me proved,
I never writ, nor no man ever loved,"
Shakespeare: Sonnet 116.

Please don't make me cry; I begged internally after the words left Haven's pressed lips, and he handed over a charming copy of *Love Poems and Sonnets of Willam Shakespeare.* My heart flutter.

"Haven, I'm so sorry for the trouble I'm causing."

"You're worth all the trouble, skirt, but you shouldn't assume," He joked before I shut him up with a kiss, his lips like french vanilla ice cream melting into mine.

"I'm glad you think so because I worry about you. Please under-stand that my feelings for you are unmatched. You never had to be under a spell to love me unconditionally. I appreciate you more than you'll ever know," and he kissed me,

"We're stronger together, skirt, we know that. And, well, I have an entire lifetime to appreciate unconditionally." I became lost in his eyes, and I nearly keeled over. He tried reaching for one more kiss as we said goodnight, but I twisted the doorknob and fell back into the house, blowing him a kiss before closing the door shut.

Leyla's birthday morning.

Leyla's fever had set into her, minutes after her birthday hour, early that bright morning. I was in bed with her and was awoken by her erratic movements just before sunrise. She was having a horrific nightmare, and I watched her panic in her sleep. I sat up, shaking her out of it when her eyes shot open. A neon lilac light appeared in her eyes as if Leyla was pulling it in. *The curse.* Standing on the tips of her toes in the most fluid way possible, she glowed, levitating into the sun rays that leaked from the window.

"Leyla! Ley!" I tried snapping her out of it, but she was in deep. Her face was pale, and she looked pained. Suddenly she began to tremble while her eyes continued to glow. The way she hated but shamelessly enjoyed the sexually charged energy erupting inside her was shocking. Her body fell into gravity, and she landed on the bed. Her fever was increasing. The owl hooting outside the window ultimately gave me flashbacks of the heart on fire syndrome. The first fever set into her as she tore at her clothes, stripping herself nude and moaning from unprovoked pleasure. Finally, Charlotte and Dean came in, pushing me aside.

Leyla and I had planned to sunbathe on my uncle's boat dock all afternoon, and now I only worried if she would awake from the curse slumber. Dean says Leyla's fever will take hours to subside. So Leyla was stuck in bed, sick as a dog, but with hot flashes of sexual urgency and blistering screaming pain. I wanted to be there for Leyla, Misael, and Charlotte wanted me out of the house.

They said they had it under control, only I knew what she was going through, and I could help with my healing magic. But the adults advised that it would be a terrible idea and would only weaken me. Misael continued to urge me out of the house. Finally caving in, I took a ride with Dean up the mountains.

"You have a revival practice later. I expect you at three," You could tell Dean's thoughts were turning as he dropped me off. I agreed before I went and checked on my garden gates to ensure they were secure and untouched. The magic built into it from my mother and ancestors was unbreakable, but a piece of me always needed the reassurance. I walked through the grassy, unkempt backyard. It didn't look like last summer, full of life and innocence.

The dock boggled in the murky lake water. The sun was beating down 100-degrees. This summer has been sweltering, and today was no exception. I threw down a towel and pulled off my cover-up. Not a minute later, I got that, *someone's watching me,* cringe down my back. I looked around. Nothing crazy. Only nature. I slipped sunglasses on, and my eyes skipped around the perimeter once more— no one I could see or hear, and confirmed. Maybe I was losing it, shrugging before laying down. I hit the music playlist, adjusted my headphones, and settled in a relaxing tanning state.

I basked in the sun, and for hours now, I felt myself blossoming as I shifted all my thoughts to Haven, and my plan to master revival, later that day. I focused on the sound of the coiling waves rocking the dock underneath me, and it gave me dirty reminiscing thoughts of that day in the creek, entwined with Haven in the water. These were the thoughts I fought off regularly, but now that I was utterly alone, *all aside from that funny feeling of being watched,* I had an excuse to obsess over the sexual fantasy. I reapplied coconut tanning oil on my hot, toasted skin as the radio app on my phone kicked off a sultry vibe that would fuel the fire that set in me.

That moment he had me pressed against the rock, with his giant boa pressing against my pearl like it was no big deal. The way he dangled me underneath him. His eyes were sparkling with the water. My hands slowly slipped away with my thoughts; I started thinking about our first date and started to masturbate; *the way Haven looked at me that moment, he saw me in that dress. The way he tried to hide his eyes from me when we talked over that candlelit dinner. The way he danced with me and held me close, and smiled at me. The way his eyes filled with savage love and dangerous pride. The way his eyes filled with lust when I took off those stockings.* Nothing was sexier than the way he languished and craved me. His passion was sexy. My juices were flowing.

Now I could feel everything private swell up. I let my fingers glide across my wet folds, slipping back and forth between the hem underneath my bikini bottoms. It was easy to imagine Haven on top of me with my eyes closed. *He was looking at me the way he does. The way he kissed me in the truck that December night. The way he lunged into me, grappling at my skin and thighs. How erected his shaft got underneath me. Imagine feeling its entire thickness inside me.* It was all turning me on so much under that hot sun. I had to remind my-self to breathe. The thoughts only got more intense when I started to think about *how his knuckle brushed against my clit when he pulled my panties off. The way he looked at me. The way his lips softly kissed my shin and ankle. And the way he savagely sucked away my sweet juice from his fingers.* My body was ready to burst on its own. But then, **HOOT HOOT-** EH? **HOOT HOOT-**

Was that an Owl hooting?

Just as my body shook and trembled, my hands pulled away, and my body bulked up. I flicked off my sunglasses, looking up into the tree, and it was a damn Owl over me. After noticing the owl, I saw my friend, the bear, pulling off into the trail from the clearing. The owl was now gone, but a strange feeling came over me. I was suddenly curious. I watched it walk further into the woodland suspiciously as if it didn't want me to see it. The bear, odd enough, seemed too human. The more I thought about it, the stranger it seemed. How strange that this magnificent creature was spying on me, intentionally? I had to find out. I quietly pulled my boots on and slowly packed my things. I wanted to give the bear a head start. I finally ventured out into the woodland, yards from the creature. The bear walked for what felt like an hour in that blistering heat, and I followed behind as soundless as possible, trying to keep a steady pace. I used my powers to make me as invisible as the wind. I was careful not to startle or grab his attention.

The Tyson's lodge was right there at the break of the woods, and I watched the bear stop right before the break, and I watched the bear, very suddenly, shift into a man, right before my eyes. In total shock, I nearly tumbled into the ground, falling out of my protective magic. It had to be a dream, or astral projection or something. But no, the bear- **NO**- the man, was **Haven;** nude and searching for something. I stood up and walked closer to him immediately.

"Oh my God!" I startled Haven, and he jumped back, looking at me. As if we had traded eyes. He dropped a pair of gray sweats in his hands, and I could see him, fully erected. I was in shock at the sight of it. The color, the shape, the immense size. I've never seen one, and yet so defined. My cheeks flushed a balloon red, and my eyes rolled away from his naked body after he jumped in modesty. He quickly pulled the gray sweats on.

"What the *hell* are you doing here?" He yelled in a whisper.

"What the hell was that?" I whisper-yelled back.

"I **don't** know what you're talking about?" He seemed collected.

"I know what I saw. I don't fucking know, start explaining." Haven ignored me, adjusted his sweat pants, and walked out of the woods. I followed behind him, warning him that I wouldn't let this go. Haven called out to Dean once we walked into the kitchen. I stood behind him, arms crossed.

"I swear you better have a good reason why you never told me about yourself," I argued as he kept calling out for his dad, "Aye, don't start skirt- I wanted to tell you. Stop acting like a brat because I'm about to get into some deep shit over this."

Jacy came running in, pulling on a tee shirt.

"You're a fucking idiot," Haven pushed him.

"How was I supposed to know you were into voyeurism?" I flushed red, realizing the two had seen me touching myself. Not a second later, Dean walked in with Leyla and Landon. For a moment, I forgot everything and hugged Leyla, shocked to see her after the state she was in earlier. She caught me with new strength, but I knew she carried that magic in her veins. The reunion didn't last a second longer as the uproar of our messy united voices turned into a chaotic anecdote. Everyone was piling into the kitchen talking but not listening. Dean whistled loudly. Everyone stopped.

"Daya saw me shift." Haven quickly stated.

"-Everyone to the table,"

Dean didn't seem too upset. We were seated around the dining room table like some intervention. Beat red in the face, and I knew it wasn't just the heat, "-I was minding my own business **(Haven begins to chuckle)** when I caught these two perverts spying on me at the lake. I followed that damn bear and wouldn't you believe it; it is your son, the one who promised me there were no secrets between us just last night,"

"*Minding your business?* Is that right-" Haven insinuated. I was in no mood for his jokes, so I threw my shoe at him across the table, but he caught it. Dean's eyes grew big as he shot a disapproving look at his sons. Leyla's eyes grew big looking at Jacy.

"-Correction! *Haven* was spying on you. I was only looking for Daya like you asked me to, Dean." Jacy grew frustrated.

"Okay, fine. It's my fault..." Haven split the argument.

"- Daya, some branches of our ancestral tribe inherited the great gift from The Great Spirit. The gift of the shifter. Though not the purest lineage, our bloodline comes from the most respected and most trusted. My boys and I were born with that gift."

"You're *shifters?* Why didn't any of you tell me?" The intensity brewing between Haven and me nearly gave Dean whiplash.

"I wasn't allowed to tell you. Dad, please tell her,"

"My boys and I are bound to secrecy. All tribes are very protective of their ancient secrets. For us, this is one of those things. The gift of the shifter is a powerful responsibility to carry." I quickly began to understand, putting all the mysterious pieces of Haven, the wendigo, and the bear.

"So you are all *were-bears?* Or something?" The guys all laughed.

"No, our shifter form is determined by our spirit power animal. Around 14-16 years old, the boys go on their first Quests. During the Quests, the boys meditate into a sacred state and are introduced to a spirit animal that leads them from boyhood to warriorhood. The boy learns everything they need to know through the spirit animal, including their destinies. I tried to protect Haven, knowing the Quests would lead him back to you, but I couldn't keep him from his destiny. There's a lot of power behind the bear. Strength and solitude, motherhood." Haven seemed embarrassed by the motherhood part, looking off and leaning back in his chair like a kid. But he was protective, loving, and caring in that way.

"Jacy is the annoying owl?"

"-Wisdom, clarity, silence...." I thought about that Halloween night and how Jacy watched me rip apart my clothes in that forest. I wanted to die thinking of all the not-so-private moments I thought I had when I was alone. Including that recent night, I ran into the cave thinking I was alone with a bear when really, Haven was with me the entire time. "-What's that look on your face?" Haven knew what was on my mind; *the absurdity.* I looked at Jacy, cheeks still flushed, "Hey, don't look at me like that! Anytime I was snooping around, It was because I was sent by one of these two."

I was actively stressing over the boys' abilities,

"Are you going to tell me Landon shifts into a raccoon?"

They laughed except for Landon, who was offended, "You think this great-looking body shifts into a raccoon? Hell no,"

"-He's a fucking horse."

"-Horse?" I looked at Landon, and it made sense. Fast, proud, pristine, showy smile. He was an attractive and graceful being. Even right now, he was smiling so arrogantly proud and glaring at me, all nonchalant. "Energy, power, freedom, all me, baby." Landon massaged his chest conceitedly. All while, Leyla seemed smitten and wondrous of all three boys. She had that lush, lust-for-life look in her eyes. A feeling I knew way too well.

"And you, Dean?" I had grown curious.

"The wolf. Leadership, and intelligence."

I agreed, "-Does Misael know?" They all looked at Landon.

"Remember when I bailed on our track meet and got kicked off the team? Well, I was serious when I said I hadn't been feeling good.

Leyla was with me. She was helping me get home when I shifted. So she got Misa so he could help me."

"Ley?" My attention shot to her.

"Dad told me about Landon. He was waiting for Landon to shift, and we got very close over the summer. I'm sorry."

"-Wait, you were hanging out with Landon too?"

Jacy questioned her,

"Why didn't you tell me?" I questioned Landon,

"I trusted Leyla because I was in love with her," is what he spit out. The underlying jealousy shook the mood a bit. Not even I had expected to feel this way. After dating Landon for almost two years, I was honestly mad that he would keep this from me. I couldn't help but feel strange. His answer made me sad, "-Okay, this is weird..." I looked at Landon seriously. Ominous energy floated about as the Five of us stared at one another with incriminating glares.

"What?" I asked, noticing all eyes were on me. Haven's eyes strayed to the ground. It was clouded with black. Whatever it was, he didn't want to talk about it, and it made him angrier. His body disengaged, and how quickly he disconnected blew fear in me. "Moboyas cursed Haven with one of the most painful curses to exist among our people. It possesses the mind and soul with insatiable greed, cannibalism, and jealousy. Lately, the curse has prevented Haven from shifting into his power animal more often than usual. Instead, it feeds off his worst triggers and habits, like a parasite. Mostly the jealousy that triggers him. If he shifts into the wendigo in an unwavering rage, he'll kill you, engulfing your soul; and shifting into the wendigo permanently, taking the form of a dark and bitter winter. It will be an excruciating force to carry all his pain inside of him. That night in the winter, he nearly lost himself completely."

Dean pulled out an old book and slid it across the table. It had no title. I took the book and began to flip through the pages. Margin notes with images of the same repulsive, foul smelled creature that nearly burned me to death in my nightmares. The one that has been chasing and burning everything down to the ground. I pointed to the beast, setting the book down before me.

"That thing comes after me in my dreams,"

Haven took my wrist and studied the scar before kicking back his seat and abruptly storming out. Jacy and Landon went after him, and I stayed behind with Dean and Leyla and reflected on how Haven's body caved into him and the sound of his bones cracking. His eyes clouded an evil gray cloud—the screeching from the pain. I had caused all of this fighting, "I can't let that happen to him. How can we break his curse."

"*WE* can't. Haven's jealousy has fed into the curse too many times. Haven wants to beat this curse, he has to do it himself, and he knows that. All the Quests that boy has done, he still doesn't get it. You can learn to revive, but it won't mean much if he can not learn to control his inner demons and keep alignment. If he continues to allow this monster to feed off of his weaknesses, he won't be able to fight off the final Wendigo transformation, which will happen when he takes your virginity,"

Haven watched me from the window. He looked at me with such serious worry in his eyes.

"Over the past months, I've fallen in deep love with Haven. He's brave, he's honest, and he loves me. It doesn't matter what the curse is capable of Dean. I know what Haven is capable of, especially if it means saving me. I'm not afraid of him. I trust him. I know Haven could beat this, even if he doesn't think so," Dean smiled light-heartedly and agreed, "-Well, Daya, you should bring Haven along to the clearing and practice revival,"

Not long after, I stood near the woodland, looking out to the purity of the forest before us. The birds chirped as I stood in silence for a moment. Haven swept my hair to one side, pulled me in close, and laid his lips down softly on my neck. Goosebumps formed as his lips whispered, "I'm sorry I couldn't tell you."

"I get it, and I'm not mad, but I doubt you'll turn into a monster,"

"That's not funny, Daya." He wasn't in the mood for that.

"I trust the bear inside you. I wished you trusted yourself,"

"I don't fully trust myself when I'm alone with you, but I'll learn... so spend the night with me tonight,"

18

Revival

"-You're not concentrating hard enough, babe."

We had arrived at the clearing over three hours ago, and since, I had Leyla, Jacy, and Haven ankle-deep in drowning mud. They did what they could to encourage my magic, but their efforts were only getting on my nerves. I couldn't seem to revive the land. So finally, I took to my hands and knees at the center of the lonely raven field, and I tried reversing whatever I did to flood the land, but it seemed to worsen, and the others were actively yelling at me about it. "Shut up!" My plea echoed through the woodlands across the way. I closed my eyes, kneeling deeper into the waterlogged rich soil. The excess water rose over my wrists. With my cemi dug into the ground, I tried concentrating on birth, growth, and my crop ancestor. *In my mind, I can see all of the tiny grass seedlings form in the soil and birth spontaneously. I pictured it growing wildly, abundantly, thick, and ravishingly—trees, shrubs, grass, moss, insects, flowers.* Yet, only a single blade of grass rose from the murky mud when I opened my eyes. I could hear Haven in a low chuckle,

"-I don't think you're concentrating enough."

And a wave of frustration took over as I hopped off my muddy knees. Cheeks flushed under the heat. I pushed and hit him. All he could do was laugh at me. He threw me over his shoulders but instantly slipped in the mud, and we both went crashing down. Leyla and Jacy screamed in entertainment, pointing and laughing like 3rd graders. I wiped my muddy hands across his once-white tee. Smiling mischievously, he smirked in return, leaning his head back and cringing to the damaging stains.

"You're going to regret that skirt,"

"-You're going to regret blowing my concentration." He tried sitting up, but I pushed him back down into the mud. My strength enticed him; I could feel him growing underneath me. He began to kiss me, and in response, I began to rub myself against his body. He moaned, praising me on top of him.

"-Maybe you can't concentrate because you two can't stop dry-humping every five minutes," Jacy yelled.

"How about you give us some privacy! I'll get her to bloom!"

Haven and I had a good laugh about it.

"That's your problem. You two never take anything seriously."

Haven and I were slowly losing in this dangerous game of chicken. Since reconciling, we haven't been able to keep our hands off each other. I pulled off my swim cover, showing my human body in a tiny red bikini. They were just at his eye level. I watched as Haven reached, wanting to engulf my entire nipple in his mouth. I smack away his hand, rubbing my sex flower on him more. He leaned up onto his elbows, threw back his head, and his eyes rolled. I knew we had to stop this messing around, yet I got off on him more. He gripped my ass aggressively and latched on my neck with his lips. His muddy hands took in my hips and helped me thrust deeper on him. I could feel the warm wetness in my bikini bottom flowing from me as he licked across my collar bone, I was peaking, and it was coming out as a moan,

"Cut it out! Before you cause an accidental homicide!" Jacy interrupted for a second time. The words were like a screeching halt to a record player. Suddenly Haven stopped. His hands went up in the air, and he pulled away from me.

"-I appreciate the cock block," Haven pushed me off of him, creating distance. I watched him adjust his sweats as I let my knees slowly drift apart, trying to give him a peek of what awaited him. He anxiously knocked my knees back and looked away, "We can't keep playing these limit games. We're going to go too far."

"Good. I want to push the boundaries with you."

"Seriously, Dayanara, it's dangerous. We can't be doing this if it will cost your life. I have self-control, but you don't, and one day you're going to push me, and I won't be able to stop."

"So what, get lost in me." It nearly came out in a moan. Haven smacked my knees closed when he saw them drift apart. Enough with my teasing; he was about to stand up when I pounced back on him, trying to weigh him down by suffocating him with my breasts. He was resilient as he nodded to my trickery and proceeded to use his strength to lift us both off the ground.

"Come on, Daya, why can't you concentrate?"

"Because... I want you to fuck me. I'm frustrated." I vented.

"I'm frustrated too, but you got this, babe. Trust me. I deal with much worse, like blue balls. I think you can handle it."

"Just because I don't have balls doesn't mean my parts don't get blue... Come on. I'm tired of ringing the devil's doorbell every night. It would feel so much better if it were you..."

Embarrassment flushed his face red.

"Put all that creative energy into your magic. Once you master the revival, I can give you what you want. I have an idea; let's meditate," Haven took my hand and led me farther out into the dark field. He stared at me before pushing down on my shoulders until I knelt before him. My lips aligned with his belt buckle, and that monstrous bulge locked away—looking up at him with begging eyes, needing just a taste. He bit his lip with pity, and his thumb stroked my cheek. I could suddenly hear him in my thoughts, *'relax.'* Then he slowly came down to his knees, meeting me at eye level. He swooned himself, straddling behind and pulling me into him. His lips harbored over my ears and neck. He whispered, "Close your eyes." He moved his mud-ridden fingertips down my curves. I closed my eyes and concentrated on breathing, and so did he. It motivated the electricity within us.

I listened to his heart as he held me in the mud. He pressed on me again before seeping our fingers deeper into the wetland. Our hands meshed in the earth. He leaned into the nook of my neck.

"-Sometimes, I think about watching you erupt from all the euphoria gushing from your body. I'm going to bury my soul so deep inside yours that your soul catches fire in a way that you'll never feel again. I want to explore your entire being as in-depth as possible. Let us take time to *really* feel each other." Haven's whispers and the visualizations I perceived were making me rise fast. I could barely sit still, but I had to find a way to relax if I wanted this to work, so I heard him, felt the lust I was feeling, held it, and balanced it. I could feel my magic tingle in my fingertips as if it were trying to jump-start. The more I settled into a state of no time and space; I did not acknowledge that deep desire for rioting sex, the more energy built up in my palms, and I used the love for the sound of Haven's heartbeat to multiply the power. My honest love for him was starting to weigh down that hyper-sexual anxiety.

We meditated in the field for nearly an hour, and all was well until we felt an overflowing of dense, stagnant energy. I violently pushed the electricity into the ground as Haven pressed against me. He held my hands down in the mud and kissed my neck; my privates pulsated like a ticking time bomb, his tongue traced the curves of my neck. I knew I couldn't hold myself together any longer. I couldn't help but moan, and his hand clapped over my mouth, mud and all. *"Shh -you're going to get me in trouble,"* he complained while snickering. I could still feel his heart continue to speed. Finally, he placed his hand over my rapid heart, and my world became still.

"Calm down..." I felt his arms collapse over me, and his warm hand over my heart suddenly stung like morphine through my body, paralyzing every anxious bone within me. I was calm. Now all my power radiates around us. The power orb grew, engulfing us. My passion rushed through my veins, overflowing from my finger-tips. I could feel our powers connect and shift, entwine and absorb. It was controlled but still wild. We wallowed in it for a moment.

"...Daya, open your eyes," *We were shining like new world gold, trying hard to balance this orb of magnetic energy around us. Inside, all sparkled with a tranquil sound of twinkling. Sparks ignited when Haven smiled at me. I cracked a smile. Solid earth formed underneath, layered grass grew wildly, and stems appeared. He held my hand and kissed me. More flowers grew. But we were absorbing the magic so suddenly, and all faded into the nothingness,* like a popped bubble. Before us in the mud, nothing more but three blades of grass; **Fuck.** Haven and I looked at each other skeptically. While it seemed useless, the magic we've conjured together was authentic, nonetheless.

"There's progress. We will try again. We're almost there."

The sun went down quickly with music, rum shots, and deep conversations. The gratitude I had inside for my experiences over the past months anchored in me and grounded me. Soon enough, my magic began to rush through my veins like a river, purposely. Considering why we found ourselves here, we didn't light a fire, but we hung out in the late contrasting dusk and kept the headlights on as Haven, and I went back into the sad, broken field.

I let his hand go and sprinted into the darkness. Haven playfully chased behind into the murky, wet field. I jumped onto him as he crashed into me. We both went tumbling down into the mud again. But now we just laid there, flat out, side by side, giggling like kids. All Haven wanted to do was hold me in the warm mud. Whispering the lyrics to the song that played on the radio onto my lips, I let him go on, serenading my vibrations. His fingers traced over my face, my cheeks red and breath of hot rum. He watched the shadows on my face attentively. My eyes illuminated lilac and honey, still ablaze inside. I gave him a sexy smirk, "-Don't get any ideas, skirt." He could feel the magic zooming in my trembles, and I laughed at the ideas floating in my mind. The sky was majestic above. Deep and rich orange-red, purple, and navy into a dusk striding sky. The night fell quickly soon after.

"I'm thinking of what Dean said that night at Wolf cliff. Maybe the energy you feed off me might not be **good** enough,"

He surprised me when he spoke, "Haven, your power is the most electrifying and potent energy to ever swim through my body, neither good nor bad. It's all just **you**. You make me stronger. Too strong, perhaps. I can be very delicate. Your power could be overbearing sometimes. My garden requires a balance of power and love, like water and sun. One can't overpower the other."

"I don't want to be the reason why you can't create,"

My eyebrow raised. He cracked a light smile and rolled his eyes.

"You know what I mean. I still have my memories of us, and I had a backlash of a time I wanted you to show me a trick, and you didn't want to. So I got mad, and I ripped a dandelion's head-"

"-Haven, you're spazzing. That happened a few weeks ago."

"No, this was different. I was eight, and you were like five; you didn't want to play, but I forced you into doing magic for me. You were mad, but you fixed the flower anyway. Unconditionally. It made me realize that I thought I'd been protecting myself when I was mean to you. I've always pushed you around, and that's never been fair. You've always been good to me. I'm sorry about being so possessive and controlling. I only want to love you," He reached for a strand of hair, "I kept the stem; so it could remind me to be gentle with you, always. I want you to trust me," My heart melted as I watched Haven pull out the old and dead Red Hibiscus stem from his pocket. It was so fragile as he held it out for me. I giggle. He was crazy, and I loved it because we were finally in sync. Then, looking at him, I pulled out the hibiscus flower head from my bikini top, right near my heart, all brown and dead.

"I'll fix the flower for you, but promise to play nice?"

"Always, skirt." He kissed his fingertips and slapped at his heart.

I put the hibiscus back together in a healing power orb within my hands that formed reasonably effortlessly in the mud with him. All I felt was love while staring into his enchanted eyes as he watched my magic. Everything we loved about each other drove the passion behind our madness, which geared our infinite power. I let the orb continue to glow in my hands. Allured, this glowing ball of energy healed the flower. All that love and passion was in the globe, fermenting the magic within. It was the most beautiful magic I have ever seen. Haven couldn't keep his eyes from it either as the flower mended itself back together. Each stitch had double the strength. We watched the flower take energy, power, and stiffen. Revived, the flower glowed a moment and then floated down, heavenly, into Haven's hand. Good as new.

Haven didn't say anything as he was too mesmerized, but he did kiss me with an unyielding passion under the night sky—the spark of his kiss illuminated through me, and suddenly a bursting rumbling underneath our bodies. The soil was seething, healing underneath and preparing to create again, and new and healthy forestland emerged. Trees, grass, and moss. Flowers, bark, spiderwebs, dew drops. Shrubs and bushes, vines. The insects and animals slowly came behind. Tons of flowers grew underneath us as we lay there kissing. Leyla and Jacy started whistling and cheering excitedly. We opened our eyes to a forest enchantment. Haven pulled my muddy body up onto him and kissed me victoriously.

I did it. I mastered revival.

"I knew you could," Haven whispered on my lips.

"Daca Taino!" Leyla cheered from Jacy's jeep.

"Taino Daca!" I cheered back.

As the night sky formed above, we watched the revival of the land flourish in contentment. But I was beginning to feel nervous. It's been a good day, and now there were no distractions from thinking about how I'd be spending the night with him in his bed.

When we got back to the Tyson home, Dean was brewing tea in the kitchen. He stared at us at first, wondering if he should ask, but instead, he brushed away curiosity and rolled his shoulders. Once we were back at Dean's house, Leyla and Jacy went off on their own into the forest trail. Much more reserved; I had felt Leyla's urgency to be alone with him for hours now, and she nearly gargled out the rush. Everyone seemed to be fading away in moments.

Landon sighed miserably at the moon through the kitchen window. It had to be hard losing two girls to your fairly 'new' brothers, you barely knew. Nonetheless, Landon was resilient and thought he had it figured out. The truth was, he didn't at all, and I believe it was sinking into him that moment when Dean handed him a warm cup of tea and patted his shoulder. They exchanged comforting glances, and Landon said his goodnights. He seemed excited about the Quest he was leaving on in the morning. Dean warned us once more to be responsible before following Landon.

Now Haven and I were standing in silence, wondering what to do next, "-I'm sure you want to shower. I have some sweats; they'll be pretty big on you, but," we snickered. He pinched at my bare side. Blushing, I innocently looked up at him. For a moment, we just smiled at each other. We held a stare like we were afraid to look away. His eyes were milk ivory and royal blue, once again. "Come on. I'll show you my bedroom." He cocked his head in the direction of the hallway. I swallowed hard, nodding, and followed him down the hallway to a dark corner. Haven stopped in front of a hidden door. He leaned into its frame as he glazed me with his eyes. My heart was beating recklessly from the way he stared at me, right before he lured me into the ground of the house.

Haven's room was expansive, with a super tall ceiling and lots of open space. It was dingy and smelled of virgin forest and natural musk. The north side wall had a huge hole punch through, big enough for a giant bear to bust through. The foundation was gray and sturdy, only ravished by nature. Mother earth seemed to seep into the room from the missing chunk in the wall like a time canal, right from the pure outside. It reminded me of a cave. There was half carpet that ombre into grass, moss, then dirt. Rocks and boulders scattered. Flowers, shrubs, and mushrooms. Timeless, like my garden. It was like his garden, and I fell in love.

"*WOW*," Pressed on, I paced about the open space. Hands in his pockets, he followed my dancing feet like a wolf and prey.

"Where do you sleep?" My throat knotted like the nervous twisting of my hair endings. My eyes flashed his eyes as I shot him with an arrow. He, too, tried swallowing down a rope as I watched him point to a substantial bed-like boulder at the corner of the room. I could see his messy blankets and pillows spilled over it. I walked over to a corner of the room that felt more humanized. It was that corner where he kept all his stuff. I stood beside the *'boulder bed.'*

It stood over five feet from the ground and laid thirteen feet wide; in a perfectly weathered down rectangle shape. I was holding in his scent from the blankets lingering. I wanted to tangle in those waves of blankets with him so bad, but I looked around the dim room some more. Glossy guitars anchored on the wall, a stereo system was hanging, a bench press and a dusty, crowded dresser stacked with books, cologne, and other personal things. Stacks and stacks of old rock and roll vinyl records. Bushes and shrubs; moss and spider webs, but no closets. It was quiet. I embraced Haven's personality through these private walls until he killed the silence that had been biting at him since my last faint words.

"-If you're not comfortable, we can sleep in the guest room."

"You're not kicking me out; I love it here," He relaxed substantially after watching my eyes glow.

"Well then, my bathroom is right there..."

Before us, an open bathroom with no walls. It was all clean and made of amber and golden river rock tile and oak-like, built-in, and freshly new—also the only corner with decent lighting. There was a sink, toilet, cabinets, and large majestic walk-in shower. It was all there but with no private walls. Instead, it had an oversized showerhead hanging from above, clean towels folded, and neatly placed on the side table. Although someone had punched a fresh hole through the finished tile in the shower, duct tape stretched over the gaping hole. "-You can go ahead whenever you're ready." He said as I looked at him with timid eyes before walking away towards his dresser. He seemed to be preoccupying himself on purpose, so I went ahead and started the shower. He took his time, keeping his eyes far from me. Despite my nerves in a frenzy, I was way ahead of him. Slipping off my muddy bikini, I tossed it aside and stepped under the steaming showerhead. Immediately, I closed my eyes, and my mind was racing, knowing I was standing naked. Moments passed in silence, and I could only feel his eyes vibing on my skin. I simmered in his euphoric stare before I opened my eyes. I stared into the gaping hole in the tile before me.

"What happened here?" I asked as he seemed to be straightening up his already neat room.

"Nothing- I tripped... hand went through the thing."

I shrugged and washed my hair, lathered my body with soap, and rinsed off. Still, I felt Haven watch my naked wet body. The heat from his eyes started to poke at my desires, a feeling I was holding down as I found myself covering my yoni. Flushed, I looked at him, luring him into the shower. His grin grew, coast to coast. Then, standing there all muddy and awkward, he flushed pink and shook his head, bashfully looking down like an 8-year-old.

"I'm going to use Jacy's room-" He nearly flew up the stairs.

I found the clothes Haven left out for me. A gray tee shirt and navy sweats. We were right. His clothes were huge on me. I walked around his room; my fingers traced his things. I finally found some deodorant and a hairbrush and brushed out my knots. I sprayed on some of his cologne and smelled it off my tee-shirt. I paced around, still looking. His rich taste in rock music ringed across the walls. His room reflected everything I loved about him. Funny, he was reading *The Taming of the Shrew.* I reached for the book when he finally came thumping down the stairs. He chuckled and chuckled, "That's big on you." He shook his head as I pulled the sweat pants up. I pushed him aside and walked around his room.

"I hope you're not a 'Netflix and chill' type."

"Mostly, I'm a *'drown in music and chill'* kind of guy."

I turned on his stereo. Music flowed through the airwaves,

"Do you play?" I pointed to the guitars mounted on the wall.

"Yes." He looked vulnerable. He cracked a nervous smile, and I took that moment to admire him. Fresh out of the shower, hair slicked back wet. He wore a plain tee and sweats that matched mine. He checked me up and down before randomly pulling at the waistband strings at the center of my sweats. He pulled and tied them tight into a bow as if he was locking up my virtue. I looked up at him, "So, can you turn into a bear on command?"

"Yes… It doesn't hurt, and yes, I have to be naked to shift."

"Can you show me sometime?"

"How about tomorrow? The sooner I get it out of your system, the better. Hey, can you decorate my room with your magic? It's dull down here. It could use your magic touch."

"Only if you play for me,"

"Okay…" He walked over to his wall and took down a guitar as I headed toward the open hole in the wall that showcased the majestic nightly woodland from the inside. I stopped before the outside. Haven sat down on the ground behind me and began to play his guitar. I spotted a tiny seedling in the peaceful night, picked it up, and multiplied it into many with my magic hands. I whispered wishes into them before I tossed them about, sprinkling some love dust as they took root, magically burying themselves into the dirt. The grass grew thicker instantly, filling all the bald spots. Chamomile and dandelions sprouted—tons of them. I added roses, vines, baby breaths, more dandelions, and some lavender near his bed. Then a burst of Red hibiscus and Ceiba tree grew behind the boulder bed. Suddenly, I realized the music had stopped, and I felt Haven's hand grab ahold of my waist from behind. Aroused by my skills as we watched the flowers bloom in the dark.

"I'll be able to feel you in here now,"

"Trust me. I don't need to do this trick to do that."

"I am not breaking." Haven tried to reassure himself before he kissed me intensely. Then, he quickly took my anxious body into his trembling hands and carried me to his bedrock. He laid me down on his bed and turned down the lights. It was more comfortable than I thought- with the soft cushions and magical flowers blossoming on top. We rolled around a moment, kissing and interlocking until he reached back for the wave of blankets.

Under the thick blankets, he crawled up near me. *Was he really lying beside me?* Awkward and quiet, I could feel him anxiously shaking his foot underneath the blanket. When his foot brushed against mine, it brought us to look at each other. It was innocent. We annoyed each other with nudges and light jokes, laughing until we were still again. "You okay?" he whispered in the dark.

"Yeah. I'm just cold." His warm feet glided over mine. It was mostly dark, but some holes in the walls brought in the silver moonlight. My nervous hands wandered through the blankets to take his hand, but I came across my lace panties engulfed in the cotton blanket, my underwear he stole on our date. He looked at me innocently, "What? You're my girl, right?"

"Damn Tyson men." I flung the thong at him, and he caught it, securing it underneath his pillow. I lured him back into my eyes.

A kiss. A hug. A touch. *Anything?* No. He was holding back.

"You can come closer. I don't bite, you know."

"-But I do. Do you want to watch a movie?" I pointed at the massive hole in the wall. Haven quickly realized the midnight sky was already a movie, and the moon was the star of the show. I felt his hands crawl toward me under the blankets, pulling me into him like a suction cup. So perfectly together, like curves in a puzzle piece. He pulled my face back to him, nearly crushing me, "I always want to be this close to you. I wish I could keep you this close and this safe *always*." He whispered in the stillness.

"We could be like this every night, now that I've learned revival." He smiled as if he was thinking the same thing,

"When you appeared in my visions, I knew what you were doing there. I fought so hard not to become so curious about you, but you would haunt me regardless. The Quests became the only way I could learn about you, but I couldn't do anything to help or protect you. That part killed me, but the first time I saw you running with Landon, that was a different emotion. I *had* to follow you two because Landon never showed up in my visions before, and I didn't trust him. Once, you had a track meet coming up, and Landon offered to train with you. You were always so distracting in spank shorts. I still remember because I was upset, but I could hear what he was thinking. I could see the way he looked at you. It killed me more to watch you flirt back. He tried to steal a kiss at some point, and you dodged him but slipped and twisted your ankle. Do you remember that?"

It was familiar. Everything Haven was talking about had happened. I was distracting, in a sports bra and skin-hugging spanks, sweating. Landon was richly green-eyed. I was caving in to his spell and twisted my ankle while trying to dodge him from groping me when we were alone on the trail. I flushed, recalling how unknowingly heartstruck I was over Landon at the time.

"-I couldn't run that meet; my uncle was pissed."

"Yeah, I know. I wanted to kill him. I wanted to catch you, but my Power Spirit stopped me before I could. I wasn't allowed to touch you. Then I heard Dean say, *'Don't touch her... you'll hurt her.'* So I pulled away from you. Watching you fall for Landon, Landon coming to your rescue, wasn't easy for me. Over the years, I had become so jealous of Landon I hadn't realized what I had done to myself until it was too late. I knew I had to be careful if I ever had the opportunity to be in your graces. When I found out he was my brother, that hurt, but it motivated me to be better, not just you, but for him too. And yes, I tried to punch Landon because he was kissing you back, but I didn't want to kill him. Dean said he was proud of me. It could have been a lot worse. Daya, I haven't been trusting of you, Landon, or myself. I'm not going to let useless human emotions rob our sacred world," I touched his face. Haven had been tormented by his demons. I've been too selfish to understand.

"I was never meant to love anyone, yet I love you deeply."

"I felt it when you looked at me Halloween night. That wasn't easy to witness. There was a lot of throwing shit, yelling, and fighting. I think I was kicked out of your house, if I remember right. The next day I told your uncle that I'd break his nose if I didn't get to talk to you. But it was too late. You were already snooping."

"-Should have seen that coming from your Quests." I giggled.

"Not all the Quests were about you, brat. Most were to teach me important life lessons. I had to learn to be the Power Spirit. Life Lessons. Tough ones about my mother and Landon and the wendigo. Some were about my toxic habits and behaviors,"

"-Like smoking?" He chuckled.

"Yes, like smoking. And jealousy and anger. I'll admit, though, my most intense Quests centered around you. I started making excuses to travel to New York on *camping trips.* I don't regret what I've done; I needed a real look at you. Tell me you couldn't fight that urge to look me in my face that first time?" He was right. The anticipation of looking at Haven face to face was stellar after finding out about him. I remember the dinner party, how hard I fought not to look at him, and how hard I fought to pull away.

"...You rolled your eyes at me," I chuckled.

"Because you were fighting so hard not to look in front of Landon, and I just wanted you to do it. I hadn't realized how mean I became, just trying to get you to notice me. I haven't been completely myself. You were right when you said, I request and never return, but I want to make it up to you. We have all the time we need, now that I'm here with you,"

"I love you," I told him as he stashed his eyes into a hideaway,

"I love you too, skirt." He held me close, mending our bodies as one. I closed my eyes as he kissed my neck, and we drifted to sleep.

19

Poetic Analgesic

Lighting sparked across the open void like flashlights, and so the last fever began to run through me that early morning. I slipped into erotic dyspareunia right before Haven's eyes. I was again feeling like I was going through a withdrawal of love and sex. Something was pulling out of me, and it was electrifyingly painful. Hot flashes, trembling, gripping the sheets on the bed. I was lucid sleeping, and even though the rain came pouring down, I could hear the night outside, and it sounded serene. And I knew I wasn't alone because I had Haven, and he took care of me and protected me under the purple and black skies rumbling and howling outside. He kept me stable until, quite suddenly, the fever made me slip into a poetic slumber, and then I was dreaming,

- As a child, I ran towards the river, recklessly in a yellow daisy dress; Haven was chasing behind like a wild goose chase, just eight years old, catching me before I could fall into the river banks. I hugged him with appreciation, but as I held on to him, I felt a sadness arise within him. I asked him, "Why are you so sad," He confessed that he fell asleep and ruined the front garden. So, I stuck my hands into the soil. Flowers were

now sprouting from my balled fists. I forced the flowers into his hands, and we trailed back to the garden he had destroyed. He followed behind. I bent over the destroyed plants and brought the dead scraps back to life. Brighter, prettier. A new garden grew, "All fixed," I smiled. Haven was amazed by my magical skills, so he showed me his magical skill and shapeshifted into a baby cub. He brushed up me aside of me, and colorful sparks ignited. We laughed; I reached to pat the top of his head, and he softly growled. He watched me build a bright bed of flowers. We laid in the flowers and looked up at the bluish sky above.

The serene morning break came, and birds chirped near the opened wall that let in the sweet breeze. It was the refreshing breeze that awoke me from my feverish coma. Something seemed different about that summer morning. Something extraordinarily peaceful. My heart didn't need to jump at the thought of Haven because I found him sleeping peacefully beside me, *my guardian angel.* His black hair waved perfectly to one side, his soft skin like buttermilk silk in the morning light, and his soft lips tempting. I reached for the time. **7:23 a.m.** Too early to disrupt this serene morning. I put the phone down, and before settling back into the blankets, Haven's dragging arms pulled me back to him. Snuggled up to his nook, he kept his eyes shut as if he wanted to keep dreaming with me in his arms. I could feel the closeness of his morning wood poking me from behind. He was careful not to get closer but hesitant to pull away. I teased him a bit. He raised his eyebrows, "Hmm, don't do that. You might wake up the," he said sheepishly. He was smirking and peeking through heavy eyelids for a reaction.

"What if I want to?"

"-Woman, you have no idea what I went through last night. Please, be nice to me today," he begged, but I had to tease him one last time. My hand slipped down his chest. He smiled in his daze,

"-Oh, it looks like it's already up." I brought my hand to the rim of the elastic of his sweats just before he grabbed my hand.

"Hardly," he smirked, opening his eyes and sitting up.

"Can we stay in bed for a while?" I watched as he pulled his tee-shirt from the bed corner and pulled it on, "Can't, we have some business. Last night, I had a weird dream that I met your parents," I sat back in awe but more restless.

"Come again?" Unsure of what I heard.

"Yeah. I was finally able to walk into your garden while astral projecting. I was looking around when your mom wandered into the garden to warn me about Moboyas. And then he showed up in the garden realm. He knew I was your suitor, and he challenged me to fight the Wendigo before him. I won, but he wasn't satisfied with the fair win. He said the real fight would be after I take you as a wife. But I'm ready, I killed it once, and I'll kill it for good. But first, we have to go back to your uncle's house and get into your garden; I have to make sure I can shift in your realm."

It suddenly hit me; how close we were to our deaths. After I take my vows and Haven takes my virginity, we will be dead. It was a scary thought that made me somewhat sad, and Haven read me well. I gulped, softly pinching the skin on his callused hands.

"Are you afraid, Daya? Of dying?"

"Yes," I admitted honestly.

"I'm fucking scared too. It's weird, right? -But don't worry, we'll be afraid together." I looked at him, and he kissed my hand.

"Haven, can we just lay here until noon? Then, I'll be good," He agreed, and so we lay in bed, talking and joking, wrapped in blankets. He calmed my stormy head and spoiled me with kisses and thoughts of our future. As always, after a fever, I never felt better. Haven pulled me back to the end, where he held me until there was a knock at the bedroom door, and moments later, in came Dean. We sat up from the bed, Haven swaying my hair to one side,

"Rough night?" Dean asked as he came closer.

"Actually, no... I had a great doctor." I smiled at Haven as he handed me fresh water. He shifted towards Dean but took my hand.

"That was the last fever... and she mastered revival last night. We're ready." He proudly informed Dean, "I know, I saw the forest; it's more beautiful reborn than before its death. Congratulations, I'm going to start the preparations for the ceremony,"

After Dean left, we finally got up from our slack and took a cold shower together. We did nothing more than kiss and touch. We seemed to have control of ourselves instead of one another. Being with him like this felt so natural. We couldn't be more in sync. As we dried off, he watched my body and pulled me in to kiss some more. As his eyes glistened the erotic milky blue color, he kissed me one last time before hiking up some dry shorts. After a colorful breakfast with the family, Haven took me on a ride through the Adirondacks nearby. He was blaring his music while my hand interlocked with his. The breeze whisked through my hair, and the sun shone classically in the northern sky. It was so beautiful and peaceful. The scenery was like a watercolor painting done before your eyes by *Jacob Van Ruisdael,* soaking in colorful nature with Haven. We stopped at roadside vendors and snacked on ice cream and cheese fries. Then, we went back into Grey Wolf Hollow and up that ominous mountain towards Misael's lodge home.

It no longer looked like home but a war zone. Haven parked right outside the outskirts of my uncle's driveway. His truck was still parked where I had last seen it. The cabin castle was a reasonable distance away but too big to ignore, even hidden behind trees. I winced at the sight of it. "Come on," Haven said after taking my hand, dragging me alongside him. While Haven seemed to walk fearlessly onto my uncle's property, I tipped-toed around on eggshells. I felt his presence as he stared at us with gruesome raven eyes from the 3rd story window.

I froze and tugged on Haven's arm, "He's watching," I warned. Haven stopped and looked up at him. "Don't worry about him. He's not our problem anymore. He knew we were coming, and he can't do anything about it." I peered back to my uncle, gripping harder onto Haven. Misael made me nervous, and he knew it, but I continued to follow Haven to the garden. Then, finally, we reached the break into the woods, and I could see the familiar gates. I was so happy to see it, and I ran to it. Haven sauntered behind me. My fingers glided across the old metal of the gates, chipping off old dried paint. I pulled the gate lever and softly swung the doors open. *Wait. Where was my Garden?* My entire magical realm was gone. I walked through the gate only to walk further into the same northern forest. My heart dropped, and my throat got dried.

"Where is it?" I rushed to tears. My magical garden was gone. I could still feel it, but it wasn't here. I looked around aimlessly. Sicken and broken by the vacancy of my once beloved magical space. Haven trailed in beyond the gates after me. He was there to catch me before my knees touched the dirt and lifted me, holding me tall. **FUCK.** It was Misael's doing. I knew because he watched from the window, smiling down on me like he had done some real sketchy shit. "Misael!" I sprinted back towards the house. Haven ran after me and caged me in his arms, pulling me away, "No, Daya, leave him be. That's what he wants, a reaction."

"Haven, you don't understand," The more I fought him, the tighter he held on to me, determined to keep me close.

"Trust me, Daya, I do. But we already won. Let's get out of here. Maybe my dad has something in one of his books that can help us find it or bring it back to you." I was still easing out all the anger. Haven's soul searchers seemed to calm me instantly. Haven was right; seeking revenge was a terrible idea. After giving me a reassuring kiss, I conceded, and instead, we left the Manigualt lodge for good. I took one last glance at the place I used to call home. I was so angry about many things, mostly Misael's rejection. But he'll know it someday, just not today.

The sky was an ombre film; orange, light blue, royal blue, navy. Fall was approaching, so the sun began to tap out earlier. And as the sun very lightly fell, we made it back to the Tyson home. Jacy came jogging down the stairs with a stack of dusty books when we got inside. His face was long and tired. He was unshaven, and his lining eyelids were bloodshot red, like a drunk. "I found the books you texted me," Haven thanked Jacy as he took the books from him. We stood in silence until Haven asked him, "Are you okay?" And so Jacy replied in an unsure tone, "I'm doing just fine. Don't worry about us. You two will be happy, and we're all happy for you." Haven stared at Jacy sternly and patted his shoulder.

"You're the wisest and strongest person I know. I wish I could be there for you," Haven looked and sounded sad. Leaving his family behind seemed to be much harder for him. They were, after all, the only ones supporting our divine connection. "We have Dean. I hate him right now, but we're Tyson's. We'll find a way to be okay."

I pulled away while the two brothers had their moment, but Haven found me in his bedroom not long after. I had kicked my shoes off and got comfortable right there on the soft green natural ground, in the middle of the room, with Dean's collection of books. We began to do some research. For hours we read. We were romping through the ancient crisp book pages, looking for anything that could help. When those books failed, Haven went up to his dad's studies and grabbed a couple of Dean's notebooks. Notes from curses and spells and diseases he has dealt with during his career. It was there that we found an entire section for *Binding Anais Garden.*

At first, there wasn't much to go on, but the further we read, the further we learned. "It says here, if you already have Atabey's magic within, your true intention will always guide you to your magic realm, even if hidden out of spite." Haven skimmed through the last pages, his back against the boulder, reading.

"Great, how do I do it?" I asked as I caught up to him.

"It doesn't say. It just says meditation. Maybe if you play around with the magic a little bit." He suggested, closing the book and tossing it on the dresser. He took my hand and dragged me near the woodsy part of his room. He grounded me down into the earth and collided with me. Face-to-face, we began to meditate together as we did in the forest field. As always, Haven Tyson was right. After several hours, we found a doorway within the projection of our auras. I stood from sitting and looked around to the bits of magic I had already spread over Haven's room the night before. The magic around his room was bright and waving. I started to conjure up my magic. I dropped to my knees. Again, I began to place spells around Haven's room, with intentions to find my garden,

Or even make a new portal and garden.

It started as tiny streams of water sprouting from the healthy, vibrant grass. Flowers came next. Pretty colorful ones everywhere. And then Moss. Vines grew and berry bushes. Trees were born before our eyes. The massive mountain of blankets on the boulder-bed slipped off rapidly, and a thick and silky bed of white lilies sprouted with scattered red hibiscus in the mix. They were slither-ing vines with lightning bugs sleeping, wildly hanging above the bed like a chandelier. Haven and I looked at each other, "I knew you would make magic in my bed, but not like this," He joked.

Looking around at my beautiful work growing, hoping a door would appear. Instead, the room glittered and twinkled. It was a job well done. But not well enough. There was no rainforest, palm trees, no beach sand, or the smell of salt waves, no Coqui's crying, and no moon over El Morro. We still weren't in my garden, and that was a problem. I kicked rocks,

"I guess we'll wait and see what happens," I was skeptical,

"Your magic is everywhere here. If we can't find the garden, at least we have my cave. As long as we're together, we can make it happen." Haven had a decent point. It was his cave, but perfect nonetheless. As I walked around, Haven suddenly stopped me,

"-Daya!" He cautiously threw his hands up and stared at something behind me, "Do you see that?" Curious, he came running directly at me and fast. It was too late to stop him as he crashed into me. I fell back into glittering soft white sand. My fingers rummaged the warm ivory, and I sat myself up. I was staring up at a bright and heated Taino sky—the sound of the lagoon water in waves just feet away. The palm leaves heaving over and the smell of the deep blue ocean; I was home. I was in my garden.

But how? And where was Haven?

I stood up and looked around. Everything looked and seemed normal. Exactly how I left it. Except. Well, except for the sky. It's not the rich and honey drip Amber and fire on cool indigo, deep cobalt sky. It was ugly. The bright resilient sunshine gleamed but like a cushioned button pinned on to the wisp stretched clouds of smoke grays; steel and pigeons and blues of a dark kind. A storm was slowly coming. It won't rain now but indeed within the next few hours. The wind picked up. I was howling a whistle of warning. My hair fluttered around. No birds, lizards, or creatures roamed. I could hear the crashing waves of the rattled ocean beyond the sand. It was all a poetic song of pity. My father's wrath would soon engulf everything. The sadness sunk in. As my fingers skimmed the stone of the fountain, I found a flat box floating in the water and reached for it—a note on top of it, "*Dayanara, A wedding gift, love*

Mami," I slipped the box under my arm as I slipped a single tear of appreciation for my mother. But then an ominous feeling looted in the air—the stank stench of rage. Moboyas was invading my space. I could feel his darkness already seeping into the garden. I walked towards a light, back to where I had fallen in, and instantly found myself in Haven's bedroom. There, he stood in awe.

"Babe, are you okay?" he pulled me into his arms, instantly inspecting me for bumps and bruises.

"Yeah," I held the gift I had retrieved from the garden tightly to my chest, dropped to the floor, and began to cry. Slowly, Haven sat down on the ground next to me and pulled me into him, "Don't worry. We're not out of time. It'll happen at the right time, my love. The best plans are usually unplanned, don't you think-"

I looked at him with glowing eyes. He was right.

"-What did you find?" He asked, tapping the box. I shrugged.

"A gift from my mom,"

Haven smiled at my words and then revealed a pearl wedding ring. I smiled back at him, and he slid the ring on me. I kissed his lips, and he windshield wiped away my tears with his palms before pulling me in closer. He lifted my chin with his index finger,

"We have our parent's blessings. It's all we need,"

"But we should say goodbye to our family." I reminded Haven.

"Don't worry. Dean's planning a dinner party. We need more than 10 minutes before committing suicide."

I looked at him disapprovingly, but it was honest.

20

Superior Emotions

The evening sun was still hanging over this deadly dusk.

As Charlotte cooked, everyone was hanging around the kitchen, pouring drinks, and Haven's uncle Shane tipped off the jukebox. Haven and I agreed to Dean's subtle wedding plans; a small death day dinner with the family before Dean's soul-binding ritual in the privacy of the heart-shaped meadow. We were excited about the union and got closer to our divine 'heaven with each hour.'

Although Haven's first business order was food, we all gathered around an intimate 'family' table. Haven sat me on his lap as he hauled back three courses, laughing and joking with our family. He and Landon were even getting along, reminiscing of good old days when they hated each other. Haven was already accepting of our fate, more than I had been. More or less because of Misael and how he refused to support my decision. When it became quiet, Haven flashed his eyes into mine, checking in. He saw sadness, and I tried to hide, gazing down. Finally, he lifted my chin and forced me at eye level. He smiled a weak but compassionate smile, "Don't be sad," he whispered reassuringly. Our eyes both shot down to our hands interlocking. Sitting there helplessly and recklessly love drunk at the same time. It didn't matter how I felt that moment because I knew with Haven, I felt safe and happy.

"Let's be alone somewhere," I begged in a whisper. Haven laughed, looking away. I knew he was feeling just as love-drunk as me; his pale face was flushed pink and blotchy cheeks. Still, he looked like Heaven. Haven towered above me, carrying me away, ignoring everyone as he rushed us out the door and into the quiet and still backyard. He pulled me into the dark shadows of the flourishing nature. Moonlight was all around us. Finally, we were alone. Haven pulled me to dance, taking me into his hands, "Dean uses this quote from *Rumi,* which says-

'Your task is not to seek for love but merely to seek and find all the barriers within yourself that you have built against it.'

- Rumi.

-Now I realize what he meant all those years; I've struggled between being a selfish fucking kid and a kid who's willing to carry the world for everyone but broken heartedly. It's all about being entitled, and it's about feeling like you don't deserve something, even someone. Sometimes we can be our own worst enemy and stand in our way. We create our obstacles right before our path. We set standards and even set ourselves up when things don't go the way we think they should. Life is not supposed to be like that, Daya. Things never go according to a 'plan.' I never appreciated the 'not knowing,' as much as I do now. That's because it took the right person, and that person was you, and know you deserve to be happy because your soul is pure light. I appreciate you if anything-"

Haven recklessly made my heart chakra flex as he fixed on me with honest azure eyes. He smirked a sexy smirk, beautiful but rugged, confident like the nightly breeze, sending shivers through my body as he danced with me. He didn't kiss me. Not yet. Instead, he lifted me onto his boots, and I interlaced over his crown before he carried me further into the shadows and lifted me onto the wood picnic table as his lips savaged onto mine. Our passion for each other was the drug we couldn't wait to inject after allowing the anticipation of our bodies and souls as one, patiently waiting the last hours. He looked hungry, in need of my sweet sugar venom. Once he started kissing me, he couldn't stop; pushing yearningly into me. If he wanted, he could have me that moment.

The buttons of my dress popped off, from the bottom up to my hip. Haven's eyes clung on helplessly to the sight of my legs. His hands ran smoothly up them like a rapid upward stream, pressing into my skin and sending rigid euphoric electricity through his touch. He kissed me and then bit my neck, and I moaned into his ear. His hands cupped under my ass, and he pulled me into him closer. My knees went up as his lips wandered from my neck to my chest. He held me with one hand at the small of my back. My dress fell loosely apart, revealing my breast as he went further down. Every deep inhale he took in was pulling in my essence, and he was trying to hold it in, like a long pull off a danky joint. My scent was encouraging him. Finally, when I couldn't hold back the sexual cries and whimpers of his teasing, he slowed down until he gently pulled away. I looked at him, grinning in the moonlight, "What?"

"Are you kidding me? You are so loud..." he snickered in the dark.

"I seriously can't help it; you feel so nice."

"We're not doing any more of this until *after* the ritual. One hour more won't kill us," *Ugh, why?* Haven intervened with common sense. Disappointment read across my face, more so in my deep lilac eyes. I reached for his belt buckle, and he pulled away but kissed me sweetly. Finally, his bold and stern look made me concede. He was still admiring me in the moonlight. He brushed the hair from my eye before he slowly slipped up the sleeves to my dress, dressing me.

We looked down to my legs wide open, his knees in between. His hand tapped my legs closed, "I don't need to rush things with you. You know that." I was frustrated, flipping my hair to one side. I had nothing to say. He slowly peeled me off the table and pulled me towards the house. Haven stopped before the entrance and pushed me up against the frame. He kissed my neck. My hands pulled at his waist, rubbing his deliciousness onto me, licking and kissing on my neck sent waves of sweet juice down my thighs. I was nearly biting my lips so I wouldn't let it out.

I couldn't let it out.

And then I let it out; a sweet yelp of bliss. His hand lightly slapped onto my mouth, holding my moans back, except he wouldn't stop. He kept kissing and feeling up over the thin fabric of my red button-down maxi dress. He showed self-control, so I slipped my two fingers into my wet panties and touched my drenched clit, collecting sweet honey nectar. He looked down at me as I slipped my fingers inside and out. My eyes rolled back, and I could feel his heavy breathing. He pushed against me and immediately grabbed my hand. He brought my dripping fingers to his hungry lips; his eyes were glowing rich gold, and he growled in awe of my actions. Then, while staring at me slowly, he put my fingers into his mouth and sucked up my sweet nectar. Licking at my fingers like I was dripping butter pecan ice cream. His mouth watered to the taste, slurping and sucking it down,

"Now go and get dressed. We're going for a run."

Woody nightshade so sits there and sonder.

In a couple of hours, Haven and I would be dead, and everyone else would be going to bed. It was a scary thought, I had to admit. But, Monachopsis settled into my bones at the right moment when Haven and I held onto each other. It wasn't in his arms that felt out of place. It was the both of us together, out of place in this world. Somehow we have caught up with its timeless end, and there was no more for us here, in this dimension. We had our heavenly paradise, and we didn't need anything or anyone. There were many ways to describe it, but in plain text, *Fuck this place.*

Ironic. The rain started to pour right before Haven, and I went back into the house. The days I spent without Haven was of beauty and sunny summer days. Now, we were to marry, and it seemed as though Moboyas decided to crash the party early. Darkness all around, and rain slapping into puddles. But with it, a silver lining. None of the nights before this have ever felt tranquil and calm. We were running towards something all this time, and now we were still. This weather may be honest. If it didn't rain with good intentions, the future ahead wouldn't be all rainbows and sunshine.

Everyone seemed to be running around that last hour, despite the crappy rain outside. I curled into a ball in the middle of the bathtub, letting the steamy water run over my crown and wash my body in the dark. I let all the fear and doubt flush down the drain. Usually, the term is, I have nothing left to lose. But in my case, I had one more thing to lose. I spent preparing the last hour before midnight alone, and it went as slow as it could feel. I didn't take much time getting dressed. By then, Charlotte and Leyla came up to help me. They were quiet, and I found it strange. But Charlotte used red paint to mark my face and body with sacred symbols and designs. My wedding dress was only a high waistband mesh maxi skirt that flowed past my feet, trailing a small train behind. My long smooth legs peered from the double slits of the dress. With it, a classic tribal bandeau top. I was all in white—no glitz and glam like the Hollywood movies we watched; It was thin, plain, but perfect, and I decided to go barefoot.

Fifteen minutes. Counting down, I could only pace back and forth and stare at nothing else except for my mother's gift, as it sat there in a sleek box on the dresser. I was a nervous wreck. My eyes widened the minute Charlotte tapped on the door, " The rain has stopped," I nodded as I watched her take the sacred wedding gift from my mother. They had arranged for Landon to escort me to Haven on ATV, so I greeted him by the opened side door. It blew in a fresh breeze as he slowly turned to me,

"Hey," When he finally looked at me, my hands clasped to my dropped jaw—the return of sad and angry sable eyes. I tugged at my chest. "-Landon," He didn't need to tell me. I was already familiar with the pain, and now I wondered if Leyla was truly in love with Jacy and why was Landon sable-eyed? I reached for him, but he pulled away. "Don't worry about me, Daya; I'm fine ... you look so beautiful," It was a strange feeling, Landon admiring me before marrying me off to his brother. He reached over, brisking my cheek with his knuckles. I closed my eyes. I couldn't show how his touch made me feel. My lips curled in, and my gut felt like the food processor was blending it; mixed emotions.

"This is terrible," I whispered, but he didn't seem like he was in the mood for pity. Instead, Landon carried himself with a power he had never had before. A passion passed down from one brother to another. He ripped his eyes from me and back to the still night, "Lucky for me, Tyson men were born with curses too. Just have to figure it out and keep Misael as far away as possible." He seemed sure of himself but felt cold. I swallowed hard, knowing it wouldn't be easy for him. Finally, I cleared my throat, "Landon, please watch over Leyla?" He looked at me sternly. Waves of blue trying to break from the ebony. "Don't worry, Daya, we will," Landon put all my final anxieties and worries to rest. I was more than confident that Leyla was in the best hands possible.

Five minutes. We drove through a familiar path in the woods. A course I had run down many nights before with Haven. Passing by each tree, new and old, was like reliving my life. We have engraved every detail of our love story in this forest, down to every tree Haven ever pushed me against, every moss gushing boulder we've kissed on, and every fallen rotten trunk we've lept over. True love, sewed in very root weaved into this rich earth. Our foot's prints weren't there anymore, but I knew where we were heading. Slowly, the ATV pushed over wet logs and rocks with thick, damp, tall grass. The clearing was just up ahead. As Landon slowly drove into the heart-shaped field, I relived that moment Haven first noticed its shape. Finally, we got closer, and I saw them.

Dean was standing just before the rushing waters with Jacy, Leyla, and Haven. Haven had his back towards me, and I could see his tall but graceful silhouette ahead. I closed my eyes. I needed patience. Trying to calm down this beating heart, my toes dug into the soil, and I released all the tension I held inside. Even so, I couldn't breathe. Was I sinking? Was I dying? "Daya, calm down… he thinks your perfect." Landon's words were able to stop every rushing thought through my head. Landon let me recompose myself before I gripped his arm again. Now I could breathe.

Haven was stunning in the moonlight, in a blue plaid single-breasted vest, long sleeve white button-up underneath, sand tan slacks; his sleeves rolled up, and he was wearing knee-high fishing boots in the midst of the after rain. Feet away, Landon released me the minute Haven turned to me. Unable to withstand another moment, I collided into Haven's open arms. He was elated at the sight of me. His eyes glossed over, honest and adoring, 'Wow,' he whispered. The meadow was glowing with lightning bugs underneath a star-ridden Midnight sky. It was influential on the darkness from the dark woodlands, hovering like a cave. Haven's chest was rising and collapsing at the same rate as mine when he took my hand and, without another word, pulled me down to kneeling on soggy ground, staring into each other's eyes.

Dean began the ceremony with a blessed scarlet rope that bounded our hands together. With our eyes closed, our natural spirits glowed and glistened within. Against the wind, Dean spoke of beauty and wisdom. He talked of destiny and lovers of peaceful earth ascending beyond a world too small for them. We felt the presence of The Great Spirit among Atabey and Anais's spirit. It was all around us. Landon presented Haven with a beautiful Native Headdress and placed it at his crown. Then Leyla opened my mother's box. Inside, a beautiful white headdress made of the rarest albino peacock and parrot feathers. Glittering its aura as Leyla came over with it, she gracefully placed it on my crown. Haven's eyes marveled in blue and white as Dean blessed upon our *forbidden* union. Binding our hearts and souls for what will be, *always.* He sealed the bind with prosperity, everlasting love, abundance, and peace. Our shine glittered into one another under that earthly moonlight, and he gave me his soul in exchange for mine. Our union, lastly, sealed over with an igniting kiss. We couldn't describe the emotion we found at that moment. Yet, it was precisely the superior emotion we chased after. The marriage of our souls ended our lives but allowed us to begin another. We were suddenly dead alone on bending knee, bound together.

Everyone was gone. It felt still, but the wind blew around our numb bodies. Haven cupped my hands into his and placed them over his heart. He wasn't moving. His heart. His breathing. His veins. All still. His hand took in my neck. He checked for a pulse as I felt up his forearm muscle, searching for his. We both were dead. Yet, Haven, his touch, and his voice all felt alive to me. Just as I did to him. We no longer existed in the realm on earth. And even in death, Haven seemed mesmerized by me.

Haven managed to pull himself up, hauling me to my feet with him and releasing the bind on our hands. "Where they go?" We were both quiet as our heads arched around, looking for a sign of life. The wind blew an echoing silence of vacancy that we couldn't feel, only see. "-What now?" I looked up at Haven. He grinned as he pulled away and kicked off his rubber boots, "Let's go for a run."

Haven took off running into the woods, and I followed behind. We ran freely, with no one to find us or even come looking. We were way beyond the abyss of the forest night. In the quiet, we played a game of tag. Stopping between oak and pine to lock lips whenever we could. Despite not having a pulse, adrenaline pushed through us with electricity. We didn't stop running until Haven ran into his bedroom from the break in the forest, hurdling through the foundation hole. He caught my speed as I tumbled right into his arms. My toes were on tips when he came into me for a demanding sweet kiss. Our eyes locked together, dull and dead but raging with passionate concentrated love, in scorching balls of fire. He kissed me slowly as he pulled me deeper into his magical bedroom. My eyes reflected all the illuminating candles scattered. The flowers were as fresh as they were when born.

I walked over to the wall where I had found my garden realm and dazzled my fingers down the drywall. It was no longer there. I steered away from the wall and to Haven popping the champagne open. He put on soft music and handed me the bottle of champagne. His hands shook nervously, "I hate tailored suits. I'm too big for this shit," Haven joked as he loosened up the buttoned vest. The button-up stuck to the creases of his sweaty body. Bottle in hand, I took a sip from it without my eyes leaving him. His face was solid, jawline running sharp. The thought of jumping his bones hasn't left my mind since we left the field. I wanted to jump in him like an ocean and slip into the trenches of his bones.

Haven read my body. He was staring like a wide eye deer caught in headlights, feet away with his hands on his collar. The flame flickered in them as I took him off guard. I tried to stick the champagne bottle on the shelf, but it fell anyway, and neither cared. Haven reached out and grabbed me by the waist. Our hips were magnets as he softly swiped away my tousled curls from my face. He kissed my lips with a rich passion. Then, he began to kiss down my neck. My fingers dug into his skin, slowly letting the anxiety sink. When I pulled from his kiss, he could see it in my eyes, "-there's no need to rush," his fingers brushed over my shoulders, smearing the red paint across my skin. The feeling sank more into me,

"Haven, I don't want to be a spaz, but this paint all over; it only makes me feel like we're doing another ritual. I don't want this to feel like that." He looked down to our muddy knees. Haven nodded before he carried me to the bathroom. "I'm going to get some wine from upstairs," He touched my cheek. *I'm so immature,* I thought, as he slid his hands in his pocket and started up the staircase. I pinned up my long flowy hair before testing the hot shower. It was burning, but I couldn't feel it—any of it. I was numb. My hair had turned from slight waves into perfect, wild curly locks with the moisture in the nightly air. I lather on the soap, rinsing off all the red and white paint. The symbols melted away with the water, and I watched the dirt and red ink swirl down the drain.

No more rituals. No more malevolent spells. I couldn't even feel the charm inside anymore. As if it left with my soul at the binding ceremony. Not one ounce of magic in my entire being. I should be panicking that I couldn't feel anything, somewhat. But, I had Haven, and everything he was, made me feel just enough frenzy to engage the real magic I left in his cave. All the love and glory, and all strength. We were minutes away from making love, and not even death took away its anxiety. It wasn't like the rush we got from pushing the boundaries. This time we were going all the way for real. I wasn't going to jump into this as I tried an hour ago. I needed his hand to hold while I walked further into this darkness.

I slipped into a white silk robe that dropped to the ground and let my hair fall from its pin-up. The air was so hollow. I peered from the corner of the bathroom opening, and there Haven stood in the middle of his room barefoot. No vest or tie. His button-up was undone, showing off his body. He had blown out all the candles but one vibrant flame that flickered in the middle of everything.

The moon's light peered in, and that divine silver struck him perfectly where Haven stood. He was still. Nervous. I could tell how he was chainsmoking that cigar and pacing about, taking in the smoke but nothing coming out. We were both nervous wrecks. Good, I thought. I am not alone. I slowly walked over to where he stood. His eyes shot up at me. Those rich blue eyes never danced with so much moonlight until now,

"-I turned off the candles; it looked too ritualistic."

There was a romantic grinding in my frozen heart as he reached for me; I wasn't sure if it was real or not. "-I'm scared, Haven." I whispered in his arms. *Odd.* His lips seemed to quiver as I said that. "We can dance if you want to," His words were perfect. The music was still playing, and when I laced my fingers into his jet black hair, he knew I had taken the invitation. He sucked my body to him, and we slow danced. Haven had always been a great dancer. Even being so tall, his lean body permanently moved fluidly and gracefully. He held my body close. He made sure I could feel every part of him push against me. I could feel my body slowly warming up. His one hand held my neck, his other pressing my hips into him. Our eyes stuck. Nothing else seemed to exist.

"Never was there a time when you and I didn't exist, nor will there ever be a time when we ceased to exist,"

Bhagavad Gita.

His fingers traced away to the outline of my body shape before he lifted me onto his long body. I kissed him again as I collapsed my long legs around him, straddling tightly. We both had to be blistering cold, but we couldn't feel it as I got lost in his lips, and he carried me to the flower-covered bed, laying me down on fluffy red hibiscus and white lilies. It was dark, but the lightning bugs had given off enough illumination. Bright enough to reach this dark corner. The flowers had to feel silky and soft, but I wouldn't know because I couldn't feel it either. I watched Haven pull his shirt off and toss it into the heaving black background. "You okay?" He whispered, concerned for me. "Yeah. I'm okay," I muttered as Haven hovered over me in plank, his hands in the flowers. He looked down at my shaking hands as I nervously undid the knot in my robe. I watched the shadows from the flares of the flames dance along with his divine being. I was slowly but surely, surrendering, and his hollowness could only feel that much.

Haven placed his hand over my chest. He slowly feathered it over my heart and, with his fingertips, peeled away the robe, sliding it over and down my shoulders and revealing my raw glowing skin. His eyes gleamed over my incarnate luminous body. He was struck stupid with eyes of wonder and fascination. I reached for his waist and pulled apart his belt. Undoing his button and zipper, I admired his being right back. I pulled off what I could, but Haven did the rest. I had to admit, it was a little awkward as he moved around above me, trying to ace the pants and briefs, but we both laughed in the comfort of each other as he finally kicked them off.

Haven went down onto elbows in plank, his natural naked body now laying over mine. He didn't feel as heavy as I remembered. Haven was near to weightless as his thumb traced my lips. He licked his lips and, as his lips electrocuted mine, all seemed to fade away.

Suddenly that rolling, loud desire came flooding back. For a moment, I did feel something underneath all the paralysis. Haven caved into me some more as his thumb traced over a single tear down the curve of my cheek, erasing its existence.

"... I'm -ah, follow you. Okay," I trembled in tone.

Haven kissed me reassuringly. I felt his knees part mine as he snuggled in between them. His face dove into my neck, and his lips began to invade my body. His weight pushed my legs further apart. His hands grappled all over my naked body as I could feel his pelvis mesh with mine. It would have felt warm if I could feel it. Instead, I still couldn't feel a thing. Until he slipped inside me, I didn't remember how intimidatingly well endowed his shaft was; I felt all of it when he got inside me. Slippery but struggling for a fit. My lungs sucked up like a syringe trying to find the room for him. The pressure was like electricity but felt so amazing.

I was *breathing,* so heavy. I think. Trying to relax, the shock of Haven pushing forced me to take ease into exhaling. It didn't matter anymore, as he was already in and knocking down my walls. Slowly at first, as he moaned, and my fingers brushed over his lips. Our chest collapsed and collided simultaneously, and that's when I began to feel my heart chakra revving with each thrust. We were burning up. Evasive tingling all over every stretch of nerves through our bodies. From my toes to the tips of my soft hair. Euphoric-inducing breaks every time he pushed into me. So hard, but so slowly, so he could feel every part of me coming back to life on him, reviving one another, Like Narcan into cocaine rolling high.

His tongue found its way to my nipple, licking and biting. I glorified Haven's titan body and all the pleasure he gave me without holding back—nothing of how I imagined it. The real thing was denser, better, more intense. A black strand of hair fell over his glossy blue eye, with the look of pure sexual bliss and gratification; he never looked any sexier than he did swaying on top of me. I had been whimpering from the pain and pleasure, but now I was moaning pretty loud, and so was he. He couldn't bear to look away from my body exploding from the oxytocin, and now his grunts were coming out uncontrollably. An incoming shaking from within, so powerful my legs trembled. He was heavy on me, sinking. He felt it too. He eased off of me, holding himself up with one arm in plank again so he could praise all of me while he continued to spark inside of me. His grunts still escaped him despite how hard he tried to keep quiet. Whatever I was doing to him, he couldn't handle it. Finally, he collapsed beside me and pulled me on top; without pulling out of the mission. I struggled for a moment, uneasy and dreading gravity as I slipped down him.

The burning energy inside manifested over us. I felt so good, I rolled my hips majestically on him; I don't even know where the skill came from; but slow, real slow. Quiet enough to nearly make him cry. He was gasping to stop, but I shut him up with my hands over his lips and continued until Haven flipped me back onto my back, and this time he pulled out but re-entered me recklessly. He smashed himself inside, over and over. My head tossed back in severe orgasm, pounding my fist on his chest. He hit the same spot twice more before we cussed at the moon, cumming together. Letting it all go like a river, I followed right behind him.

Our breathing huffed through the night. Heavy and defined, seizing in the thickening air. Are we alive? Our hearts were racing again. I touched his hot face, both of us sweating, and he kissed my hand. Neither of us could stop smiling. Then, giggling, he came collapsing to the side of me. We were both in wonder-lust shock. I felt like I was burning up—our bodies steaming in the cold air like melting butter on pancakes.

"Wow... Fucking worth it." His running mind broke the silence.

We looked at each other and laughed. Then, reaching for my hand, I could feel the heat of his blood coursing through him. I cupped his hand and brought it to my chest. There were no answers to the questions that formed in our minds. But where there once was a hollowness, a warm thickness settled. Almost uneasy. Haven felt it too. "I love you." Haven protectively pulled me under his arms, glancing around suspiciously, as we laid naked in the flowers. I told him I loved him as our bare skin rippled with goosebumps. We felt the bitter cold that blew into our cave—the crisp smell of dying wet leaves and pine cones. The air was eerie. There was more to come, but it was peaceful laying there in the safety of Haven's arms. "Are you okay? Did I hurt you?"

He had no reason to be concerned. I felt perfect for the first time, "You felt good, and I feel good," His eyebrow raised, and he smirked. Neither of us anticipated the silence that quickly seeped in after. We wallowed in solitude, lost in thought. Until, "-Daya, I have to tell you something," He broke the perfect silence. I looked at him, worried from his troubling tone, "-When we were running in the woods, I tried shifting. I can't shift into my Bear Spirit in this dimension we're in." That was a profound revelation. I pulled the white silk sheet along to cover my nakedness,

"Why didn't you tell me?"

"I didn't want to worry you,"

I could feel an argument brewing by the waves of his tone.

"That's something we should worry about, isn't it?"

My tone caused him to exhale deeply, "It's the only way I'll kill the wendigo," Lighting his cigarette, he stared off.

"If my father shows, I will sacrifice myself for your soul."

"-The hell you are," He fought with me,

"Your not supposed to be trapped here, where ever we are,"

"Neither are you, Daya, but we're here together, and I'll take that. I'm already pissed, so leave it at that, I love you, I don't want to fight-" he chucked the cigarette to the ground, "-this is not up for discussion- I followed you here, I'm not leaving without you, and you're not going anywhere without me. I'll find a way to shift, Daya. Just promise me you won't do anything stupid,"

Pulling at my hand, Haven begged, but I stayed quiet. After everything I've been through with Haven, this was a perfect ending. If he couldn't save me from my father's fate, I didn't want him jumping in after me. My father's magic would destroy every beautiful part of him. But, of course, he knew what I was thinking, "You jump, I'm jumping." He proclaimed, laying back into the flower bed.

There was no use arguing with him. Even after death, he was a hothead and a dummy. But I loved him, almost too much. So it was quiet, but not still. Haven's hands came for my body underneath the bedsheet, and he pulled me into him; the wind blew recklessly outside, and the rain poured. Haven was right, I felt like we were already in paradise, lying with him while the rain poured was serene. I was ready for real make up sex, and that read in my lilac eyes.

Haven kissed my neck, and his fingertips wandered down my body until his thumb pressed my love button, and his tongue was in my ear. He knew my body much more in-depth, so I closed my eyes and relaxed into euphoria, forgetting our problems as Haven pulled the sheet from me to watch his magic come over my body. Heavy rain fell through the hole in the ceiling and poured onto my body. He continued to watch me squirm under his hypnotic touch.

I squealed on the verge of orgasm, trying to get him to stop, but he pinned my hands down and sucked on my ear lobe.

"Hold on," He played with me more before climbing back on top of my body. He very smugly parted my legs. The way I yearned for him to ravish me again made him smirk, and he knocked my knees further apart, rubbing his shaft over my juicing lips. He came back into me, dominating me more aggressively than before, and I loved it. We was taking out our frustration; my arms snaked between his, and I let him deeper inside. This second time around felt different. There was no nervousness nor hesitation. It felt so good. We were tumbling into the wild, with our bodies entangled on the flower bed. He gave me complete control as he always wanted, and the whole place shook and burst into flames, Engulfing us.

21

Taino Ever After...

I see why they call red ants *fire ants*—a swarm; No- an invading army biting every stretched inch of me. That's how it felt when the fire consumed us mid-creating. If it weren't for the sounds of drums and the howling of a conch shell, I'd thought we were dying again. But when the flames set aside, Haven and I were laying in that glittering silver sand, looking up to the wrecked garden sky that seemed to be just as bipolar as Haven and I. *Orange and yellow* colliding with *heavy gray and navy*. In the distance, a hurricane storm approached rapidly. I reached for Haven's extending hand as he helped me up to my bare feet, dressed in our proper Indigenous attire and red paint. The ground trembled, and before our eyes, a platform emerged from the sand before us— the growing thrones, perfectly fitted for Taino Gods and Goddesses.

Unmoved, Atabey, glowing in a glittering orange-pink aura. Yocahu in a clear and bright but glittered light. More rumbling. The Zeni Entourage. Deities filled the space around us. **More rumbling.** Another throne appeared. One of molten hot lava. Raven black with structured bones and skulls embedded. My father's, I assumed by its ugliness as it grew. Moboyas appeared sitting in it, amused by his entrance. His cheekbones rose to the sight of me. He crackled a menacing giggle that started low but quickly echoed—a shot of thunder and cracks of lightning,

"My *broken doll*," Moboyas spoke, "-you are more of me than you'll ever know, little bat." He rose and snapped. A dusting of the colorful kind shook down, and there my mother stood. A sight for sore eyes, but a prisoner, dressed in red silks with heavy chains at her wrists and ankles. The energy of Moboyas melted away after a weltering bursting wind came from the abyss.

The colorful, lively fluttering of neon butterflies, petals and berries, bubble bees, nuts, and seeds. A glowing heavenly light as the skeleton. A very sophisticated and tamed wind could only be the *Great Spirit.* So powerful. Beautiful. Colorful and full of life. It whisked around Haven several times before the Spirit pulled away and dreamed into the thick air.

It was invisible, but you felt it there, especially around Haven.

From the Great Spirit came woodland animals in pairs of two. Squirrels. Deer. They all came forward. A vibrant large white wolf approached within a blue aura; with him, a beautiful divine white horse, and in a nearby tree, a beautiful white Owl hooted, alongside a beautiful maroon hummingbird. *Our family-* by the way, Haven found comfort in Jacy's hooting. The air settled now that our audience was there. My once-thriving garden was slowly rotting and falling to pieces. It was now a specter stadium for these deities and creatures. The Great Spirit blew. It spoke to Yocahu.

Yocahu, as always, has been a powerful ancestor, aside from mother Atabey, who claimed more strength as the feminine energy. As should be. No one dares his authority, which has made him rather bored. He swallowed his wine, "Yocahu! True Spirit of the Taino people! I have tried to keep from the affairs of Moboyas.

However, *mother Goddess Atabey* has taken pity on the half mortal-Goddess princess." The Owl hooted, intense and electrifying. Moboyas looked down with a dirty look of disgust.

"Moboyas, the True Powerful God of Death, Darkness, Destruction. I claim the child of my own making. Birthed by this mortal Queen after she was given to me as a sacramental gift by our people; as goes the curse plagued upon every living bloodline princess. Dayanara is to return to the realm of *Turey* before tainting the *sacred Taino bloodline.* Except, my child has entwined her fate with that of the *Great Spirit.* Regardless, I come to take what's mine."

"I'm here to protect the Spirit of Dayanara!" Haven intercepted.

"So- we meet again, the Spirit of the Bear." Moboyas chuckled more violently than before, "The curse already branded her soul. Her life on earth has ended, as did yours. You are of no real value to me. But Dayanara, she is precious to me." Atabey stood up and Clapped hard. Yocahu, sitting like he was about to fall asleep from all the boredom, looked up at his Queen and sat straight.

"-Quite frankly- Moboyas, you're getting on my nerves. Dayanara's earthly life has ended, and she has been birthed into the realm, as did the boy. But that doesn't mean their souls can't be together. If the Goddess can prove she's worthy of creating a world of her own, she should be allowed to walk that plane forever. If she truly carries the unconditional true love magic, she claims,"

"-What about the boy?" Moboyas pointed to Haven, and The Great Spirit blew with intention. Finally, it spoke, and they listened. Things seemed to be in an uproar for a moment as the energy thickened and looks of suspicion and distrust shot everywhere.

"-I'll bless the binding!" Yocahu spoke, and Moboyas lost himself.

"Travesty! This union between two energies birthed into the worlds of two different Superior Gods is a travesty. She is a Taino star seedling and belongs with her kind,"

"Know no truth but the sacred truth Mother Atabey speaks. Love is truth. Dayanara and Haven have been brought together in sacred union to teach the power of *perfect,* unconditional love. This is not a travesty, but a union blessed, binding forever, the most powerful and divine spiritual shifts in the Universe. Only through the conflicting bloodlines did they learn to love in a way much more patient and kinder than most. Giving hope to our descendants-"

"You can not interfere with what had always been! The betrayal should turn their hearts to stone," Moboyas yelled at the wrong God. Fury and flames flared about the gods' perfect facial structure. But his buck-up seemed to diminish when Yocahu rose to eye level.

"I shall do as I please! Who are you but a weaker God of the dark kind, beneath my golden feet, overlooked in this perfect realm with disgust. You are unworthy to stand before a being as Superior as I. You are so bored Moboyas, enough to bother with the fairs of frail and impractical immortals. Dayanara and Haven have already ascended into their divine beings; let the little bat go." My father kept shut at his superior's will, "-The boy will be blessed and will enter the garden world of Dayanara *AFTER* he proves himself worthy of our young star seed. If Moboyas wishes to challenge the boy to a duel, Dayanara shall prove her gift of Atabey. If successful, they shall be granted peace and reward in the garden realm forever. Does anyone object?" Yocahu demanded,

"I Do!" Haven growled. I looked at him anxiously. If Yocahu was powerful and intimidating enough to shut Moboyas up, I didn't want Haven talking back to him. But there he was, "-I want to win back my Bride… and Queen Anais under the same conditions." Haven stepped closer to him. The audience, just as I, gasped in shock. Yocahu laughed in sudden entertainment,

"Spoken like a true warrior, I see. I like him. So, you wish to alter the challenge?" Yocahu was hoping he heard correctly.

"-Nonsense!" My father screeched. Smacking down his staff that echoed a rumbling underneath. But Haven didn't back down, and Yocahu supported him. Moboyas was just about to speak when he held his tongue back. Slowly his eyes gleamed. He sat back on his throne of oozing black lava and thought a moment,

"Fine -**Two.** Two, you shall fight—the jealous wendigo and the wendigo of hate and vengeance; at the same time - If you fail, I take you and your *FATHERS* soul." Haven didn't think twice.

Very quickly, Haven replied with, "*Deal.*"

I ran to him. There was no way he could do this. *He couldn't even shift,* "What are you doing?" I cried. He could gamble with my soul all he wanted, but how dare he gamble with the souls of our parents. "Trust me, Daya-" His eyes seemed so sure of it. He knew what he was doing and didn't wait for me to agree. Instead, he kissed me hard before pushing me aside and stomping closer to Moboyas. They looked at each other with a thick intensity that stilled the arena. *My father snapped his fingers again.*

A flame appeared before Haven and traveled in a large circumferencing circle around us, and a dusty battleground formed at the center beneath our feet. Moboyas face was etched up above, like a watcher in the troubled sky. His horrid chuckle rumbled with the storm clouds, his grin projected wide across the sky. He was going to cheat, and he wanted everyone to know it. Atabey stomped her foot and crossed her arms while Yocahu tried to calm her. We felt the Great Spirit blast wind throughout the arena. Suddenly two different colored lights shot from Moboyas evil eyes in the sky like meteors. *One green. The other is yellow.*

Jurakan and Guabancex, crashing into the battlefield before us. Terror in Haven's eyes as he ran close to protect me. Rumbling lightning clouds formed. The wind stole our attention as speeding winds of *one-eighty MPH* howled, *clashing and colliding* into trees. Everything was ripping apart too fast. Debris flew all around. The God of Hurricane and the Goddess of scorned Wind was now standing in the circle. The skies became black, and the creatures and birds that came with the Great Spirit hovered for cover. In the pouring rain, a holographic movie played in the storm clouds above like a movie—*every moment of betrayal.*

Every single lie. Every single trick. Every Curse.

Every spell meant to keep Haven and me apart. In the beginning, every single intimate moment I had with Landon played. *The first time he asked me out—the first date. Our track runs. The first time he held my hand, and I kissed him. Our ATV summer rides at Wolf Cliff. 4ᵗʰ of July. Homecomings. Games. Hector's. The moment he gave me the engagement ring. What a sensitive moment it was for me. And even that night in his truck, as I tried to force myself on him. I was cringing to every word spoken, every touch witnessed.*

I wanted to throw up, but Haven was already doing that. **Vomiting.** Hot danky tar-like acid spewed all over the sand, instantly burning away like acid. He shook with fury. His wrath slowly crept from his limbs. *The Sable eyes returned for a moment.* Haven endured the excruciating pain as the oozing sappy wendigo emerged from within him, first, through his sharp eyes, and then he bled from his nose and ears and dripped from his fingertips like lava. Finally, Haven fell to the ground, violent enough to knock it out of him, but only in convulsions. And so it came out slithering willingly, in the form of two ugly and morbid long *Boa reptilians.*

Haven's eyes retreated to blue. The darkness had escaped from his being, and he was utterly free from it. I ran over to him and helped him to his feet, but soon after, we were stuck watching the two giant snakes slither across the arena and over to Jurakan and Guabancex, steadily waiting. The snakes slithered up their leg. They bit venom into the deities as the snakes made their way up their necks and into their mouth. Finally, the God and Goddess swallowed the snake's whole.

First, their eyes came, like Obsidian rocks. *Hard and cold.* Their limbs began to crackle and break. The wendigo Spirit consumed the deities like a blood fusion infecting every atom of their higher beings. The tar pulsated and grew like wildfire. Their skin *ripped and stretched.* Their masses were eaten alive like carnivorous parasites feasting till they were only rotting bone. And still, the bones cracked and extended and grew into two malformed, unnaturally lanky *monstrous beings.* These tall, emaciated, bony coal creatures dripped of that nasty acid tar. With teeth of shattered glass and slicing thorns. A disfigured flesh-less gaunt face, the skull half stag, and falling molding skin; half deity with massive bat wings, large horns of a demon, and claws of an eagle, ready to rip out an artery and consume. Their mouths were dripping with hot black spit, and their eyes ravaged sable. With every drop of venom spit to the ground from their harsh mouth, these humanoid zombie-like creatures were birthed, rising from the mix of the sand like bubblegum to your shoe, hungry and rabid. They moved around like crackheads, fast and agile. They sniffed about for something they could sink their teeth into, and their eyes rolled onto me.

The Great Spirit whirled around Haven several times until it lifted his large manly body into the air as if abducted. The Great Spirit blew a blue blast of energy into Haven like *blue sapphires and blue fluorite floods.* Haven swallowed it up, slowly being weighed back down to the ground. He opened his eyes, crashing blue ocean waves. *Glowing and pulsating.*

Thunder rolled, lightning flashed, and rain poured into the arena.

A flood formed of the evil minion creatures, and it began to charge towards me, drawing closer and closer like water down a drain. My heart stopped at the unfairness of the fight, but Haven had no fear as he ran right into the threat. He charged into the darkness, fighting the toxic energies off as best he could. Haven's blows were waving fluidly. Then, with supernatural power, Haven broke the creatures' limbs instantaneously, massacring them as if each were obstacles he had dealt with his whole life. Even when he might slip up and become victimized, Haven focused on his goal and nothing more. *I pushed him through.* And Haven never stopped, using one creature to shield and destroy the other, using one as a weapon against the other. Haven showed his honor and courage as he defeated his fears, making them puff into gray dusting and dissolving until nothing was left. The crowd cheered as Haven stumbled about the arena, harmed but surviving, trying to regain the energy and power that he lost from the wounds of his offenders. He looked around to the deities, his angelic face tired but proud.

The rain poured down harder.

Moboyas was infuriated. The flames around the arena flickered harder. The two wendigo spirits that possessed the deities were now starving. Their gluttonous hunger was slithering closer. Then, purely out of defense, Haven stretched out and lifted. *A spark explosion of all blue and silver dust flashed* before us, and suddenly *a vast FUCKING* **BEAR** appeared, stomping onto the battlegrounds with electroplating power. Everything rumbled and shook. The energies chomped their scissoring teeth harshly as they neared the majestic glowing super bear. Haven's bear Spirit looked angered, as I never saw it so violent other than in that first nightmare. The two came closer, snapping for a taste of my overruling power. But, instead, Haven roared a warning. They danced around in ritual before the starving wendigo's jumped for a bite. One caught on Haven's leg, but he kicked it away as he pushed the other one hard enough to send it flying some great distance. Then, he turned to the one that bit him and began to fight with it. The other regained its stance and came charging toward him as his back was turned. I watched in horror as the two wendigo energies attacked him together. Haven sent one flying. The other biting into him again. They fought until Haven was jumped from behind the other a second time. Again they had Haven on the ground. Together, they both rammed into his neck, biting him simultaneously. He roared in pain and fell to the ground. They tried chewing away at him, but Haven was relentless. He refused to relinquish his power as he continued to fight.

I had to find a way to intervene. If Moboyas was going to cheat, then so will I. *I could distract both energies using my powers.* I began to manipulate the rain and wind. The wendigo-possessed deities noticed I was using the elements against them. The large hail, sticks, and twigs caught into their faces, the ground underneath the monsters rattling and sinking. I made it pour over them. Every shot that I took with my powers seemed to weaken the creatures. I was taking away all its energy and transmuting the energy into love. Finally, one of them wasn't having it. It released its grip on Haven and turned to me. It came charging, and I embraced myself as it pulled its limbs closer, crawling at full speed like a spider. Flashbacks of the winter made my heart pound harder as it came closer.

Before it could sink its teeth into me, I threw my hands up and a force field formed around me, protecting me from its fangs. I had my eyes closed, so I didn't realize I had used magic to defend myself at first. Until I opened my eyes. The bubble was time-sensitive. On the outside, things were moving at a languid pace. I watched as the wendigo tried penetrating the bubble with his useless teeth. Unfortunately, it was so distracted it didn't notice that Haven had taken a fatal bite into the other wendigo, ripping the creature apart into lifeless dust that disappeared into the wind. Nothing would stop him from doing the same to the jealous wendigo energy.

I watched Haven grab the creature with his teeth and take it apart before launching it to the other side. The wendigo weakened more with each blow until Haven had the wendigo on its knees. His claws were tearing it, and Haven was finishing off the wendigo, but before he could kill it for good, the wendigo slammed its sharp claws into Haven's chest. I could see Haven hold back the pain with a thick control. And even though Haven was seriously injured, he jumped at the last attempt to kill the monster. Finally, Haven gathered his might and strength, stood up tall, and brought the wendigo up in the air before splitting the creature in half with his teeth and sharp claws. The wendigo whistled out a cry of defeat before it collapsed violently and disappeared into nothing but dust.

Haven let out a vicious roar of Victory.

A roar that sent electricity under the feet of every deity.

Everything was still. Speechless. Everyone, including Moboyas, as Haven instantaneous shifted back into his ascended form and fell to the ground. He was bleeding from his wounds and lost consciousness. I released the protection force field and ran to him.

Shocked, Yocahu and Atabey stood up, wondering if Haven could fight the death coming for him. I pulled his head onto my lap. He was nearly lifeless. I begged him to keep awake as everyone watched. On the verge of giving up—a glimpse of confidence.

Revival. I whispered onto his lips with such intention that I felt a rumbling in my heart chakra spewed in the form of green loving energy and soothing blue energy from my fingertips.

The storm clouds retracted, and the flames blew out. Everything cleared as quickly as it came. The Taino sun appeared again, with its rainbow evening sky, as beautiful as it ever was, and the sea was silently calm. The wrath of Moboyas destroyed everything.

I pulled Haven deeper into my embrace. I dug my face into his heavy chest. ***Revival,*** my heart pleaded. I refused to let Haven die in my arms. After all, he has done to protect me. All he ever wanted was to be near me. To love me, even if it meant at a distance or through another. He didn't care as long as he could protect me, despite knowing that I could defend myself all along. I was angry but felt no need to dwell or wallow in guilt. No. He wasn't gone, and that was a genuine feeling. My infinite appreciation, in tears.

I wanted him back, and right now.

I thought deeply of the moment I laid eyes on him. That split smile he gave me across the table at the dinner party. The way he flexed his arm muscle that day, we argued in the kitchen. How he stared at me the moment I opened my eyes at Hector's and found him hovering over me. Amazing how relenting we were both were. Haven was always tenacious about our relationship. We had our moments but never gave up.

Then, my extravagant power radiated over him. My reflecting thoughts were helping Haven heal. All that thundering passion, hidden deep inside the depths of me with my uncle's magic, fully unlocked. Everything I've felt for him drove right into Haven's chakras. The magic he sparked in me mended him. The glowing grew like a ball of fire. I was giving him life and to all that once lived and prospered in my garden. I stuck my hands into the ground and swooned my magic throughout the soil, watching everything heal and revive. Then, the entire arena cleared with a blinding blast of ivory and golden light. Moboyas was gone. The Zeni's and deities were all suddenly gone. The Great Spirit was gone.

A new Garden is reborn underneath us. I held onto Haven, looking around to the garden, more radiant and prosperous than before. The smell of the pure ocean and the fruits luscious than ever. I cracked a smile through the tears, watching all Haven's color come to life. His fingertips grazed my jaw as he stared with mesmerizing blue eyes. He's been watching for a while. His fingers tangled in my hair as I chuckled. Then, all he could do was pull to kiss me.

Haven pulled me into the glittering ivory sand and rapidly pushed me onto my back. The two of us admired each other before I frantically checked his wounds. *He had none; he had healed.* Haven seemed in the best health ever and looked at me with familiar milky blue eyes. His one brow raised. Our bodies pulled in even closer. My visions of wonder gleamed over him. He had that smirk that made me crazy, but the look in our eyes held no suspicion. Our bodies were quickly entwining. *He was here, in my world. Alone. With me.* Haven's hands tore apart at my attire; I tossed away the headdress. He made sure all stripped from me but his pearl band. I ripped off his apron as he threw his weight on me. His sandy fingers took my body into his. He raised my hands above me and held them down.

"So I guess I owe you for saving my life Daya," He wouldn't let me speak as he ravished me; his hands split my knees apart. His tongue wiggled over my abs, and my giggles quickly turned into moans as he came in to devour my sex mound with his hungry lips and tongue. He was finally able to ravish me entirely without feeling like he would lose me completely. I still blush at the thought of how Haven made me feel that first time we made love in our garden. That pastel rainbow in the Paradiso sky never looked so damn beautiful. EVER. It could be because it was my first time seeing it with him. Or it could have been the orgasm I had while staring at it. All I know is that there was nowhere else I would rather be but here with Haven Tyson. *My blue-eyed forbidden love.*

Several Long weeks Later.

I watched the sweat drip from Haven's golden body as he worked all damn day around the garden in the sun, rebuilding our home. I didn't mind not having the shelter for the time being. We loved finding new places to sleep and making love every night under the stars. There were always new places to discover in our realm, and Haven was the perfect exploration partner.

In our *Land of Peace and Reward, we lived an eternal life* in a universe where all the Taino princesses who successfully helped heal the bloodlines live in their gardens with their true forbidden loves.

Love was about Teamwork. Prosperity was about teamwork. Yocahu, like many other ascended ancestors, was beginning to lose faith in his earthly people. People have grown so angry from betrayal, and no one cared to heal the trauma. True love is rare but possible if we learn to understand and forgive. If we become who we are, honestly. Learn to compromise and trust. Don't give up so easily; *if it's broken, fix it. If not, don't toy with it. Allow it to heal.* Love, very passionately, but consciously. It will be worth it.

They granted my mother her freedom. Yocahu blessed Haven, so he could keep and bring his gifts into our world, and Haven blessed my world with his spirit and powers and became our garden's protector. We were timeless and free. Our attraction and connection seem stronger here than they had been on earth. The tropical heat and sweet air were of no help. Either it set a lovely sexy mood that dragged all day or made us irritable where we would bicker and still end up under a Ceiba tree making up. It didn't matter where. Our world was our bed. Under bushes. Over flower beds. In the trees.

Where ever our hearts seemed to spark up.

"What are you staring at?" He caught me staring at his body from a tree above. I could feel myself flare up with desire, and my legs began to shake. A river was already beginning to flow.

"Are you going to stay up there all day and read?" He walked over and tossed me a half-bitten mango. I looked down at him,

"Let's go for a run,"

We ran through the rainforest, and when it began to pour fresh rain, Haven used his powers to bring us back into the Northern forest, to the same place we fell in love. The sound of parrots, rain frogs, and lizards turned into Owls hooting and crickets. I followed behind him to the heart shape meadow. Hiding in the tall grass, he jumped me like a lion on gazelle, and we rolled in the grass. We looked up, and the sunset was especially wondrous. I couldn't understand why and I was stuck on questioning it. The colors were so magnetic. I couldn't take my eyes off it even with Haven's organic body before me, now standing in the rushing river.

"Daya, are you seeing this?" Haven pointed up to the sky. A rich maroon-colored *Hummingbird* was flying above us. "-I haven't seen one like that before," The bird left a colorful chem-trail painted across the sky. Haven turned to me, sizing up my body and reaching for my hand, "Come here, gorgeous. You look delectable."

I looked at his tempting body, ready to jump his bones as he pulled me further into the water depths. As he kissed my neck, my eyes stayed focused on the sunset, but his lips were so intoxicating, and I closed my eyes in utter pleasure. **Until**

"OH-MY-GOD!" A familiar voice went off like an alarm in the garden, and my eyes jolted open. Haven's jaw dropped simultaneously. He was staring intensely behind me as if he was looking at a ghost. I quickly turned behind me, and I walked closer to the silhouette in the shadows. No, it just couldn't be?

"LEYLA?"